TEMPTED BY
THE BRIDESMAID

BY
ANNIE O'NEIL

MILLS &
BOON

Published in Great Britain 2017
By Mills & Boon, an imprint of HarperCollins*Publishers*
1 London Bridge Street, London, SE1 9GF

© 2017 Annie O'Neil

ISBN: 978-0-263-92659-0

Our policy is to use papers that are natural, renewable and recyclable
products and made from wood grown in sustainable forests. The logging
and manufacturing processes conform to the legal environmental
regulations of the country of origin.

Printed and bound in Spain
by CPI, Barcelona

Dear Reader,

Welcome to the first story of what I'm hoping you will think is a magical trip to Italy.

When I was dreaming up the perfect location for Luca, my tall, dark and dangerously handsome hero, I came across a website filled to the brim with photos of beautiful 'ghost towns' in Italy and simply had no choice but to get him to move into one.

This was an interesting book for me to write as it's the first time I've had a heroine who prefers working with dogs to people. After all, they're not only man's best friend, right? (*My* dogs are totally up there in the besties category.) And it took one very special human to bring Fran around to her HEA.

Enjoy—and don't be shy about getting in touch. You can reach me at annieoneilbooks.com, on Twitter @annieoneilbooks, or find me on Facebook…

Annie O' xx

Annie O'Neil spent most of her childhood with her leg draped over the family rocking chair and a book in her hand. Novels, baking, and writing too much teenage angst poetry ate up most of her youth. Now Annie splits her time between corralling her husband into helping her with their cows, baking, reading, barrel racing (not really!) and spending some very happy hours at her computer, writing.

This book could go to no other
than Jorja and Grissom—my own fluffy hounds
who are always there when I need them…
and sometimes when I don't!

Furry friends…simply the best!

CHAPTER ONE

IT FELT AS if she were watching the world through a fishbowl. Everything was distorted. Sight. Sound. Fran would have paid a million dollars to be anywhere else right now.

Church silence was crushing. Especially under the circumstances.

Fran looked across to the groomsmen. Surely there was an ally within that pack of immaculately suited Italian gentry who...?

Hmm... Not you, not you, not you... Oh!

Fran caught eyes with one of them. Gorgeous, like the rest, but his brow was definitely more furrowed, the espresso-rich eyes a bit more demanding than the others... Oh! Was that a scar? She hadn't noticed last night at the candlelit cocktail party. *Interesting.* She wondered what it would feel like to—

"Ahem!" The priest—or was he a bishop?—cleared his throat pointedly.

Why had she raised her hand? This wasn't school— it was a church!

This wasn't even Fran's wedding, and yet the hundreds of pairs of eyes belonging to each and every esteemed guest sitting in Venice's ridiculously beautiful basilica were trained on *her*. Little ol' Francesca "Fran" Martinelli, formerly of Queens, New York, now of…well… nowhere, really. It was just her, the dogs, a duffel bag stuffed to the hilt with more dog toys than clothes and the very, *very* pretty bridesmaid's dress she was wearing.

Putting it on, she'd actually felt girlie! Feminine. It would be back to her usual jeans and T-shirt tomorrow, though, when she showed up for her new mystery job. In the meantime, she was failing at how to be a perfect bridesmaid on an epic scale.

Fran's fingers plucked at the diaphanous fabric of her azure dress and she finally braved looking straight into the dark brown eyes of her dearest childhood friend, Princess Beatrice Vittoria di Jesolo.

The crowning glory of their shared teenage years had been flunking out of finishing school together in Switzerland. That sun-soaked afternoon playing hooky had been an absolute blast. Sure, they'd been caught, but did anyone really *care* if you could walk with a book on your head?

Their friendship had survived the headmistress dressing them down in front of their more civilized classmates, grass stains on their jeans, scrapes on their hands and knees from scrabbling around in the mountains making daisy chains and laughing until tears shot straight out of their eyes… But this moment—the one where Fran was ruining her best friend's wedding in front of the whole universe—this might very well spell the end of their friendship. The one thing she could rely on in her life.

Fran squeezed her eyes tight against Bea's inquiring gaze. The entire veil-covered, bouquet-holding, finger-waiting-for-a-ring-on-it image was branded onto her memory bank. Never mind the fact that there were official photographers lurking behind every marble pillar, and hundreds of guests—including dozens of members of Europe's royal families—filling the pews to overflowing, not to mention the countless media representatives waiting outside to film the happy power couple once they had been pronounced husband and wife.

Which they would be doing in about ten minutes or so unless she got her act together and did something!

"What exactly is your objection?" asked the man with the mystery scar through gritted teeth. In English. Which was nice.

Not because Fran's Italian was rusty—it was all she and her father ever spoke at home…when she *was* at home—but because it meant not every single person in the church would know that she'd just caught Bea's fiancé playing tonsil tennis with someone who wasn't Bea.

She stared into the man's dark eyes. Did *he* know? Did he care that the man he was standing up for in front of Italy's prime guest list was a lying cheat?

"If you could just speak up, dear," the priest tacked on, a bit more gently.

Maybe the priest didn't want to know specifically what her objection was—was choosing instead just to get the general gist that everything wasn't on the up-and-up. That or he would clap his hands, smile and say "Surprise! I saw them, too. The wedding's off because the groom's a cheat. He's just been having it off with the maid of dishonor in the passage to the doge's palace. So…who's ready for lunch?"

After another quick eye-scrunch, Fran eased one eye open and scanned the scene.

Nope. Beatrice was still standing next to her future husband, just about to be married. All doe-eyed and… well…maybe not totally doe-eyed. Beatrice had always been the pragmatic one. But—*oh, Dio! C'è una volpe sciolto nel pollaio*, as her father said whenever things were completely off-kilter. Which they were. Right now. Right here. A fox was loose in the hen house of Venice's most holy building, where a certain groom should have been hit by a lightning bolt or something by now.

On the plus side, Fran had the perfect position to give the groom the evil eye. Marco Rodolfo. Heir apparent to some royal title or other, here in the Most Serene Republic of Venice, and recent ascendant to the throne of a ridiculously huge fortune.

Money wasn't everything. She knew that from bitter experience. Truth was a far more valuable commodity. At least she hoped that was what Bea would think when she finally managed to open her mouth and speak.

Maybe she could laser beam a confession out of him...

The groom looked across at Fran...caught her gaze... and smiled. In its smarmy wake she could have sworn that a glint, a zap of light striking a sharp blade, shot across at her.

Go on, the smile said. *I dare you.*

Marco "The Wolf" Rodolfo.

The wolf indeed. He hadn't even bothered with the sheep's clothing. If she looked closely, would she see extra-long incisors? *All the better to eat you—*

"Per favore, signorina?"

A swirl of perfectly coiffured heads whipped her way as the priest gave her an imploring look. Or was he a cardinal? She really should have polished up her knowledge of the finer details of her Catholic childhood. Church, family dinners, tradition... They'd all slipped away when her mother had left for husband number two and her father had disappeared with a swan dive into his work.

"Francesca!" Bea growled through a fixed smile. "Any clues?"

Santo cielo! This was exactly the reason her father had held her at arm's length all these years. She couldn't keep her mouth shut, could she? Always had to speak the truth, no matter what the consequences.

"Francesca?"

"He's—" Fran's index finger took on a life of its own and she watched as it started lifting from her side to point at the reason why Bea's wedding shouldn't go ahead. She couldn't even look at the maid of honor he'd been having his wicked way with. What was her name? Marina? Something like that. The exact sort of woman who always made her feel more tomboy than Tinker Bell. Ebony tresses to her derriere. Willowy figure. Cheekbones and full lips that gave her an aloof look. Or maybe she looked that way because she actually *was* aloof.

She was insincere and a fiancé thief—that much was certain. Since when did Bea hang out with such super-modelesque women anyhow?

Society weddings.

Total. Nightmare.

Last night, in their two seconds alone, Bea had muttered something about out-of-control guest lists, her mother and bloodline obligations. All this while staring longingly at Fran's glass of champagne and then abruptly calling it a night. Not exactly the picture of a bride on the brink of a lifetime of bliss. A bride on the brink of disaster, more like.

"Francesca, say something!"

All Fran could do was stare wide-eyed at her friend.

Her beautiful, kind, honest, wouldn't-hurt-a-fly, take-no-prisoners friend. This was life being mean. Cruel, actually. When she'd seen Mommy kissing someone who definitely hadn't been Santa Claus and told her father about it, how had she been meant to know that her mother would leave her father and break his heart?

Would Bea stay friends with the messenger now, or hate her forever? A bit like Fran's father had hated her since his marriage blew apart no matter how hard she'd tried to gain his approval. A tiny hit of warmth tickled around her heart. They were going to try again. *Soon.* He'd promised.

The tickle turned ice-cold at another throat-clearing prompt from Mr. Sexy.

Why, why, why was *she* the one who caught all the cheaters in the world?

All the eyes on her felt like laser beams.

Including the eyes of the mystery groomsman who she really *would* have liked to get to know a bit better if things had been different. *Typical.* Timing was definitely not her forte. What was his name? Something sensual. Definitely not Ugolino, as her aunt had mysteriously called her son. No…it was something more… *toothsome.* A name that tantalized your tongue, like amaretto or a perfectly textured gelato. Cool and warming all at once. Something like the ancient city of…

Luca! That was his name.

Luca. He was filling out his made-to-measure suit with the lean, assured presence of a man who knew his mind. His crisp white shirt collar highlighted the warm olive tone of his skin and the five-o'clock shadow that was already hinting at making an appearance, despite the fact it was still morning. He looked like a man who would call a spade a spade.

Which might explain why he was staring daggers at her. Strangely, the glaring didn't detract from his left-of-center good looks. He wasn't one of those calendar-ready men whose perfection was more off-putting than alluring. Sure, he had the cheekbones, the inky dark hair and brown eyes that held the mysteries of the universe in them, but he also had that scar. A jagged one that looked as if it could tell a story or two. It dissected his left eyebrow, skipped the eye, then shot along his cheek. If she wasn't wrong, there were a few tiny ones along his chin, too. Little faint scars she might almost have reached out and touched—if his lips hadn't been moving.

"*Per amor del cielo!* Put these poor people out of their misery!"

Fran blinked. Enigmatic-scar man was right.

She looked to his left. The priest-bishop-cardinal was speaking to her again. Asking her to clarify why she believed this happy couple should not lawfully be joined in marriage. Murmurs of dismay were audibly rippling through the church behind her. Part of her was certain she could hear howls from the paparazzi as they waited outside to pounce.

Clammy prickles of panic threatened to consume her brain.

Friends didn't let friends marry philandering liars. Right? Then again, what did *she* know? She was Italian by birth, but raised in America. Maybe a little last-minute nookie right before you married your long-term intended was the done thing in these social circles filled with family names that went back a dozen generations or more. It wasn't illegal, but… Oh, this was ranking up there in worst-moments-ever territory!

Fran sucked in a deep breath. It was the do-or-die

moment. Her heart was careening around her chest so haphazardly she wouldn't have been surprised if it had flown straight out of her throat, but instead out came words. And before she could stop herself, she heard herself saying to Beatrice, "He's… You can't marry him!"

CHAPTER TWO

"*BASTA!*" QUICK AS a flash, Luca shuttled the key play-
ers in this farce to the back of the altar, then down a
narrow marble passageway until they reached an open
but mercifully private corridor.

"Her dress was up and Marco—"

"*Per favore.* I implore you to just…*stop.*" Luca
whirled around, only to receive a full-body blow from
the blonde bridesmaid. As quickly as the raft of sensations from holding her in his arms hit him she pressed
away from him—*hard.*

"I'm just trying—" Bea's friend clamped her full,
pink lips tight when her eyes met his.

The rest of the party was moving down the corridor
as Luca wrestled with her revelation. "Do you have *any*
idea what you've done? The damage you've caused?"

Stillness enveloped her as his words seemed to take
hold.

Such was the power of the moment, Luca was hur-
tled back to a time and place when he, too, had been
incapable of motion. Only there had been a doctor *and*
a priest then.

Stillness had been the only way to let the news sink
in.

Mother. Father. His sister, her husband—all of them

save his beautiful niece. Gone. And *he'd* been the one behind the wheel.

He closed his eyes and willed the memory away, forcing himself to focus on the bridesmaid in front of him. Still utterly stationary—a deer in the headlights.

Another time, another place he would have said she was pretty. Beautiful, even. Honey-gold hair. Full, almost-pouty lips he didn't think had more than a slick of gloss on them. Eyes so blue he would have sworn they were a perfect match to the Adriatic Sea not a handful of meters from the basilica.

"Don't you dare—" She took in a jagged breath, tears filming her eyes. "Don't you *dare* tell me I don't understand what speaking up means."

Luca's gut tightened as she spoke. Behind those tears there was nothing but honesty. The type of honesty that would change everything.

His mind reeled through the facts. Beatrice was one of his most respected friends. They'd known each other all their lives and had been even closer during med school. Their career trajectories had shot them off in opposite directions, much to their parents' chagrin. He'd not missed their hints, their hopes that their friendship would blossom into something more.

Beautiful as Beatrice was, theirs would always be a platonic relationship. When she'd taken up with Marco he'd almost been relieved. *Si*, he had a playboy's reputation, but he was a grown man now. A prince with an aristocratic duty to fulfill—a legacy to uphold. When Marco had asked him to be best man he'd been honored. Proud, even, to play a role in Beatrice's wedding.

Cheating just minutes before he was due to marry? What kind of man would *do* that?

He shot a glance at Marco, who was raising his hands

in protest before launching into an impassioned appeal to both Bea and the cardinal.

Marco and a bridesmaid in a premarital clinch? As much as he hated to admit it, he couldn't imagine it was the type of thing a true friend would conjure up just to add some drama to Italy's most talked-about wedding.

He glanced down at her hands, each clutching a fist-ful of the fairy-tale fabric billowing out from her dress in the light wind. No rings.

A Cinderella story, perhaps? The not-so-ugly step-sister throwing a spanner into the works, hoping to catch the eye of the Prince?

Each time she pulled at her dress she revealed the fact that she was actually wearing flip-flops in lieu of any Italian woman's obligatory heels. No glass slippers, then. Just rainbow-painted toes that would have brought the twitch of a smile to his lips if his mind hadn't been racing for ways to fend off disaster.

She'd be far less high maintenance than his only-the-best-will-do girlfriend.

He shook off this reminder that he and Marina needed "a talk" and forced himself to meet the blonde's gaze again. Tearstained but defiant. A surge of compassion shot through him. If what she was saying was true she was a messenger who wouldn't escape unscathed.

"I saw them!" she insisted, tendrils of blond hair coming loose from the intricate hairdo the half-dozen or so bridesmaids were all wearing. All of the brides-maids including *his* girlfriend. "It's not like you're the one who's been cheated on," she whisper-hissed, her blue eyes flicking toward Beatrice, who, unlike her, was remaining stoically tear-free.

Luca took hold of her elbow and steered her farther away from the small group, doing his best to ignore how soft her skin felt under the work-hardened pads of his fingertips. Quite a change from the soft-as-a-surgeon's hands he'd been so proud of. Funny what a bit of unexpected tragedy could do to a man.

"Perhaps we should leave the bride and groom to chat with the cardinal." A shard of discord lodged in his spine as he heard himself speak. It had been in the icy tone he'd only ever heard come out of his mouth once before. The day his father had confessed he'd gambled away the last of the family's savings.

"I'm Francesca, by the way," she said, as if adding a personal touch would blunt the edges of this unbelievable scenario. Or perhaps she was grasping at straws, just as he was. "I think I saw you at the cocktail party last night."

"I would say it's a pleasure to meet you, but…"

She waved away his platitudes. They both knew they were beyond social niceties.

"Francesca…" He drew her name out on the premise of buying time. He caught himself tasting it upon his tongue as one might bite into a lemon on a dare, surprised to find it sweet when he had been expecting the bitterness of pith, the sourness of an unripe fruit.

Focus, man.

Luca clenched his jaw so tightly he saw Francesca's eyes flick to the telltale twitch in his cheek. The one with the scar.

Let her stare.

He swallowed down the hit of bile that came with the thought. He knew better than most that nothing good came from a life built on illusion.

"I don't think I need to remind you what our roles are here. I promised to be best man at this wedding. To vouch for the man about to marry our mutual friend."

He moved closer toward her and caught a gentle waft of something. Honeysuckle with a hint of grass? His eyes met hers and for a moment…one solitary moment… they were connected. Magnetically. Sensually.

Luca stepped back and gave his jaw a rough scrub, far too aware that Francesca had felt it, too.

"There is no one in the world I would defend more than Bea." Francesca's words shattered the moment, forcing him to confront reality. "And, believe me, of all the people standing here I *know* how awful this is."

Something in her eyes told him she wasn't lying. Something in his heart told him he already knew the truth.

"I'd want to know," she insisted. "Wouldn't you?"

Luca looked away from the clear blue appeal in her eyes, redirecting the daggers he was shooting toward her to the elaborately painted ceiling of the marble-and-flagstone passageway. The hundreds of years it had taken to build the basilica evaporated to nothing in comparison to the milliseconds it had taken to grind this wedding to a halt.

A wedding. A marriage. It was meant to last a lifetime.

"Of course I'd want to know," he bit out. "But your claims are too far-fetched. The place where you're saying you saw them is not even private."

"I know! It doesn't mean it didn't happen."

Francesca's eyes widened and the tears resting on her eyelids cascaded onto her cheeks before zipping down to her chin and plopping unceremoniously into the hollow of her throat. Luca only just stopped himself from lifting both his hands to her collarbone and swiping them away with his thumbs. First one, then the other…

Perhaps tracing the path of one of those tears slipping straight between the soft swell and lift of—

Focus!

"Which one was it? Which woman?"

Francesca's blue eyes, darkened with emotion, flicked up and to the right. "She had dark hair. Black."

The information began to register in slow motion. Not Suzette…a flame-bright redhead. And the others were barely into their teens.

Elimination left him with only one option.

A fleeting conversation with his girlfriend came back to him. One in which he'd said he was going to be too busy with the clinic to come to the wedding. Marina had been fine with it. Had agreed, in fact. *So* much work at the clinic, she'd said. And then it all fell into place. The little white lies. The deceptions. The ever-increasing radio silences he hadn't really noticed in advance of the clinic's opening day.

A coldness took hold of his entire chest. An internal ice storm wrought its damage as the news fully penetrated.

"My girlfriend was *not* having sex with Marco."

Francesca's eyes pinged wide, a hit of shock shuddering down her spine before she managed to respond.

"Your girlfriend? That's… *Wow.*" She shook her head in disbelief. "For the record, she is an idiot. If you were *my* boyfriend, lock and key might be more—"

Luca held up a hand. He didn't want to hear it.

It was difficult to know whether to be self-righteous or furious. In Rome, his relationships had hardly warranted the title. Since moving back to Mont di Mare…

The home truths hit hard and fast. Sure, Marina had been complaining that she wasn't the center of his universe lately, but any fool—anyone with a heart beating in their chest—could have seen that his priorities were not wooing and winning right now.

He owed every spare ounce of his energy to his niece. The one person who'd suffered the most in that horrific car accident. His beautiful, headstrong niece, confined to a wheelchair evermore.

He looked across at Marco. The sting of betrayal hit hard and fast.

He and Marina had never been written in the stars—but *Beatrice*? A true princess if ever there was one. She was shaking her head. Holding up a hand so that Marco would stop his heated entreaty. From where Luca was standing it didn't look as if the wedding would go ahead.

He swore under his breath. He had trusted Marco to treat Bea well—cautioned him about his rakish past and then congratulated him with every fiber of his being when at long last he'd announced his engagement to Princess Beatrice Vittoria di Jesolo.

The three of them had shared the same upbringing. Privileged. Exclusive. Full of expectation—no, more than that, full of *obligation* that they would follow in their ancestors' footsteps. Marry well. Breed more titled babies.

Luca might have considered the same future for himself before the accident. But that had all changed now. Little wonder Marina had strayed. He'd kept her at arm's length. Farther away. It was surprising she had stayed any time at all.

"Why don't you go and get her? Ask her yourself?" Francesca wasn't even bothering to swipe at the tears streaking her mascara across her cheeks.

"You're absolutely positive?"

Even as the hollow-sounding words left his mouth he knew they were true. There weren't that many women wandering around the basilica in swirls of weightless ocean-blue fabric. And there was only one bridesmaid with raven hair. The same immaculate silky hair he'd been forbidden from touching that morning when Marina had popped into the hotel suite to grab the diamante clutch bag she'd left while she was at the hairdresser's. Not so immaculate when she'd appeared at the altar, looking rosy cheeked and more alive than he'd seen her in months, if he was being honest.

"I—I can go get her for you, if you like," Francesca offered after hiccuping a few more tears away.

He had to hand it to her. The poor woman was crying her eyes out, but she knew how to stand her ground.

"Why don't I go find her?" Her fingers started doing a little nervous dance in the direction of the church, where everyone was still waiting.

"No offense, but you are the *last* person I would ever ask to help me."

"Isn't it better to know the truth than to live a lie?"

Luca swore softly and turned away. She was hitting just about every button he didn't care to admit he had. Truth. Deceit. Honesty. Lies. Weakness.

He had no time in his life for weakness. No capacity for lies.

He forced himself to look Francesca in the eye, knowing there wasn't an iota of kindness in his gaze. But he still couldn't give in to the innate need to feel empathy for the position she'd been put in. Or compassion for the tears rising again and again, glossing her eyes and then falling in a steady trickle along her tear-soaked face. How easy it would be to lift a finger and just…

Magari!

Shooting the messenger was a fool's errand, but he didn't know how else to react… A knife of rage swept through him. If he never thought about Marina or Marco again it would be too soon.

"It didn't seem like it was the first time," Francesca continued, her husky voice starting to break in a vain attempt to salve the ever-deepening wound. "I'm happy to go and get her if you want."

"Basta! Per favore!"

No need to paint a picture. He almost envied Francesca. Seeing in an instant what he should have known for weeks. He should have ended it before she'd even thought to stray.

"If you want, I'll do it. Go and get her. I would do it for any friend."

Francesca shifted from one foot to the other, eyes glued to his, waiting for his response. He'd be grateful for this one day, but right now Francesca was the devil's messenger and he'd heard enough.

The words came to him—jagged icicles shooting straight from his arctic heart. "I know you mean well, Francesca, but you and I will *never* be friends."

Shell-shocked. That was how Bea had looked for the rest of the day. Not that Fran could blame her. Talk about living a nightmare. She knew better than most that coming to terms with deception on that kind of scale could take years. A lifetime, even, if her father's damaged heart was anything to go by.

From the look on Luca's face when they'd finally parted at the basilica he was going to need *two* lifetimes to get over his girlfriend's betrayal. Good thing they wouldn't be crossing paths anytime soon.

"Want me to see if I can find a case of prosecco lying around? A karaoke machine? We could sing it out and down some fizz."

Fran scanned the hotel suite. The caterers had long been sent away, the decorations had been removed and the staff instructed to keep any and all lurking paparazzi as far away as possible…

"No, thanks, *cara*. Maybe some water?" Bea asked.

"On it."

As she poured a glass of her friend's favorite—sparkling water from the alpine region of Italy—Fran was even more in awe of her friend's strength. All tucked up in bed, makeup removed, dress unceremoniously wilting like a deflated meringue in the bathroom, Bea looked exhausted, but not defeated.

"Want to tell me anything about this mystery job I'm due to start tomorrow?"

"No." Bea took a big gulp of water and grinned, obviously grateful for the change of topic. "Although it *will* make use of both your physio skills and the assistance dogs."

Fran frowned. "I thought you said she had a doctor looking after her?"

Bea blinked, but said nothing.

"The girl's in a wheelchair, right? Lower extremities paralyzed?"

"Yeah, but…" Bea tipped her head to the side and gave her friend a hard look. "You're not going to waste all those years of practicing physio are you?"

"What? Because the person I was stupid enough to go into business with saw me as a limitless supply of cash?"

"You're clear of that, though, aren't you?"

Fran grunted.

People? Disappointing. Dogs? They never asked for a thing. Except maybe a good scratch around the ears.

"Are you sure you're all right?" Fran flipped the topic

back to Bea. "Don't you want to stay in the palazzo with your family?"

"And listen to my mother screech on about the disaster of the century? How I've ruined the family's name. The family's genetic line. Any chance of happiness for the di Jesolos forever and ever. Not a chance. Besides—" she scanned the sumptuous surroundings of the room "—your suite is great and I'd much rather be with you, even if the place *does* smell all doggy."

"Does not." Fran swiped at the air between them with a grin. She'd washed the dogs to within an inch of their lives before they'd checked into Venice's fanciest hotel. A little trust-fund treat to herself before heading out to this mystery village where Bea had organized her summer job.

"You don't need to watch over me, you know," Bea chided gently. "I'm not going to do anything drastic. And you *are* allowed to take the dress off. Don't know if you've heard, but the wedding's off!"

"Just wanted to get my money's worth!" Fran said, knowing the quip was as lame as it sounded.

The truth was, she hadn't felt so pretty in…*years*, really. When your workaholic dad bought your clothes from the local menswear shop, there was only so much ironic style a girl could pull off. When she'd graduated to buying her own clothes it had felt like a betrayal even to glance at something pink and frilly. It wasn't *practical*.

"Not exactly what a proper engineer would wear, Frannie!"

So much for *that* pipe dream! It had died along with a thousand others before she'd found her niche in the world of physiotherapy and then, even more perfectly, in assistance-dog training. *Dogs.* They were who she liked to spend her time with. They were unconditionally loyal and always ridiculously happy to see her. When she had to hand over these two dogs to her mystery charge at the end of the summer...

Fran swallowed down another rush of tears. Bea shouldn't have to be the one being stoic here. "I'm so sorry, Bea. About doing things the way I did. There just wasn't time to catch you after I'd seen them, and before I knew it, we were all up there at the altar and—"

"I'm not sorry at all." Bea said. "I'm glad you said something. Grateful you had the courage when no one else did."

"That's pretty magnanimous for someone who just found out they were being cheated on!"

"Others knew. All along. Even my mother." Bea chased up the comment with a little typical eye roll.

Fran's hands flew to cover her mouth. *Wow*. That was just... *Wow*.

"They were all so desperate for me to be one half of the most enviable couple in Europe. Even if it came at a cost." She shuddered away the thought. "You were the only one today who was a true friend."

Fran's tear ducts couldn't hold back any longer.

"How can you be so nice about everything when I've ruined the best day of your life?"

"*Amore!* Stop. You were *not* the one who ruined the day. Besides, I'm pretty sure there will be another best day of my life," Bea added, with a hint of something left unsaid in her voice.

"Since I barely see you once a year, it would've been nice to be honest about something else. Like how ridiculously beautiful you looked today."

Fran's heart rose into her throat as at long last Bea's eyes finally clouded with tears.

"Everyone has their secrets," Bea whispered.

"Including you?"

Bea looked away. Fair enough. There had to be a full-blown tropical storm going on in that head of hers right now, and if she wanted to keep her thoughts to herself, she was most deserving. Thank heavens her family had the financial comfort to sort out the mess The Wolf's infidelity would leave in its wake.

"You all ready for your new job?" Bea turned back toward her with a soft smile.

"Yes!" She gave an excited clap of her hands. The two dogs she had trained up for this job were amazing. "Not that you've told me much about the new boss, apart from the pro bono bit. I can't *believe* you offered to pay me."

Beatrice scrunched her features together. "Best not to mention that."

"I have no problem doing it for free. You know that. If I could've lived in one place for more than five minutes over the past few years, I would've set up a charitable trust through Martinelli Motors years ago, but…"

"*He* was too busy making his mark?"

"As ever. We don't have ancient family lineage to rely on like you do."

"*Ugh.* Don't remind me."

"Sorry…" Fran cringed, then held her arms open wide to the heavens. "Please help me stop sticking my foot in my mouth today!" She dropped her arms and pulled her friend into a hug. "Ever wished you'd just stayed in England?"

Bea's eyes clouded and again she looked away. This time Fran had *definitely* said the wrong thing, brought up memories best left undisturbed.

"That was…" Bea began, stopping to take a faltering

breath. "That was a very special time and place. Those kinds of moments only come once in a lifetime."

Fran pulled back from the hug and looked at her friend, lips pressed tight together. She wouldn't mention Jamie's name if Beatrice didn't. The poor girl had been through enough today without rehashing romances of years gone by.

"Right!" Fran put on a jaunty grin. "Time to totally change the topic! Now, as my best friend, won't you please give me just a teensy, tiny hint about my new boss so I don't ruin things in the first five minutes?"

"*You're* the one who wanted a mystery assignment!"

"I didn't want them to know who *I* was—not the other way around!" Fran shot Bea a playful glower.

She'd already been burned by a business partner who had known she was heiress to her father's electric-car empire. And when it came to her social life, people invariably got the wrong idea. Expected something… *someone*…more glamorous, witty, attention seeking, party mad.

It was why she'd given up physio altogether. Dogs didn't give a damn about who she was so long as she was kind and gave them dinner. If only her new boss was a pooch! She giggled at the thought of a dog in a three-piece suit and a monocle.

"What's so funny?" Bea asked.

"C'mon…just give me a little new-boss hint," Fran cajoled, pinching her fingers together so barely a sheet of paper could pass between them.

Bea shook her head no. "I've told you all you need to know. The girl's a teenager. She's been in a wheelchair for a couple of years now. Paraplegic after a bad car accident. Very bad. Her uncle—"

"Ooh! There's an enigmatic *uncle*?"

"Something like that," Bea intoned, wagging her finger. "No hints. They need the dog so she can be more independent."

"*She* needs the dog."

"Right. That's what I said."

"You said *they* need the dog," Fran wheedled, hoping to get a bit more information, but Bea just made an invisible zip across her lips. *No more.*

"That's not tons to go on, you know. I've been forced to bring two dogs to make sure I've got the right one!"

"Forced?" Bea cackled. "Since when have you had to be *forced* to travel with more than one dog?"

"C'mon…" Fran put her hands into a prayer position. "Just tell me what her parents are like—"

Beatrice held up her hand. "No parents. They both died in the same accident."

"Ouch." Fran winced. She'd lost her mother to divorce and her father to work. Losing them for real must be devastating.

"So does that mean this devilishly handsome uncle plays a big role in her life?"

"No one said he was handsome!" Bea admonished. "And remember—good things come to those who wait!"

Bea took on a mysterious air and, if Fran wasn't mistaken, there was also an elusive something else she couldn't quite put her finger on. How could a person *glow* when their whole life had just been ripped out from beneath them? Bea was in a league of her own. There weren't too many people who would set up a dream job for a friend who was known to dip in and out of her life like a yo-yo.

"Well, even if her uncle is a big, hairy-eared ogre, I can't wait. Nothing beats matching the right pooch to the right patient." Fran couldn't stop herself from clapping a bit more, drawing the attention of her two stalwart companions. "C'mere, pups! Help me tuck in Her Majesty."

Bea batted at the air between them. "No more royal speak! I don't want to be reminded."

"What?" Fran fell into their lifelong patter. "The fact that you're so royal you'd probably bleed fleurs-de-lys?"

"That's the French, idiot!"

"What do Italian royals bleed, then? Truffles?"

"Ha!" Bea giggled, reaching out a hand to give Fran's a big squeeze. "It's not truffle season. It's tabloid season. And they're *definitely* going to have a field day with this. I can't even bear to think about it." She threw her arm across her eyes and sank back into the downy pillow. "What do you think they'll say? Princess left at the altar, now weeping truffle tears?"

Fran pulled her friend up by her hands and gave her a hug. It was awful seeing her beautiful dark eyes cloud over with sadness. "How about some honey?" she suggested, signaling to the two big dogs to come over to the bedside. "That mountain honey you gave me from the Dolomites was amazing."

"From the resort?" Bea's eyes lit up at the thought. "It's one of the most beautiful places in the world. Maybe…"

"Maybe what?" Fran knew the tendrils of a new idea when she saw one.

"Maybe I'll pull a Frannie!"

"What does *that* mean?" She put on an expression of mock horror, fully aware that it wasn't masking her defensive reaction.

She knew exactly what it meant. A lifetime of trying to get her father's attention and failing had turned her into a wanderer. Staying too long in any one place meant getting attached. And that meant getting hurt.

"Don't get upset. I envy you. Your ability to just pick up and go. Disappear. Reinvent yourself. Maybe it's time *I* went and did something new."

Fran goldfished for a minute.

"That phase of my life might be over," she hedged. "Once this summer's done and dusted I'm going home."

"*Home*, home?" Bea sat up straight, eyes wide with shock. "I thought you said you'd never settle down there."

"Dad's offered to help me set up a full-time assistance-dogs training center—"

"You've never accepted his money before! What's the catch?"

"You mean what's going to be different this time?" Fran said, surprised at the note of shyness in her voice.

Bea nodded. She was the one who had always been there on the end of a phone when Fran had called in tears. *Again.*

"We spent a week together before I came over."

"A *week*?" Bea's eyes widened in surprise. "That's huge for you two. He wasn't in the office the whole time?"

"Nope! We actually went to a car show together."

Bea pursed her lips together. Not impressed.

"I know. I know," Fran protested, before admitting, "He had a little run-in with the pearly gates."

"Fran! Why didn't you *tell* me?"

"It turned out to be one of those cases of indigestion disguising itself as a heart attack, but it seems to have been a lightbulb moment for him. Made him reassess how he does things."

"You mean how he's neglected his only daughter most of his life?"

"It wasn't *that* bad."

"Francesca Martinelli, don't you *dare* tell me your heart wasn't broken time and time again by your father choosing work over spending time with you."

Fran met her friend's gaze—saw the unflinching truth in it, the same solid friendship and loyalty she'd shown her from the day they'd met at boarding school.

"I know. But this time it really *is* different."

"Frannie…" Bea's brow furrowed. "He took you to a *car* show. You *hate* cars!"

"It was an antique car show. Not a single electric car in sight."

Bea gave a low whistle. "Will wonders never cease?"

"Martinelli Motors is doing so well it could probably run itself."

"No surprise there. But I'm still amazed he took time off. It must've been one heck of a health scare."

Fran nodded. She knew Bea's wariness was legitimate. The number of times Fran had thought *this* would be the time her father finally made good on his promise to spend some quality father-daughter time…

"It was actually quite sweet. I got to learn a lot more about him as we journeyed through time via the cars." She smiled at the memory of a Model T that had elicited a story about one of his cousins driving up a mountainside backward because the engine had only been strong enough in reverse. "Even though we all know cars aren't my passion, I learned more about him in that one weekend than I have…*ever*, really."

He'd thought he was going to die—late at night, alone in his office. And it had made him change direction, hadn't it? Forced him to realize a factory couldn't give hugs or bake your favorite cookies or help you out when you were elderly and in need of some genuine TLC or a trip down memory lane.

"We've even been having phone calls and video-link chats since I left. Every day."

Bea nodded. Impressed now. "Well, if those two hounds of yours are anything to go by, it'll be a successful business in no time. Who knows? I might need one of those itty-bitty handbag assistance dogs to keep me chirpy!"

"Ooh! That's their specialty. Want a display?" Without waiting for an answer, she signaled directions at her specially trained pooches, "Come on, pups! Bedtime for Bea!"

Fran was rewarded with a full peal of Beatrice's giggles when the dogs went up on their hind legs on either side of the bed and pulled at the soft duvet until it was right up to her chin.

Snuggled up under her covers, Bea turned her kind eyes toward Fran. "*Grazie*, Francesca. You're the best. Mamma has promised caffe latte and your favorite *brioche con cioccolata* if we head over to the palazzo tomorrow morning."

"I'll be up early, so don't worry about me. I'll just grab something from this enormous fruit bowl before I shoot off." She feigned trying to lift the huge bowl and failing. "Better save my back. I've got to be there at nine. Fit and well!"

"At Clinica Mont di Mare?"

"Aha! I *knew* I'd get something from you beyond the sat-nav coordinates!"

Bea gave her a sidelong glance, then shook her head. "All I'm going to say is keep an open mind."

"Sounds a bit scary."

Bea gave her hand a squeeze. "Of all the people in the world, I know you're the best one for this particular job."

"Thanks, friend."

Fran fought the tickle of tears in her throat. Bea was

her absolute best friend and she trusted her implicitly. The fact Bea was still speaking to her after today's debacle made her heart squeeze tight.

"Un bacione." She dropped a kiss on her friend's forehead and gave her hand a final squeeze before heading to her own bedroom and climbing into the antique wrought iron–framed bed.

"Freda, come! Covers!" *Might as well get as much practice in as possible.*

The fluffy Bernese mountain dog padded over, did as she had been bid, then received a big ol' cuddle. Fran adored Freda, with her big brown eyes. The three-year-old dog was ever patient, ever kind. In contrast to the other full-of-beans dog she'd brought along.

"Edison! Come, boy!"

The chocolate Lab lolloped up to the side of the bed to receive his own cuddle, before flopping down in a contented pile of brown fur alongside Freda.

The best of friends. Just like her and Bea. It would be so hard to say goodbye.

Never mind. Tomorrow was a new beginning.

Exactly what she needed after a certain someone's face had been burned into her memory forever.

"You and I will never be friends."

Luca's hardened features pinged into her mind's eye. No matter the set of his jaw, she'd seen kindness in his eyes. Disbelief at what was happening. And resignation. A trinity of emotions that had pulled at her heartstrings and then yanked hard, cinching them in a tight noose. No matter how foul he'd been, she knew she would always feel compassion for him. Always wonder if he'd found someone worthy of his love.

CHAPTER THREE

"*How* MUCH?" LUCA's jaw clenched tight. He was barely able to conceal his disbelief. Another *five million* to get a swathe of family suites prepared?

He looked at the sober-faced contractor. He was the best, and his family had worked with the Montovano family for years. In other words, five million was a steal.

Five million he didn't have, thanks to his father's late nights at the poker table. Very nice poker tables, in the French Riviera's most exclusive casinos. Casinos where losing was always an option.

Luca's eyes flicked up to the pure blue sky above him. Now that his father was pushing piles of chips up there, somewhere in the heavenly hereafter, it wasn't worth holding on to the anger anymore. The bitterness.

His gaze realigned with the village—his inheritance...his millstone. Finding peace was difficult when he had a paraplegic niece to care for and a half-built clinic he was supposed to open in a week's time.

Basta! He shook off the ill will. Nothing would get in the way of providing for Pia. Bringing her every happiness he could afford. Be it sunshine or some much-needed savings—he would give her whatever he had. After the losses she'd suffered...

"Dottore?" The contractor's voice jarred him back into the moment.

"Looks like we're going to have to do it in phases, Piero. *Mi perdoni.*"

Luca didn't even bother with a smile—they both knew it wouldn't be genuine—and shook hands with the disappointed contractor. They walked out to the main gate, where he had parked. Luca remained in the open courtyard as the van slowly worked its way along the kilometer-long bridge that joined the mountaintop village to the fertile seaside valley below.

He took in a deep breath of air—just now hinting at all the wildflowers on the brink of appearing. It was rare for him to take a moment like this—a few seconds of peace before heading back into the building site that needed to be transformed into an elite rehabilitation clinic in one week's time.

He scanned the broad valley below him. Where the hell was this dog specialist? Time was money. Money he didn't have to spare. Not that Canny Canines was charging him. Bea had said something about fulfilling pro bono quotas and rescue dogs, but it hadn't sat entirely right with him. He might have strained the seams of his bag of ducats to the limit, but he wasn't in the habit of accepting charity. Not yet anyway.

The jarring clang of a scaffolding rail reverberated against the stone walls of the medieval village along with a gust of blue language. Luca's fists tightened. He willed it to be the sound of intention rather than disaster. There was no time for mistakes—even less for catastrophe.

Sucking in another deep breath, Luca turned around to face the arched stone entryway that led into the renamed "city." Microcity, more like. Civita di Montovano di Marino. His family's name bore the legacy of a bustling medieval village perched atop this seaside mountain— once thriving in the trades of the day, but now left to fade away to nothing after two World Wars had shaken nearly every family from its charitable embrace.

Just another one of Italy's innumerable ghost towns— barely able to sustain the livelihood of one family, let alone the hundred or so who had lived there so many years ago.

But in one week's time all that would change, when the Clinica Mont di Mare opened its doors to its first five patients. All wheelchair bound. All teenagers. Just like his niece. Only, unlike his niece, *they* all had parents. Families willing to dedicate their time and energy to trying rehabilitation one more time when all the hospitals had said there was no more hope.

A sharp laugh rasped against his throat. After the accident, that was exactly what the doctors at the hospital working with Pia had said. "She'll just have to resign herself to having little to no strength."

Screw that.

Montovanos didn't resign themselves to anything. They fought back. *Hard.*

His hand crept up to the thin raised line of his scar and took its well-traveled route from chin to throat. A permanent reminder of the promise he'd made to his family to save their legacy.

"Zio! Are they here yet?"

Luca looked up and smiled. Pia might not be his kid, but she had *his* blood pumping through her veins. Type A positive. Two liters' worth. Montovano di Marino blood. She was a dead ringer for her mother—his sister—but from the way she was haphazardly bumping and whizzing her way along the cobbled street instead of the wheelchair-ready side path to get to their favorite lookout site, he was pretty sure she'd inherited her bravura from him.

Pride swelled in him as he watched her now—two years after being released from hospital—surpassing each of his expectations with ease.

Breathless, his niece finally arrived beside him. "Move over, Zio Luca. I want to see when she gets here."

"What makes you so sure the trainer is a she?"

"Must be my teenage superpowers." Pia smirked. "And also Bea told me it was a she. Girl power!"

Another deep hit of pride struck him in the chest as he watched her execute a crazy three-point turn any Paralympian would have been hard-pressed to rival and then punch up into the morning sunshine, shouting positive affirmations.

"Never let her down. You're all she has now."

The words pounded his conscience as if he'd heard them only yesterday. His sister's last plea before her fight for survival had been lost.

His little ray of sunshine.

A furnace blast of determination was more like it.

Pia wanted—*needed*—to prove to herself that she could do everything on her own. Her C5 vertebra fracture might have left her paralyzed from the waist down, but it hadn't crushed her spirits as she'd powered through the initial stages of recovery at the same time as dealing with the loss of her parents and grandparents all in one deadly car crash. She had even spoken of training for the Paralympics.

And then early-onset rheumatoid arthritis had thrown a spanner in the works. Hence the dog.

They both scanned the approaching roads. One from the north, the other from the south and their own road—

a straight line from the *civita* to the sea, right in the middle. There was the usual collection of delivery vehicles and medical staff preparing the facility for its opening. And inspectors. Endless numbers of inspectors.

He was a doctor, for heaven's sake—not a bureaucrat.

"Just think, Pia...in one short week that road and this sky will be busy with arriving patients. Ambulances, helicopters..."

She let out a wistful sigh. "Friends!"

"Patients," he reminded her sternly, lips twitching against the smile he'd rather give.

"I know, Uncle Luca. But isn't it part of the Clinica Mont di Mare's ethos that rehab covers all the bases. And that means having friends—like me!"

"Remember, *chiara*, they won't all be as well-adjusted and conversation starved as you."

He gave her plaits a tug, only to have his hand swatted away. She was sixteen. Too old for that sort of thing. Too young to find him interesting 24/7. Having other teens here would be good for her.

"They're all in wheelchairs, right?"

"You know as well as I do they are. And thank you for being a guinea pig for all the doctors here in advance of their coming."

"Anything for Mont di Mare!" Pia's face lit up, then just as quickly clouded. "Do you think they'll try to take my dog? The other patients, I mean? What if they need the dog more than I do?"

Luca shook his head. "No. Absolutely not. This is solely for *you*."

"What if they get jealous and want one, too?"

"That's a bridge to cross further down the line, Pia. Besides," he added gently, "they'll have their families with them."

"I have *you*!" Pia riposted loyally.

"And I have you." He reached out a hand and she met it for a fist bump—still determined to make him hip.

Hard graft for Pia, given everything he'd been dealing with over the past few months in the lead-up to opening the clinic. Endless logistics. Paint samples. Cement grades. Accessibility ramps. Safety rails. And the list went on. It was as if he was missing a part of himself, not being able to practice medicine.

It's what your family would have wanted. You're doing it for them. Medicine will wait.

"Do you think that's her?" Pia's voice rose with excitement.

In the distance they could see a sky blue 4x4 coming along the road from the north, with a telltale blinking light. It was turning left.

"Can't you remember anything about her at all?" Pia looked up at him, eyes sparkling with excitement.

"Sorry, *amore*. Beatrice didn't say much. Just said it was a friend she'd stake our own friendship on."

"Wow! Beatrice is an amazing friend. That means a lot. Not like—" Pia stopped herself and grimaced an apology. "I mean, Marina was never really very nice anyway! You deserve better."

He grunted. There wasn't much to say on the matter. Not anymore. His thoughts were all for Bea and her privacy. He'd offered her a cottage up here at Mont di Mare, but she'd said she needed some serious alone time.

"Do you know what Dr. Murro and I called Marina?" Pia asked, a mischievous smile tweaking at the edges of her sparkle-glossed lips.

He shook his head. "Do I *want* to know?"

"Medusa!" She put her hands up beside her head and

turned them into a tangle of serpents, all the while making creepy snake faces.

"Charming, *chiara*. Next time you go to the gym to work with Dr. Murro, please do tell him that perhaps a bit less chat about my defunct love life and a splash more work might be in order."

"Zio!" Pia widened her big puppy-dog eyes. "We can't help it if she was horrible."

Luca gave one of her plaits another playful tug. Just what a man needed. To find out that no one liked his girlfriend all along. Then again...being upset about Marina was pretty much the last thing on his mind. Making the clinic a running, functioning entity was most important.

Six months. That was how far what little money he had left would last before the bank made good on their promise to repossess what had been under his family's care for generations.

Pia shrugged unapologetically, then pulled the pair of binoculars she always had looped around her neck up to her eyes, to track the car that was still making its way toward the turnoff to Mont di Mare.

"I hope Freda looks exactly like she did in the pictures Bea forwarded. And Edison. He's *definitely* a he, and Freda's a she, but I'm glad the trainer is a she, too."

"Why's that?"

"It'll be nice to have a grown-up friend."

"You have me!"

"I know, but..." Her eyes flicked away from his.

She'd always been so good about making him feel worthy of the enormous role of caring for her. And yet at moments like these...he knew there were gaps to be filled.

"It'll be nice to have a girl to talk to about...you know...*things*."

Luca looked away. Of *course* she could do with a woman in her life. Someone to fill even a small portion of the hole left when her mother had been killed in that insane accident. A massive truck hurtling toward them from the other side of the tunnel with nowhere else to go...

"Zio! I think I see Freda!"

"Who's Freda?"

"Freda's the *dog*!"

"Right."

"And it *is* a her! She's a *her*!"

"Who? The dog?"

"The *trainer*!"

Pia was clapping with excitement now and Luca couldn't help but crack a smile. His first genuine one in the last twenty-four hours.

"*Zio!* Comb your hair. She's almost here!"

Luca laughed outright. Fat lot of good a comb would do with the rest of him covered in sawdust and paint.

A far cry from his Armani-suited and booted days at his consultancy in Rome. The one none of his colleagues had been able to believe he'd just up and leave for a life in the hinterlands. He wouldn't have wished the life lessons he'd had to learn that night on anyone. His cross to bear. The suits were moth food as far as he was concerned.

He tugged both hands through his hair and messed it up werewolf-style.

"Suitable?"

Pia gave his "makeover" the kind of studious inspection to which only a sixteen-year-old could add gravitas, then rolled her eyes.

"It's not *my* fault if you're a fashion plate," he teased.

"I'm trying to save you from yourself," Pia shot back. "What if she's a beautiful blonde and you fall in love?"

"Nice try, Pia. I'm officially off the market."

"Officially off your rocker, more like," she muttered with an eye roll. "Look! They're turning onto the bridge!"

He spotted the vehicle, then looked out beyond the road and took in the sparkle of the sun upon the Adriatic Sea. Italy's most famed coastline. Croatia and Montenegro were somewhere out there in the distance. Dozens of ports where the world's billionaires parked their superyachts. The price tag of just one of those would have him up and running in no time.

He gave himself a short sharp shake. This wasn't the time for self-pity or envy. It was time to prove he was worthy of the name he'd been given. The name he hoped would stay on this village he now called home.

"Shall we go and greet our new guest?" Luca flourished a hand in the direction of the approaching vehicle, even though his niece already had the wheels of her chair in motion.

Fran had to remind herself to breathe. Way up there on the hilltop was the most beautiful village she'd ever seen. Golden stone. Archways everywhere. The hillsides were terraced in graduated "shelves." If one could define countless acres of verdant wildflower meadows and a generous sprinkling of olive trees to be the "shelves" of a mountainside.

It was almost impossible to focus on driving, let alone the figures coming into view in the courtyard at the end of the bridge. She rolled down the window to inhale a deep breath of air. Meadow grass. The tang of the sea. The sweetness of fruit ripening on trees.

Heaven.

For the first time in just about forever, Fran wondered how she was going to find the strength to leave.

Was that…? *Wait a minute.*

All the air shot out of her lungs.

Long, lean and dark haired was no anomaly in Italy, but she recognized this particular long, lean, dark-haired man. As she clapped eyes on the tall figure jogging alongside the beaming girl in the wheelchair, her heart rate shot into overdrive.

Fight or flight kicked in like something crazy. Her skin went hot and cold, then hot again. Not that it had *anything* to do with the picture-perfect jawline and cheekbones now squaring off in front of her SUV.

No *wonder* Beatrice had been all mysterious and tight-lipped last night.

Un-freakin'-believable.

Mr. You-and-I-Will-Never-Be-Friends was her new boss.

Chills skittered along her arms as their gazes caught and locked.

From the steely look in his eyes he hadn't exactly erased her from *his* memory either.

From the flip-flop of warmth in her tummy, her body hadn't forgotten all that glossy dark hair, tousled like a lusty he-man ready to drag her into a cave and—

Silver linings, Fran. Think of the silver linings. He hates you, so flirting isn't something you need to worry about.

The dogs were both standing up in the back now, mouths open, tongues hanging out as if smiling in anticipation of meeting Pia. Trust *them* to remember they were here to help—not ogle the local talent.

Take a deep breath... One...two...three... Here goes nothing.

She pulled the car up to where the pair were waiting, then jumped out and ran around the back to the dogs. The dogs would be the perfect buffer for meeting—

"Francesca."

Gulp! His voice was still all melted chocolate and a splash of whiskey. Or was it grappa because they were in Italy? Whatever. It was all late-night radio and she liked it. Precisely the reason to pretend she didn't by saying absolutely nothing.

"We meet again."

Mmm-hmm. All she could do was nod. Luca had looked a treat in his fancy-schmancy suit yesterday, but now, with a bit of sawdust... *Mmm.* The sleeves of his chambray shirt were rolled up enough to show forearms that had done hard graft...and he wore a pair of hip-riding moleskin trousers that looked as if they'd seen their fair share of DIY...

Mamma mia!

Of all the completely gorgeous, compellingly enigmatic Italians needing an assistance dog for his...

"Allow me to introduce my niece, Pia."

Fran shook herself out of her reverie.

Niece! Nieces were nice.

"Yes! Pia—of course." She swept a few stray wisps of hair behind her ear and turned her full attention on the teenager whose smile was near enough splitting her face in two. "I bet you're far more interested in meeting these two than me."

They all turned to face the back of her SUV, where two big furry heads were panting away in anticipation of meeting their new charge. Fran deftly unlocked the internal cage after commanding the two canines to sit.

"If you'd just back your chair up a bit, Pia. They are both really excited to meet you."

"Both?" Luca's voice shuddered down her spine.

"Yes, both," she answered as solidly as she could. "Not everyone gets off on the right foot when they first meet."

She lifted her gaze to meet his.

Luca's eyebrow quirked.

"Is that so? I thought dogs were instinctive about knowing a good match."

"*Dogs* are," Fran parried, with a little press and push of her lips. "People sometimes need a second chance to get things right."

Luca's eyebrow dipped, then arced again, and just when she was expecting a cutting remark she saw it— the kindness she'd knew she'd seen lurking somewhere in those smoky brown eyes of his.

"Zio! Leave Françesca alone. I want to see the dogs!"

Grateful for the reprieve from this verbal fencing, Fran turned her focus to a starry-eyed Pia as her eyes pinged from one dog to the other.

"Aren't they a bit…big?" Luca stepped forward, his presence feeling about a thousand times more powerful than either dog did to Fran.

"Zio Luca! No!" Pia protested. "They are perfect. Both of them!"

"She's actually right." Fran shrugged an apology. "When Bea explained that your village offered unique challenges in the navigating department, I thought a mountain dog would be perfect."

"You mean the big one?" Pia pointed at Freda, the Bernese.

"I sure do." She shot a glance toward Luca, who had

moved back from his protective position but still held a wary look in his eye.

She always forgot that to a person who wasn't used to dogs a Bernese could seem enormous. *Baby pony* was an oft-heard phrase when mountain dog "virgins" first saw them.

"Come along, Freda. Let's say hello to Pia."

"Surely Labs are more reliable. In terms of character." Luca stepped forward again, just managing to slot himself between Fran and Pia before she asked the dog to jump out.

Fran bit down hard on the inside of her cheek before replying. "Both dogs are extremely gentle and come with my one hundred percent guarantee."

"And what exactly is *that* worth?" Luca arced an eyebrow, daring her to name a number.

Fran's blood boiled. She wasn't here to prove herself to anyone. She was here to help. How *dare* he put her to some sort of ridiculous test of worth?

"I'll leave right now, if you think that's what's best. But I can guarantee that by the end of the day you will see a change in your niece's life. And as it is Pia's life we're talking about, perhaps *she* should be the one who is deciding."

They both turned to look at her, but when his niece opened her mouth to interject, Luca held out a hand to stop her.

"As her guardian, I make all the decisions for Pia's welfare."

"As an experienced trainer, I know you'd be making a mistake by turning me away."

Luca's inky, dark eyes stayed glued to hers, his face completely immovable. She felt as if she was clashing with a gladiator. One false move and—*crack!*—down she'd go. It didn't stop her from wanting to reach out and touch that salt-and-pepper stubble of his, though. Soft or scratchy...?

"You and I will never be friends."

"So?" Defiance saturated Fran's posture, but she didn't care. "Are you happy for me to unload them? Start bringing some empowerment to your niece's life?"

Without a backward glance Fran quickly clipped leads onto the dogs, and silently commanded them to jump down, approach Pia and present their paws for a handshake.

Pia laughed, delightedly taking each dog's paw for a shake, then giving their heads an adoring pat.

"Zio! *Per favore!* Can they all stay forever?" Pia's plaits flipped from one shoulder to the next as she looked between the two dogs and then beamed up at Fran as if she were a fairy godmother, complete with a magic wand. Which was nice. It was good to have someone rooting for her when the other person looked as if he'd happily tip her off the side of the mountain.

Fran turned toward Luca and crossed her arms. "Two against one?"

"Four against one," Pia said, then quickly tacked on in a gentler plea. "If that's okay, Zio? Can they at least stay until the end of the day?"

Luca's hands slipped to his hips as if he were reaching for invisible holsters. A small gust of wind rustled his already tousled hair. Off in the distance, Fran saw a rising plume of dust, as if a band of horses and *banditos* were heading their way to intervene. A showdown at dawn—minus the weapons and the sunrise.

"I promise you'll see a difference. In an hour, even."

Luca's eyelids lowered to half-mast as his glance

skidded away from her toward the dogs and then back to her.

Too much? *Oh, jinks.* How was she going to tell her father she'd messed up Canny Canines before she'd even had a chance to begin? Yes, she wanted to go back—but not with her proverbial tail between her legs.

"*Per favore*, Francesca." Luca affected a courtly bow, though the charm didn't quite make it to his eyes. "My niece seems to want to give you a tour. Please. Allow us to show you around our humble abode."

He stood up to his full height, brow furrowed tight at the bridge of his aquiline nose.

"Then we'll talk."

CHAPTER FOUR

FRAN'S GAZE CAUGHT with Luca's. If he wasn't being sincere, she was out of here.

What? And run home to Daddy a failure before you've even begun?

She forced herself to look deep into the mahogany darkness of his irises and seek answers. He didn't look away this time. He held his ground—eyes glued to hers—as if he knew what she was looking for.

Somewhere between the crackle of "I dare you to fail" and the burn of "she's all I've got," Fran found what she needed. The answer. How she knew that Luca was hiding a good man deep within that flinty exterior of his was beyond her—but she did.

"Luca, I just wanted—"

Of all the times for her backside to vibrate!

"Can you excuse me for just a moment?" Fran tugged her cell phone out of her back pocket, instructed the dogs to stay with Pia and Luca, then scooted off to the far end of the village's central plaza, where their tour of the "humble abode" was just wrapping up.

"Beatrice?" She didn't wait for a reply. "You are truly the evilest friend I have ever had the privilege of knowing."

Bea's wicked cackle trilled down the line. "I guess you've met the baron, then?"

"The baron?"

"Luca. Il Barone Montovano di Marino. Didn't I tell you he was a baron?"

She'd been at her lippiest, sassiest best with a *baron*?

"Princess Beatrice, you know blinking well you didn't tell me *anything*! And, yes. Since you ask, we *have* met, formed an instant kinship, become blood siblings and vowed to be the absolute best of friends forever and ever."

There was a beat.

Too sarcastic?

"Well, make sure you use an antiseptic wipe. It would be a shame if your new BFF had to chop off your finger because of a case of sepsis," Bea said without a hint of apology. Then she added, "I *knew* you two would get along."

"Yeah. Like water and oil."

"Oh, don't be ridiculous. He enjoys being a baron as much as you love being sole heiress to Martinelli Motors, so cool your jets. You two will hit it off. Mark my words."

Hmm… Time would have to be the arbiter on that one.

"Everything okay with you?"

"What do you think of Mont di Mare? Pretty impressive, eh?"

"Nice dodge, my friend." Fran tugged at her ponytail before deftly knotting it into a bun at the base of her neck. "Tell me you're all right and then I'll tell you how meeting Luca really went. Thunder and lightning are your two clues."

She glanced across at Luca and her eyes went wide.

He was kneeling beside the dogs, calling out half-hearted protests as Edison gave him a good old-fashioned face cleaning while Freda kept trying to put her paws on his shoulders for a hug. Pia's eyes were lit up bright. Not so brooding and glowering after all, then…

"Everything's fine, Fran. I'm planning an escape under the cover of darkness!"

Hearing Bea add melodramatic dum-dah-dum-dum noises was all the reassurance Fran needed. She was smarting, but she'd be fine.

"Any clues about where you're headed? I hear Transylvania's nice this year."

"Ha-ha. Vampires aren't my style."

"*No one* has your amount of style. Or class," Fran insisted.

"No need to fluff my ego, Fran. I'm going to be fine."

"You're amazing, Bea. Seriously. I don't think I'd be as calm and collected in your shoes."

"It's…it's a relief, really. My only goal is to get through the next few months with no paparazzi. Yours should be to get Luca to cook his stuffed pumpkin flowers for you. *Delicioso!*"

"He cooks?"

"Like a dream."

Fran grinned at the sound of Beatrice kissing the tips of her fingers.

"And just remember, Frannie, his bark is worse than his bite. He's a pussycat, really,"

Fran muttered a few disbelieving words to the contrary, but something in her fluttered as she caught sight of Luca trying—and failing—to get the dogs to stop chasing him.

Maybe he was just taking out his frustration about

Marina on her. He wouldn't be the first man she'd met who'd dealt with a broken heart by taking it out on her.

Dads are different, Fran.

Besides. Something told her Luca wasn't exactly brokenhearted about Marina.

"Steel exterior. Molten heart," Beatrice insisted. "You two'll be friends before you know it."

Humph. Doubtful.

She looked over and saw Luca, lying flat on his back, with the dogs appearing to give him some sort of chest compressions. Seeing him all silly and smiley made him...

"Beautiful..."

"He *is* a hottie, isn't he?" Bea teased.

"The place—not the man," Fran swiftly corrected.

"As I said," her friend teased, "time will change all that. You'll be fine. Just remember—Luca's the hawk... Pia's his fledgling. She's his number one concern. You get that right, your summer will be golden."

Fran shot a look up to the pure blue sky, hoping there was someone up there watching out for her. She had a feeling she'd need all the help she could get this summer.

"You *sure* you don't want to come up here to Mont di Mare? Luca told me he'd offered you an invitation."

"No, *chiara*. I'm all right. Just be there on the end of the phone if I need you?"

"Always."

"*Un bacione*, Fran. *Ciao!*"

"*Ciao, ciao!* Be safe."

She clicked the phone off and cast a final wish up to the heavens that Bea would find somewhere beautiful and private to heal. When she dropped her gaze, her eyes met and clashed with Luca's. Goose bumps ran across her arms as she watched the shutters slam down, cloaking the warm, loving man she'd just caught a glimpse of.

Never you mind, Il Barone. I'll show you everything I'm made of and then some.

"Bea." Fran held up the phone, toward him, as if it would prove their mutual friend had been on the line.

"Ending your friendship after yesterday's debacle?"

From the sharp intake of breath and the hollowing of Francesca's cheeks Luca knew he'd pushed it too far. Been too brusque. *Again.*

"Quite the opposite," she replied evenly, her eyes darting about the courtyard until they lit on some bloodred roses. A beautiful contrast to her honey-tanned skin. She bent forward, then stopped herself, giving him a sidelong glance. "I trust there aren't any rules against smelling the roses here?"

Her blue eyes widened, daring him to say otherwise.

He looked away as she called the dogs to heel, only to catch a don't-be-so-grumpy glare from his niece. A sharp reminder of who he was doing this for. All of it. When life ripped your entire family away from you except for one precious soul you cherished it. And he was making a hash of that, as well. Too out of practice. Too many of his earlier years spent being intent on the wrong goals. If he'd known the learning curve to making things right would be so hard…

He'd still be doing it. Even if it meant putting up with Little Miss Ray of Sunshine for the next two months. Pia seemed smitten and that was what counted.

Despite himself, Luca's eyes were drawn to Francesca like a feline to catnip. The fullness of her lips was darkened to a deep emotional red. Not a speck of any other makeup. Jeans and a baseball shirt that teased at the edges of her shoulders. Her blond hair was pulled back from her face in a thick ponytail that swished between her shoulder blades when she walked. Not that he'd been watching her closely… Her shoes were practical leather ankle boots, similar to the boots horsey types wore. Funny… He could easily picture her riding a horse along the mountain trails. Something he and his sister had often done, disappearing for hours at a time, stuffing themselves with wild berries and drinking straight from the mountain streams.

Those days were gone now. Long gone. Just as Francesca's fripperies from yesterday's wedding had all but disappeared. No more soft pink nail polish. No eye shadow, mascara. All of it cleared away to show off her distinct natural beauty. The countryside suited her. Mont di Mare suited her—as if an Old Master had painted her there and just changed her clothing with the passage of time…

"Freda. Edison." Fran commanded the dogs to sit with a gesture, shot Luca an over-the-shoulder wait-for-it-look, then a mischievous grin to Pia. She whipped out her fingers pistol-style and "shot" each of the dogs, who instantly rolled over and played dead.

Pia was consumed by gales of laughter and Fran's lips had parted into a full-fledged smile. One a movie star would have paid a lot for.

"Is there anything *useful* they can do?"

"Zio Luca!" Pia swiped at the air between them. "What *has* got into you today?"

"I'm just waiting to see if Francesca has something helpful to show us. What was it? An hour, she said, and we'd see a change?"

"She made me laugh," Pia growled.

He opened his mouth to protest. Surely he and Pia

had laughed… No. Not so much. Especially in the weeks since the bank had slapped the deadline on him. Six months or *finito*.

"Pia—" Fran took a couple of steps forward "—could I use your binoculars for a minute?"

"*Si*, of course." She untangled the strap from her plaits and handed them to Fran.

Without a second glance at Luca, Fran took a scan around the plaza.

"Can you distract the dogs for a minute?"

Pia obliged as Fran jogged over to a small olive tree and hung the binoculars on a low branch, then jogged back.

"Freda." She signaled to Pia's neck. "Where are the binoculars?"

Luca watched wordlessly as the dog took a quick sniff of Pia, did a quick zigzag around the courtyard, abruptly loped over to the olive tree, spotted and tugged down the binoculars by their strap, then padded back, offering the binoculars to a delighted Pia.

"Impressive," he acquiesced. "But hardly a life changer."

Fran pushed her lips forward into a little moue. One that said, *You ain't seen nothin' yet, cowboy.*

He folded his arms and rocked his weight back onto his heels. *Go on*, his stance said. *Prove it.*

A flare of irritation lit up her eyes, bringing a smile to his lips. He got to her as much as she got to him. A Mutual Aggravation Society.

In quick succession Fran ran both dogs through a number of tasks. She had Pia wheel around the courtyard, dropping various items. The dogs picked them all up. They found exits from the courtyard on command. The dogs pushed the wheelchair from one point to another, navigating it around the low-slung branches of the various fruit trees dappling the area.

Fran slipped each dog into a harness and had them take turns pulling Pia on various routes around the courtyard, stopping at one point to pick up a set of keys that had slipped from Luca's pocket. The display culminated in each dog barreling out of the courtyard and returning two minutes later, triumphant, with their water bowls tucked in their mouths, and then dropping them at Fran's feet.

She turned to him, arms crossed in satisfaction. "Proof enough for you?" The arc in her eyebrow dared him to say otherwise.

He made a noncommittal noise, his eyes glued to Fran's, as sharp hit after hit of connection exploded in his chest. He rammed the sensations to the background. Work and Pia. His only two concerns. Francesca brought chaos in her wake. She teased too cruelly at his instinctive urges to pull her in close and taste exactly what those full lips of hers—

"They're *amazing*, Zio! Aren't they amazing? We should get dogs for all the patients! Wouldn't that be just the best?" Pia reeled off her praises, failing to notice the crackle of electricity surging between her uncle and Fran.

He took a step back to break the connection. "Bravo, Francesca." Luca gave a stilted clap, trying to ignore his niece's ebullient response. "I'm sorry to bring the display to an end, but I'm afraid my niece has to spend some time with her tutor."

"It's English lessons, Zio. I could practice with Francesca, *si*?"

"No," he answered in his most pronounced Italian accent. The role of cantankerous uncle was coming to him a bit too fluidly, but needs must. Their world had mayhem enough without a canine-training Mary Poppins running around the place with fairy dust and moonbeams.

Although it was better than Marina's preference, that the village be revamped into an exclusive hotel. Little wonder she'd chosen Marco. He had glitz and glamour down to a T.

Pia gave an exasperated sigh but turned her wheelchair toward the arched stone passageway that led to their private quarters before abruptly spinning around. "Can they—will the dogs be able to come with me?"

"Absolutely." Fran nodded with a quick backward glance to check that it was okay with Luca.

He nodded.

"They are *your* buddies now. Freda is the one I thought might best suit your needs, but it's a good idea to spend time with both of them. We can meet later and talk about things you specifically need help with and start to set up a training routine. Sound good?"

"Cramp!" Pia screamed suddenly, her hands seizing into gnarled fists. "Cramp!"

Without a second glance Fran was on her knees in front of Pia, cupping her hands together, kneading one, then the other, tension knotting her brow as tears formed in Pia's eyes.

"Do you have any heat wraps?" She glanced up at Luca, completely oblivious to the shock in his eyes.

"Let me." Luca reached out to take his niece's slender hands, noting as he did the expert efficiency with which Fran massaged Pia's fingers.

"I'm a physiotherapist. It's fine," Fran said.

"Certified by the University of Life?"

"Harvard," she snapped back. "Good enough for

you?" She continued massaging Pia's hands. "You'd be best getting those heat wraps."

"*I* decide what's best for my niece—not you."

"Zio, *please*," Pia pleaded through her tears. "Francesca is doing fine. Please can you get the wraps?"

"I've got a sock filled with rice in my car, if there's a microwave nearby. You just throw the sock in for a—"

"I have appropriate heat wraps. I just—" *I just don't want to leave her with you.* Though unspoken, the words crackled in the air between them.

Francesca continued her fluid movements, but turned her head to face him. "She will be safe with me," she said, more solidly than he'd thought possible. "I will take care of her."

He looked at his niece, her features crumpled in pain, and made the decision.

He ran.

The sooner he left, the sooner he would be back.

A dog trainer *and* a physio? There was a story there. But it was one that would have to wait.

A few minutes later he returned, astonished to see Pia's face wreathed in smiles, her hands lodged in the Bernese mountain dog's "armpits."

"Stand-in heat pads." Fran shrugged, pushing up from her knees at the foot of Pia's wheelchair.

"Rendering these unnecessary?" Luca held up the hot packs he'd already cracked so that they'd be ready for action.

"Sorry." Fran shrugged again and turned to her dogs with a grin, seemingly oblivious to the thousands of dark thoughts that had run through his head as he'd raced to the clinic, pawed through the storage cupboards, then raced back only to find his efforts had been for naught.

"I brought you some electrolyte water, too, Pia. In case you were dehydrated."

"Is she on any medication?"

Luca's eyes widened. "I have brought her what she needs. Pia's on a couple of things for her paraplegia, but other than that has made the choice not to start on any medication until she absolutely has to."

"Right *here*, Zio Luca. No need to talk about me as if I'm invisible!"

"I've got some great cream recipes we can make up that might help," Fran said to Pia, barely acknowledging Luca. "I bet there are loads of medicinal herbs and flowers growing out there. The dogs and I can forage for you!"

"That'd be great!" Pia enthused.

"Here." Luca took his niece's hands in his and wove the heat pad between them. "Better?"

Pia nodded, then turned away.

"Fran?"

Luca watched as Pia looked up at Fran with a shy look he rarely saw from his niece.

"I'm glad you're here."

"Me, too," Fran replied straight away, then looked up, her azure eyes meeting Luca's as powerfully as a bolt of lightning. There was a connection there. A vivid, primal, deep-seated connection.

One he was going to have to bury in order to survive.

Once Pia had left, her hands wrapped around a heat pad, the tutor in control of the wheelchair and the dogs trotting merrily behind, Fran and Luca eyed each other warily.

A lion and a tigress vying for supremacy. Or a truce?

Fran broke the silence "It's very beautiful up here."

"Far too much room for improvement," he countered, wincing when he saw she'd taken it personally.

Luca put on his "bright" voice, knowing it would sound a bit strangled, but he wasn't ready for making nice with Fran. Might not ever be.

"Shall we get you and your things to your quarters?"

"If that means I'm staying?"

He shot her a noncommittal look. "It's a long walk. Plenty of time to change my mind."

The incident with Pia had shaken him. He was his niece's warrior—her defense against the countless aches and pains she'd had to tackle and overcome since the accident. Getting her an assistance dog was one thing. Seeing her reach to someone else for help...

It hurt.

More than leaving his exclusive reconstructive surgery clinic in Rome to bring his niece here had hurt. More than discovering, once he'd arrived, that his father had leveraged Mont di Mare to within an inch of its life. More than staring daily at the scar he would never fix, keeping it as a reminder—a vivid, daily reminder—of the promises he'd made to do his very best for Pia.

"Hello? Luca?" Fran was waving her hand in front of his face. "You've obviously got things on your mind, and about *this* much patience for me—" She pinched at a smidgen of air, then crushed it between her fingers. "So if you'd just point the way, I'm sure I can find it myself."

"No, you can't."

He bit back a smile as Fran bridled at his pronouncement.

"I happen to have a very good sense of direction."

"I'm sure you do, but we haven't put any signs up on the doors, so it'll be tricky for you to find your cottage."

"Cottage?" Fran's eyes widened in delight as she

tugged a couple of medium-sized tote bags out of the truck onto the stone plaza.

She did that a lot. As if everything new was a pleasure rather than a burden. Each corner turned was a moment of thrilling excitement rather than full of the dread that enveloped him whenever a foreman or a staffer headed his way with a purposeful gait and an I-need-to-bend-your-ear-for-a-minute look in his eye.

Fatigue. That was all it was. The clinic was a massive project. The ramifications of failing were too weighty to bear.

"Shall we?"

Fran gave him a wary look, shifting her weight so that her crossed arms formed a protective shield. "Look. I know we didn't get off to a very good start yesterday."

"That would be putting it mildly." They were past niceties. She might as well know she could count him out of her new-friend posse.

"I'm really, truly, incredibly sorry about what happened, but—no offense—I'm much sorrier for Bea, who has to deal with all the mess left by that ratbag fiancé of hers."

"Ratbag?" Luca quirked an eyebrow. Honesty. He liked that in a woman.

"Ratbag," Beatrice replied solidly.

"At last." He picked up one of her bags from the ground where she'd let them drop. "Something we agree on."

"Phew!" She gave a melodramatic swipe of her brow before picking up the other tote bag and running along after him. "And I just want to say I am genuinely grateful for the chance to experiment up here with Pia and the dogs."

"Experiment?" Luca dropped the bag and turned on

her. "I don't have time for *experiments*! I need exacting, perfect, unrelentingly driven, skill-based superiority in *everything*. In *everyone* who comes through these gates! Doctors, nurses, cleaners and, most of all, *you*! You are the one person I'm relying on most to help!"

Fran's jaw dropped open, her eyes widening as the stream of vitriol continued.

As the words poured out and he felt his gestures grow more emphatic Luca abruptly clamped his lips tight and stuffed his fists into his pockets. Baring his heart to Bea in the form of this tirade was as good as…as good as showing his hand.

He almost laughed at the irony. His poker face was as poor as his father's. His father had lost the family fortune. Had *he* just lost Pia's shot at a bit of independence? Some much-deserved fun?

Extraordinarily, Francesca just stood there. Dry-eyed. Patient. Listening to his tongue-lashing as if in fact he was calmly explaining that he was terribly sorry, but he'd been under tremendous pressure owing to the imminent launch of the clinic and, as a result, his concern for his niece and her welfare was escalating. That it pained him to admit it, but he needed support. He needed *her*.

"Feel better?" Fran finally asked after the silence between them had grown heavy with expectation.

"Not really," Luca answered, furious with himself for letting down his guard. He reached for her bags again. "Let's get on with this, shall we? I've already wasted too much time today."

Fran held her ground. "I want you to know I'm willing to stake everything I am on those dogs."

"And what *is* that exactly? Beyond, of course, wedding whistle-blower and circus-trick performer?"

"That's not fair."

"My time is precious, signorina—I'm afraid I didn't catch your surname."

Fran's eyes narrowed. Her teeth took part of her full lip captive, unfurling it bit by bit.

"Martinelli."

When she said it, he saw a change in her. A hint of something he knew *he* saw when he bothered to look at his own reflection in the mirror. Not the scar. The pain. The pain that came from no longer being part of something he should have cherished so much more than he had.

Family.

One simple word that equaled a heady combination of love, guilt, trying to do better and not getting a single damn thing right.

"Looks like there's a story there," Luca said.

She shrugged.

"Complicated?"

"Very." Her lips pressed forward before thinning into a tight smile.

Luca tipped his chin in understanding. "Looks like we've found *two* things in common."

If there was anyone who grasped *complicated*, it was him.

"Let's cut across here." Luca pointed toward a short covered alley. "It's the long way around."

Fran arched an eyebrow at him.

"I like to get to know my staff."

"I'm not charging you, so technically I'm not staff."

"I can fire you, so technically you *are*. My niece is the single most important person to me in this world. If I'm not happy, you're gone."

Free or not, he wasn't letting just *anyone* get involved with Pia.

"My niece seems to like you. I have yet to be persuaded. With the clinic opening, and no time to look for someone else, I'll give you a chance to prove me wrong."

"And for that I humbly thank you, my lord." An effervescent laugh burbled up and out of Fran's throat as she went into a deep curtsy. "Or is it *Your Excellency*? How *does* one address a baron?"

If he hadn't been so irritated, he would have laughed. She was right to mock him. The arrogance! Since when had he become such a stuck-up prig?

"It's Luca," he said finally, willing himself not to smile. "That's all you need to know."

"Got it." Fran winked, tapping the side of her nose. "Your undercover name."

"Something like that."

He pointed her toward the path they'd need to take to her cottage. Close to his cottage. *Too* close, he realized now. Yet another note for his to-do list: *don't get attached. She'll be gone soon enough.*

CHAPTER FIVE

"DID BEA TELL you anything about me?" Fran asked once they'd walked for a bit in silence, stopping at a bench overlooking the peaks and folds of the surrounding countryside. She focused on a field full of sunflowers. A reminder of all the good she hoped would come of moving back home.

"No. Why?" Luca eyes narrowed, interesting little crinkles fanning out from the corners of his eyes as he tried to figure it out on his own.

"Well, for starters, my full name is Francesca Lisbetta Martinelli." Fran gave him a moment before asking, "Nothing?"

"I've not got all day, Francesca." A flicker of impatience crossed his features.

"Vincente Martinelli... Lui è mio padre."

Saying it in Italian seemed to come more naturally. She and her father spoke it at home. She might as well pronounce her paternity in his native tongue.

"Basta! No? Really?"

A panoply of reaction passed across Luca's face. It was a little bit like watching a short film. Such an interesting face. Not just the scar, which she was aching to touch. There were other stories there. Stories she'd love to hear if only her presence didn't drive him so batty.

"So that makes you…?"

"The daughter of a billionaire."

A flash of understanding lit up his eyes, then disappeared so quickly she thought she'd imagined it.

"And your point is…?" Luca spun his finger in a keep-talking swirl, then gave his watch a sharp tap.

Not the usual reaction. That was nice. Most people wanted to know why she didn't walk around dripping in jewels and designer labels.

"I'm moving home at the end of the summer."

"And…?" Luca's impatience was growing.

"I've not lived there for a long time. Or ever accepted my father's help. But this time…this time he's going to invest in my business."

"The dogs?" Luca's eyebrows lifted.

He obviously thought it was a weird choice, but it wasn't his money, so…

"The point being I've never accepted money from him. *Ever.* And I'm not going home with a fail on my books before I've even started."

Luca blinked, processing that.

"Why are you accepting his help now?"

"Because I want my dad back in my life. And I want him to be proud of me. I believe in what I'm doing this time."

"*This* time?" A flash of concern darkened his features.

"I used to be a physiotherapist. Well, physio and hydrotherapy."

"Why did you give it up?"

She considered him for a moment. He didn't need to know the whole story. Going into business with a "friend" only to discover he'd thought being partners with her meant tapping into her father's wealth.

"One of my patients asked me to help a dog with arthritis. Working with dogs seemed more…"

"Satisfying?" Luca suggested.

"Sounds like the voice of experience," she countered, unwilling to tell Luca how betrayed she'd felt. How hurt. She'd wanted to go to her father, but had felt too ridiculous to confess how foolish she'd been. The last thing she expected from Luca—or anyone—was sympathy. Being an heiress was hardly tragic. Just…*tricky*.

"So you just abandoned your patients? Left on a whim?"

"No. I oversaw their treatment until I could transfer them all to someone I trusted."

"A boyfriend?"

Where had *that* come from?

"My mentor. She took on each and every patient."

"And once you'd shaken off your responsibilities—"

"I didn't shake them off!" Fran protested.

"You left."

"I was young."

"And why should I believe you won't do the same to Pia?"

"You're just going to have to trust me."

Luca's jaw tightened. *Trust*. That was what it was going to boil down to.

"Why should I trust you?"

"I did what was right yesterday, even though it could have cost me the friendship I hold dearest in my heart." Fran's eyes clouded with more emotion than she'd hoped to betray. She swallowed it down and continued, "That, and the second I saw *you* were the person I'd be working for I could've turned the car around and left right then and there. But the dogs seemed excited. They like

Pia. Which makes sense. They seem to like *you*. Which makes less sense. But I trust them. Dogs are loyal."

"Three," Luca said grimly.

"Three?"

"Three things we agree on. Dogs are the only sentient creatures who have any loyalty. Excluding, of course, my niece. If she can stick with me, she can stick with anyone."

"Ah! Finally admitting you're a bit of a Mr. Cranky Pants, then?"

Fran teased at the corner of her T-shirt. Had she overstepped the mark with that one?

"Not a chance, *carina*."

Fran looked up at his change of tone and was caught completely off balance as Luca flashed her a wicked smile.

Santo cielo! A swirl of sparks swept through Fran's tummy, lighting up all sorts of places she'd rather not think about when she was trying to be serious and grown-up. Sort of. Maybe…

"Whatever." She clucked dismissively, feeling a bit more like herself. "Just you wait. Beatrice has assured me we'll be friends. That'll be my summer challenge."

Luca grunted. "We're a long way from friends, *bellissima*. And we're nearly at your cottage." He tipped his head toward a wooden door.

Shame she couldn't convince him to stand there all day. Backlit by the sun. Hair tousled by the gentle breeze. The outline of his body looking rugged and capable. The perfect alpha male to have a summer romance with and then get on with the rest of her life.

As if *that* would ever happen.

"Any final tidbits of wisdom about assistance dogs you want to impart before I drop you off at your cottage?"

"So you're going to let me stay?"

She watched as he processed her question—his teeth biting together, his jaw giving that telltale stress twitch along the line of his scar, his lips parting to demand one last task.

"Give me one word to describe the change you see in your customers once they have a Fran Special."

One word?

"Wait—give me a minute." She scrunched her eyelids tight in order to think and came up blank. In a panic, she looked up into Luca's espresso-dark gaze and it came to her. "Breathtaking."

Just like you, bellissima.

The words popped into Luca's mind and near enough escaped his lips as Fran's blue eyes lit up, her cheeks flushing with pleasure and undiluted pride in what she did.

It was the same sensation *he* felt when a reconstruction surgery had gone to plan. Particularly when a patient picked up a mirror for the first time and, eyes brightening, exclaimed, "It's the old me!" That was far better than the enhancement surgeries that paid the bills. If Mont di Mare could one day do charitable cases, that would be a dream come true.

He shook the thought away. An impossibility right now. A far-off dream.

"So, what's your decision?"

Luca shook his head, temporarily confused. "What decision?"

"Are you going to let me stay—" she swung her thumb toward the village entryway "—or do we have to drag these bags back to my car and pick up the dogs so I can hoof it?"

Pragmatics told him to send her away.

Fran was chaos. He needed peace.

But a splinter of doubt pierced through his more reasoned side.

Perhaps it *wasn't* chaos she brought. Perhaps it was… possibility. And that meant change. Never easy, but sometimes necessary.

The look of glee on his niece's face when she'd seen not only the dogs but Fran had tugged at his sensibilities. Not to mention the sheer expectation on Fran's face now, which was making too great a play on his heartstrings. The strings of the heart he was beginning to realize had never quite regained its usual cheerful cadence since the accident. The very same heart he felt opening, just a sliver, to this ray of joy standing before him. Besides, *he* didn't have to spend time with her. Pia did.

"Si." He gave Fran a quick nod before adding wryly. "Pia might disown me if I say otherwise."

A whoop that might have filled a football stadium flew out of Fran's throat and she immediately launched into some sort of whirling happy dance, the likes of which, he was quite sure, the streets of Mont di Mare had never seen.

Oh, Dio!

Had he *really* just welcomed Hurricane Fran into their lives?

Dance finished, Fran eventually came to a standstill, chest heaving with excitement, eyes alight with the power of that single yes.

"Really?" Endearingly, her voice hit the higher altitudes of her range and her fingers went all pitter-patter happy. "I promise you won't regret it. And when Pia's at school I will *totally* help with painting or putting up

wallpaper or making beds—anything you need. I'll even change bedpans when the patients arrive if it will help."

"We have moved a bit beyond bedpans in terms of patient care."

"Cool." Fran was unfazed. "Whatever the least favorite jobs are, count me in."

He began to shake his head no, but she stopped him with a finger on his lips.

"I won't take no for an answer. You're helping me more than you know, and from what I've gleaned—" they both turned to watch yet another delivery truck begin its way up the bridge toward the clinic "—you have a lot to do. Another pair of hands isn't going to hurt anything, is it? Three years of boarding school has ensured my hospital corners are excellent in the bed-making department."

"How's your grouting?" he asked, in a tone more suited to a master tiler than a doctor doing his best to bring a thousand loose ends together into one beautiful tapestry.

"Unparalleled!" she shot back without the blink of an eye. "My sanding skills are a bit rusty, but I know my way around a mop and bucket something serious."

A sudden urge to pull Fran into his arms seized Luca. If he had Fran on his side she'd no doubt start spreading her pixie dust and turn the entire workload from a burden into an adventure. Why *shouldn't* he have a partner in crime?

Because the bank was threatening to take it all away.

If you'd paid more attention to your father, seen how low he was feeling...

Their gazes connected, meshing in a taut sensation of heightened awareness, powerful currents of electricity surging between the pair of them. Holding them together as one. Sensations he hadn't felt for a long time charged through him, lighting up parts of his body to a wattage he hadn't felt in even longer.

The buzzing of his phone checked the sensations. The raw attraction.

He glanced at the screen.

Work.

The consultant for one of his patients who'd be flying in by helicopter a week from today.

Fun and spontaneity would have to wait.

The first hit of genuine attraction he'd felt in years would have to go untended.

He had bills to pay.

"*Scusi.* I've got to take this."

"Of course." Fran's smile bore the same shade of disappointment he felt in his marrow. "Patients come first."

He took a few steps away, the smile he'd so recently worn eradicated without a trace. "*Si*, Dr. Firenze. How can I help you?"

CHAPTER SIX

THE WEEK HAD passed in a blur. An adrenaline-fueled blur that was about to culminate in the arrival of his first five patients. T minus eighteen hours and counting.

Luca pulled the weights out of their packaging and began lining them up on the rack. These would all be in use soon.

He sat back on his heels and scanned the rehab gym. Gleaming weights machines. Several pairs of handrails ready to bear the weight of patients ready to be put to the test.

The doctor in him itched to get back to work. Not the doctor who'd worn the fancy suits and tended to Rome's image-conscious elite. The doctor who'd re-trained at night after working all day with his niece. The doctor who'd poured every last cent he had into getting to this point.

At least Pia and Fran had been so engrossed in working with the dogs that Luca hadn't had to add the guilt of neglecting his niece to everything else he was feeling. And, in fairness to Fran, she'd gone above and beyond being an assistance-dog trainer this past week. Any spare moment she'd had away from Pia and the dogs had, true to her word, been spent doing anything and everything she could to get the clinic to the gleaming, immaculate state of readiness it was in now.

"Are you ready for the big reveal?" Fran appeared in the doorway, a mischievous smile making her look more imp than workhorse.

"Does Pia really need to do this *now*? Half of Mont di Mare still isn't renovated. I haven't checked the patients' rooms or the family quarters yet, and there are still—"

"C'mon!" Fran held up a hand, then arced her arm, waving for him to join her. "This means a lot to her— and I have an idea about the other thing. The unrenovated tidbits."

"How unusual," he answered drily.

Tidbits.

Half the village, more like: ten family houses, ten more patient rooms and the same number again for common rooms and treatment facilities. *Tidbits.* Only an American! He checked himself. Only an *optimist* like Fran would call the amount of work left to be done tidbits. The same projects that buoyed her up near enough pinned him to the ground with worry. What had *possessed* him to turn one of the least disabled-friendly places in the universe into a specialized clinic for disabled people?

Optimism?

Necessity?

"All right." He pushed up from the floor once the final row of weights had been laid out. "Let's hear it, Little Miss Creativity."

"Ha-ha. Very funny, Signor White-Walls-or-Bust." She fluttered her lashes. "It's not *my* fault the spirit of Italy's esteemed relationship with beauty and art courses through my veins and not yours."

Luca watched, unexpectedly transfixed as Fran struck a modeling pose, swooshing her hair up and over one shoulder as she skidded her slender fingers along the length of her athletic figure, eventually coming to rest on her thigh.

He tried to tamp down the flare of heat rising within him.

A lab coat would be most convenient right about now.

He cleared his throat. There were things to do. A clinic to open. This mysterious "reveal" to witness. No doubt another one of Pia's feats with her dogs rather than Francesca reenacting Salome's Dance of the Seven Veils.

He considered the swish of her derriere as she turned to walk down the hall.

Pity.

Where *had* he put those lab coats?

She glanced over her shoulder. "I'll spell out my idea on the way, and you can let me know if it's a yea or a nay by the time we get there." Fran glanced back again, eyes widening as he remained glued to the spot for no apparent reason. "It's our *thing*! Walking, talking, deciding. Remember?"

Just one week together and they had a "thing"? He rolled his eyes.

She dropped him a wink.

A flirtatious wink.

Was that the tip of her tongue peeking out between her teeth, giving the bow and dip of her top lip a surreptitious lick?

Sleep. That was what he needed. A good night's sleep and he'd be seeing things more clearly.

"All right, then. What's this grand idea of yours?"

"Well!" She wove her hands together underneath her chin. "I know you're rehab royalty—"

"Along with a team of highly trained experts," Luca interrupted.

She didn't need to know he'd been dubbed the King of Collagen before the accident had pushed him away from plastics to spinal injury rehabilitation. He probably would have carried on with plastics forever until— *bam!* In thirty horrifying seconds his life had changed.

He shook his head against the rising bile, forcing himself to focus on what Fran was saying.

"I read all of the bios for your clinicians last night, and there is some serious brainpower in play here." She dropped her hands. "Anyhow, I was thinking about the psychological advantages of being part of things here."

Luca gave her a sidelong look. "Do you mean you or the patients? All your chipping in has been much appreciated, Francesca. The painting, making the beds as promised… But if you read the résumés properly you will have noticed we have two very experienced psychiatrists on the team."

"I'm not talking about me and a paint roller. I'm thinking more hands-on stuff for the patients. There *is* the itty-bitty problem of half your village needing a splash more work done to it."

Her lips widened into an apologetic wince-smile.

"How very…politic, Signorina Martinelli. I presume your plan includes *you* wrapping everything up nicely before your intended departure date?"

The smile dropped from Fran's face as quickly as the light fled from her eyes.

Luca could have kicked himself. Still shooting the messenger. Fran had been a trouper, working as hard as his paid staffers—if not harder—to get everything shipshape for the opening. She didn't deserve to be on the sharp end of his mood. Particularly seeing as he wasn't entirely sure he wasn't behaving like a boor in order to fight off the deepening attraction he felt to his resident sunflower.

"*Per favore*, Francesca." He forced himself to grind out the plea. "Please tell me your idea."

"Why, thank you very much!" She rubbed her hands together excitedly. "I can't really take credit for the idea, though. The other day I was watching online videos— you know, those feel-good ones where human spirit triumphs over adversity and you end up crying because people are so amazing?"

She looked across at the dubious expression he knew he was wearing and qualified her statement.

"The ones that make *me* cry anyway. So, there was this huge pile of bricks and a guy in a wheelchair— totally hot. Completely good-looking. Like you. But he was more…uh…*Nordic*."

She stopped, took a step back to consider him, and as their eyes caught a streak of pink blossomed on her cheeks.

"Let's not get carried away, here, Fran. Shall we?"

He gestured that they should continue along the stone-slab route they were making short work of. Fran scuttled ahead, rabbiting on about the video and only occasionally looking back at him. He was surprised to find he was smiling. At her unquenchable thirst for life? Or the fact she thought he was good-looking?

Foolish, really.

He shoved the thoughts away and forced himself to listen to her suggestion. It was the least he could do after his abrupt behavior.

By the time they reached the archway leading out

to the bridge he'd been more than persuaded. Her idea was a good one.

"So what you're saying is if the patients—no matter what their background—put some actual graft into refurbishing the rest of the village, they'll be happier?"

"Precisely. I mean, this guy—totally paralyzed from the waist down—made just about the coolest fireplace out of bricks and mortar that I've ever seen. He *made* something. Crafted it with his own hands. Something many able-bodied people wouldn't even dream of starting, let alone finishing. I'm completely happy to oversee the project, of course. I know your team's hands are full."

She stood before him, blue eyes bright with expectation. Hope.

Tempting...

Pragmatics forced his hand.

"I hate to rain on your parade, Francesca, but there are thousands of other considerations. Health and safety, for one. You don't know how many inspections I have to deal with already—if I were to add patients to the mix of some already dangerous situations, I—"

He stopped himself. He'd been about to say he couldn't afford the insurance. Truth was he could hardly afford *any* of this. But turning it all over to the bank just so it could be demolished was out of the question. The clinic simply *had* to be a success.

"Look—" Fran raised her hands in a hear-me-out gesture "—I know what you're saying, and the idea definitely needs to be fleshed out. Especially as a lot of your patients are on the young side, right?"

"All of them." Luca nodded. "Teenagers."

"I'm not talking about everyone building stone walls or pizza ovens—although that *would* be a totally great idea. Can you imagine it? Pizza under the stars! What teenager doesn't love pizza?"

Luca glanced at his watch and spun his finger in a let's-get-on-with-it gesture, all the while trying his best not to get caught up in her enthusiasm.

His focus had to be X-ray machines. Crucial rehabilitation equipment being properly installed. Clipboards! If he'd known just how many clipboards he'd need when he'd started this pie-in-the-sky project...

"Sorry." She threw him an apologetic look. "I've just—I've just fallen a little bit in love with this place and it's hard to fight the enthusiasm, you know?"

Of course he knew. And her enthusiasm—despite his best efforts to be stoically distant—had touched his heart. His passion for the place was why he'd started the project in the first place. But now, with bills to pay and the bank breathing down his neck...

"I'm afraid it'll have to go on the pipe dreams list, Francesca."

Fran's disappointed expression soon brightened into something else. Inspiration.

"I've got an even better idea. I bet you there are any number of craftsmen who would love to come up here and work. True Italian craftsmen who wouldn't mind passing on some of their expertise to willing apprentices. Leather. Glass. Embossing. Calligraphy. I once saw an entire wall done in a painted leather wallpaper. It was amazing."

"We are *not* covering the walls in leather wallpaper, Fran."

"All right Mr. Grumpy. They don't have to be leather. Who cares what the patients do as long as they're happy? Even if it's just throwing a bit of paint on a wall. In the nicest way possible, of course," she finished with a polished smile.

"And what makes you think working on a building site will be an effective remedy for their ailments in comparison with the unparalleled medical attention they will be receiving here—*if* you ever let me get back to work, that is?"

Fran looked at him as if he was crazy.

"Who *doesn't* feel the satisfaction of a job well-done? Of knowing you've made an actual difference to somewhere this special. I mean, you must be *bursting* with pride."

A crackle of irritation flared in him.

"Francesca, the only thing I'm bursting with is the desire to untangle myself from this ridiculous conversation and get back to—"

Luca stopped in his tracks as they turned the corner of the archway into the main courtyard. Emotions ricocheted across his chest in hot thuds of recognition.

Humility. Pride. Achievement.

All the staff were assembled in the center of the broad arc—an impressive crowd of applauding doctors, rehab therapists, X-ray technicians and countless others. In the center was Pia and the two dogs. When her eyes lit on him she whispered a quick command to the dogs, each holding the end of a thick blue ribbon in their mouths, and they went in separate directions until it was taut and he could read the message on it. *"Bravo! I nostri migliori auguroni, Dr. Montovano!"*

The unfamiliar tickle of emotion teased at the back of Luca's throat.

Congratulations on a job well-done.

No one had done anything like this for him. *Ever.* His partners at the plastic surgery clinic had always mocked him for his pro bono cases. For bringing a bit of pride back into the life of a child with a birth defect or a scar that might have changed their lives forever. *Money!* they'd said. *The high life!*

He looked across at Fran. A flush of pleasure played across her cheeks as she watched him take it all in. The ridiculous conversation they'd been having made sense now. A distraction. Typical Fran. Perfection and mayhem in one maddening and beautiful package.

He felt torn. The sentiment of the moment was pure kindness.

"Zio! Come! Look at the food Fran has organized! It's all from artisan specialists in Tuscany!" Pia wheeled over to him and took his hand.

Behind the doctors and other medical practitioners— a team of about thirty, who were now reliant on him and the success of the clinic—were two trestle tables heaving under the weight of a bounty of antipasti, salads, savory tarts. All the regional specialties—and the people who had made them. Anything and everything a red-blooded Italian would crave if he were away from home.

He gruffly cleared his throat, giving them all a nod of thanks for their contributions.

More cries of *"Bravo!"* and *"Auguroni!"* filled the air.

He waved off the applause with a quick comment about how they were a team. How they all deserved a pat on the back for pulling together in the same way generations of villagers had back in the day when someone had been fool enough to start carving into the side of this blasted mountain and call it home.

Looking around at the smiling faces, hearing the laughter, feeling the buzz of anticipation in the air, he allowed himself a brief moment of elation. If he could hold on to that feeling—

Luca's eyes lit upon Fran, the only woman in the world who would have bothered to make this moment happen.

Something deep within him twisted and ached. Longed to have a spare ounce of energy, an unfettered moment to explore…test the waters and see what would happen if he and Fran were to—

Enough.

He couldn't even hold on to a girlfriend he'd no plans to marry, let alone pay enough attention to his niece.

Pia and the clinic. His two priorities. Everything else—everyone else—would have to wait.

Fran saw the lift in Luca's eyes as he scanned the team. The glint of renewed energy. The gratifying blaze of pride. She hoped he knew just how proud all of these people were of *him*. Of the life he'd brought not only to Mont di Mare but to the community as a whole. A center of excellence, right here in their own little hideaway nook of Italy!

"Cut the ribbon!"

The call originated from Pia, but soon everyone was chanting it.

A nurse ran up to Luca with a small pair of surgical scissors from her hip kit when Pia put out a panicked call that she'd remembered the ribbon but not the scissors. The dogs were instructed to stand at either side of the archway in front of Luca, and as the scissors swept through the silken sash, marking this historic moment, Luca's eyes met Fran's.

It was impossible to read his expression, but the effect his gaze had upon her body was hard to deny. The explosion of internal fireworks. Her bloodstream soaring in temperature. The roar in her ears while the rest of her body filled with a showering cascade of never-ending sparks. The feeling that she was less mortal than she had been before.

She gave herself a sharp shake.

She was here to do a job. Not to get all doe-eyed over the boss man. And yet…was that a hint of softness in Luca's gaze? A concession that she might *not* be the thorn in his side he'd initially pegged her to be.

Little sparkles of pleasure swirled around her belly at the thought. Sparkles she was going to have to round up and tame if doing her job and leaving this place with her heart intact were her intentions.

She felt a set of familiar fingers giving her hand a tug.

Pia. Her golden-hearted charge. The entire point of her being there.

"What do you say we get some food?" Fran asked.

"Sounds good to me." Pia swirled her chair around then looked up at her. "Fran?"

"Mmm-hmm?" Fran pulled her attention back from another surreptitious glance in Luca's direction.

"You're good for him, you know."

"Beg pardon?" Fran's attention was fully on Pia now.

"Uncle Luca. He's a bit like me, I think."

Fran swallowed a disbelieving laugh out of respect for Pia's serious tone. "In what way?"

Pia's expression turned suddenly shy, and her fingers teased at the belt that held her petite torso in place against the low back of her chair.

"He's a bit lonely, I think. He works so hard. And with all the pressure my…my condition must put on him I can't help but worry that he's going to work himself to death. I know he loves medicine and everything, but what if this is all too much for him? What if…?" Pia's voice broke, though she maintained eye contact and tried again. "What if…?"

Fran's heart felt as though it were going to burst with compassion when Pia's eyes filled with tears. The amount of loss the poor girl had endured and now she feared losing her uncle, as well? She saw that Luca was trying to spend time with Pia, but she also knew the long hours he put in with the clinic. It was exactly what had happened with her father and his cars. Even when he was at home he wasn't really there. And getting access to his heart was near impossible.

Fran pulled Pia's hands into hers and gave each set of the girl's knuckles a quick kiss. "Don't you worry, *amore*. As long as I'm here we'll make sure your uncle is looked after."

No matter how hard a task it was.

They both looked across to where Luca was standing. He'd stepped away from the crowd now, and a smattering of antipasti was near enough tipping off the plate he barely seemed to notice he was holding.

The team of doctors and support staff had all formed groups, or were crowding around the table, piling delicacies onto their own plates. Luca's body was drawn up to his full height. Six feet of *leave me alone*. His attention was utterly unwavering as he gazed upon the clinic's entryway. His expression was hooded, once again, heavy with the burden of all that had yet to be done.

CHAPTER SEVEN

LUCA SAW THE helicopter before he heard it. A tiny speck heading in from Florence—the whirring blades, the long body of a medical helicopter with its telltale red cross on the undercarriage coming into view as it crested the "hills," as Francesca insisted upon calling them.

As if his thinking her name had conjured her up, she appeared by his side. "Are you excited?"

"Focused. I have my first surgery today. Shouldn't you be working with Pia? Where are the dogs?"

Fran gave him a sidelong look, clearly unimpressed by his curt tone. "They're with her algebra tutor. Pia wanted me to give you this." She handed him an envelope, but not before shooting him a ha!-take-that look. "She wanted to wish you luck," she continued. "As do I."

Luca pushed the card into his pocket, returning his gaze to the approaching helicopter.

This is work. Fran is...pleasure. There's no room for pleasure in my life.

Despite himself, he turned and watched Fran as she tracked the arrival of the *elicottero*, her chin tipped up toward the sky, the movement elongating the length of her slender neck, the fine outline of her face, the sweet spot where her neck met her jaw. If he were to kiss her there would she groan or whimper with pleasure?

Would her legs slip up and around his waist, tugging him in deeper, more fully into her, so that with each thrust he took—

"Dr. Montovano?"

"*Si*, Elisa?" He stopped and corrected himself. "Dr. Sovani. What can I do for you?"

Luca forced his attention to narrow and focus as the doctor rattled through the plans for their patient's arrival and presurgical procedures. He didn't miss Fran's fingers sweeping up to cover the twist of her lips—a snigger at his obviously divided attentions.

She'd obviously caught him staring. Seen the desire in his eyes.

Something in him snapped. Didn't she *know* how vital today was for him and the clinic? The bank had already been on the phone that morning to remind him. *Tick-tock.*

"Miss Martinelli, do you mind? We've got a surgery to prepare for."

She didn't say a word. Didn't have to. Disdain for his dismissive tone was written all over her face.

"Did you want Paolo to go up to the main buildings first, or to his quarters?" Dr. Sovani asked.

"We should get him straight to a prep room." Luca blinkered his vision, forced himself to train his eyes on Elisa's clipboard. "He'll be tired after his journey, and his family would no doubt like to see him settled. The operation isn't for a couple of hours, and we'll need him at his strongest. Are his parents in the chopper with him?"

"They're arriving by car."

As if on cue, a couple appeared in the archway leading to the helicopter landing area, two young children alongside them, all eyes trained on the sky as their loved one approached.

The instant the helicopter touched down, the air was filled with rapid-fire instructions, questions and action.

Fran was nowhere to be seen.

"*Ciao*, Paolo." Luca strode to the teenager's side once the heli-medics had lifted him into his wheelchair and ensured the helmet protecting his skull was in place. "What do you say we head to the clinic and get you settled?"

If Pia hadn't asked, Fran wouldn't have dreamed of stepping foot anywhere near the clinic. But she'd pleaded with Fran to let her take a break from her studies and watch her uncle in surgery. Now that they were here, in the observation room, she had to admit it was amazing.

"Can you turn the speaker up, please, Francesca?" Pia's fingers were covering her mouth, and her body was taut, as if she were watching a blockbuster movie, not a surgery meant to restore a portion of a patient's skull.

"Do you know what happened to him?" Fran asked.

"I don't know the whole story, but he was in a *moto* accident, I think. A year ago. They had to take out part of his skull because of the swelling. The surgeons in Florence said Zio Luca would be the best person to replace it, so they've waited until now. The last thing he needed was a terrible surgeon *and* to be left with a dent in his head!"

Fran smiled at the pride in Pia's voice. Of *course* she was proud. Her surgeon uncle was finally doing what he loved best. Fran could see that now. Sure, he had held his own with a hammer, and seemed to have no problem understanding complicated spreadsheets—

but this... Seeing him here in the operating theater was mesmerizing.

The assured sound of his voice as he spoke to the nurses turned her knees to putty, and the exacting movement of his hands was both delicate and confident. It was little wonder he'd seemed like a pent-up ball of frustration in the week leading up to the clinic's opening. He hadn't been doing what he obviously did best: medicine.

"Francesca?" Pia was tapping a finger on her hand.

"Yes—sorry. What is it, *amore*?"

Pia giggled, then singsonged, "Someone's got a crush on Zio Luca!"

"I do *not*!" Fran protested. A bit too hotly, maybe. Just a little. But in a never-ever-going-to-happen kind of way. A flight of fancy.

"Just as well." Pia returned her gaze to the OR window as if she saw that sort of thing all the time. "He's a terrible boyfriend. Too bad you're the only girlfriend I like."

"And you can carry on liking me. Just not as your uncle's girlfriend."

"Maybe not *now*..." Pia teased, her eyes still glued to her uncle.

Maybe not *ever*, Fran told herself, refusing to let the seeds of imagination take root. It was far too easy to imagine those hands touching her body. His full lips, now hidden behind a surgical mask, touching and tasting her own...

She froze when she realized Luca was looking at her. His eyebrows cinched together in confusion. He obviously hadn't been aware he had an audience. Then they lifted, and little crinkles appeared at the corners of his eyes as if he were smiling behind his mask.

A whirl of something heated took a tour around her chest and swirled lazily in her stomach.

All she could think of to do was to point at Pia, then give him a double thumbs-up and a cheesy grin as if he'd just managed to flip a pancake, not perform an incredibly intricate reconstructive surgery.

What an idiot!

If she'd stood even the tiniest chance of being Luca's girlfriend a second ago—not that she *wanted* to be his girlfriend—she'd definitely closed the door of opportunity right down. Luca only took people seriously if *they* were serious. Whether he thought she was cute or not was beside the point. She wanted him to take her as seriously as she took him.

Pia and the dogs. She needed to repeat it like a mantra. *Pia and the dogs.* They were her only focus. Not the other patients. Not the beautiful village. Not the tall, dark and enigmatically talented surgeon putting the final stitches into his first surgery at his new clinic.

He was a picture of utter concentration.

There wasn't room for her in his life.

Never had been.

Never would be.

The best thing she could do now was focus on getting Pia up to speed, then going home and mending fences with her father. He was the only man she should be worrying about impressing.

CHAPTER EIGHT

A SURGE OF pride filled Luca's heart on seeing the new ramps and pathways being put to use as they'd been intended.

Just a few days in and Mont di Mare felt *alive*. More dynamic than it had in years.

His sister would be so proud of what they'd done with the place. If only bank loans could be repaid with good feelings...

Never mind. Treatments were underway. However slowly, payments were starting to come in to counterbalance the flood of outgoing costs.

The surgery with Paolo had gone as smoothly as he'd hoped. The teenager was already out of Recovery, and at this very moment discussing the litany of tests he would be going through to combat further deterioration in the wake of his paralysis.

Luca itched to join Paolo's team, to be part of adding more movement to the young man's upper body after his motor scooter accident had paralyzed him from the waist down. It was a similar injury to his niece's, only he'd received next to no physio in the wake of his accident.

The lack of strength in his upper body was startling.

Just thinking about the various avenues of treatment they could explore made him smile.

"Dr. Montovano?" Elisa appeared at the doorway. "We've got Giuliana, ready to discuss her case with you."

"Great! Is she in her room?"

"No, she's over by the pool, speaking with your... your friend?"

Luca's brow cinched. "Friend?"

"You know—the one with the dogs."

"Ah. Francesca. No, she's not a friend. She's here to work with Pia."

The words hit false notes even as they came out. A familiar feeling began to take hold of him. The feeling that he'd started to let someone in and then, slowly but surely, had begun to push her away again. Just as he'd done with Marina. Just as he'd done with the women before her.

Elisa shifted uncomfortably, a soft blush coloring her cheeks. "Apologies... We weren't sure..."

"We?" Luca's alarm bells started ringing.

"The team. We didn't—she just..." Elisa's eyes scanned his office in a panic. "She seems to do a lot more than someone who is just here with the assistance dogs would."

"Yes, she's very...*American*," he said, as if it explained everything.

Elisa nodded, clearly none the wiser.

"Va bene," he said, in a tone he knew suggested otherwise. "Shall we go and have a chat with Giuliana?"

"It's all right. You can pet him if you like." Fran smiled at the teen, well aware that Giuliana's fingers had been twitching on her wheelchair arm supports ever since she and Edison had appeared in the courtyard adjacent to the infinity pool.

The pool she was absolutely dying to jump into now that summer had well and truly made an appearance.

When Giuliana's parents had mistaken her for medical staff and asked if she would look after their daughter while they went to see her room, she had said yes.

Foolish? Perhaps.

But everyone was operating at full capacity now that the clinic was open, and with Pia already busy with her studies what harm could a little babysitting do?

The dark-haired girl looked across at her with a despondent look. "It's my arms. They're just so weak."

"You've got to start somewhere," Fran reminded her gently. "Not to mention the fact you're in the perfect place to start rebuilding that strength."

Fran tried to shake away the problem with a smile, hiding an internal sympathy twinge. Giuliana's arms were strapped to stabilizing arm troughs and wrist supports on her chair. They were so thin it was almost frightening.

"Edison." Fran issued a couple of commands and the Lab bounded over and sat alongside Giuliana, so that his head was directly in line with the armrest. "Is it all right if I undo your strap?"

A hint of anxiety crossed the girl's eyes. "Are my parents back yet?"

Fran looked around, vividly aware of how restricted the poor girl's movement was. Her neck was being cradled by two contoured pads and it didn't seem as if she had the strength—let alone the capacity—to turn it left or right.

"They don't seem to be. They were going to look at your room, right?"

"*Si...*" Giuliana replied glumly. "They have to approve every single little thing before I am even allowed to see it. I can hardly believe they left me alone with *you.*"

Tough for any teen to have helicopter parents. Even harder when there was zero choice in the matter.

Fran bit her cheek when Giuliana gave the telltale eye roll of an exasperated teen. She didn't know how many times *she'd* rolled her eyes behind her dad's back when he'd made yet another unilateral decision on her behalf.

Her hand slipped to her back pocket to check her phone was still there. They hadn't talked yet today.

Time zones.

She'd call him later. Just knowing he'd pick up the phone now, close his laptop and really talk to her, made such a difference. Giuliana might find her parents annoying, but at least they were *there* for her.

"It doesn't really hurt when my hands are out of the supports..." Giuliana was saying.

"Do you mind me asking what happened?"

"Skiing." The word sounded as lifeless as the far-away look in Giuliana's eyes.

"Where was the injury?" Fran asked.

When she'd been a physio being straightforward with her questions had usually paid dividends. No need to tiptoe around patients who were facing a life of paralysis.

"Grade-four whiplash. Cervical spine fracture."

"C1?" Francesca asked, her jaw dropping. Most people would have died.

"C2."

"Oof! That must've hurt." Fran's features widened

into a "youch" face. She was still lucky. C2 fractures often resulted in fatalities.

"Quite the opposite," Giuliana answered drily. "I didn't feel a thing."

"Ha! Of course you didn't!"

Fran hooted with laughter before registering the look of disbelief on Giuliana's face. *Oops.*

"I'm sorry, *amore*. You'll have to forgive me. I'm used to talking to dogs, not humans. I am a class-A expert in Open Mouth, Insert Foot."

Giuliana considered her for a moment, then gave a wry smile. "Actually, it was my test. You just passed."

"Oh!" Fran gave a little wriggle of pride that morphed into a hunch of concern. "Wait a minute. What kind of test?"

"A test to see who will laugh at the poor crippled girl's joke."

"A joke test?"

"A litmus test," Giuliana answered solidly. "Most people don't even ask me what happened. They just look at me with big sad eyes, like I'm on the brink of death or something. I'm paralyzed. Not deaf or blind!"

And not bereft of spirit either, from the looks of things.

Fran let loose an appreciative whoop of respect. "You go, girl!" She put her hand up in a fist bump, rolled her eyes at her second idiotic move within as many minutes, then put her fist to Giuliana's anyway. "Forgive me. *Again.* You're here for the summer?"

Giuliana nodded, amusement skittering through her eyes.

"Well, I don't know what your doctor's plans are, but by the end of our stay what do you say we work toward a proper fist bump?"

"What? So you can be 'down with the kids'?" Giuliana giggled, as if the idea of Francesca being down with the kids was quite the challenge.

"Yeah!" Fran parried, striking a silly pose. "That's how I roll. Hey! I have an idea." She positioned herself so she was at eye level with Giuliana. "How crazy are you feeling today?"

"In what way?"

The teen's brow crinkled and it was all Fran could do not to reach out and give it a soothing caress. She couldn't promise the girl that everything would be all right, and nor did she have the right to do anything other than what Luca had hired her to do, but...

"Well, Edison here is my number one gentle dog..."

It wasn't a lie. Not really. Her *other* number one dog was already completely under Pia's command.

"If you'd like to pet him, it seems to me the easiest way to do it would be if we unstrapped you. I would be right behind you, supporting your elbow, and Edison is very good at holding his head still."

The glimmer of excitement in Giuliana's eyes was all the encouragement Fran needed. Ever so gently, Fran lifted the girl's frail arm out of the rest and settled it in her lap for a moment.

"Is it all right if I put a treat in your hand?" Fran asked. "It's a sure-fire way to get Edison's full attention."

"I don't know how well I'll be able to hold it."

"Not a problem. I'll support you."

Fran pinched a treat out of her belt pouch, placed it between Giuliana's fragile fingers with Edison sitting at full attention at her feet. Then Fran shifted around behind the wheelchair, so she could provide support for the girl's elbow. It surprised her to feel how rigid the poor thing's arm was—similar to some of the elderly people she'd worked with years ago. Something deep within her bridled. How awful to have to live like this with your whole life in front of you!

Don't get attached, Fran! You gave up on people for a reason. First, fix things with your father...

Her thoughts faded as instinctively she began to massage the girl's arm. Stroking and smoothing her fingers along the length of the musculature, teasing some suppleness into the brittle length of her arm.

"Come, Edison. Want a treat?"

Giuliana's hand jerked as she spoke. The treat went flying. As it arced up so, too, did Edison's snout, his jaw opening wide as he jumped up to catch it.

"What the *hell* do you think you're doing?"

Luca was thundering across the patio, his face dark as midnight.

By the time he arrived Edison was contentedly swallowing the treat he'd caught, with no detriment to Giuliana whatsoever.

"We were just—" Fran began, then she stopped as memory swept her back to her sixteenth birthday. The one her father had forgotten because it had been the same day his first car had rolled off the production line.

All day she had stayed at the factory. Doing homework...idly peeking into the kitchen at the canteen to see if anyone was secretly whipping up a birthday cake. Wandering through the advertising section on the off chance that someone had made a little—or an enormous—birthday banner to mark the day. Hanging around in the mailroom on the pretense of helping to sort the large bundle of post, only to discover that her mother had, as usual, neglected to send anything.

When at long last the first car had come off the

assembly line—that first amazing vehicle—she had been so excited she'd run up to touch it, to press her face to the window. The second her hand had touched the car her father had seized her wrist and pulled her away so hard it had hurt for a week.

He hadn't meant to hurt her. She knew that. But it was in that instant that she'd forced herself to take her first significant emotional step away from him.

That same week she had been signed up for her first round of finishing school in Switzerland. And then another and another, until the thick wedge of her self-protection had been permanently driven between them.

The flash of ire lighting up Luca's eyes was near enough identical to the one she'd seen in her father's eyes when she'd dared lay her hand on something that wasn't hers.

In Luca's eyes she'd just crossed the line.

His patient. His clinic. His future.

Her mistake.

"Dr. Montovano! Did you *see* that?"

Luca could just hear Giuliana's voice through the static roaring in his ears. He was still reeling at how careless Fran was. *Reckless!*

"*Scusi*, Giuliana. See what?" Luca forced himself to turn to his new patient, hastily removing from his eyes the daggers he'd been shooting at Fran.

This was a clinic for people with *spinal injuries*, for heaven's sake. Had she no respect for what he was trying to do here? No understanding that the slightest mishap could shut him down?

"The dog!" Giuliana said, the smile so broad across her face he hardly recognized her as the same girl captured in the glowering, unhappy photos her parents had sent. "Did you see how when I threw the treat he caught it?"

"He was catching a treat?"

"*Si, Dottore.* Of course. What did you think he was doing?"

Fran turned to him, arms crossed defensively across her chest, with a look that said, *I'd certainly like to know what it was you thought Edison was doing.*

The dog had been jumping, its mouth wide-open, teeth bared. It had looked as if it had been launching himself at the girl's hand. Which—on went a lightbulb—of *course* he had. She had been throwing a treat.

Another lightbulb joined the first.

"I thought you didn't have any movement in your arm."

"I didn't…" Giuliana replied, her expression changing as she, too, began connecting the dots of an enormous puzzle.

"Mind if I have a quick feel?" Luca knelt, and with his young patient's consent he took her arm in his hands and began to run his fingers along the different muscle and ligament groups in her forearm. Her fingers responded to a few of his manipulations. Fingers that were, according to her physio at home, completely atrophied from disuse.

"Shall we get you into one of the treatment rooms? See what may have happened there?"

"*Si.* Can Edison come, too? And Francesca? She massaged my arm before I fed Edison."

A flash of ire blinded him again for an instant.

Why couldn't Fran keep to herself?

He hesitated for a moment before looking up, forcing himself to take a slow breath. She was a trained physio. This was meant to be a place of innovation. And now that he was repainting the scene into what it had actually been, it was very likely Fran and Edison had each played a role in eliciting movement in Giuliana's arm.

By the time he lifted his eyes to offer an invitation he saw that none was necessary. Fran and Edison were disappearing through an archway leading to the wild-flower meadows.

A sour twist of enmity tightened around his heart. He didn't need to push Fran away. She had already gone.

CHAPTER NINE

A KNOCK SOUNDED on the door frame of Fran's cottage. It was so unexpected she nearly jumped out of her skin. And she was half-naked. More than half-naked, really.

The baby-doll nightgown had been a spontaneous, lacy gift to herself when she'd gone bridesmaid-dress shopping with Bea. A nod to the femininity she knew lurked somewhere inside her but that she'd never quite had the courage to explore.

"*Scusi*, Francesca, do you have a moment?"

Little frissons of awareness tickled up along her neck when she heard Luca's voice. Sprays of goose bumps followed in their wake when she turned the corner and saw him. One hand flew to cover her chest and the other stupidly groped for and tugged at the bottom-skimming hemline.

"Yes, of course. What can I help you with?"

"I think I owe you an apology."

"Ah, well…"

Please quit staring at my half-naked body.

"No need. I understand—"

"No. I was too sharp. The truth is…" Luca paused and looked up toward the stars just beginning to shine out against the night sky.

The truth is what? An icy chill spread through her. Was he going to send her away?

She nodded, tugging at the spaghetti straps of her nightdress as if the soupçon of flesh they covered would disguise the fact that the plunging neckline and tiny triangles of lace barely covering her breasts were advertising the fact she hadn't had sex in... Oh...who was counting anyway? Celibacy was the "in" thing, right? Or did the nightdress say the opposite? That she was a floozy and had been hanging out with her front door open just waiting for him to—

Stop. Just stop. Act normal. Relaxed. As if gorgeous Italian doctors who can't bear the sight of you are always popping by for a casual you're-fired chat.

"I think I know why you're here." Fran decided to fill the growing silence. "Making sure we continue in the same vein as we started, right? Frenemies forever!"

Luca's brows hitched closer together.

"Frenemies?" She tried again. "Friends who are enemies?"

He shook his head.

She shifted her shoulder straps again, trying to feel less naked.

This whole standing-here-in-silence thing was getting a little annoying. She had dignity. Brains. Self-esteem.

C'mon, Frannie. Pull it together.

"Luca, is there anything I can help you with? Some last-minute painting...?"

Still too chirpy. Dial back the cheerleader... Bring in the helpful canine-assistance trainer.

Tough when Luca was just standing there staring at her, refusing to engage in her inane one-sided conversation.

"I was not thinking frenemies. I was thinking employee."

"What?" *Unexpected.* "You want me to *work* for you?"

He nodded—yes.

"One of my physios has returned to Rome. The rural location didn't seem to suit him."

"Is he nuts?" Fran was shocked. "I mean Rome is great, but this place is just about as close to heaven as it gets! I'd stay here forever if I could. I mean, not *forever*, forever…just…"

"Francesca. *Per favore*, will you just answer the question?"

"Of course. I'll do anything to help." She held up a finger. "On one condition."

A crease of worry deepened the scar on his cheek— the one she was dying to ask about but already had a pretty good guess had something to do with his orphaned niece being in a car accident. They all added up to a picture no one would keep in their wallet.

But now wasn't the time.

"Luca, listen. I would love to do the work—but only if you let me do it gratis."

"Oh, no—"

Francesca held up a hand to protest.

"Don't take it the wrong way. This would be helping *me*."

Luca laughed, but not because he thought she was funny. "I hardly think not paying you is *helping*."

"It would." She reached out to the side table and wiggled her phone between them. "See…my dad and I have been having daily talks in advance of my return. I've been trying to convince him for years to let me do charitable work in the name of his company. If you'd let me work on the patients and make little video diaries of their progress as I went—with their permission, of course—I think it might be a way to persuade him to let me do more of the same when I get home."

"I thought you were through with treating people?"

She shrugged. "Some people are worth changing your mind for."

The words hit their mark. Luca's dark eyes sought her own and when their gazes caught and cinched tight she could hardly breathe. She'd meant *patients*. But from all the tiny hairs standing up on her arms, something was telling her there had just been a shift between them.

As suddenly as the air had gone taut between them it relaxed. As if Luca had sought and found the answer to the questions racing through his eyes. She sucked in a breath of mountain air, her heart splitting wide-open. More than she'd allowed for anyone else.

He looked tired, his hair all helter-skelter, as if he'd been repeatedly running a worried hand through it. Though he wore smart attire, he still had on paint-stained, sawdust-covered work boots.

Her eyes were trained on his boots because she wasn't brave enough to look up into those dark eyes of his again. And then she dared.

A flush of heat struck her cheeks like a slap when she realized the flash of emotion she'd seen in his eyes was the same one alight in hers.

Desire.

"I also wanted a quick word about Pia…" Luca began.

"Pia! Yes. Good. All's going blue blazes in *that* camp." She tried to strike a casual pose. Tricky when she was half-naked in front of a man whose mere presence made her nipples tighten. "I think Freda's the dog for her. Those two seem inseparable."

"Is that a good thing? Being so close?" Luca uncrossed his arms. "What about boundaries?"

Was he still talking about Pia and her dog?

"Well, boundaries are gray areas."

Luca's eyebrow arched. "Oh?"

"But they need to be clear. Boundaries definitely need to be very, very clear."

"Clear enough so that each party knows exactly what they're getting into?"

Luca reached up and rested a crooked arm along the wooden beam above her door frame. Where had stern-faced, humorless Luca gone? There wasn't time to think. Sexy Luca's sun-heated man scent was invading her senses, whooshing through her like a drug.

He definitely wasn't talking about the dogs anymore.

Just as well. There was no room for any thought in her head other than the knowledge that she wanted him. She wanted to jump into his arms, wrap her legs around his trim waist and kiss the living daylights out of him. Touch his scar. Get stubble burn. Ache between her legs from hours of lovemaking. *Hell!* She'd dance around on tiptoe for the next three weeks if he would just scoop her up and have his wicked way with her.

"How does one *establish* these boundaries?" Luca asked, the tension between them thickening with each passing moment.

Gone was the uptight, form-filling timekeeper. In his place was a sensualist. His shoulders shifted, rolling beneath the thick cotton of his shirt with the grace of a mountain lion, and his eyes were alight with need. With hunger.

Heat tickled and teased across Fran's skin, swirling and pooling between her legs.

Per amor del cielo!

Luca let the door frame take some of his weight, bringing him even closer to her.

There was no disguising her body's response to him. Goose bumps shot up her arms. Her breasts were taut, arching toward him as if they had a will of their own.

Did she really want this? Him? Maybe he was right. Clear-cut boundaries were exactly what they needed if either of them was to survive the summer. Then again, sex was an excellent way to cut tension…

No. They needed to talk this out. Like grown-ups. With clothes on.

"Did you want to…um…?"

She pointed toward the bedroom, where her bathrobe was hanging. It was a scrubby terry-cloth number covered in images of Great Danes wearing nerdy spectacles. Her gaze returned to Luca's. As the hit of electricity that only seemed to grow each time their eyes met took effect she lost the power of speech. She'd meant "should she go get her robe and so they could sit down for a talk and a coffee." Or a nightcap. Not "should they go for a roll in the hay"!

Before Fran's brain could comprehend what was happening Luca had pulled her into his arms and was lowering his mouth to hers with a heated passion she had never felt before. There was an urgency in his kisses. A thrilling assurance in his touch. As if they were long-lost lovers separated by oceans, reunited by their unquenchable thirst for each other.

The ardor pouring from his body to hers began to flow between them in an ever-growing circle—floodwaters unleashed. There was nothing chaste about their kisses.

They were needy, insatiable. Words escaped her as he tasted and explored first her lips and then her mouth with every bit as much passion as she put into touching and experiencing him. The occasional brush of stubble. The burr of a growl as she nibbled and then softly bit his lower lip before opening her mouth as he teased her lips apart with his tongue.

A soft groan escaped Fran's already kiss-bruised lips as one of Luca's hands slid to the small of her back and tugged her in tight to him; the other slipped around to the nape of her neck. She felt his fingers weave through the length of her hair, then tug it back so that her neck lay bare to him. It wasn't cruelty or domination. It was unfettered desire. The same ache rendering her both powerless and energized in his arms.

Willing away the millions of thoughts that might have shut the moment down, Fran closed her eyes and allowed the sensations of Luca's touch to spread through her veins. With the pad of his thumb he tipped her head to the side. His lips pulled away from hers. Before she had a chance to experience any loss she could feel their heated presence again, tasting and kissing the sensitive nook between her chin and neck.

His fingers moved from the back of her head to the other side of her neck, his thumb drawing along the length of her throat as his lips did the same on the exposed length of her neck. She could feel the pads of his fingers tracing from her shoulder to her collarbone, dipping down to the swell of her breasts. She couldn't help it. She arched into his hands, her body longing for more.

Unexpectedly, Luca cupped her face in both his hands and tipped his forehead to hers, his breath coming as swiftly as her heartbeat, which was racing to catch up with what was happening.

"*Scusi*, Francesca. I'm so sorry."

She heard the words but his body told a different story as his hands tugged her ever so slightly closer toward him. Her hands rose to his chest and confirmed what she'd suspected. His heart was racing as quickly as her own.

"I'm not..." she managed to whisper.

"This isn't why I came here."

"Stay." The word was out before she could stop it.

"I have nothing to offer you." Luca's voice was raw, as if the words had scraped past his throat against his will.

"I don't remember asking for anything," Fran said, her feet arching up onto tiptoe, her lips grazing his as she spoke.

"I need boundaries."

"So do I."

Fran meant the words with all her heart. She felt as if her whole body was on fire, and without protecting her heart she'd never survive the summer.

Luca held her out at arm's length, examining her face as if his life depended upon it.

"What did you say we were?"

Fran ran their conversation through her head at lightning speed, then laughed. "Frenemies?"

Luca nodded. "Will that do?"

"Colleagues by day, lovers by night?" she countered.

He nodded his assent. "No more talking."

Their lips met again, to explosive effect. In just those few moments his touch had already changed. Where there had been tentative exploration now there was fire behind his kisses. Intimacy. As if each erotically charged touch was laying claim to her, physically altering the chemical makeup of her bloodstream. What had once felt heavy now became light. Effervescent, even. In each other's arms they were no longer bound to the earth. They were in orbit—two celestial bodies exploring, teasing, coaxing, arousing.

Fran's breasts were swollen with longing, her nipples taut against the sheer lace of her nightgown. As Luca's hand swept across her bottom his fingers just grazed the sensitive pulsing between her legs, forcing her to bite back a cry of pleasure. He drew his fingers up and along her spine, rendering her core completely molten. She'd experienced lust in the past, but now she became vividly aware that she had never known desire. Not like this. She'd never craved a man's touch as much as she yearned for Luca's.

"Mio piccola passerotta..."

Fran felt Luca's breath glide along her neck as he whispered into her ear. *His little sparrow.* If anyone in the world could make her feel like a delicate bird in flight...

Don't think. Just be.

Abruptly she tugged her fingers down the back of his neck, the pressure of her nails eliciting a groan of pleasure as once again he tipped her head back and dropped kisses along the length of her neck, his fingers tracing the delicate dips and swells of her décolletage.

Fran inhaled deeply—everything about this moment would form the scent palate she would return to when the day came she had to leave. Late-night jasmine. Pepper. Wood shavings. The sun-warmed heat of early summer and tanned skin.

She tipped her head forward as Luca's hands slid along her sides and pulled her close to his chest. Another scent she'd remember forever. One very particular chest, attached to the most intriguing man she had ever laid eyes on.

A particle of insecurity lodged itself in her heart as she became aware of his hands sweeping along the curve of her shoulders to her arms. It took a second to connect mind and body. He was holding her out—away from him—so that he could tip her chin up and their eyes would meet.

And when they did it was like a lightning strike.

One so powerful she knew what she was feeling was more than chemical.

"You must want something. Everyone does."

Respect. Love. Of course she wanted love. Marriage. Family. The whole nine yards one day. But Luca was the worst person in the world to start *that* sort of craziness with. And the last.

"We couldn't have met at a worse time," he continued.

"Or in a less promising way," she reminded him, unable to keep that moment at the basilica from popping into her mind. "You and I will never be friends."

Oh, the irony! And look at them now, woven into one another's arms as if their being together had been predestined.

And that was when it hit her. What it was she wanted from a relationship.

To be lit up from within as she had been these last few precious moments. To feel elemental. Woven into the very fabric of someone else's being.

She lowered her eyelids to half-mast. Luca didn't need access to the tempest flaring between her heart and mind.

Her heart was near enough thumping out of her chest. She'd never done anything this...*intentional* before. Offering herself to him only to zip up what was left of her heart and take it away at the end of the summer.

She looked at Luca, all super masculine and reserved. Every bit the courtly gent by day, but by night a wild boy up for a bit of rough and tumble, if his kisses were anything to go by. His five-o'clock shadow was thick with the late hour, cheekbones taut, lips bloodred from their kisses. The scar she was longing not only to trace with her finger but her tongue...

"Let's do it." She moved her hand into the thin wedge of space between them. "Frenemies. Boundary hunters. Whatever you like. Shake on it?"

Luca didn't want to shake hands. He wanted to take possession of her. Become intimately acquainted with every particle of Francesca he could get his hands on. He wanted to touch and caress all that he could see and all that he couldn't beneath the tiny bits of fabric that made up her excuse for a nightgown. To disappear in her beauty and reemerge fortified and vital. Ready to take on anyone and anything.

Fran's hand pressed against his chest as he pulled her tight to him so she could feel the effect she had on him. Her eyes widened and a distinctly saucy laugh burbled up from her throat. She wanted him as much as he wanted her. He could see it in her eyes, feel it in the tipped points of her nipples as they abraded his chest when she wriggled in his arms.

"I've got something better than a handshake in mind for you," he murmured.

"Oh, *do* you now?"

Fran's feline eyes were sultry. She tipped her chin toward him with a smile edging onto the corners of her lips. A naughty smile.

Dio! She was beautiful.

In one swift move he kicked the door shut with his booted foot, swept her up into his arms and carried her without further ceremony straight to her bedroom.

She whooped when he all but tossed her onto the mattress, showing scant restraint as he stretched out alongside her. He was clearly enjoying the soft groan of pleasure he elicited when he ran a hand over the tips of her breasts before brusquely pushing aside the tiny triangles of lace and lowering his lips onto first one, then the other taut nipple, his tongue circling the deep pink of her areolae as he leisurely slid his hand across her belly and down to rest between her legs.

Luca's breath caught, his lips just barely touching her nipple, as Fran pressed against his fingers. She grabbed for his free hand, drawing each of his fingers, one at a time, into her mouth, giving each one a wicked swirl of the tongue, a teasing lick and a suck.

Forcing himself to ignore the growing intensity building below his waistline, Luca slid his fingers beneath the thin strip at the base of Fran's panties, delighting in the heated dew of her response to his touch. He had become utterly consumed with bringing her pleasure.

So responsive to his touch was she, he had to check himself again and again not to move too rapidly. To draw out her pleasure for as long as he could. When at last her body grew taut with expectation and desire, he unleashed his hands from their earlier restraint, let his mouth explore the most tender nooks of her belly, licking and teasing at the very tip of her most sensitive area until she cried out with pleasure and release.

Fran grabbed the sides of his face and roughly pulled his mouth toward hers. "Naked. Now!" were the only two words he could make out between her cries of pleasure as he dipped his fingers in farther, teasing and tempting her to reach another climax.

"Protection?"

An impressive stream of Italian gutter talk flowed as Fran lurched out of the bed, ran to the bathroom, clattered through who knew what at a high rate of knots and reappeared in the doorway, framed by the soft light of the bathroom, with a triumphant smile on her face and a small packet held between two fingers.

"Bridesmaid favors! Now, take off your clothes," Fran commanded, already taking deliberate steps toward the bed. *"Now."*

A broad smile peeled his lips apart. This made a nice change from the needy women he tended to attract. The ones who wanted the title, the property, but not the work that came along with the mantle he'd been forced to wear.

"Is this how it's going to work?" Luca asked, propping himself up on an elbow as he watched her approach like a lioness about to pounce for the kill. "You giving me orders?"

"Tonight it is." Fran straddled him in one fluid move, the bold glint in her eyes hinting at pleasures yet to unfold.

He needed this. He needed *her*.

"Well, then…" Luca arched an eyebrow at her and began unbuttoning his shirt. "I suppose it would be foolish not to oblige."

Fran batted his hands away and ripped off the rest of the buttons of his shirt, her hands swirling possessively across the expanse of his chest.

"Yes," she murmured as she pushed him back on the

bed and began lowering herself along the full length of his body, exploring with her lips as much as with her hands. "It would."

Two, maybe three hours later—Luca didn't know; he'd entirely lost track of time—he slipped out from beneath the covers, trying his best not to disturb Francesca.

All the tiptoeing came to nothing when he picked up his trousers and his belt buckle clattered against the tile flooring. A quick glance toward the bed and he could see one bright blue eye peeking out at him amidst a tangle of blond hair.

"Pia?" she asked.

Luca nodded.

The single word had contained no animosity. Only understanding. His main priority was his niece. Luxurious mornings in bed would never be on his menu, and Fran would have to understand that was his reality.

He swept his fingers through her hair, dropped a kiss on her forehead and left without saying a word.

Outside, he sucked in the night air as if he'd been suffocating.

A night like that...

He wanted more.

Much more.

He tried as best he could to push the thoughts—the desire—away. There was no chance he could make peace with giving in to these precious green shoots, the chance at something new blossoming in a place where he'd thought love would only wither and die.

With his niece to provide for, wanting and having had become two very different things. He could want, but he definitely couldn't have. Fran would just have to understand that.

CHAPTER TEN

A SHOT OF irritation lanced through Luca's already frazzled nerves. Spreadsheets taunted him from his computer screen. Stacks of bills sat alongside ledgers he knew he couldn't reconcile. He barked a hollow laugh into the room.

This must be how his father had felt when his business was failing. Alone. Horrified by the ramifications of what would happen if he admitted his failure to his family. To those he loved the most in the world.

Another peal of hysterics echoed down the corner.

Since when did hydrotherapy sessions contain so much *laughter*?

He pushed back from his desk in frustration. He knew the exact moment. Ever since he'd gone to Francesca. Vulnerable. Heart in hand. Needing help. Needing *her*.

A shot of desire coursed through him and just as quickly iced it.

Their nights together were...otherworldly. Never before had he met his match as he had with Francesca. The pure alpha male in him loved hearing her call his name as he pleasured her. Loved teasing and taunting just a little longer as she begged him to enter her. Even now, fully clothed, he could conjure up the sensation of Fran's nails scratching along the length of his back as he thrust deeply into her until the pair of them both cried out in a shared ecstasy.

If only he hadn't gone to her to ask for help. Help she'd given willingly. Gladly, even. But it made him feel weak. It ate at his pride and filled him with yet another measure of self-loathing he'd yet to conquer.

He was meant to be shouldering the load. Righting wrongs *he* had set in motion.

Paolo's triumphant cry of "I did it!" pierced through to his consciousness.

Pride was his enemy. The devil on his shoulder drowning out the man he'd buried somewhere deep inside him, who knew having Fran here was exactly what the patients needed. What *he* needed.

The Francesca Effect, the staff were calling it.

Yes, the patients worked hard, but they also laughed and cheered, and a few had even cried in moments of triumph they had never thought they'd achieve.

Like a moth to a flame he found himself drawn to the hydrotherapy room.

He looked through the glass window running the length of the indoor pool and ground his teeth together.

Even in a functional one-piece swimsuit she was beautiful. Her hair was in Heidi plaits, trailing behind her in the water as she faced Paolo in his chair, stretching from side to side of the pool along with him, keeping up a steady flow of encouragement. Silly jokes. Pointing out every time he'd done well. Reached further. Done more. Aimed higher.

Luca pressed his head to the glass and as he did so, Fran turned to him, her blue eyes lighting up and her smile growing even broader.

He wanted to smile, too. His heart pounded in his

chest, demanding some sort of response, yet all he could do was grind his teeth tighter together.

How could he let her know? This beautiful, carefree, intelligent, loving woman to whom he could lay no claim... How could he let her know the simple truth?

He turned away before he could see the questions deepen in her pure blue eyes and strode to his office, slamming the door shut behind him and returning to his desk.

Try as he might, the columns and figures blurred together. He pressed his fingertips to his forehead, trying to massage some sort of meaning into them.

It was pointless, really. No matter which way he rearranged them—no matter how many times he added them up—the answer was always the same.

It wouldn't last.

Couldn't last.

And the sooner he came to terms with that, the better.

"How's your grip? Still strong?" Fran wheeled herself around in Pia's wheelchair to the edge of the pool.

Pia looked up at Fran from where she was being towed along the shallow end of the pool's edge and grinned. "I think Freda is doing most of the work here, but I'm still hanging on." She faked letting go of the mop head Fran had rigged up as a steering wheel between her and Freda.

"Ha-ha. Better not let your uncle see that."

"You mean Zio the Thundercloud?"

"Yeah." Fran did her best to stay neutral. "Him."

She and Luca had rigorously stuck to their boundaries over the past week.

Lover by night—ridiculously fabulous.

Physio and hydrotherapist by day—so much more rewarding than she'd remembered. Teenagers were a hoot.

And, of course, assistance-dog trainer by afternoon.

Although Pia was doing well, Fran had resorted to inventing hybrid physio-hydro-canine combo therapies. If the teen kept it up, Fran would be extraneous before long and would be able to go home.

Home.

Three weeks ago it had been all she could dream of. Her dad. Her new business. But now leaving Mont di Mare seemed more punishment than pleasure.

"How are your wheelchair skills coming along?" Pia teased, openly laughing when Fran tried to mimic her teenage charge and pop a wheelie but failed.

"I've still got a way to go to be on par with you."

"You could always get in a car accident that pretty much ruins your life. Then you'd catch up pretty quick," Pia shot back.

From the shocked look on Pia's face Fran knew the teen hadn't meant the words as they'd sounded. Dark. Angry.

"*Scusi*, Francesca. I didn't mean—"

"Hey…" Fran held up her hands. "This is a safe zone." She drew an invisible circle around the pool area, where she knew it would just be the two of them for the next hour or so as Luca and the rest of the staff were still neck-deep in appointments in the main clinic buildings. "You can say whatever you like. Better out than in, right?"

"Anything?" Pia asked incredulously.

"Anything." Fran gave a definitive nod.

What *she* wouldn't have done to have had an older woman in her life when she was growing up. Someone to confide in. To ask those awkward girl questions that adolescence unearthed.

"Do you think I will ever be able to do more in this pool than be dragged back and forth by Freda?" Pia's face shifted from plaintive to apologetic in an instant. "Not that I don't totally love her. Or this. Or being here with you. It's just…sometimes it's really frustrating."

Fran nodded. It was impossible to imagine. She could just step up and out of the wheelchair whenever she chose and dive into the pool. Do a cartwheel. Anything.

She considered Pia for a moment, then focused on the path Freda was taking, back and forth along the length of the pool.

"It's too bad we can't get Edison in there. He would tow you around like a motorboat!"

The second the words were out of her mouth Fran regretted saying them. From the ear-to-ear grin on Pia's face it was more than obvious that to her being pulled around at high speed sounded great.

"That would be amazing! Zio Luca would—"

"Go apoplectic with rage," Francesca finished for her.

"It's not like anyone else is using the pool." Pia splashed a bit of water toward her.

"Yet," Fran intoned meaningfully, lifting her face up to the sun. "But once everyone's properly settled this place will be more popular than the walk-in refrigerator."

"You mean wheel-in, don't you, Fran?" Pia teased.

"Si. Of course. Wheel-in fridge. Either way, I don't think your uncle would be happy to know the pool maintenance guy might be scooping dog hair out of the filters."

"We could do it! *I'd* do it. All I'd have to do is lie on the ground before I get in my chair and just fish it all out. Excellent upper body strengthening opportunity." Pia smiled cheekily. "He would never have to know."

Fran gave her a sidelong glance. "I think you know as well as I do that your uncle is all seeing, all knowing." She pointed up to the security camera she was praying he wasn't keeping an eye on.

"He's a pussycat, really."

"Mountain lion, more like."

A sexy mountain lion, with far too much weight on his shoulders.

He shouldn't have to do all this alone. If only she could stay. Share the load.

She wheeled the chair around in a few idle circles, unable to stop a sigh heaving out of her chest. Edison appeared with a ball in his mouth, his permanently worried-looking eyebrows jigging up and down above his amber eyes.

"Don't worry, boy," she whispered into the soft fold of his ear. "I'm not sad. I'm...*perplexed*. Wanna play catch?"

Back and forth went the ball and the dog. Back and forth. Just like her thoughts.

It wasn't as if she wanted to win Luca's heart or anything. She just really believed in everything he was doing here at the clinic.

Boundaries.

A sudden frisson swept through her as her thoughts slipped far too easily back to the bedroom. Had she actually bitten into his shoulder last night, when the explosion of their mutual climax had hit the heavens and returned her to earth in thousands of glittery, grinning pieces?

She threw the ball again. Harder this time.

Edison duly loped off. Returned. Totally obedient.

"C'mon, boy. Drop the ball. There's a good boy," she cooed. "You *always* do everything I ask."

Her eyes pinged wide. Was that why she'd switched to dogs? Because they always did what she wanted? That couldn't possibly be what she was hoping for in a man. *Obedience?*

No! Ridiculous. She wanted a man with his own mind, his own interests—but his heart? She wanted that to beat solely for *her*. And no matter how smitten Luca seemed between the hours of 10 p.m. and whenever they'd exhausted each other, she knew his heart was well and truly off-limits.

"Good boy. Drop the ball." This time she threw it extra hard, her eyes widening in horror when she saw where it had landed. At the far end of the very pristine, very new, entirely immaculate swimming pool...now getting dive-bombed by a thrilled Labrador.

Pia was nearly crying with laughter.

"Can he pull me around now, Francesca? *Per favore? Bravo*, Edison! *Vieni qui.*"

"No way!" Fran whispered as if it would make the scenario disappear.

She pulled off the sundress she was wearing over her bikini and dove into the pool, as if she would be able to magnetically draw any loose hairs Edison might be leaving in his wake.

"Edison! *Out!*"

"Edison, *vieni qui!*" Pia repeated. More adamantly this time. "You know..." Pia went on slowly, avoiding eye contact with Fran as she spoke, "Zio Luca didn't say *specifically* that I was meant to have just one assistance dog. You said yourself you'd brought two to see which one I hit it off with the best, and, well...it's not like everyone has just *one* best friend, right?"

"It is pretty standard. Having just the one."

"*What* about life up here at Mont di Mare is standard?" Pia appealed.

Fran couldn't help laughing. She knew exactly where Pia was coming from. It *was* otherworldly up here.

She took a few strokes in Pia's direction, to where Edison was merrily paddling around her. She watched as the teen lay back in the water, her slim legs floating up to the surface. Her fingers pitter-patted on the water's surface, and all the while she was humming a pop tune as she worked on her argument. She looked like any normal kid having a float in a pool—if you ignored the harness and pole contraption she was still holding on to, the life vests, and the float around her neck for an extra "just in case."

"Won't Edison miss Freda?" Pia asked eventually. "I mean, they both spend most of their time with me now, so it wouldn't be like keeping both would be that strange."

"What? And leave me all alone?" Fran had meant it as a jest, but the reality of returning to the States alone…

Ugh. Boundaries, Francesca. Boundaries!

She dunked herself under the surface of the water to mask the rush of emotion. She was meant to be Pia's sounding board, not the other way around. She whooshed up and out of the pool, pulled a huge bath towel around her and plonked herself down in Pia's chair, calling Edison out of the pool.

Staying or going, Luca would kill her if he saw a dog in his fancy pool.

"Just remember, Fran, *you* can get up out of that chair anytime you want and just walk away," Pia sternly reminded her. "I'm stuck in it forever."

The words all but ejected Fran straight out of the chair and into the pool.

She looked from Pia to Edison, his furry legs pedaling at the sky as he rolled on the grass, rubbing the pool water off his back. Then to Freda, who always looked as if she was smiling, happy as ever to stand or walk by Pia's side.

The thought of life without Freda and Edison was sobering. But that was how it worked.

You train them, you hand them over, you move on.

Normally she was fine with it. But this time it didn't feel right.

"Don't you think you should try asking?" Pia let go of the mop handle and folded her hands in the prayer position before quickly grabbing it again. "It'd be better coming from you."

"Me?" A cackle of disbelief followed the wide-eyed yeah-right look Fran threw Pia's way. "I think pleading for favors from your uncle is more *your* turf."

Pia made a pouty face, then quickly popped on a smile. "Take me to the edge!"

"What? The far edge?" The one overhanging the sheer drop of the mountain. "Not a chance!"

"I bet Edison would do it if we were here alone," Pia grumped.

"And what makes you think your uncle would be thrilled about you being in the pool on your own."

"That's exactly the point! I wouldn't *be* on my own. Edison could tow me around, and if anything went wrong, Freda could run for help." Pia's features widened, then threatened to crumple. "For once I could feel like a normal kid. Just *once*."

"Pia, I really don't think…"

Once more Pia pressed her hands into the prayer position. "*Per favore*, Francesca. Help the poor little orphan girl on the mountaintop."

"Just the once?" Fran finally conceded.

She knew she was supposed to be the older, wiser person in this scenario. At twenty-nine years old she was hardly old enough to be her mother, but she felt protective of Pia. She could say, hand on her heart, that she loved her. Even if she *was* extra cheeky. Demanding. Unbelievably capable of getting her to take risks she knew Luca would frown upon.

She glanced at the sheer drop at the edge of the infinity pool.

Luca was going to kill her. Well and truly kill her.

"C'mon, you wily minx. I'm going to get you out of here. Let go of the pole and grab hold of my neck."

"I'm not wily!" Pia feigned a hurt look. "I'm...*cunning*."

"That you are." She reached out to Pia and unclipped the pole from Freda.

"You promised!"

"What exactly did you promise?"

Pia and Fran froze, then slowly shifted their gazes from each other to the pair of leather shoes attached to a familiar pair of long legs, which were, in turn, supporting a terrific torso—lovely clothed or unclothed—topped off by one very unamused face.

"Francesca? What did you promise my niece?"

"I promised to keep her hair dry!" Fran chirped.

"*Si*, Zio. That's exactly what she promised. And to keep me safe and out of harm's way." Pia added, tightening her hold on Fran's neck as she did.

"That's us! Two little safety nuts!" Fran grinned while Pia maintained a frantic nodding, as if it would erase everything else from Luca's mind.

Two inane, grinning bobbleheads, still neck-deep in the pool. Which was another issue. If she stepped out any farther, he would see her breasts had pinged to full Luca-alert position.

She narrowed her gaze and dared a quick scan. Damn, that man was head to toe desirable. Even when he was glowering at her.

"And the dog?" Luca couldn't resist tipping his head toward the Lab merrily paddling around the pool. "Is he part of the safety plan?"

"Absolutely...not..."

Fran slipped Pia's arms more securely around her neck and walked her toward the shallow end of the pool. With each step she took, Luca couldn't help but think he was watching a beach-rescue video. In slow motion.

With that barely there bikini on—

Dio mio.

"What *were* your plans to get Pia out of the pool?" Luca heard the bite in his voice and detested himself for it. But he'd been scared. He'd heard screams and had feared the worst.

Lungs heaving with the effort of reaching the pool to save his niece, he felt the burn as he surveyed the scene now. His niece had been in gales of laughter. All because of Fran. Of course. Francesca wasn't just a ray of sunshine—she was a cascade of light. Wherever she went.

"We actually practiced it a lot at the beginning of the session," Fran said, rattling off a technique she'd seen on the internet.

"Aren't you meant to be studying?" He zeroed in on Pia, feeling less like a loving uncle and more like an officer in the Gulag.

"I finished early. Fran helped me with my trigonometry. And it was such a lovely day…"

"How did you get her in?" Luca asked Fran, not entirely certain he wanted to know.

Pia peeked out from behind Fran's head once again. "I swan-dived."

"You *what*?" His voice dropped in disbelief. "The only way you could have done that is if—"

"I tipped her in," Fran interjected, her expression every bit as stoic as an elite soldier caught going a step too far by the drill sergeant.

"Pia said she knew how to swim—that it was her favorite part of rehab when you were still in Rome—so I tipped her in. And because she's such an amazingly graceful girl she turned it into a swan dive!"

"She could've been—"

"What? Paralyzed?" Pia cut in. "Uncle Luca, it's okay. There is no way Edison, Freda or Fran would've let me drown. Besides, it felt amazing. Like I was whole again."

He looked to Fran, saw her teeth biting down on her lip so hard the flesh paled around it. Then he saw the defiance in her eyes.

C'mon. Do it. I dare you to take away this moment from your niece.

Didn't she realize his niece was the only person he had left in the world, and that to chuck her into a swimming pool without the necessary precautions was sheer madness?

"Don't move. I'll go and get one of the portable hoists. I hope I can trust you to respect my wishes for just a few moments?"

His back stiffened as a peal of nervous giggles followed him when he about-faced and began stomping off. Then it struck him. Fran had done it again. Found exactly the sort of moments he'd been hoping for Pia would have here at Mont di Mare. Happy ones. Discovery. Trying new things. Making the village a home as well as his place of work.

His pace slowed. What sort of life was he giving his niece here? Did he even know what Pia wanted to do when she grew up? When was the last time they'd sat down and eaten a normal dinner together? As a family?

An image of the three of them sitting down—Fran, Pia and Luca—enjoying a meal together put a lift in his step. And then just as quickly weighed it down. They weren't a family. It was just him and Pia, and he was barely succeeding at that. And as for the clinic—the bank was still nipping at his heels, getting ever closer.

When he returned a few minutes later with the hoist he saw Pia on the top step at the side of the pool, tugging herself into her wheelchair with a small grunt and a smiley, "Voilà!" She looked him in the eye as he approached. "See? I didn't need you after all."

He forced a smile, knowing full well it didn't reach his eyes. Not because he wasn't happy for her, but because he was furious with himself for being so blind.

Letting her fend for herself was the only way to build Pia's confidence. It was the entire raison d'être of the clinic. How had he lost sight of the endgame so quickly?

When his eyes met and meshed with Fran's a rush of emotion hit him so hard he could barely breathe. Half of him resented her for being there for his niece. The other half was grateful. If only he'd had a chance to grieve for all that he had lost—not just in the accident, but in the years that followed. His spontaneity. His voracious appetite for experimental treatments. His passion for life. His capacity to love.

Perhaps then he would be whole again.

"Would you like to take Pia back to the house?" Fran finally asked. "I'm happy to bring the hoist back to the clinic."

It was an olive branch. She was trying to bring him closer to Pia, not divide them. He was grateful for the gesture.

"*Grazie*, Fran. See you tomorrow at the clinic?"

She knew what he was saying. They wouldn't meet tonight. He simply couldn't. Not with the demons he was battling.

"Of course," she replied, her eyes darting away in an attempt to hide the hurt he'd seen in an instant. "Tomorrow at the clinic."

He just caught Pia rolling her eyes at him, then putting her hands out. *Do something! Fix it!* her expression screamed.

But all he was capable of was letting Francesca walk away.

CHAPTER ELEVEN

"HERE'S THE BREAK POINT."

Luca followed Dr. Murro's finger as he pointed out the T11 vertebra on the X-ray.

"Hard to miss, isn't it?" he replied grimly. "Severed right in two. No chance of recovering function below the waist." Luca shook his head. Off-road vehicles could be dangerous things. "She's lucky the vertebra didn't rupture her aorta."

"Has Francesca done any work with her?"

"I don't think so." Luca shook his head. "She usually submits a report as soon as she's worked with a patient, and I haven't seen one for Maria yet."

"She'll be staying on?"

"Who? Maria? Of course. She's only just arrived."

"Francesca," Dr. Murro corrected.

Ah. That was a more complicated answer.

"The whole staff seem to have really taken to her," Dr. Murro continued.

So have I. Too much.

"She has commitments back in the States, making it impossible."

"Shame. Someone like that—a triple threat—is going to be difficult to replace."

"Triple threat?" He'd not heard that turn of phrase before.

"Physio, hydro and canine therapist in one. She's a league above most. A real asset to Mont di Mare."

"That she is," Luca conceded. "That she is…"

A sharp knock sounded on the exam room door. "Dr. Montovano? It's Cara Bianchi. Francesca has found her out by the meadows, indicating with possible autonomic dysreflexia."

Luca shot from his chair. "Where is she? Have you brought her in?"

"*Si*. One of the doctors is seeing her now, in the Fiore Suite, but it's probably best if *you* take a look."

"On my way." He stopped at the doorway, "Dr. Murro, are you all right to meet with Maria? Talk through her treatment program?"

"Absolutely, Doctor. And if you could send Francesca to meet me when you're done, that'd be great. Well-done for hiring her, by the way. She's a real catch."

Luca nodded, striding out of the office before the scowl hit his lips.

Francesca was more than an asset. She was a woman. One who once you caught hold of, you'd be a fool ever to let go. But he would have to do just that if he was ever going to stand on his own two feet. Provide for his niece. Be the man his family had always believed him to be.

Doctors and nurses were already surrounding Cara on an exam table, where Francesca and a nurse were holding the girl in an upright position.

"She's bradycardic. Blood pressure is one-four-five over ninety-seven," the nurse said as soon as she saw Luca enter.

"Any nasal stuffiness? Nausea?" Luca asked.

"No, but she's complained to Francesca about a headache."

He glanced to Fran, who gave a quick affirmative nod.

"When I saw the goose bumps on Cara's knees and felt how clammy her skin was I brought her in here."

"My head is killing me! And my eyes feel all prickly!" Cara wailed from the exam table. "All I wanted to do was lie in the meadow!"

"It's all right… We'll ease the pain. Can we get an ice compress for Cara's face, please?" Luca smiled when he saw that one was being slipped in place before he'd finished speaking. "Autonomic dysreflexia." He gave Fran a grateful nod. "You were right. Can we strap her in and tilt the exam table up?"

"Has anyone checked her urinary bag?"

"Just emptied it. She had a full bladder."

"Bowels need emptying? Any cuts, bruises? Other injuries?"

"Nothing that I could see," said Fran. "But Cara hadn't voided her bladder in a while and was lying down, which I'm guessing exacerbated the symptoms."

She looked to Luca for confirmation. A hit of color pinked up her cheeks when their eyes met.

"Exactly right," Luca confirmed grimly.

It sounded like a simple enough problem, but for a paraplegic it was potentially lethal. Francesca had done well. His eyes met hers and he hoped she could read the gratitude in them.

"That's all it was?" Cara's voice turned plaintive as she scanned the faces in the room. "I just had to pee but it felt like I was going to die?"

"That's the long and short of it, Cara. If you like…" Luca flashed the group a smile, trying to bring some levity to the room, and dropped Cara a quick wink. What he had to say next was a hard bit of information to swallow. Something she'd have to live with for the rest of her life. "Tell the others it was autonomic dys-reflexia. Sounds much cooler." The smile dropped from his lips. "But you should also tell them how quickly it can turn critical. All those symptoms are warning signs of a much more serious response."

"Like what?" Her eyebrows shot up.

"Internal bleeding, stroke and even death." He let the words settle before he continued. These kids already had so much to deal with. Worrying about dying simply because their brain couldn't get the message that they needed to pee seemed cruel. Cara had been snowboarding less than a year ago, and now the rest of her life would involve wheelchairs, assistance and terrifying moments like these that, if she were left unattended, might lead to her death.

"You use intermittent catheterization, right?" Luca asked.

Cara nodded, a film of tears fogging her eyes.

Luca turned to the staff. No need for an audience. "I think we're good here. Cara and I might just have a bit of a chat and then…"

He scanned the collected staff including Gianfranco Torino—a GP who had retrained in psychotherapy when he'd suffered his own irrecoverable spinal injury. He, too, would be in a wheelchair for the rest of his life.

"Dr. Torino, would you be able to meet up with Cara later today? Maybe for an afternoon roll around the gardens?"

"Absolutely." Dr. Torino gave Cara a warm smile. "Three o'clock at the pergola? Is that enough time?"

Cara nodded. "*Si*, Dr. Torino. *Grazie*."

"*Prego*, Cara. See you then."

Luca scanned the staff, everyone of them focused on Cara as a unit.

This is the Mont di Mare I imagined.

His eyes lit on Francesca, who lifted her gaze from Cara's hair. She'd been running her fingers through the girl's long dark locks. Soothing. Caressing. When she saw him looking at her and smiled, it felt as if the heat of the sun was exploding in his chest.

Perfection.

And perfectly distracting. Smiles didn't pay bills. Patients did.

He moved his hands in a short, sharp clap. Too loud for the medium-sized exam room. Too late to do anything about it.

"All right, everyone. I think Cara and I need to chat over a couple of things."

Cara reached over her shoulder and grabbed Francesca's hand, shooting Luca an anxious look. "Can Fran stay? She was going to plait my hair—right, Francesca?"

"Ah! You're a hairdresser now?"

He saw the flutter of confusion in Fran's eyes and then the moment she made her decision.

"One of my hidden talents." She gave Cara a complicit wink and gathered her hair together as if it were a beautiful bouquet of wildflowers. "I promise I won't distract you from what you two are talking about."

Her pure blue eyes met his. There were a thousand reasons he should say no, she couldn't stay, and one single reason to say yes. His patient.

The motivation behind everything. Not Fran. Not desire. Not love.

The thought froze him solid for an instant, but quickly he forced himself into motion.

"I may need you to help for a moment before the hairstyling session begins."

"Of course," Fran replied. "Anything you need."

Despite himself, he risked another glance into her eyes and saw she meant it. She wasn't there to take. To demand. To change him. She was simply there to help.

Removing the cold compress from Cara's face, Luca ran a hand across the girl's brow, satisfied the hot flush was now under control. With Fran's help, they triple-checked for bedsores and ensured her clothing was fitting comfortably. A tight drawstring on a pair of trousers could trigger one of these potentially deadly incidents.

Once they were settled, and Fran had magicked a hairbrush from somewhere, he brought over the portable blood-pressure gauge, straddled a stool and wheeled himself over to Cara.

"Arm." He gave her a smile and held out the cuff.

"You already took my blood pressure."

"It's good to do it every five minutes or so when this happens. Here—let's slip your legs over the edge of the table to help your blood pressure. C'mon. Stretch your arm out."

Cara obliged him with a reluctant grin and soon he was pumping up the pressure in the cuff.

"I know you've had a lot to get used to since the accident, and this is another one of those scary learning curves. Basically, your bladder can't tell your brain it's full, so it's best if you have some sort of schedule. Have you ever set up a regular voiding timetable?"

"I did for the couple of months I was back in school, but over the summer I guess I let it lapse a bit." She shot him a guilty look.

"Did your doctors explain what might happen if your bladder was full and you didn't empty it?"

Another guilty look chased up the first. "I forget..."

"They're pretty strong symptoms—as you just found out. I know you've only been here a few days, but if you have a voiding timeline in your schedule it's a good idea to follow it."

"I was just waiting for my parents to go. You know—making the most of the time they were here."

"I thought you were out in the field on your own? That Francesca found you?"

Instinctively, his eyes flicked up to Fran's. The soft smile playing on her lips as she listened to them talk reminded him to do the same. A smiling doctor was much easier to listen to than the furrowed-brow grump he'd been of late.

Cara was remaining stoically tight-lipped.

"Either way, here's what's happening. Autonomic dysreflexia is your body's response to something happening below your injury level. You're a C6, C7 complete, right?"

Cara gave him a wry grin. "Can't get anything past you, can I, Dr. M?"

"Let's hope not, if it means getting you to a place where you're in charge of your own life. So." He gave the reading on the gauge a satisfied nod and took off the cuff. "I'm sure you've heard it before, but this time let it sink in. There are any number of things that can kick off an AD response. Overfull bladder or bowel."

"Ew!"

"I know—it's gross."

"No grosser than picking up dog poop who knows how many times a day!"

* * *

Fran's fingers flew to cover her mouth. *Oops!* So much for staying out of the doctor-patient talk!

Cara gave her a toothy grin. One Fran was pretty sure contained a bit of bravura.

"Actually…do you think an assistance dog would be able to remind me?" Cara had switched from doleful teen to bargaining expert.

Ah! *That* was why the teen had asked her to stay. Not for her sure-handed approach to a fishtail braid.

"That's not really my terrain." Luca pressed his lips together. "Francesca?"

Fran shook her head in surprise. Was Luca *including* her in this?

"Sorry, hon. What exactly is it you want to know?"

"If an assistance dog—one like Edison, maybe— were to help me, couldn't he remind me of things?"

Fran's instinct was to look to Luca, seek guidance. But to her surprise he just smiled, then widened and raised his hands, as if opening the forum to include her.

She gulped. This was… This was getting *involved.* Becoming interwoven in the fabric of things here on a level she'd told herself was a danger zone. A little dog training here. A bit of physio there. But advising a patient…?

"Francesca?" Luca prompted. "This is your area of expertise."

Dropping her gaze from his, she stared at the plait her fingers was weaving by rote and started speaking.

"Of course assistance dogs can certainly respond to alarms, and help you to remain upright in your wheelchair if you were ever to slump down. They can do a lot. But this sounds to me like something you and Dr. Montovano had better work out."

"But couldn't a dog have told you if I was dead or dying?"

"You mean when I found you out in the field? Absolutely. It would've barked. Tried to get someone to come and see you straightaway."

"Like Lassie?" Cara's voice squeaked with excitement. "If you hadn't found me then a dog could have saved my life!"

"Well…" Fran's fingers finished off the plait and she swirled a tiny elastic band she'd dug out of her pocket onto the end.

She'd overstepped the boundaries before. She really didn't want to do it again.

"Cara, you're with us for the rest of the summer, right?" Luca interjected. *Mercifully.*

Cara nodded.

"How about you and Fran spend a bit of time with Pia's dogs—if it's all right with Pia, of course. See how you go. I'm sure assistance dogs suit some people and aren't quite right for others. Am I right, Francesca?"

She'd expected to see some sort of triumph in his eyes. A way to catch her out. But there was nothing there but kindness. Possibility. Respect.

And for one perfect moment she was lost in the dark chocolate twinkle holding her rapt like a… Ha! The irony. Like a giddy teen.

Her phone buzzed. She glanced at the screen and frowned. Her father didn't normally ring this early.

"Sorry, I've just—"

Luca waved her apologies away. "I think Cara and I have plenty to talk about."

She gave Cara a quick wave, then accepted the call, closing the door softly behind her as she went.

"Si, Papa? Va tutto bene?"

CHAPTER TWELVE

"GOT A MINUTE?"

Fran looked up to find Luca at her doorway, striking the pose that had reduced her to a pool of melted butter a handful of weeks ago—arm resting on the low sling of the beam above her door frame, body outlined by the setting sun.

If she knew how, she'd let out a low whistle of appreciation and give him a one-liner an old-time Hollywood starlet would envy.

Somehow she found her voice. "I was just opening a bottle of wine. Fancy a glass?"

Luca didn't answer straight away, his eyes narrowing slightly as if inspecting her for ulterior motives. Which only succeeded in making her think of all the illicit things she could do with him right here and now, if only he'd duck his head, step inside her cottage and kick the door shut behind him.

Desire flared up hot and intense within her.

Bad brain. Naughty thoughts. Quit staring at the sexy doctor.

"*Grazie.* I'd love a glass of wine."

Good, brain. Excellent thoughts. Run to the bedroom to check it doesn't look like a hurricane has hit it.

"Mind if we sit out here? On the bench?"

What? Does not compute.

Then again, not a lot of what passed between them computed. Their tempestuous nights of lovemaking chased up by…absolutely nothing. No talks. No explanations. Just complicated silences.

Perhaps a talk was exactly what they needed.

"Here." Fran threw him a couple of pillows from the sofa. "Makes it comfier."

She pulled on a light sweater, grabbed another glass and cascaded an arc of gorgeous red wine into the goblet, all the while rearranging her features into something she hoped looked like casual delight that Luca had chosen sitting outside on a bench over ripping off his clothes.

"Everything all right with your phone call?" he asked.

"Mmm, yes." She quickly swallowed down a spicy gulp of Dutch courage, then topped up her glass. "It was my father."

"All's going well on the home front?"

"Very. So good, in fact, he'd like to come over."

She stepped outside the cottage in time to see Luca's eyes widen in surprise.

"I know. It freaked me out, too. My dad's never visited me before. Must be all these video calls we've had. I've been showing him Mont di Mare."

"Oh?" Luca's tone was unreadable. "Did he like what he saw?"

"Very much."

She looked up into Luca's eyes as she handed him his glass. His hand brushed hers, lingering just a fraction of a second longer than necessary, and with the connection a rush of heated sparks raced up her arm and circled around her heart.

"How did your day go with Pia?"

Luca stared deep into his wineglass before taking a thoughtful draught, tasting it fully before swallowing it down.

Had he felt it, too?

"Really well," Fran managed as nonchalantly as she could, tucking her feet up under her on the broad wooden bench. "She and the dogs have a whale of a time together."

"I meant as regards the training."

Killjoy! It wasn't her fault that their being together made them all fizzy and full of lust and desire and... and other things.

"Getting along with the dogs is part of the training," Fran began carefully. "If they don't sync—you know, make a love match as it were—the relationship isn't going to work out."

"A love match?"

"For lack of a better turn of phrase," Fran mumbled.

Could she be digging herself into a bigger hole? It wasn't as if she—*oh, no.*

She looked at him, then away and back again, before realizing what had been happening to her for these past few weeks.

She had fallen in love with Luca. It was mad. And foolish. And totally never going to happen. But—

Did he feel the same way?

She turned to him, seeking answers, only to catch Luca's gaze dropping to her mouth as her lips grazed the edge of her wineglass. An urge to throw caution to the wind took hold of her. Why shouldn't she just go for it? Fling her glass away and climb onto his lap so he could claim what was already his?

His lips parted.

For an instant she was certain she could see it in Luca's eyes, too. The exact same exhilarating rush of realization that he'd found love in the least likely of places. With the least likely of people.

He hesitated.

Was he...? Was he about to tell her he loved her, too?

"What are the actual *practical* things Pia is taking away from this? What, *precisely*, are you enabling her to do by having a dog?"

Fran's heart plummeted, finding itself on all too familiar terrain. She was a solitary girl, seeking her place in the world, only to realize she'd read the wrong page. *Again.*

She scrunched her eyes tight, conjuring up an image of Freda and Edison. She could do with a dose of canine cuddles right now.

"If you'd been spending any time with Pia, you probably would've noticed for yourself," she snapped.

Luca's eyes widened at the level of heat in her voice.

Tough. You just broke my heart.

She looked away, drew in a deep lungful of mountain air and forced it out slowly before continuing.

"Pia and Freda have already mastered a lot of the drop-and-retrieve tasks that will help in her day-to-day life. Right now we're working on Freda responding to very specific verbal commands."

"Like what?" Luca asked—with genuine interest rather than the disdain she'd been expecting. *Good.* At least she'd made some sort of a mark.

Ha! Take that, you doubting...sexy Italian, you.

"Freda can go and get other patients, for example. By name. Scent, really. It's amazing how quickly they learn who is who."

"Why would Pia want her to fetch other patients?"

"Oh…I don't know." Fran took a big gulp of wine before answering that one. "Maybe she's enjoying having some people to spend time with. Friends."

"What would she—" Luca began, then stopped himself, his jaw tensing as his lips pressed together and thinned.

Fran gulped down the rest of her wine, then stood up, hands on hips, to face Luca.

"It may not be my place to say this, but you're letting your niece grow up without you. Take it from me. Once that opportunity is gone, it's hard to claw it back."

A complication of emotions crossed Luca's face as he looked up at her. As if he was having a fight with himself.

"You're right. It's not your place."

Something deep within her flared, hot and fierce.

"That may be so, but let me tell you this. Crush the hearts of all the women you want, Luca Montovano. I'll be fine. *We'll* be fine. But Pia…? You're all she has. You lose this chance to show her you love her and you might lose her for good."

Luca looked away, a searing blast of emotion pounding the breath out of his chest in one sharp, unforgiving blow.

Lose Pia?

Unthinkable.

And what had Fran meant about crushing hearts? Marina wasn't crushed—

"I'll be fine," she'd said.

Did Fran *love* him? Had she invested her heart in those nights they had spent together? Nights he hadn't acknowledged since…since she had become a vital part of his work team. One of the people he kept at arm's length in preparation for the bank's inevitable foreclosure.

He knew she enjoyed sparring with him, working with him—but love? It wasn't something he had ever allowed himself to consider. Not with so much at stake.

He looked back at her, saw her eyes blazing with indignation. The fury of a child who had been where Pia was now. The rage of a woman who loved a man who could never love her in return.

He pushed himself up to standing after placing his drained glass on the floor and faced her. "You're a very brave woman, Francesca Martinelli."

She shifted her feet, eyes held wide-open as they had been on the very first day they'd met. When she'd been the only one courageous enough to stop her friend from doing something she'd regret forever.

"You never shy away from hard truths, do you, Francesca?"

She gave her head a little shake in agreement.

Luca couldn't help but give a self-effacing laugh. "I suspect moments like these are why Beatrice always speaks so highly of you. Why she insisted you come up here. She said you'd be good for me."

"She did?" Fran's eyes brightened, endearing her to him more than he should allow.

"Often," he said. "And with great affection."

He fought the urge to reach out and touch Fran. Stroke a finger along the length of her jawline. Smooth the back of his hand along the downy softness of her cheek.

"That's good," Fran whispered.

Whether she was referring to Beatrice or to the frisson fizzing between them, Luca couldn't tell. How it had shifted from rage to zingy chemistry, he didn't know, but it had.

Luca took a step back, intentionally breaking the moment in two, and gave his thoughts over to Beatrice—his dear friend who'd all but had the world ripped out from under her feet and yet had remained true, kind. A loving friend who had never, even in her darkest hour, withdrawn her emotions as he so often did. Barring his heart from the aches and pains that loving someone entailed.

"If you don't mind me saying something…" Fran began tentatively.

"Why stop now?" He opened his palms. An invitation for her to continue.

Fran blushed, but continued, "Marina didn't really seem your type. Or deserve you, for that matter."

Before he thought better of it, he asked, "And what exactly is it that *I* deserve?"

They both stopped and stared at each other in a moment of mutual recognition. Of course Francesca was a better choice. The natural choice.

A choice he didn't have the freedom to make.

"Marina just seemed… She seemed to be after something more…*fantasy*. Like in a fairy tale. With cocktails and fast cars."

"That sounds about right," Luca conceded. "You're not like that, though, are you?"

Fran squirmed under his gaze and he didn't blame her. He didn't have the ability to disguise the desire he knew was burning in his eyes. But he couldn't offer her what she deserved. His heart.

He turned to face the view, breaking a moment that

would only have led to more heartache. "It's probably just as well we're talking about my relationship failures."

"Why's that?" Fran looked away, then dropped down onto the bench, carefully rearranging the pebbles at her feet with her toe.

"I know my behavior over the past few weeks or so has been…confusing, to say the least."

"Are you saying our being together was a mistake?" Defensiveness laced her words and tightened the folding of her arms across her chest.

"No. No, *chiara*." He joined her on the bench and reached out a hand to cup her chin, so that she could see straight into his heart when he spoke. "Being with you was…bittersweet."

She swallowed. He forced himself to hold his ground, letting his hand shift from her chin to her arms, which he gently unlaced, taking both of her hands in his.

"I liked the idea of having a summer romance with you."

"Past tense?" she asked, with her usual unflinching desire to hear the truth.

"Yes." He owed it to her.

"I thought… I thought you enjoyed being with me."

Little crinkles appeared at the top of her nose as the sparks in her eyes flared in protest. A swell of emotion tightened in his throat. "I did. More than I should have, given the circumstances."

"Which are…?" Francesca barely got the words out before choking back a small cry of protest.

His fingers twitched and his hands balled into fists. He didn't want to cause her pain. Far from it.

"You said yourself you have to go home."

"Not for another few weeks!"

"Francesca, Mont di Mare may not *be* here in a few weeks."

A silence rang between them so powerfully Francesca felt her skin practically reverberate with the impact of his words.

"What do you mean?"

"The bank." He spat the word out as if it were poison, then swept an arm along the length of the village. "The bank will own all of this in a few weeks if I don't turn things around."

She shook her head as if he'd just spoken in a foreign tongue. "I don't understand…"

"You don't need to." He bit the words out one by one, as if he were actually shouldering the weight of the mountain as he did so. "My focus needs to be entirely on the clinic, and what little time I have left in my day—as you so rightly pointed out—I need to give to Pia. She's all I have."

"You know you could have more," Fran asserted.

"Only to have you disappear at the end of the summer, along with Mont di Mare?" He didn't pause to let Fran answer, and his voice softened as he offered her what little consolation he could. "I've experienced enough loss to last a lifetime, *amore*. I don't think I could bear any more."

A dog's bark filtered into the fabric of the night sounds. It reminded him that he'd delivered the death knell to any future between them. The least he could do was soften the blow.

"I meant to say the reason I was asking so much about the dogs is that after our session with Cara a couple of other patients were asking whether or not they might have one, too. If it suits you, you could look into supplying them with assistance canines before the summer is out."

* * *

Fran didn't know whether to be elated or furious, given the circumstances. Shell-shocked was about as close as she could come.

Luca was about to lose the entire village and still his thoughts were on his patients?

Her heart bled for him, and then just as quickly tightened in a sharp twist of anguish.

Why couldn't he afford *her* the same courtesy?

Take a risk.

Chance his heart on love.

She stared at him, searching his dark eyes for answers.

How could he just stand there like that? All business and attention to detail when everything he'd worked so hard for was slipping away.

Wasn't he full of rage? Of fight? *Why* wouldn't he let her love him? Take the blows of an unfair world alongside him?

She stared at Luca, amazed to see the light burning in his eyes turn icy cold.

Perhaps he was right. He was giving her a chance to cut her losses. Preserve what was left of her heart. Do her job, then get on with her life—just as she'd planned.

She forced on her most businesslike tone. He wanted facts? He could *have* facts.

"You know it takes more than a couple of weeks to find the right dogs, let alone train them up, right? It requires skill. Precision. Plus, I adopt dogs from local shelters, so sometimes there are additional factors to consider. What if the patient doesn't take to the dog and I can't bring it back to the States? I could hardly return it to the shelter afterward, could I? Having given it a glimpse of another life?"

Luca stared at her. Completely unmoved.

Fran continued. "Dogs are loyal, even if people aren't, and I don't play emotional bingo. With anyone."

It was vaguely satisfying to finally see a glint of discord in Luca's eyes.

Vaguely.

There was no glory in one-upping a man whose world was about to collapse in on him.

She bent and picked up his wineglass from the ground, then took a definitive step toward her doorway before turning to address him again.

"I *will* speak with your administrator about patients looking to work with an assistance dog and see if there's someone local who can be brought in. It would be foolish to invest in something I won't be able to see through to the bitter end. If you'll excuse me?"

She scooted around Luca and into her cottage before she could catch another glimpse of those beautiful dark eyes of his, silently cursing herself, her life—anything she could think of—as she shut the door behind her.

Leaning against the thick, time-worn oak, she let a deep sigh heave out of her chest.

As painful as it was for her to admit, Luca was right. There was too much at stake for him to worry about foolish things like a summer romance. She was going home. She'd promised her father—just as he had promised her.

The only thing she could do now was follow the advice she'd given to Luca. Spend her time building a life she wouldn't regret.

A flicker of an idea came to her, but just as quickly as it caught and flared brightly, she blew it out.

She wasn't ready to ask her father for help. Not yet. But a talk...

She could do with a talk right now.

She swiped at the number and smiled as the phone began to ring.

Before, she had always turned to Bea, but now, hearing her father's voice brighten when he picked up the phone, she let gratitude flood into her heart that, step by step, they were forging a real relationship.

CHAPTER THIRTEEN

LUCA FROWNED. HE'D caught a glimpse of her. As per usual, no matter how stealthily Fran passed, he always knew when she was near. It was a sixth sense he'd grown all too aware of.

He glanced up at the clock. It was past seven. A lovely evening. Well after rehab hours. The residents were all back in their villas, Pia was tucked up with the dogs, watching a film, and here he was hunkered over a pile of papers, brow furrowed, one hand ramming his hair away from his forehead, the other spread wide against the mahogany sheen of the large desk he commanded. Taut. Ready for action. Poised like a reluctant but honorable admiral, helming a ship when duty called.

"Fran!"

He called out her name before he thought better of it. Unlike Francesca, who, true to her word, had maintained an entirely professional demeanor in the weeks following their talk, Luca had behaved like a bear with a sore head.

A golden halo of hair appeared, then her bright eyes peeped around the edge of his door frame like a curious kitten—tempted, but not quite brave enough to enter the lion's lair.

Luca gazed at her for a moment, just enjoying the

chance to drink her in. Those blue eyes of hers were skidding around his office as if trying to memorize it. Or maybe that was just him hoping. It wouldn't be long now before she left.

Her loose blond curls rested atop the soft slope of her bare shoulders. The tiny string straps of her sundress reminded him of...too much.

He pushed the pile of papers away, against his better judgment, and rose. "Fancy a walk? I could do with some fresh air."

She shot him a wary look, then nodded. Reluctantly.

They strolled for a few minutes in a surprisingly comfortable silence. Strands of music, television and laughter ribboned out from the villas along with wafts of home-cooked food.

Fran broke the silence. "That smells good."

"My mother used to call the scents up here 'the real Italy.'" Luca laughed softly at the memory.

"In my house that was store-bought macaroni and cheese!" Fran huffed out a laugh that was utterly bereft of joy.

Her response to his throwaway comment was a stark reminder to Luca that he did have blessings to count. Proper childhood memories. Family, laughter, love and joy.

"So what were they? Those scents of the real Italy?" Fran asked.

"Oh, let's see..." He stopped and closed his eyes for a moment, letting the memories comes to him. "Torn basil leaves. The ripest of tomatoes. Freshly baked focaccia. *Dio*, the bread alone was enough to bring you to your knees. Signora Levazzo!" The memory came to him vividly. "Signora Levazzo's focaccia was the envy of all the villagers. She had a secret weapon."

"Which was...?" Fran asked.

"Her son's olive oil. He had a set of olive trees he always used. Slightly more peppery than anyone else's. No one knows how he did it, but—oh!" He pressed his fingers to his lips and kissed them. *"Delicioso!"*

"Sounds lovely."

He didn't miss the hint of wistfulness in her voice. Or the pang in his heart that she hadn't enjoyed those simple but so-perfect pleasures in her own childhood. From the smattering of comments he'd pieced together, she hadn't had much of a childhood at all.

"They were unforgettable summers." Luca looked up to the sky, unsuccessfully fighting the rush of bitterness sweeping in to darken the fond memories. "And to think I told them to sell it all."

"Who? Your family?" Fran's brow crinkled.

He nodded. "We spent all our summers here. Well..." He held up his index finger. "Everyone but me once I'd turned eighteen."

"What happened then?" Fran asked, her eyes following the line of his hand as he indicated that they should follow a path leading to the outer wall of the village.

"The usual things that happen to an eighteen-year-old male. Girls. Motorcycles. University. Medicine."

Fran laughed, taking a quick, shy glimpse up toward him. "I don't think most eighteen-year-old males are drawn to medicine."

"Well...I always like to be different."

"You definitely are that," Fran said, almost swallowing the words even as she did. "And it was plastics you went into?"

"Reconstructive surgery," he corrected, then amended his brusque answer. "I did plastics to feed my taste for the high life. Reconstructive surgery to feed my soul."

Fran shot him a questioning glance.

"I did a lot of pro bono cases back then. Cleft palates. Children who'd been disfigured in accidents. That sort of thing."

He felt Fran's eyes travel to his scar and turned away. He'd never remove his scar. Not after what he'd done.

Abruptly Fran stopped and knelt, plucking at a few tiny flowers. She held them up when he asked if she was making a posy.

"Daisy chain," she explained, turning her focus to joining the flowers together. "It's fun. You should try it."

"I don't do *fun*," Luca shot back.

"I know." Fran pressed her heels into the ground and rose to her full height. "That's why I said it."

Luca turned away to face the setting sun.

He shouldn't have to live like this, she thought. All stoic, full of to-do lists and health-and-safety warnings. He was a kind, generous man who—when he dared to let the mask drop—was doing his best to stay afloat and do well by his niece. And failing at both because he insisted upon doing it alone.

She placed the finished daisy chain atop her head, then reached out to grab his hand before he strode off beyond her reach. His heart might not be free to love her, but he didn't have to do this alone.

"Talk to me."

A groan of frustration tightened Luca's throat around his Adam's apple. If he hadn't squeezed her fingers as he made the animalistic cry, she would have left immediately. But when his fingers curled around hers and pressed into the back of her palm, she knew it was his way of doing the best he could—the only way he knew how.

"C'mon…" She tried again. "Fair is fair. You got *my* life story on my first day here."

When she sent him a playful wink she received a taut grimace in place of the smile she'd hoped to see.

"I was looking after my niece. Ensuring you weren't some lunatic Bea had sent my way."

Fran clucked her tongue. "First of all, Bea would never do that. And, second of all, I think you know I've encountered enough crazy in my life for you to feel safe in the knowledge I will pass no judgment when I hear your story."

Was that…? Had he just…? Was that the hint of a smile? No. He gave a shake of his head.

Frustration tightened in her chest. What would it take to get this man to trust her?

"Listen. Of all the people up here in this incredible, wonderful center of healing you've created, you seem to be the only one not getting any better."

She ignored his sharp look and continued.

"I'm probably the only one here who knows exactly what it's like to butt heads with their own destiny. My dad's due any day now and I'm already quaking in my boots. Please…" She gave his hand a tight squeeze. "Just lay your cards on the table and see what happens."

A rancorous laugh unfurled from deep within him. "Oh, *chiara*. If only you knew how apt your choice of words was…"

"Well, I *would* know if you told me." Despite all her efforts to rein in her emotions, she couldn't help giving the ground a good stamp with her foot.

Luca arced an eyebrow at her. "It's not a very nice story."

"Nor is mine. It's not like I'm made of glass, Luca. I'm flesh and blood. Just like you."

Luca's lips remained firmly clamped shut.

"You've already had my body!" she finally cried out in sheer frustration. "What do you *want*? Blood?"

CHAPTER FOURTEEN

LUCA WHEELED ON FRAN, his features turning dark, almost savage in their intensity. "I didn't ask for anything from you, *chiara*. Not one kiss. Not one cent. Remember that when you're gone."

Shock whipped anything Fran might have said in response straight out of her throat. She felt her mouth go dry and, despite the warmth of the summer's evening, she shivered as the blood drained from her face when he continued.

"Don't think I haven't seen it."

"Seen what?" Fran looked around her, as if the answer might pop out from behind a bush. She was absolutely bewildered.

"I *know* how you speak of Mont di Mare. How you've made this place into some sort of Shangri-la. A place where nothing can go wrong. Where everything is perfect and rose-colored. You don't get to do that. Not without knowing the facts."

Luca drew in a sharp breath, the air near enough slicing his throat as it filled his lungs.

What the hell?

After a summer of holding it all in, he couldn't contain his rage any longer.

Losing Fran, the clinic—perhaps even Pia if she saw the shell of a man he'd turned into—was more than he could take.

He began pacing on the outcrop where they'd stopped. And talking. Talking as if his life depended upon it.

"Thanks to my father's time at the poker tables, I am in debt up to my eyeballs. Worse. Drowning."

It was an admission he'd never made aloud.

He was shocked to see compassion in Fran's eyes when he'd been so brutal. Even more, they bore no pity.

It was what he had feared most. The pitying looks. He'd had enough of those at the funeral. The funeral in which he had buried his mother, his father, his sister and brother-in-law all in one awful, heart-wrenching day. A day he never wanted to remember, though he knew slamming the door shut on those memories only left them to fester. To rear their ugly heads as they were doing now.

He glanced across at Fran again. Surely she would shrink away from him at some point. As the facts of the story began to sink in. As the knowledge that *he* was to blame for everything that had come his way became clear.

Astonishingly, she seemed more clear-eyed and steady than he had ever seen her. As if his lashing out at her had been an unwelcome shock, but not unexpected.

"How did you open the clinic without assets?"

Fran's question pulled him back to the facts—however unsavory they were to confront.

"I had saved a fair amount when I working in Rome."

Her eyebrows lifted in surprise.

"Plastic surgery brings in a lot of money when you're willing to put in the hours. That, and some of the doctors here are actually operating as private practices, so they came with their own equipment. Thanks to Bea, I learned about and applied for a few grants. Historic building restoration and the like. The rest..." He swallowed down the sour memories of learning just how far into penury his father had sunk. "Let's just say what's left of my soul belongs to the devil."

"I doubt that's true, Luca. You're too good a man to compromise your principles."

Surprisingly, Fran's face was a picture of earnestness rather than horror. As if she held out hope that the clinic could still be saved.

"Not me—my father. But I'm sure I can shoulder a large portion of the blame for that, as well. To cut a long story short—if I don't make a profit from the clinic very, very soon it will go to Nartoli Banking. My father leveraged the place."

"What will happen?"

"They'll repossess it." The emotion had drained from his voice now. "In a few weeks, most likely. Sell it to an investor, who will most likely raze the village, turn the site into a modern hotel. *Exclusive*, of course," he added with an embittered laugh.

He thought of Mont di Mare—the historic cottages and stone buildings, the gardens and archways—all of it being obliterated to make way for a glitzy glass-and-steel hotel aimed at the world's rich and careless...

"Is it essential to have the clinic here?" she asked. "I mean, it's obviously beautiful, and just the view alone is healing, but...could you not have set up the clinic in Rome?"

Fran's voice was soft. Nonjudgmental. She wasn't accusing him of making the wrong decision, just trying to paint a picture. She wanted to understand.

"Revitalizing the village had always been my sister and mother's dream," he finally admitted.

"As a clinic?"

He shook his head. "A holiday destination, summer homes—that sort of thing. They even toyed with the idea of trying to revamp it into a living, working village. One with specialized craftsmen—and women," he added quickly, when he saw Fran's lips purse and then spread into a gentle smile at his correction. "Similar ideas to what you had, minus the patients. A place where craftspeople could live and create traditional works of art and wares. Do you know how hard it is to find a genuine blacksmith these days?"

Fran shook her head, then quirked an eyebrow. "About as hard as finding world peace?"

He laughed. Couldn't help it. And was grateful for the release.

Fran lowered herself onto a broad boulder, her legs swinging over the edge as she looked out into the valley below.

Hands on his hips, he scanned the outlook, fully aware that this was most likely one of the last days he could call the view his own.

"This is the first time I've heard you speak about your family," Fran said when he eventually sat down alongside her.

"Pia is my family. I don't even deserve *her*."

He looked across in time to see Fran shake off his words, the hurt he'd caused because he wouldn't—*couldn't*—love her, too.

"I just meant—"

"I know what you meant," he cut in harshly. "I'm sorry, Fran. I know you're all about healing old wounds, making amends with your father and all that, but it's too late for me."

"How do you know that?"

He saw something in her then. A steely determination to see this through with him, no matter how ugly.

"You want the whole story?"

She nodded.

"All right—well, the beginning's pretty easy. Happy childhood. Wonderful mother. Doting father. They would've loved me to take up a bit more of the whole Baron Montovano thing, but they never pressed when they saw medicine was my passion. My sister and mother looked after things here. Had the vision. My father was a proud man. Passionate and very much in love with my mother. A few years ago, when his business ventures started going south along with the rest of the world's, he went into a panic."

"About what?"

"He became convinced he was going to die before my mother."

"Was he sick?" Fran asked.

"No." He corrected himself. "Or not that I was aware of. He and I weren't exactly close by then, and even if I'd asked him, he wouldn't have come to me for a medical exam."

"How do you know that?"

"Because he told me." Luca scraped his hand against the sharp edge of the stone he sat upon, not caring if it lacerated his skin. The cut would hurt less than the words his father had shouted in rage that night at the casino.

"You are the last person I would come to for help. The last person in the world."

"My mother and my sister were his world. He would've done anything for them."

"I bet the same was true for you."

"Don't speak of what you don't know, *chiara*. Do you know how he showed his love? His loyalty to his family? By taking to the craps table. The poker table. Baccarat. Anything to try to scrape back the money he had lost in business. But instead of securing a healthy nest egg, he lost. Lost it all."

Fran's fingers flew to cover her mouth, but to her credit she didn't say a word.

"Just over two years ago I received a call from a casino in Monaco, asking if I could come and collect him. His pockets were empty and it was either me bailing him out or they'd put him in prison for the night."

He looked up to the sky, completely unadulterated by city lights, and soaked it in.

"I drove from Roma straight to Florence, where my mother and sister were. We decided to all go together. Show our support."

He kept his gaze on the sky. There was no chance he could look into Fran's eyes and get through this part of the story without completely breaking down.

"So we all climbed into the car and drove through the night to go and pick up my wayward father in Monte Carlo."

"You *drove*?" Fran asked incredulously.

"The things you do for love," Luca answered softly. He would have done anything for his father. Walked there if he'd needed to. Oh! How he wished he'd walked.

"What happened when you reached him?"

"He was furious at first. Blaming everything on me. For abandoning the family."

"By working in medicine?" Fran shook her head, as

if trying to make sense of it all. "Didn't he know about the charity work you did?"

"No." Luca scraped his other hand along the rough surface of the granite. "It didn't suit my image for people to know, so I never really talked about it."

He tugged a hand through his hair, grateful for the deepening darkness. With any luck, it was hiding the waves of emotion crossing his face at the memory of his father eventually breaking down. Sobbing with relief and sorrow at the pain he had brought to his own family.

"Then we all piled back into my car." He laughed at the memory. They'd been jam-packed in that thing. Like sardines, his mother had kept saying. A motley crew, they'd been. Tearful. Laughing. Up and down the emotional roller coaster until they had all sagged with fatigue.

"Pia, you will be unsurprised to hear, was ever the diplomat. She kept everyone talking about what we were going to make for dinner when we got back to Italy. And it was somewhere around a very vibrant discussion about eggplant parmigiana—"

Luca stopped. This was the hardest part. Pieces of information still only came to him in fragments. His hands on the steering wheel. Entering the tunnel. The articulated truck crossing the median strip—

Mercifully, Pia's memory of the accident had never returned. He prayed, for her sake, that it never would.

"The truck driver must've fallen asleep. That route is renowned for it. Up and over the mountains. Lots of tunnels. We were all tired, too. I'd been driving all day. All night. It was why we'd forced ourselves to keep talking, inventing ridiculous recipes to try when we got home."

Luca felt his voice grow jagged with emotion. Each word became weighted in his chest, as if the words themselves were physical burdens he'd been carrying all these years.

"He just careened straight into us. There was nothing I could do!" The words scraped against his throat as though they were being torn from his chest.

Without even noticing her moving, he suddenly felt Francesca's arms around him, and after years of holding back the bone-shaking grief of loss—nearly his entire family gone in one sickeningly powerful blow—he wept.

Luca hardly knew how much time had passed when at long last his breath steadied and the reddened edges of his eyes dried.

Fran had not said a single word through his outpouring. No trite placations. No overused sayings to try to soothe away a pain that could never be fully healed. Although now his silent grief had become a sorrow shared. It was Fran's gift to him. He could see it in her eyes, glistening with the tears she had not let herself shed, as he wept in the silvery, ethereal light of the moon.

"So that's where this came from?" Fran reached out and gently ran her finger along his scar.

He nodded, catching her hand beneath his own. He'd never thought of it as disfiguring. More as one of life's cruel reminders that he had debts to pay—both literal and figurative.

"If there's anything I can do—" Fran began, stopping abruptly when he dropped her hand as if it had scalded him.

Her touch hadn't. But her words had.

After all that didn't she see this was *his* burden to bear? His cross to carry alone?

"You've done more than enough, Francesca."

She blinked, and something he couldn't quite read

had changed in her eyes when she opened them again. "I hope you're saying that in a good way."

"As best I know how. Now..." He pushed himself up, offering her a hand so that she could rise more easily from their mountainside perch. "I'd best be off. See my niece. *Buonasera.*"

He left a bemused Francesca at her doorway, not daring to let himself dip down and give her cheek a kiss. He'd said too much. Bared too much of his heart.

He had three minutes—the length of the walk between her cottage and his own—to pull himself back together. Make a man out of himself again before he saw Pia.

How would he tell her he was going to lose this place to the bank?

Again, his eyes returned to the stars, searching for answers.

God willing, he would never have to say a word.

Fran pulled a blanket over her shoulders and curled up in the window seat. The way her mind was buzzing, sleep was going to be a hard-won commodity. Nearly as impossible as it had been to say good-night to Luca.

Never before had she been so moved as when she and Luca had held each other and he'd finally given in to the years of grief he'd held pent up inside him.

If only—

No.

She gave herself a sharp shake, willing the tears forming in her eyes to disappear. If Luca could be so strong under such heartrending circumstances, she would strive to be the same. Never before had she held someone in such high regard. Never before had she felt such compassion, such love, for one man.

Even if he couldn't return her love he'd shown her the power of sacrifice. Sacrifices she was willing to make even if it cost her her heart.

Shivering a bit, she pulled the blanket closer around her shoulders, willing her body to recapture the sense of warmth she'd felt when she had held Luca.

She had half a mind to call Bea, desperate to brainstorm with someone. Come up with something, *anything* that would help save Mont di Mare from the bank. But Bea had enough on her plate without this to worry about.

Then the lightning-bolt moment came.

She *did* know one person whose entire life had been fueled by the betrayal of another. Who had poured his every energy into exacting revenge by succeeding in his own right.

Her tummy lurched, then tightened as her nerves collected into one jangling ball in her chest, but she picked up her phone anyway.

Courage.

That was what Luca had. In spades.

Strength.

She dialed the number. Took a deep breath…

Forgiveness.

Luca had so many reasons to let his heart turn black, and through everything all she had seen was compassion and—

"*Si, pronto?*"

Love.

"*Papa, è Francesca. Va bene?*"

CHAPTER FIFTEEN

"THAT WAS AN excellent session, Giuliana. Are you pleased with your progress?"

Luca took a seat beside the girl as she wheeled her chair into the shade of the pergola after Dr. Torino had headed back to the gym.

"Si." Her eyes glistened with pride. "All the therapists and doctors here have been amazing. I can't believe how quickly I've gained in strength. Don't let Fran go back to America."

The smile dropped from his eyes. "I'm afraid I don't have much control over that."

"I'm sure if you asked her..."

Luca tsk-tsked and shook his head. "We're not talking about Fran right now—we're talking about you and your progress."

He didn't want Fran to go. But he was hardly going to beg her to stay on a sinking ship.

"Dai. Facci vedere i muscoli."

Despite his grim mood, Luca smiled as Giuliana pushed back her T-shirt and flexed her slender bicep.

He gave it an appreciative squeeze. *"Va bene,* Giuliana. You'll be winning arm wrestling matches soon."

This was the fun part. The satisfying part of being a doctor. Happy patients. Positive results.

"You're not finding the full days of rehab too tiring?"

Giuliana gave the exasperated sigh of a teenager. "No more than I'm supposed to!"

"Excellent. You're a star patient."

Giuliana giggled, waving away his praise. "That's not hard when there's only five of us. Besides—" she fixed Luca with a narrow-eyed gaze "—I have it on good authority you say that to everyone."

"Guilty." Luca shot her an apologetic grin. "You're all making me—the clinic—look really good."

"Ciao, Pia!"

Luca turned in the direction Giuliana was waving— something she hadn't been able to do when she'd arrived here—the smile dropping from his lips again when he saw Fran corralling his niece and her dogs into the large courtyard. Giuliana called out a greeting again, and Pia quickly changed course toward them.

Fran's eyes caught his but she didn't cross over. Not that he blamed her.

"Scusi, Dr. Montovano, Pia is going to show me some things with the dogs."

"No problem." Luca grinned—not that Giuliana was hanging around to see if he wanted her to stay.

"Dr. Montovano?" His administrative assistant appeared by his side with a note in her hand.

"Si, Rosa?"

"We've got a patient who would like to be transferred here. His parents, actually. They say their son has lost hope."

"We don't have room," he said by rote, giving his head a shake, though his mind was already spinning with ways to make it possible. It wasn't the money— though that would help. It was the hope part. When a patient had lost hope...

"They're asking for intensive. Maybe a month."

We may not have a month.

"Perhaps if he came for a day. A chance to see the other patients so he doesn't feel so alone," Rosa persisted.

"What's his case history?"

He shouldn't ask. Knowing more about the patient would make him want to help.

A shard of frustration tugged his brows together. His gut was telling him to say yes. The staff had already made it clear they would be fine working with more patients. It was simply a question of finding the room. He and Pia could move out of *their* house, but after so much disruption he hated to move her again.

Out of the corner of his eye he could see Fran approaching the pergola as the girls and the dogs disappeared, leaving gales of laughter in their wake. Fran's cottage was wheelchair friendly. Close enough to the clinic's hub to access all the facilities easily.

"It's just the three of them, you say?"

"Three of who?" Fran asked.

"A new patient and his parents," Rosa jumped in.

"No. *Not* a new patient. I'm afraid it won't work," Luca interjected. "There's nowhere for him to stay."

"How about my cottage?"

Fran looked between the two of them, as if they were both ridiculous for not thinking of it in the first place.

"You would give up your cottage?" Rosa's eyes lit with relief.

"Of course I would. Anything! I'd leave right now if that helped."

"And abandon Pia?" Luca shook his head. "Leave her with the job half-done—not to mention the other patients you've taken on—before your contract is up?"

Fran's eyes shot to his, striking him like a viper. Neither of them was talking about Pia and he knew it.

"I'm hardly *abandoning* anything. I only have a few days left anyway."

Of course she would leave. What had he thought would happen after last night? Had he really thought ripping his heart open and letting his whole sorry story pour out would keep her here? *No.* Quite the opposite. He hadn't thought at all. He most likely repulsed her now.

"I would *never* let my patients down," Fran shot back before he could get a word in. "I'm talking about the cottage. I can stay anywhere. The patients can't."

He waited for her to state the obvious. That he needed the money. He needed *her.*

"Rosa." He forced himself to speak calmly. "Would you please give us a moment to discuss Miss Martinelli's housing arrangements?"

"Of course, Dr. Montovano."

If he wasn't mistaken, Rosa gave the tiniest hint of a smile before she reluctantly headed back to the office. Italians loved a passionate fight, and from the speed of the blood coursing through his veins this was set to be explosive.

"So, what's your big plan? To camp out on one of the sun loungers? Or are you going to whip one of the cottages into shape with one of your feel-good projects?"

Luca knew he was being unreasonable. Knew there was bite in his bark.

"I'll stay in town. Commute in like the other doctors. Besides, with my father coming—"

"What?"

"My father. You know he's coming."

Luca shook his head. He remembered her mentioning something about a visit, but it hadn't really registered. He couldn't believe Fran would humiliate him like this. Show a half-finished clinic to a man renowned for his exacting attention to detail. A man who with a few swift strokes of his keyboard could save the clinic from oblivion. Fran's father was the last person on earth he wanted crossing the entryway to Mont di Mare.

"Why would you do that? Why would you invite him here?"

Fran took a step away from Luca, as if the question had physically repelled her.

"He's my *father*. He wants to see the clinic. Meet the people I've been talking about all summer. You of all people should know how important family is."

Luca looked at her as if she'd slapped him. Her remorse was instant, but it was too late to make apologies. The warmth she had once seen in Luca's eyes turned into inaccessible black, his pupils meshing with his irises as if there would never be enough light for him to see any good in the world. Any hope.

His lip curled in disgust, as if by inviting her father here she had betrayed him. "What's the point in bringing him here if all you're going to do is leave? Showing Daddy what a good little girl he's raised?"

"You don't mean that."

"Oh, I do, *chiara*." He closed the gap between them with one long-legged stride. "Has this been *fun* for you? Playing at a mountainside clinic while the rest of us are struggling to survive?"

Fran opened her mouth to answer, then thought better of it. Her heart ached for Luca. Ached to tell him everything—but not in the state he was in now. Unbending. Proud. Hurt. There was hurt coursing around that bloodstream of his—she knew it—but it didn't change the facts. She loved him, but if inviting her father here meant losing Luca but saving the clinic, then so be it. Her father was coming whether Luca liked it or not.

"Tell the new patient to come." She forced her voice to sound steady.

"For how long, Francesca? Where's your crystal ball? A day? A week? How many days do you foresee here before I have to tell this miserable wheelchair-bound boy and everyone else here that they will all have to go?"

"Whatever you feel is best. Now, if you'll excuse me, I have a patient appointment to keep."

Fran forced herself to turn away and walk calmly toward the clinic, trying her very best not to let Luca see that her knees were about to give way beneath her.

She knew anger and fear were fueling Luca's hateful comments. Of *course* she wanted the clinic to flourish. She wanted everything in the world for him. She wanted *him*!

Couldn't he see it in her eyes? In her heart?

Leaving wasn't the plan. *Staying* was the plan. The dream.

But her father was a facts man. He needed to see things for himself. Touch the stone. Scour the books. Observe the work. He'd never invest in a dream he didn't think could become a reality. And for the first time since she'd rung her father and asked him to jump on a plane as soon as possible, she felt a tremor of fear begin to shake inside her, forcing her to ask herself the same question again and again.

What have I done?

CHAPTER SIXTEEN

LUCA RUBBED THE kink out of his neck. A night in his office hadn't achieved anything other than darkening his already-foul mood.

"They're just about to land, Dr. Montovano," a nurse called out to him.

He pushed up and away from his desk and strode toward the helicopter-landing site.

Against his better judgment, he had approved the new patient's arrival.

It was Francesca's doing. Of course.

Not literally, but he'd heard her voice in his head each and every time he'd tried to say no. If he was going to go down, he might as well go down in flames.

He looked up to the sky to see if he could catch a glimpse of the chopper. They usually headed in from Florence, but this sound came from the east. Nearer to the seaside airport.

Unusual.

It was all unusual. This hospital transfer was happening much earlier than normal.

He huffed out a laugh. As the patient's stay would no doubt be short, they could at least eke a few more sessions out of his early arrival.

See? He shot a glance toward the bright sky. *I'm still capable of seeing the silver lining.*

The whirring blades of the helicopter strobed against the rays of sun hitting his face. He closed his eyes against the glare, taking a precious moment to relish the fact that the clinic was still here to help. Might still make a difference.

A day? A week? He didn't know how long he'd have with this boy, but he would do everything in his power to show him that giving up without a fight was sounding a death knell. And dying young...? That wasn't going to happen on *his* watch.

By the time the chopper landed, he had realigned his features into those of a benign clinician. Just as well. The first face he saw was his patient's.

A scowling teenage boy who looked intent on proving that nothing and no one would improve his lot in life.

Luca stepped toward the helicopter with a grim smile.

Giancarlo Salvi. Seventeen years old. An able-bodied teen turned quadriplegic after a late-night joyride went horrifically wrong.

He took another step forward and saw the boy's scowl deepen. And why wouldn't it? Luca was able-bodied. Strong. Vital. *He* had the ability to walk toward things—and away from them.

The moment froze in Luca's mind—crystalizing as if it were a beacon of truth.

No matter how powerless he felt, he still had choices.

Energy shot into his limbs, and without further ado he helped the crew unstrap Giancarlo's wheelchair.

Destiny wasn't just something you haphazardly fell into.

Destiny was something you shaped.

* * *

Fran tucked herself behind a thick cascade of greenery near the pergola when she heard voices. The last thing she wanted to do was distract Luca during this crucial time. Or drag out the duffel bag she'd hastily jammed her things into before cleaning her cottage to gleaming perfection before the new family arrived.

She needed to get it to the car so she could meet her father at the nearby airport. He'd called a few minutes ago and asked for a ride. Something about the helicopter he'd chartered being delayed. The excuse sounded sketchy, but maybe it was his way of having some alone time before he saw the clinic.

A nervous shudder went through her. Once she'd brought her father here, Luca might well decide he never wanted to speak to her again. But if that was the cost of keeping the clinic alive, she could just about live with herself.

Fran let the stone wall behind her take her weight for a moment as she fought the sting of tears. When she'd invited her father here, to see if he thought the clinic was worth investing in, she'd thought she was doing the right thing. Now she was riddled with doubt.

Her father liked cars, not people. His passion wasn't health care. Or dogs. The only reason he'd said he would invest in Canny Canines was to finally bring his daughter home.

She swiped at her eyes when she heard voices on the other side of the wall. The last thing she needed was to have a member of the staff—or worse, Luca—find her blubbering away.

She tuned in to the female voices. A pair of nurses whispering something about the newly arrived patient insisting the helicopter must stay until he had deemed the place "worthy."

Fran's blood boiled on Luca's behalf. The place was *exemplary*!

Her jaw set tight as she tugged Edison in closer to her and listened more closely when the voices changed.

"This is where most of our patients like to spend their downtime."

Fran peered out from behind the froth of summer blossoms at the sound of Luca's voice. He was just a few meters away, guiding a teenage boy and his parents through the archway and out to the walled garden with the pool. This area always won people's hearts. An infinity pool on the side of a mountain overlooking the sea… What wasn't to love?

"You've got to be kidding me." Disdain dripped from the teenage boy's every word. "Your paralyzed patients hang out by the *pool*? Why? So they can see what everyone else gets to do for fun?"

Luca eyed the boy silently for a while. He didn't need to check Giancarlo's charts to know fear of failure was behind the boy's words. It was obvious that whatever treatment he'd been receiving had been palliative at best.

"Didn't your previous physio involve any pool time?" Luca asked finally. The bulk of his patients had done at least a trial run in a pool, if not an entire program of hydrotherapy.

"*Si,* Dr. Montovano." The boy's voice still dripped with disdain. "They just threw us quadriplegics in the pool and whoever bobbed up first won a prize."

"Giancarlo! *Amore*, he's trying to help." His mother admonished her son in a hushed tone, but her flush of embarrassment betrayed the frustration she was obviously feeling.

Despite himself, Luca felt for her. A parent trying to do her best in an already bad situation. His thoughts shot to Fran. She'd been doing the same thing. Taking a bad situation and doing her very best to make it better.

Why hadn't he given her a chance to explain?

"Not all patients are necessarily up to pool work. Isn't that right, Dr. Montovano? My son's concerns *are* valid."

Luca nodded in Giancarlo's father's direction and gave his chin a thoughtful stroke, trying his best to look neutral as he processed the parents' different approaches to their boy's disability.

The father was accepting his son's bitterness. Failure. As if it were a done deal.

The mother? He could see her love knew no boundaries. That she was willing to give anything a shot if it meant bringing back her little boy.

"Not all facilities are equipped to deal with patients in hydrotherapy scenarios. We're one of the lucky ones."

"Lucky enough to be on a mountaintop and hide all of us cripples away, you mean."

Luca stared into Giancarlo's eyes, not liking what he saw. The bitterness. Rage. The loss of hope. All reflected back at him as if they were mirrors into his own soul.

A movement caught his attention. Edison. The Labrador was running into the garden, chasing after a tennis ball.

"You let *dogs* roam around here?" Giancarlo still sounded irritable, but the tiniest bit of light in his voice and the flash of interest in his otherwise-dull eyes told Luca all he needed to know. He still had hope. Despite everything, the boy still had hope.

Luca looked up and saw Fran slowly walking toward them, her hand making a sharp signal to Edison that he should sit in front of Giancarlo's chair.

The parents were looking between Luca and Fran for answers. Was this her way of asking him not to give up hope?

"*Buongiorno.* I seem to have lost track of my assistance dog." Fran unleashed her warm smile, instantly relaxing Giancarlo's parents.

The Fran Effect.

"*Per favore.* Allow me to introduce Francesca Martinelli—"

"Like the cars?" Giancarlo interrupted, the first hint of a smile discernible on his face.

"Exactly like the cars." Fran nodded. Then smiled.

Better than sunshine.

The next twenty minutes or so passed in a blur as Edison became the center of attention.

Giancarlo's parents watched, wide-eyed, as Fran and the assistance dog exhibited a wide array of skills. Holding the boy upright if necessary. Retrieving objects and placing them in Giancarlo's hands. Manipulating his electric wheelchair around hard-to-negotiate corners. Going for help if necessary. She was bringing smiles to the lips of three people who Luca was certain hadn't known much, if any, happiness in the months since their lives had been changed forever.

By the time Fran had finished with her display, the Salvis—including Giancarlo—were committed to staying.

"Let me organize one of the other doctors to show you around." Luca heard the note of caution in his own voice. Fran had performed a miracle and still he wasn't happy. What was wrong with him?

Once Dr. Murro had been found and was showing the Salvis around the facilities, Luca wheeled on Fran.

"What the *hell* do you think you're doing?"

Bewilderment swept across Fran's features. "What do you mean? I was helping! Didn't you want them to stay?"

"Not this way. Not when I don't know how long I can offer them treatment. Don't you see what you've done?"

"Offered him hope? Offered him a new way of looking at the world?" Defiance rang in her every word.

"Stop!" He spoke too harshly, too cruelly for someone who felt as if his heart was breaking.

Fatigue hit him like a ton of bricks. This couldn't go on. He only had so much energy, and what little of it was left would have to go to Pia and the clinic.

"Will you please just stop?"

Francesca looked at him, her eyes held wide as if a blink would shatter her into a million pieces.

In them—in those crystal-clear blue eyes of hers—he saw myriad messages. Confusion. Tenderness. Pain.

She turned away without a word, and as she disappeared around the corner he knew in the very core of his being what the universe had been screaming at him all these weeks—he was in love with Fran.

"Dr. Montovano?"

A knock sounded at Luca's office door. Enzo Fratelli, one of the physios, cracked the door open a bit wider, obviously hoping for an invitation to come in.

"Si?" Luca flipped over the pile of paperwork he'd been working on. No point in Enzo seeing all the red ink. Not before he'd found a way to tell the staff.

"We all want you to know we appreciate how much

work you've been putting into getting the clinic up and running."

Luca pushed back from the desk, suddenly too tired to pretend any longer. "Is it worth it, Enzo? Really?"

He gestured for his colleague to sit down. He knew he'd given up a lot to come and work here—a life in Florence, assured work at a busy hospital.

"*Si, Dottore.* Of course it is." Enzo sat down, concern pressing his brows together. "What makes you doubt it?"

Money. Debt. The idea of doing this whole damn thing without Francesca to remind him of the bright side.

"What if I've been wrong?"

"About what?"

"The location. About having the clinic here at Mont di Mare."

"But that's half the draw. Surely you of all people would see that?"

Luca nodded, looking away from the appeal in the young man's eyes.

"I'm not saying the idea of the clinic needs to come to an end. Perhaps we'd be better off relocating to a city. Florence. Or Rome, maybe."

"I don't understand." Enzo shook his head. "This is your family's land, no? Your heritage." He opened his arms wide. "Being up here at Mont di Mare, breathing the mountain air, seeing the sea, being part of the sky, the meadows—all of it—is every bit as healing as the work I do in the physio rooms."

He tipped his head to the side, as if trying to get a new perspective on Luca. See him afresh.

"You've been working too hard, Dr. Montovano. Surely now that Francesca's father is here you can relax a little. Go enjoy a prosecco on the terrace—"

Everything inside him grew rigid. He'd not yet given himself a chance to process his feelings about Fran—about loving her—and now her father was here.

It didn't matter now whether or not *he* wanted her to stay. With her father here to influence—to persuade, see things through a cooler lens—everything would change.

"Where are they?" Luca strode out from behind his desk.

Enzo put up his hands and took a couple of steps back. "*Scusi, per favore, Dottore.* I thought you knew. She's showing him around the clinic now. Lovely time of day—seeing the sunset from up here."

Luca didn't hear what else Enzo was saying. He was running down the corridor, his blood racing so hot and fast he was surprised he could still see. It didn't matter. Blind. Breathless. However he found her, all he knew was one thing. He had to find Fran.

"Did you notice this, Papa? The date carved into the beam?"

Francesca watched as her father lifted his fingers and touched the date almost reverently.

"It's very beautiful, Francesca. How old did you say the village was?"

"It's medieval."

Francesca whirled around and all but collided with Luca. Her heart rate shot into hyperdrive and the power of speech simply left her. She'd been hoping Luca would stay holed up in the main clinic building, like he usually did, while she gave her father the grand tour. If her pitch was successful she could at least leave with a clean conscience, if not an unbroken heart.

"*Scusi?*" Fran's father turned, too. "You are?"

"Papa," Fran interjected, "this is Luca Montovano.

Remember I told you about him? The clinic director. Luca, this is my father, Vincente Martinelli."

The men introduced themselves with a sharp handshake and the type of solid eye contact that seemed more gladiatorial than friendly.

"It's a delight to have you here, Mr. Martinelli," Luca said solidly, his eyes not affording her even the most cursory of glances. "I suppose Francesca has told you what a mark she has made here?"

Fran felt heat creep into her cheeks as the two most important men in her life turned toward her. She didn't like being the center of attention at the best of times, and it was all she could do to keep her feet from whipping around and pulling her away toward the wildflower meadows she'd grown to love so much. Wildflowers she'd never see again if her father took the bait.

"Of course." Her father gave Luca a discerning look. "Francesca has spent most of my time here so far singing your praises."

"Papa!" Fran protested. Feebly.

She knew as well as he did that she'd been completely transparent. Glowing like a love-struck teen despite every effort to present the clinic as an outstanding business opportunity.

"I was simply…simply making the point that the entire vision here at Mont di Mare is Luca's. From the cobblestones to the first-class clinic. None of this would exist without his insight. His…um…"

Stop talking, Fran.

No, don't!

This is your last chance.

And so she plowed on. Detailing the clinic's mission. The work they'd done so far. The work she would have loved to do if she could stay, but she knew with

Luca's talent he'd surely find more therapists. The best, of course. Only the best.

Despite the charge of adrenaline coursing through her, Fran saw that Luca's eyes softened as she spoke. The gentle light that warmed the espresso darkness of his irises got brighter and brighter as she carried on. Her eyes dipped to his mouth. Those beautiful lips she would never be able to kiss again.

Forcing herself to meet Luca's gaze, Fran charged ahead with her final appeal. If her father saw what she did in Luca he would do the right thing and accept her offer to leave today in exchange for starting a charitable foundation to support the clinic.

"Like yours, Papa, Luca's drive is pretty much unparalleled. In such a short time he has...he has... He's..."

Completely stolen my heart.

Luca's eyes widened slightly, his right eyebrow making that delightful little questioning arc she'd grown to enjoy watching out for whenever his curiosity was piqued.

"I've never seen anyone render my daughter speechless, Dr. Montovano. You seem to have made quite an impact."

"She's made a similar impression," Luca replied, his eyes never leaving hers as he spoke.

"Francesca is very loyal. Always has been," her father replied with a decisive nod.

And then Luca saw it.

The switch.

One moment Francesca was looking into his eyes as if her life depended upon it, and the next...

There wasn't a soul in the world except for her father. The very light in Francesca's eyes changed when her gaze shifted to her father. A steely determination replaced the gentle glow.

Thank goodness he hadn't dropped to his knees. Begged her to marry him as he wanted to.

We could do it. Together we could do anything we put our hearts and minds to.

This was his fault. He'd cut too deep to hold on to her affections. Been too harsh. She was a gentle soul who needed to be cared for as generously as she was generous in giving her heart to others. Again, he'd taken a bad situation and made it worse. *So* much worse.

The clinic had been meant to redeem him, not ruin him.

Luca's lungs strained against the pain. As if his heart was being ripped from his chest.

"Per favore," he finally managed. "Do continue with your tour. I wouldn't want you to miss anything before you both return to the States."

"Return?" Vincente turned to his daughter. "Haven't you spoken with him?"

Fran opened her mouth to try to explain but, much to her horror, her father beat her to it.

This wasn't the way it was meant to happen. She was supposed to be on a plane, heading far, far away from the man who had stolen her heart, before he knew she'd made one last-ditch effort to help.

"Si, Dottore," her father began. "My daughter, as you have obviously come to discover, is fueled by grand thoughts and ideas. She called me with a simple proposal."

"Which is…?"

Fran shivered to hear the chill in Luca's voice. She

hadn't done it to hurt him. Far from it. She'd done it for *love*! Emotion choked the words in her throat and all she could do was watch, wide-eyed, as her father continued.

"Francesca said your clinic could do with a large financial injection. A way to get more rooms prepared for patients and increase cash flow. One of the ideas she suggested was to run her own business from here."

"Is this true?"

Luca turned to her, forcing her to meet his gaze.

Fran nodded, wishing the mountain would swallow her up and leave her in darkness. She was no business mogul. It was just an idea.

"It won't work. A single investment," her father continued, seemingly oblivious to the heartbreak happening right in front of him.

"Papa—no!"

"Hear me out, Frannie, I didn't get where I am today by being sentimental."

Fran's eyes darted toward Luca. He'd drawn himself to his full height, dark eyes flashing with emotion. He gave a curt nod. He'd hear her father out, but she knew any love he might have had for her was gone.

"Martinelli Motors isn't all about cars. Did you know this, Dr. Montovano?"

"I'm afraid I didn't. Fran hasn't told me much about you at all."

A hint of coldness shivered down Fran's spine. How could she? She barely knew her father.

"How would you feel about Francesca managing a charitable trust on behalf of Martinelli Motors here at the clinic? As well as her assistance-dog business."

"Papa?" A flutter of hope lit up Francesca's eyes while Luca remained stoically silent.

"Fran's been talking about starting a trust for ages,

and I have to say I didn't put much stock in it. But now that I've seen the clinic, the passion with which my daughter approaches the business—"

"This is *not* her business," Luca interrupted.

"No, not now—but if I were to put money into it then she would, of course, become a partner."

"I think there's been a misunderstanding," Luca said, his eyes once again glued to Fran. "There is no part of this business that is for sale."

A pin might have dropped in a city two hundred miles away and Fran would have heard it in the silence that followed.

"Are you crazy?" Fran finally regained the power of speech, her eyes appealing to Luca to use common sense. *She* was the emotional one. Not him.

His refusal to answer made her even angrier. Now he was just being plain old stubborn.

"Papa. *Don't* let him refuse your offer. The clinic needs the trust. I will do anything to make that happen."

Much to her astonishment, her father raised his hand in protest. "I think Luca knows his own mind well enough. I'm not going to force the money down the poor man's throat."

Luca gave him a curt nod of thanks, then turned to walk away.

"Luca, please—wait!"

"I think I've heard enough." He began to stride toward the far end of the village.

"Luca, please," Fran pleaded once they were out of earshot of her father. "None of that went the way it was meant to."

He turned on her, chest heaving with exertion. Fran pulled herself up short, teetering on her tiptoes, reaching out toward him to try to gain her balance.

And that was when it dawned on him.

A truth so vivid it near enough brought him to his knees. He'd been fighting the wrong battle. Fighting a truth that had raged like a tempest within him from the day he'd laid eyes on her.

Love was about faith. Deep-seated belief. And trust.

Fran would never ask her father—a man with whom she was only just beginning to have a proper relationship—to pour money into something, *someone*, she didn't believe in. She saw something in *him*. Trusted *him*.

And here she was, after all the horrible things he had said to her, reaching out with nothing but love in her eyes.

He held out his hands to her and pulled her to him. With every fiber of his being he loved her.

He cupped her face with his hands and tipped his forehead to hers. "Francesca, I've been a fool. You aren't trying to take anything from me, are you?"

"Of course not," she whispered. "I love you."

"How?" His hands dropped to her shoulders and he held her out so she could take a good look at him. "*How* can you love me when I have been so horrible?"

A gentle smile played upon her lips before she answered. "Everything you do is motivated by love."

"And how do you come to that conclusion, my little ray of sunshine?"

"Because a lesser man would have given up long ago," she said, giving a decisive nod. Her voice grew clearer, stronger, as she continued. "A lesser man would've stayed in Rome. Put his niece in a home. Hidden from everything he was ashamed of. Instead you confront the things you hate most about yourself on a daily basis."

"I owe it to Pia—"

"You didn't owe her an entire *clinic*!" Fran said, the light and humor he so loved finally returning to her eyes.

"But her mother, her grandparents—it was *my* fault they were all in that car."

"It wasn't your fault the truck lost control. You didn't make it cross the median strip. You didn't ask it to crash into you! I know it was awful, but it was *not* your fault."

Luca pulled her close to him, feeling her heart thud against his chest. He drew his fingers through her hair and asked aloud the question he'd wondered again and again.

"How can I deserve you?"

Fran pulled back, eyelids dropped to half-mast, and quirked an eyebrow. "You don't—yet."

"I beg to differ, *amore*, but you are standing in my arms."

"That doesn't mean we've made any decisions yet, does it?"

"About what?"

"About my business. Canny Canines. If you think I'm going to give it up just because you've won my heart you've got another think coming."

"Does this mean I'm going to have to go groveling to your father?"

Fran crinkled her nose. "I thought you didn't want his money?"

"I don't," Luca admitted. "But I *do* want something far more precious to him than any amount of money he has."

A twinkle lit up Francesca's eye. "Oh, yes? And what could *that* possibly be?"

"I think you know exactly what I'm talking about,

Francesca Martinelli." He pulled back from her, folding her small hands between his as he knelt on the ground in front of her. "I would very much like it if you would consider becoming Francesca Montovano."

Fran's eyes filled with tears as she nodded. "Yes. Yes, please. I'd love to."

Luca rose to his feet, picked Francesca up and twirled her around, whooping to the heavens all the while.

When he put her down he tipped his head toward her and murmured, "As you're going to be staying awhile, I suppose it would be a good idea for you to agree with your father about the whole Martinelli Trust thing."

Fran's tooth captured her lower lip and he felt her fingers pressing into his hands.

"Do you mean it?"

"I can hardly refuse the opportunity to help needy children, can I?"

"Luca Montovano…" Fran sighed as she rose on tiptoe to give him the softest kiss he'd ever known, "I'm going to love you until the end of time."

He cinched his arms around her waist, pulling her in for a kiss so rich with meaning there was no mistaking how long he would love her in return.

"Forever and ever, *amore*. Until the end of time."

Two years later

"Dante!" Fran clicked her fingers, a proud smile lighting up her face as the dog padded off to the opposite side of the patio and returned with her padded shoulder bag.

"Is he getting so heavy that you can't get out of your chair?" Luca laughed, taking the diaper bag from their latest canine family member and handing it to his wife with a tender smile.

Fran gazed down into the eyes of her son—a teeny-tiny replica of his father.

"Pia's been bringing him to the gym. Getting the other patients to use him as a weight!"

She laughed at the memory of one of the poor girls straining to lift him to shoulder height, Pia leaning forward, her hands ready if he dropped more than a millimeter.

"I think he gains a kilo every other day!" She tickled the tiny tip of his nose. "Besides, why would I want to move when I have everything I need right here?"

"And what's that?" Luca asked, settling into the patio chair alongside Francesca.

"You know exactly what I mean, but as you've asked, I will tell you." Fran held up a hand and ticked off her list on her fingers. "A gorgeous man, a big furry dog, the most handsome son a woman could ask for and, of course, the view."

She reached out her hand, closing her eyes tight as the tickle of sparks that still tingled and delighted her each and every time she and Luca touched took effect.

"The view *is* rather spectacular," Luca said.

When she opened her eyes she saw he wasn't facing the mountains, nor the broad, lush valleys below them, not even the sea sparkling in the early morning sun. Luca—her husband, her love—was looking directly into her eyes.

* * * * *

CLAIMING
HIS PREGNANT
PRINCESS

BY
ANNIE O'NEIL

Published in Great Britain 2017
By Mills & Boon, an imprint of HarperCollins*Publishers*
1 London Bridge Street, London, SE1 9GF

© 2017 Annie O'Neil

ISBN: 978-0-263-92659-0

Our policy is to use papers that are natural, renewable and recyclable
products and made from wood grown in sustainable forests. The logging
and manufacturing processes conform to the legal environmental
regulations of the country of origin.

Printed and bound in Spain
by CPI, Barcelona

Dear Reader,

I don't know why—sometimes the world just works in mysterious ways—but these two characters came to me *so* easily. I just loved them—and their obvious love for one another.

There are times in life, aren't there, when we get ourselves in a pickle? Sometimes we aren't even sure how it's worked out that way. This is one of those times for Beatrice…and it's one heck of a pickle. *Huge!*

I really hope you enjoy both Bea's and Jamie's journeys, at the conclusion of my duet, and seeing how two friends from two totally different backgrounds find love.

Enjoy some Italian food while you're reading this, and don't be shy about getting in touch. You can reach me at annieoneilbooks.com, on Twitter @annieoneilbooks or find me on Facebook…

Annie O' xx

This book is dedicated to my great friend Jess.
She had the most epic hen do in the history of
hen parties and somehow we ended up in a three-mile parade
in the centre of a town just outside of Venice.
As you do when you're dressed as a nun and the lawfully
intended is dressed as a minx. I mean bride.

Big love, Annie O' xx

Books by Annie O'Neil

Mills & Boon Medical Romance

Paddington Children's Hospital
Healing the Sheikh's Heart

Hot Latin Docs
Santiago's Convenient Fiancée

Christmas Eve Magic
The Nightshift Before Christmas

The Monticello Baby Miracles
One Night, Twin Consequences

One Night…with Her Boss
London's Most Eligible Doctor
Her Hot Highland Doc

Visit the Author Profile page
at millsandboon.co.uk for more titles.

**Praise for
Annie O'Neil**

'This is a beautifully written story that will pull you in from
page one and keep you up late, turning the pages.'
—*Goodreads* on
Doctor…to Duchess?

**Annie O'Neil won the 2016 RoNA Rose Award
for her book *Doctor…to Duchess?***

CHAPTER ONE

"Dr. Jesolo! There's a full waiting room!"

"*Si, pronto*, Teo!" Bea poked her head out of the curtained exam space and then repeated herself in English, just in case her Australian coworker hadn't understood. "On my way."

He nodded, screwed his nose up for a minute and gave her a funny look.

She hoped her pasted-on happy face simply looked like a case of first-day jitters.

Her new colleague didn't need to know she was fighting another wave of impossible-to-quench tears.

She swiped at her eyes again and forced herself to tune in to the various conversations happening in the exam areas surrounding hers.

English, Italian, French and German. Broken arms. Asthma attacks. Altitude sickness. They were all mingled together up here in Torpisi, and she was loving every moment of it. Or would be if she could get her eyes to dry and see another patient.

That was why this multilingual, brain-stretching trauma center suited her needs to a tee.

Hormones or history. It was always a toss-up as to which would unleash the next flood.

You can do this. You're a princess! Trained in the art of...of artifice.

At least work would give her poor over-wrung tear ducts a break.

The Clinica Torpisi catered to the needs of international tourists. Ones who didn't read the gossip rags. Adrenaline junkies, fun seekers and good old-fashioned holidaymakers kept the *clinica* operating on full steam over the summer—and probably more so in the winter, when the skiing crowd came in. It was the perfect place to hide in plain sight. And to create some much-needed distraction from her real-life problems.

Zurich, Lyon, Salzburg and even Milan were only a couple of hours' drive away, but the press still hadn't caught wind of the fact that she was up here in this magical Italian mountain hideaway.

Ha! Foiled again. Just the way she liked it. They'd had their pound of flesh after the wedding nightmare. Painting a picture of her as if she'd been abandoned at the altar... The cheek! She'd been made of fool of, perhaps, but *she'd* been the one to pull off her ring and walk away.

The press might have stolen what little dignity Bea had left, but she wouldn't let them take away her precious Italy. Especially now that returning to England was out of the question.

Her fingers pressed against her lips as the strong sting of emotion teased the back of her nose again.

Ugh. She'd tried her best to shake off those memories. The ones she'd kept locked away the day since she'd agreed to her mother's harebrained plan. What a fool she'd been!

She'd had a shot of living the perfect life and had

ruined it in a vainglorious attempt to please her blue-blooded family. Power and position. It was all they'd wanted.

Well…they'd hit the tabloids, all right, just not in the way anyone had anticipated.

Hopefully the paparazzi were now too busy jetting around the globe trying to find "Italy's favorite playboy prince" to worry about *her* any longer.

Bea pulled the used paper off the exam table and stuffed it in the bin. It was her own fault this mess had blown up in her face. If she'd stayed strong, told her parents she was in love with someone else…

Inhale. Exhale.

That was in the past now. She'd made the wrong decision and now she was paying for it.

Bea took a quick scan of the room, then glanced in the mirror before heading out for her next patient, smiling ruefully as she went. Trust an Italian clinic in the middle of nowhere to have mirrors everywhere! She was willing to bet the hospital on the Austrian side of town didn't have a single one. Practical. Sensible. More her style. Maybe she should have tried to get a job there…

Her eyes flicked up to the heavens, then down again.

Quit second-guessing yourself! It's day one, and so far so good.

She forced herself to look square into the mirror at the "new" Bea.

No more Principessa Beatrice Vittoria di Jesolo, fiancée of Italy's favorite "Scoundrel Prince."

Her eyes narrowed as she recataloged those memories. Everything happened for a reason, and deep in her heart she knew marrying for tradition rather than for love would have been a huge mistake. Even if it would have made her mother happy.

A mirthless laugh leapt from her chest.

She was well and truly written out of the will now!

She shrugged her shoulders up and down, then gave her cheeks a quick pinch.

Saying goodbye to that life had been easy.

The hard part was living with herself after having let things go as far as they had.

"Dr. Jesolo?"

Bea started, and wagged her finger at herself in the mirror.

Self-pity wasn't going to help either. Work would.

"Si, sto arrivando!"

From today she was simply Dr. Bea Jesolo, trauma doctor to the fun-loving thrill seekers up here in Italy's beautiful Alpine region.

She tipped her head to the side. Now that she was a bit more used to it, she liked the pixie haircut. The gloss of platinum blond. It still caught her by surprise when she passed shop windows, but there were unexpected perks. It made her brown eyes look more like liquid shots of espresso than ever before. Not that she was on the market or anything. Just get up, work, go to bed and repeat. Which made the short, easy-to-style cut practical. Much better than the long tresses she'd grown especially for the wedding.

She gave a wayward strand a tweak, then made a silly face at herself when it bounced back out of place.

Undercover Princess.

That was this morning's newspaper headline. She'd seen it on the newsstand when she'd walked into work.

There had been a picture of heaven knew who on the front page of Italy's most popular gossip magazine. A shadowy photo showing someone—no doubt a model wearing a wig—looking furtively over her shoulder as she was swept through airport security in Germany. Or was it Holland? Utrecht? Somewhere *she* wasn't.

Undercover Princess, indeed.

She pulled her stethoscope back into place around her neck and shrugged the headline away.

It was a damn sight better than the handful she'd seen before sneaking away to lick her wounds on her brother's ridiculous superyacht for six weeks, ducking and dodging the press among the Greek islands.

There were perks to having a privileged family. And, of course, pitfalls.

Abandoned by the Wolf!

Prince Picks Fair Maid over Princess!

Altar-cation for Italy's Heartbroken Princess.

Heartbroken? Ha! Hardly.

Love-Rat Prince Crumbles at the First Hurdle

That was getting closer. Or maybe:

Pregnant Principessa Prepares for First Solo as Mama.

Not that anyone knew *that* little bit of tabloid gold. Doctor by day...

Her hand crept to her belly. Though she wasn't showing yet, she knew the little tiny bud of a baby was in there…just the size of an apple seed. Maybe a little more? Bigger, smaller… Either way she'd protect that blossoming life with every ounce of power she possessed. Hers and hers alone. How she'd go about living the rest of her life once the baby was born was a problem she hadn't yet sorted, but she'd get there. Because she didn't have much of a choice.

Bea swiped at her eyes, forced on a smile, then pulled open the curtain. Nothing like a patient to realign her focus.

"Leah Stokes?"

She scanned the room, bracing herself against the moment that someone recognized her, air straining against her lungs. Her shoulders dropped and she blew a breath slowly past her lips as all the patients looked up, shook their heads, then went back to their magazines and conversations. All except a young twentysomething woman, who was pushing herself up from her chair. She was kitted out in cycling gear and… *Oh. Ouch!*

"Looks like some serious road rash there." Bea's brow furrowed in sympathy and she quickly walked over to the woman and put her arm around her waist. "Lean on me. That's right. Just put your arm around my shoulder and let me take some of the weight."

"I don't think I can make it all the way." Leah drew in a sharp breath, tears beginning to trickle down her cheeks now that help was here.

"Can I get a hand?" Bea called out.

There were a couple of guys in rescue uniforms at the front desk. She called again to get their attention. When the closest one looked up, the blond…

Her breath caught in her throat.

He wasn't blond. His hair was hay colored—that was

how she'd always remembered it... The color of British summertime.

A perfect complement to startling green eyes.

As their gazes grazed, then caught, Bea's heart stopped beating. Just...*froze.*

She'd know that face anywhere. It had been two long years. Two painfully long years of trying to convince herself she'd done the right thing, all the while knowing she hadn't.

Fate had intervened in saving her from a loveless marriage, but what was it doing *now?*

Taunting her with what she could never have?

She blinked and looked again.

Those green eyes would haunt her until the end of time.

Before she could stop herself she spoke the name she'd thought she'd never utter again.

"Jamie?"

For a moment Jamie thought he was hallucinating. It *couldn't* be her. Beatrice was meant to be on her honeymoon right now. That and *no one* called him Jamie.

He'd gone back to James the day she'd left. He'd changed a lot of things since then.

"Jamie, is that you?"

For a moment everything blurred into the background as he looked straight into the eyes of the woman he had once thought he would spend his life with.

Still the same dark, get-lost-in-them irises, but there was something new in them. Something...*wary.* No, that wasn't right. Something...fragile. Unsure. Things he'd never seen in them before.

Her hair was different. Still short, but... Why had she gone platinum? Her formerly chestnut-brown hair, silky soft, particularly when it brushed against… A shot of heat shunted through him as powerfully as it had the first time he'd touched it. Touched *her*.

Instinct took over. She was struggling with a patient. Before he could think better of it, he was on the other side of her, calling to his colleague to find a wheelchair.

"What's your name, love?" he asked the girl, who was whispering words of encouragement to herself in English.

"Leah," Beatrice answered for her. "Leah Stokes."

Jamie hid a flinch as the sound of Beatrice's voice lanced another memory he'd sealed tight. If he'd doubted for a second that this transformed woman—the blond hair, the uncharacteristically plain clothing, the slight shadows hinting at sleepless nights—was the love of his life, he knew it now. She had a husky, made-for-late-night-radio voice that was perfect for a doctor offering words as an immediate antidote for pain. Even better for a lover whispering sweet nothings in your ear.

"The exam table isn't far away. Instead of waiting shall we—" Beatrice began.

He nodded before she'd finished. Once-familiar routines returned to him with an ease he hadn't expected. The looks that made language unnecessary. The gestures the said everything. They'd done this particular move when he'd "popped in" accidentally on purpose to help out with her trauma training. Carried patients here and there. Practiced the weave of wrists and hands. Supported each other.

"On three?" The rush of memory and emotion almost blindsided him. He'd been a fool to let her go. Not to fight harder.

But a modern-day commoner versus a latter-day prince?

There'd been no contest. He'd seen it in her eyes.

Like a fool, he looked up.

"One...two..."

He saw the words appear on her lips but could hardly hear them, such was the rush of blood charging around his head.

Never again.

That was what he'd told himself.

Never again would he let himself be so naive. So vulnerable. So in love.

As one they dipped, eyes glued to each other's, clasped one another's wrists and scooped up the patient between them, hardly feeling Leah's fingers as they pressed into their shoulders once she'd been lifted off the ground.

It definitely wasn't the way he'd imagined seeing Beatrice again. If ever.

"Just here on the exam table, *per favore*." Beatrice had shifted her gaze to her patient, her hands slipping to Leah's leg to ensure the abraded skin was kept clear of rubbing against the paper covering the table. "Thank you, Dr. Coutts."

Her dark brown eyes flitted back toward him before she returned her full attention to her patient, but in that micromoment he saw all that he needed to know. Seeing him had thrown her as off-kilter as it had him.

Whether it was a good thing or a bad thing was impossible to ascertain. At least he hadn't seen the thing he feared most: indifference. He would have packed his bags and left then and there. But something—the tiniest glimmer of something bright flickering in those espresso-rich eyes of hers—said it would be worth his while to stay.

Answers were answers, after all.

"I'll leave you to it, then," he said, tugging the curtain

around the exam table, his eyes taking just a fraction of a second longer than necessary to search her hand for the ring. Jewelry had never been his thing, but that ridiculously huge, pink cushion-cut diamond ring—a family heirloom, she'd said—was etched in his mind's eye as clearly as the day she'd told him she was moving back to Italy. *Family*, she'd said. *Obligations. Tradition.*

He yanked the curtain shut, unable to move as he processed what he'd seen. Pleasure? Pain? Satisfaction that neither of them had succeeded in gaining what they'd sought?

A chilling numbness began to creep through his veins.

No sign of a ring.

Nothing.

Each and every one of her fingers was bare.

Bea's heart was thumping so hard behind her simple cotton top she was sure her patient could see it.

Even though she had taken longer than normal to put on her hygienic gloves, Leah would have had to be blind not to notice her fingers shaking.

Jamie Coutts.

The only man who'd laid full claim to her heart.

Why wasn't he in England?

Leaving Jamie had been the most painful thing she'd ever done. The betrayal she'd seen in his eyes would stay with her forever. Having to live with it was so much worse.

"Is everything all right?" Leah asked.

"Si, va bene." Bea gave her head a quick shake, pushed her hands between her knees to steady them and reminded herself to speak English. She had a pa-

tient. Rehashing the day she'd told the man she loved she was going to marry another would have to wait.

"Let's take a look at this leg of yours." Bea gave her hands a quick check. Jitter-free. *Good.* "Cycling, was it?"

"We were coming down one of the passes," Leah confirmed, her wince deepening as Bea began gently to press the blue pads of her gloved hands along the injury. "A car came up alongside me. I panicked and hit the verge too fast."

"A fall when you're wearing these clip shoes can be tough. It looks largely superficial. Not too much bleeding. But from the swelling on your knee it looks like you took quite a blow." Bea glanced up at her, "I'm just going to take your shoes off, all right? Do you feel like anything might be broken? Sprained?"

Leah shook her head. "It's hard to say. I think it's the road rash that hurts the most, but my knee *is* throbbing!"

"Did you get any ice on it straight after you fell? A cool pack?"

"No…" Leah tugged her fingers through her short tangle of hazel curls, loosening some meadow grass as she did so, before swiping at a few more tears. "The guys had all ridden ahead. Downhill pelotons freak me out—and I wasn't carrying a first-aid kit with me. A local couple saw me fall and brought me here."

Poor thing. Left to fend for herself.

It's not any fun, is it, amore?

Bea gave her a smile. "Trying to keep up with a peloton of adrenaline junkies is tough." She pushed herself back on the wheelie stool and looked in the supplies cart for the best dressings. "I don't think you've broken anything, but it's probably worth getting some X-rays just in case."

"But we've still got four more days of riding!" Leah protested, the streaks of dirt on her face disappearing in dark trickles as her tears increased. "Richard's going to think I'm such a weakling. This was meant to be the time I showed him I could keep up with the boys."

Bea took a quick glance at Leah's fingers. Bare, just like hers. "Boyfriend?" she chanced.

"Probably not for long. He's going to think I'm such a wimp!"

"With a road rash like that?" Bea protested with a smile. "This shows *exactly* how tough you are. I've had men in here with half the scraping *your* thigh has taken, howling like babies."

"Howling?" A smile teased at Leah's lips.

"Howling," Bea confirmed with a definitive nod.

She wouldn't mind tipping back her head and letting out a full-pelt she-wolf howl herself right now, but instead she told herself off in her mother's exacting tones. *Princesses don't howl. Princesses set an example.*

She screwed her lips to the right as she forced her attention back to Leah's leg. "*Mi scusi,* I can't see what I need to dress this leg of yours in here. I want to get some alginate and silver dressings for you."

"What are those?"

"They're both pretty amazing, actually. You should get some dressings to carry in your pack. There are derivatives from algae in one of them—really good for wounds like this. Ones that ooze."

Leah sucked in her breath after touching a spot on her thigh. "It's so disgusting."

"It's not pretty now, but it will definitely heal well. Once the dressing gets wet, it will begin to form a gel and absorb any liquid from the abrasion." She pressed her hands into her knees and put on her best I-know-itstinks face. "Keeping the wound moist is essential to preventing scarring. The dressing I'm hoping to use contains silver. It's antibacterial, so it will keep the wound clean of infection." Bea tipped her head to catch Leah's eye before she rose. "Are you going to be all right for a few minutes while I get the supplies?"

Leah half nodded, her interest already diverted as she pulled her phone out of her bag and flicked on the camera app. "I'm going to send the guys some pictures. Give them a proper guilt trip for abandoning me."

"Back in a minute," Bea said unnecessarily as Leah snapped away.

No doubt the photos would be hitting all sorts of social media sites in seconds. She'd taken all those things off her *telefono* within hours of the wedding being called off. She'd even tried throwing the phone in a canal when some wily reporter had got hold of her number, but Francesca hadn't let her.

"Just put the thing on Mute or change your number," Fran had insisted. "*Use* us. Stay contactable. We want to help."

If only someone *could* help. But she and she alone had got herself into this mess.

Bea hurried into the supplies room before a fresh hit of tears glossed her eyes. She missed her best friend. Could really do with a Bea-and-Fran night on the sofa. A pizza. Box set. Bottle of wine—nope! Nix the wine. But… Oh…nix everything. Now that Fran had gone and fallen in love with Luca, and the pair of them were making a real go of the clinic at Mont di Mare, Bea would have to make do on her own. And stay busy. Extra busy. Any and all distractions were welcome.

She forced herself to focus on the shelves of supplies,

desperate to remember why she'd gone to the room in the first place.

"Hello, Beatrice."

She froze at the sound of Jamie's voice. Then, despite every single one of her senses being on high alert, she smiled. How could she have forgotten it? That Northern English lilt of his accent. The liquid edge he added to the end of her name where Italians turned it into two harsher syllables. From his tongue her named sounded like sweet mountain water...

When she turned to face him, her smile dropped instantly. Jamie's expression told her everything she needed to know.

He wasn't letting bygones stay back in England, where she'd left him some seven-hundred-odd days ago. But who was counting? Numbers meant nothing when everything about his demeanor told her it was the witching hour. Time to confront the past she'd never been able to forget.

"Since when does Italy's most pampered princess get her own supplies?"

The comment held more rancor than Jamie had hoped to achieve. He'd been aiming for a casual "fancy meeting you here," but he'd actually nailed expressing the months of bitterness he'd been unable to shake since she'd left him. True, he hadn't put up much of a fight, but she had made it more than clear that her future was in Italy. With another man.

It had blindsided him. One minute they were more in love than he could imagine a couple ever being. The next, after that sudden solo trip to Venice, her heart had belonged to another.

He'd not thought her so fickle. It had been a harsh way to learn why they called love blind.

When their gazes connected the color dropped from Beatrice's face. A part of him hated eliciting this bleak reaction—another part was pleased to see he still had an effect on her.

Ashen faced with shaking palms wasn't what he'd been hoping for… Seeing her *at all* hadn't been what he'd been hoping for…but no matter how hard he tried, no matter how many corners he'd turned since he'd left England, he didn't seem to be able to shake her. This was either kismet or some sort of hellish purgatory. From the look on her face, it wasn't the former.

Self-loathing swept through him for lashing out at Beatrice. A woman who'd done little more than proactively pursue the life she wanted. Which was more than he could say for himself.

"What are you doing here, Beatrice? Aren't you meant to be on honeymoon? Or is this part of it? Dropping in to local clinics to grace us with your largesse before embarking on a shopping spree. Dubai, perhaps? Turkey? Shouldn't you be buying silver spoons for the long line of di Jesolos yet to come into the world?"

Jamie hated himself as the vitriol poured out of him. Hated himself even more as he watched Beatrice's full lips part only to say nothing, her features crumpling in disbelief as if he'd shivved her right then and there rather than simply pointed out everything the tabloids had been crowing about. The engagement. The impending wedding. The royal babies they were hoping would quickly follow the exotic and lengthy honeymoon.

A month ago he'd refused to read anymore. He'd endured enough.

He looked deep into her eyes, willing her to tell him something. Anything to ease the pain.

As quickly as the ire had flared up in him, it disappeared.

You're not this man. She must've had her reasons.

Jamie took a step forward, his natural instinct to put a hand on Beatrice's arm—to touch her, to apologize. As he closed the space between them the handful of gel packs and silver dressings she'd been holding dropped from her fingers. They knelt simultaneously to collect them, colliding with the inevitable head bump and mumbled apologies.

Crouching on the floor, each with a hand to their forehead, they stared at one another as if waiting for the other to pounce.

By God, she is beautiful.

"You've grown your hair," she said finally.

She was so close he could kiss her. Put his hand at the nape of her neck as he'd done so many times before, draw her to him and…

She was talking about haircuts.

A haircut had been the last thing on his mind when she'd left. *Work.* Work had been all he'd had and he'd thrown himself so far into the deep end he'd been blind to everything else. Got too involved. So close he'd literally drained the blood from his own body to help ease the pain of his patient.

Elisa.

That poor little girl. They'd shared a rare blood type. Foolishly he'd thought that if he saved her life he might be able to save himself. In the end his boss had made him choose. Take a step back or leave.

So here he was in Italy, just when he'd thought he was beginning to see straight again, eye to eye with the woman who had all but sucked the marrow from his bones.

"It looks nice," Beatrice said, her finger indicating the hair he knew curled on and around his shirt collar. What was it she'd always called him? Hay head? Straw head? Something like that. Something that brought back too many memories of those perfect summer months they'd shared together.

He nodded his thanks. Blissful summers were a thing of the past. Now they were reduced to social niceties.

Fair enough. He glanced at his watch. The chopper would be leaving in five. He needed to press on.

"C'mon. Let's get these picked up. Get you back to your patient." No matter how deeply he'd been hurt, patients were the priority.

She reached forward, sucking in a sharp breath when their fingers brushed, each reaching for the same packet of dressings.

"I'm not made of poison, you know."

Beatrice's gaze shot up to meet his, those rich brown eyes of hers looking larger than ever. He couldn't tell if it was because she'd lost weight or because they were punctuated by twilight-blue shadows. Either way, she didn't look happy.

"No one knows who I am here," she bit out, her voice low and urgent as she clutched the supplies to her chest. "I would appreciate it if you could keep it that way."

A huff of disbelief emptied his chest of oxygen. Flaunting the family name was the reason she'd left him, and now she wanted to be *anonymous*?

She met his gaze as she finished scanning his uniform. "Since when do pediatricians wear high-octane rescue gear? I thought life in a children's ward was all the excitement you needed?"

"Snide comments were never your thing."

"Pushing boundaries was never *yours*."

Jamie's lungs strained against a deep breath, all the while keeping tight hold of the eye contact. He wanted her to see the man he'd become.

After a measured exhalation he let himself savor the pain of his teeth grating across his lower lip. He turned to leave, then changed his mind, throwing the words over his shoulder as if it were the most casual thing in the world to lacerate the woman he loved with words.

"People change, Dr. Jesolo. Some of us for the better."

Ten minutes later and the sting of his comment still hadn't worn off. Perhaps it never would.

And hiding in the staff room with her friendly Aussie colleague had only made things worse. He was a messenger with even more bad news.

Jamie Coutts was not just back in her life—he was her boss.

"Wait a minute, Teo." Bea held up a hand, hardly believing what she was hearing. "He's *what*?"

Teo Brandisi gave Bea a patient smile and handed her the cup of herbal tea he'd promised her hours earlier in the busy shift.

"The big boss man. The big kahuna. Mayor of medics."

"But *you* hired me."

"He was out in the field. He hands over the reins to me when he's away."

"But—"

"Quit trying to fight it, sweetheart. He's *le grand fromage*—all right? I wouldn't be working here without his approval, so if you've got a bone to pick with him, I'm recusing myself. He has my back. I have his. You got me?" Teo continued in his broad Australian accent.

Bea shook her head and waved her hands. "No, it's not that. I've nothing *against* Dr. Coutts."

Liar.

She cleared her throat, forcing herself to sound more neutral. "I just don't understand why he had to approve appointing *you* but not me."

"Foreign doctor." Teo pointed at himself. "We can't just swan in and take all the choice jobs. Even though he's English, he's been qualified to practice here for over a year."

He'd been in Italy for a year and she hadn't known.

Well…she'd done a whole lot of things *he* didn't know about, so fair was fair.

"My advice?" Teo was on a roll. "You have to suck up to people like James Coutts."

"James?"

"Yeah… Why?"

Teo scrunched up his nose and looked at her as if she was giving proof positive she was losing her marbles. Maybe she was. And if Jamie was James, and she'd shortened her name to Bea, then the only thing that was clear was that they were both trying to be someone new.

A reinvention game.

Only games were meant to be fun. And everything about seeing Jamie again was far from fun. Confronting what she'd done to him was going to be the hardest thing she'd ever done.

"Anyhoo…" Teo continued. "James has got the whole British-reserve thing going on big-time." A glint of admiration brightened his blue eyes. "The man's like an impenetrable fortress. Impossible to read. Well done!" He clapped her on the shoulder. "A gold star to Dr. Jesolo for getting under the Stone Man's skin!"

"The Stone Man?"

"Yeah. We all take bets on how many facial expressions he actually has. I'm going with three. Contemplative. Not happy. And his usual go-to face—Mr. Neutral. No reading that face. No way, no how."

Bea hid her face in the steam of her tea for a minute. Her kind, gentle Jamie was an impenetrable fortress? That wasn't like him. Then again...*she* was hardly the same. Why should *he* be?

"It's most likely a fluke. That or he doesn't like blondes?"

Teo gave her a sidelong glance as if he already knew the whole story. Could tell she was just making things up. Covering a truth she wasn't yet ready to divulge.

"Fair enough."

They stood in an awkward silence until Bea launched into a sudden interest in removing her herbal tea bag from her mug.

If Teo had known she was pregnant, she could have just blown the whole thing off as a bout of pregnancy brain. Not that she even knew if pregnancy brain hit this early. Sharp bouts of fatigue certainly had. And morning sickness. She'd never look at a hamburger the same way again! At least when she'd been on her brother's yacht she'd managed to fob off the nausea she'd felt as seasickness. Now that she was up here in the mountains she couldn't do that. It was meant to pass soon. And by the time her contract was up she'd be off to hide away the rest of her pregnancy somewhere else.

"So, on a day-to-day basis *you're* my boss?" She kept her eyes on her tea, wincing at the note of hope in her voice.

"Nope. Dr. James Coutts is your actual boss," Teo continued, after taking his shot of espresso down in one swift gulp.

Classic Italian. She would be amazed if he went back to Australia. He might be second generation in Australia, but the man had Italy in his bones.

"I step in when he's out on rescue calls, like today. The fact I was on duty when we held your interview was just a coincidence."

"So…he knew I was coming?"

The interview had been a week ago. Start date today. He'd had a whole week to come to terms with things and yet she was sure she'd seen shock in his eyes. The same shock of recognition that had reverberated through to her very core.

"He knew *someone* was coming, but he's been tied up training the emergency squads."

Her Jamie? Better-safe-than-sorry Jamie?

She'd always thought *she* was a solid rock until she'd met him. But no one had been more reliable, more sound than him.

"He's pretty good about not breathing down your neck." Teo pulled open a cupboard and began to look around for some biscuits. "And he lets staff make decisions in his absence. He's a really good guy, actually. Don't let the whole Dr. Impenetrable thing get to you."

Her lips thinned. Jamie was better than a good guy. He was the kindest man she'd ever met.

Strangely, it came as a relief to hear his bitterness seemed to be solely reserved for her. Deservedly so. How she could have dumped him just to make good on an antiquated match between her family and the Roldolfos was beyond her now. Family loyalty meant altogether different things when your blue-blooded mother was trying to uphold hundreds of years of tradition. Pass the princess baton…even if it came at her daughter's expense.

She heard Teo sigh and looked up to catch him lovingly gazing at a plate of homemade biscotti. Someone's grandmother's, no doubt. There was a lot of bragging about grandmothers up here. She missed hers. No doubt *she* would have had some wise words for the insane situation Bea was in now.

"Did you hear the crew earlier? Sounds like it was a pretty intense case," Teo continued, oblivious to the turmoil Bea was enduring.

"I didn't see any patients come down from the helipad." She shook her head in confusion.

"They dropped the patient off in Switzerland. A little kid. Five, maybe six years old—broke his leg. Compound fracture. Tib-fib job. Massive blood loss. The mother nearly lost the plot. She was attacking the staff, threatened to kill one of them if they didn't let her on the helicopt—"

"All right, all right." Bea held up a hand, feeling a swell of nausea rise and take hold as he painted the picture. "It's obvious someone's a bit jealous that *he* wasn't out on the rescue squad today."

"I'm on tomorrow." Teo gave his hands a quick excited rub. "You can sign up, too, if you like. We do it on rotation, because summers are so busy up here, but you'd probably have to do your first few with James. The man is a right daredevil when's he's wearing the old rescue gear. Biscotti?" He held out a plate filled with the oblong biscuits.

"*No, grazie.* Or, actually…" Maybe it would help settle her stomach. She took one of the crunchy biscuits and gave him a smile.

He gave the door frame a final pat and then was gone.

Bea sank into a nearby chair. As far as she was concerned, Teo could have all her emergency-rescue shifts. About eight weeks, two days and…she glanced at her watch…three hours ago she would have been all over them. High-octane rescues and first-class medical treatment? *Amazing* experiences.

Experiences she would have to miss now.

Compromising the tiny life inside her while the former love of her life looked on…

She let her head sink into her hands.

Clinica Torpisi wasn't going to be the healing hideaway she'd been hoping for.

More like hell on earth.

CHAPTER TWO

HE SAW HER across the piazza. Jamie wondered now, having adjusted to the platinum blond hair, how he hadn't noticed her instantly. He certainly had when she'd walked into Northern General. How could he not have when he'd entered the *clinica*?

Fathomless chocolate-brown eyes straight out of the Italian-nymph guidebook. Slender. The darkest chestnut hair he'd ever seen. Short, but thick enough to lose his hands in when he wanted to put his fingers against the nape of her soft, swan-like neck. Perfect raspberry-red lips. Olive skin. Carrying herself like royalty.

She was royalty.

He shook his head again.

Little wonder he hadn't recognized her straight off. He hadn't wanted to.

A bit of shock.

A splash of denial.

Hope, pain, love, despair… All those things and more made up the roiling ball of conflict burning in his heart. Most of all he just wanted to understand *why*.

He hitched his trousers onto his hips. She wasn't the only one who'd lost weight in the past couple of years.

Stop apportioning blame.

The closer he got, the more he wondered what the hell he was doing.

No. That wasn't true. Ripping off the bandage had become his modus operandi since she'd left. He might as well stick true to his course. Life wasn't sweet. Might as well get used to it.

"Mind if I join you?"

Beatrice started, as if her thoughts had been a thousand miles away. When she'd pulled him into focus he watched as she searched his face for signs of enmity. He couldn't say he blamed her. After his performance in the supplies room earlier in the day he'd hardly made a good show of the manners his mother had drilled into him.

"Please..." Beatrice pushed aside a small plate of antipasti and indicated the chair beside her. One from which he could enjoy the stunning lakeside view. One that would seat them side by side, where they wouldn't have to look into the other's eyes.

He sank into the chair, grateful for this reprieve from animosity. Perhaps a few hours apart had been what they'd each needed. Time to process.

"Is that a spritzer you're having?" He pointed at the bright orange drink on the table, the glass beaded with condensation as the final rays of sunlight disappeared behind the mountain peaks beyond the lake.

"No." She shook her head. "I never liked spritzers. Too..." Her nose crinkled as she sought the right word. "Aftertasty," she said finally, her lips tipping up into the first suggestion of a smile he'd seen. "Orange soda is my new guilty pleasure. I don't seem to be able to drink enough of it."

He was about to launch into the lecture he gave all his patients—too many fizzy drinks were bad for the bones, bad for the brain, bad for the body—but just seeing the tension release from the corners of her eyes as she lifted the glass, put her lips around the red and white stripes of the straw and drew in a cool draught made him swallow it.

He hadn't come here to deliver a lecture. He had questions. Thousands of questions.

A waiter swooped in, as they all did at this time of day, keen to get as many people as possible their drinks before the early-dining Americans began infiltrating the wide square in advance of the Europeans.

He and Beatrice both bit back smiles at the waiter's terse "Is that all for *signor*?" after he'd settled on a sparkling water.

"Going back to the clinic?" Beatrice asked.

"That obvious?"

"Mmm, 'fraid so." Beatrice looked out toward the square as she spoke. "It would be a glass of Gavi di Gavi if you were finished, wouldn't it? If…" She hesitated. "If memory serves me right."

He nodded. Surprised she'd remembered such a silly detail. Then again, there wasn't a single detail he'd forgotten about *her*. Maybe…

He rammed his knuckles into his thigh.

Maybe was for other people. He was all about sure things. And Beatrice wasn't one of them.

Jamie scrubbed a hand along his chin, then scraped his chair around on the stone cobbles until he faced her head-on.

"What are you doing here, Beatrice?"

"Well, that's a nice way to—" She stopped herself and lifted a hand so that he would give her a moment to think. Say what she really meant to.

Despite himself, he smiled. She'd always been that way. A thinker. Just like him. The more they'd learned about each other, the stronger the pull had been. Interns hadn't been meant to date residents—but try telling that to two people drawn to each other as magnetically as iron and nitrogen. Weighted and weightless. He'd felt both of those things when he'd been with her. Secure in himself as he'd never been before, and so damn happy he would have sworn his feet hadn't touched the ground after the first time he'd tasted those raspberry-ripe lips of hers.

"You *have* read the papers lately, haven't you?" Beatrice asked eventually.

"I have a hunch that world peace is a long way off, so I tend to steer clear of them." Jamie leant forward in his chair, elbows pressed to his knees. "C'mon, Beatrice. Quit throwing questions back at me. Why are you in Torpisi?"

She shook her head in disbelief. "You are the one person in the world I wish had read the tabloids and you *haven't*!" She threw her hands up in the air and gave a small isn't-the-world-ridiculous? laugh.

When their eyes met again there was kindness in hers. A tenderness reserved just for him that he might have lived on in a different time and place.

"I never got married."

She took another sip of her soft drink and looked away as casually as if she'd just told him the time. Or perhaps it was guilt that wouldn't let her meet his eye.

Jamie blinked a few times, his body utterly stationary, doing its best to ingest the news.

Despite his best efforts to remain neutral, something hardened in him. "Is this some sort of joke?"

She shook her head, seemingly confused about the question.

"Why did you do it?"

"Do what?" It was her turn to look bewildered.

"Oh, well…let's see, here, love. Quite a few things, now that I come to think of it."

He spread out his fingers and started ticking them off, his tone level, though his message was heated.

"Up and leave me for a man you didn't love. Ruin the future we'd planned together. All that to never even see it through?"

He pulled his fingers into tight fists and gave his thighs a quick drumming.

"Is this some sort of cruel game you're playing, Beatrice?"

He pushed back in his chair and rose, no longer sure he could even look her in the eye.

"If you're here to rub it in and make sure you made your impact, you can count me *out*."

"Jamie! Wait!"

Bea's voice sounded harsh to her own ears. As quickly as she'd reached out to stop Jamie from leaving she wished she'd rescinded the invitation, tightly wrapping her arms around herself to brace herself against the shards of ice coursing through her veins.

She'd betrayed too much by calling out to him. Jamie would know better than anyone that there had been pain in her voice. The ache of loss. But what was she going to do? Explain what a fool she'd been? That she'd gone and got herself pregnant at an IVF clinic in advance of her wedding so her family, the press and the whole of Italy could coo and smile over the Prince and the Principessa's "honeymoon baby"?

She was the only one in the world who knew that her fiancé—her *ex*-fiancé—was infertile, apart from a doctor whose silence had been bought. She was surprised he'd even told *her*. Perhaps their family get-togethers had begun to rely a bit too heavily on talk of children running around the palazzo, in order to cover up the obvious fact that neither of them were very much in love.

Their one joint decision: an IVF baby. Keeping it as quiet as possible. A private clinic. More paid-off doctors and nurses. An anonymous donor.

The less anyone knew, the easier it had been to go ahead with it.

Her sole investment in a relationship she had known would never claim her heart. A child… A child who had been meant to bring some light into her life.

Now it just filled her with fear. Confirmation that she'd been a fool to agree to the plan. She no longer had the support of her family and, worse, she would be a single mother in a world where it was already tough enough to survive on her own.

It hadn't felt that way when she'd been with Jamie. With him she'd felt…*invincible*.

Relief washed through her when Jamie sat down again, pressing his hips deeper into the chair, his back ramrod straight as he drained his water glass in one fluid draught before deigning to look her in the eye.

"I'm in trouble, Jamie."

As quickly as he'd tried to leave, Jamie pulled his chair up close, knees wide so they flanked hers, fingers spread as he cupped her face in both his broad hands, searching her eyes for information.

"Are you hurt? Did he hurt you?"

No, but I hurt you.

He used an index finger to swipe at a couple of errant locks of hair so his access to her eyes was unfettered. Against his better judgment—she could see that in his eyes—he traced his finger along the contour of her jawline, coming to a halt, as he had so many times before, before gently cradling the length of her neck as if he were about to lean in and kiss her.

It was like rediscovering her senses all over again. As if part of her had died the day she'd told him she was returning home to marry another man.

She blinked away the rising swell of tears.

Part of her *had* died that day. The part that believed in love conquering all. The part that believed in destiny.

"Beatrice," Jamie pressed. "Did he hurt you?"

I was a fool to have left you.

She shook her head, instantly feeling the loss of his touch when he dropped his hands, sat back in his chair and rammed them into his front pockets, as if trying to hide the fact that his long surgeon's fingers were balled into tight fists. For the second time in as many minutes. Twice as many times as she'd ever seen him make the gesture before.

He'd aged in the years since she'd seen him last. Nothing severe, as if he'd been sick or a decade had passed, but he *had* changed. His was a proper grown-up male face now, instead of holding the hints of youth she had sometimes seen at the hospital, when he'd caught her looking at him and smiled.

It felt like a million years ago. Hard to believe it was just two short years since he'd been thirty-three and she twenty-eight.

"Just a young lass, you are," he would say, and laugh whenever she whined about feeling old after a long shift. "Perfect for me," he'd say, before dropping a surreptitious kiss on her forehead in one of the busy hospital corridors. They'd been little moments in heaven. *Perfect.*

She closed her eyes against the memory, gave them a rub, then forced herself to confront the present. It was all of her own making, so she might as well see it for what it was. *Payback.*

A painful price she knew she had to pay when all she really wanted was for him to love her again as he once had.

Impossible.

Sun-tanned crinkles fanned out from Jamie's eyes, which she still wasn't quite brave enough to meet. The straw gold of his hair was interwoven with a few threads of silver. At the temples, mostly. More than she thought a man of thirty-five should have.

But what would she know? When she grew her dyed hair out again it might *all* be gray after the level of stress she'd endured these past few weeks. It was a wonder she hadn't lost the baby.

Her hands automatically crept to her stomach, one folding protectively over the other.

"Did he *hurt* you?" Jamie repeated, the air between them thick with untold truths.

"Only my pride," she conceded. "He didn't want me."

The explanation came out as false, too chirpy. She hadn't wanted Marco either. What she most likely really owed him was a thank-you letter.

"Can you believe it?" She put on a smile and grinned at the real love of her life, as if having her arranged marriage grind to a halt in front of some of Europe's most elite families had been the silliest thing to have happened to her in years.

"He should be shot."

"Jamie…" Bea shook her head. "Don't be—" She huffed out a lungful of frustration, then unfolded her arms from their tight cinch across her chest, visible proof she was trying her best to be honest with him.

Open. Vulnerable. "*Mi scusi*. I'm sorry. I don't have any right to tell you what to feel."

"You're damn right you don't," he shot back, but with less venom than before.

Something in her gave. He deserved to vent whatever amount of spleen he needed to.

"Serves you right" was probably lurking there in his throat. Along with a bit of "now you know how it feels" followed by a splash of "what goes around comes around" as a chaser.

She deserved the venom—and more.

After a moment had passed, with each of them silently collecting their thoughts, Jamie reached across and took one of her hands in his, weaving their fingers together as naturally as if they'd never been apart.

A million tiny sparks lit up inside her. A sensation she'd never once felt with her ex-fiancé.

Obligation didn't elicit rushes of desire. She'd learned that the hard way.

"Talk to me, Beatrice."

His voice was gentle. Kind. His thumb rubbed along the back of her hand as his features softened, making it clear he was present—there just for her.

In that instant she felt he was back. The man she'd met and fallen in love with in the corridors of a busy inner-city hospital tucked way up in the North of England. Their entire worlds had been each other and medicine.

She vividly remembered the first time she'd seen him. So English! *Male*. He'd exuded…*capability*. So refreshing after a lifetime of worrying about etiquette and decorum and the thousands of other silly little things that had mattered to her mother and not one jot to her.

Surviving finishing school had been down to Fran. Without her... She didn't even want to think about it.

She glanced up at Jamie. His eyes were steady... patient... She knew as well as he did that he would wait all evening if he needed to.

She lifted her gaze just in time to see the topmost arc of the sun disappear behind the mountain peaks.

"Maybe we could walk?" she suggested.

He nodded, unlacing his fingers from hers as he rose.

She curled one hand around the other in a ridiculous attempt to save the sensation.

He pointed toward the far end of the piazza. "Let's go out along the lake. Have you been to the promenade yet? Seen the boats?"

She shook her head. She'd had enough of boats and morning sickness over the past few weeks to last a lifetime. She agreed to the route anyway. It wasn't as if this was meant to be *easy*.

Every part of Jamie itched to reach out and touch Beatrice. Hold her hand. Put a protective arm around her shoulder. There was something incredibly fragile about her he wasn't sure he'd seen before. She was nursing something more than a chink in her pride. And all the rage he'd thought would come to the fore if he ever found himself in her orbit again... It was there, all right. It just wasn't ready to blow.

Instinct told him to take things slowly. And then start digging. A verbal attack would elicit nothing. As for a physical attack... If that man had laid one finger on her—

"How are you settling in here? Everyone at the clinic helping you get your bearings?"

Beatrice nodded enthusiastically. "I love it. All one day of it, that is."

He smiled at the note of genuine happiness in her voice. Excellent. The staff were making her feel at home. He fought the need to press her. To get her to spill everything. Explain how she'd found it so easy to break his heart.

"Your contract is…?"

"For the rest of the summer. I guess one of the early-summer staffers left before expected?"

"No." He shook his head. "She had a baby. Worked right up until her due date."

"Ah…"

Beatrice's gaze jumped from boat to boat moored along the quayside. Families and groups of friends were spilling out onto the promenade to find which restaurant they'd eat in tonight.

"I suppose she'll be coming back, then, after maternity leave. Although I did tell your colleague, Dr. Brandisi, that I would be happy to extend if the clinic loses any essential staff after the season ends."

"It waxes and wanes up here. There'll be a time when the summer wraps up where we hit a lull, and then ski season brings in another lot. It's usually all right with just the bare minimum of hands on deck."

Beatrice threw a quick smile his way, her lips still pressed tight, so he continued. "Mostly Italians to start, then Swiss, German, Austrian… A complete pick 'n' mix at the height of the season."

That was why he liked it. Nothing stayed the same. Change was the only thing keeping him afloat since he'd finally faced facts and left Northern General. Everything about that place had reminded him of Beatrice.

And then, after Elisa... That had been the hardest time of death he'd ever had to call.

He swallowed and pushed his finger through a small pool of lake water on the square guard railing, visibly dividing it in two.

Everything leaves its mark. And nothing stays the same.

Those were the two lessons he'd learned after Beatrice had left. Now was the time to prove it.

He rubbed his hands together and belatedly returned her smile. "So! What sort of cases have you had today? Anything juicy?"

They might as well play My Injuries Were Worse Than Yours until she was ready to talk.

The tension in Beatrice's shoulders eased and she relaxed into a proper smile. "Actually, all my cases have been really different to what I treated at home in Venice. With all the recreational sports up here I'm seeing all sorts of new things. It's made a great change."

He felt his jaw shift at the mention of "home." Home—for a few months at the end of their relationship, at least—had been their tiny little apartment, around the corner from the hospital. The one they'd vowed to stay in until they could afford one of the big, rambling stone homes on the outer reaches of the city. One of those houses that would fall apart if someone didn't give it some TLC. The kind of house where there'd be plenty of room for children to play. Not that they'd talked about the two boys and two girls they'd hoped to have one day. *Much.*

Let it go, Jamie. It was all just a pipe dream.

"Were you still working in trauma? When you came back to Italy?" he added.

"Off and on." She nodded. "But mostly I was working in a free clinic for refugees. So many people coming in on boats…"

"With all your language skills you must've been a real asset. Were you based in Venice?" He might as well try to visualize some sort of picture.

"Just outside. On the mainland." She stopped farther along the railing, where the view to the lake and the mountains beyond was unimpeded by boats, and drew in a deep breath, curling her fingers around the cool metal until her knuckles were pale.

The deepening colors of the early-evening sky rendered the lake a dark blue—so dark it was hard to imagine how deep it might be. Fathomless.

"It was relentless. Working there. The poverty. The sickness. The number of lives lost all in the pursuit of a dream."

"Happiness?" he asked softly.

"Freedom."

When she turned to him the hit of connection was so powerful he almost stumbled. It was as if she was trying to tell him something. That her moving back to Italy had been a mistake? That she wished she could turn back time as much as he did?

"Do you miss it? Working at the refugee clinic?" he qualified.

If she was going to up and leave again, he had to know. Had to reassemble the wall he'd been building brick by brick around his heart only to have the foundations crumble to bits when she'd walked back into his life.

She turned her head, resting her chin on her shoulder, and looked at him.

"No." Her head shook a little. "I mean, it was obviously rewarding. But I don't miss being there. Venice…"

Something in him gave. His breath began filling his lungs a bit more deeply.

"What drew you up here to our little Alpine retreat?"

He leant against the railing, unsurprised to see her give him a sideways double take.

Nice one, Jamie. Super casual. Not.

"I used to come up here to one of my cousins' places. Skiing. The next valley over, actually," she corrected herself, then continued, her eyes softening into a faraway smile. "One year I brought Fran with me. Remember Francesca? My mad friend from America? I don't think you met her, but she was—" Beatrice stopped, the smile dropping from her eyes. "We saw each other recently. She's getting married."

"Ah." Jamie nodded.

What was he meant to say to that? *Congratulations, I wish I was, too?* He elbowed the rancorous thoughts away and reharnessed himself to the light-banter variety of conversational tactics.

"Wasn't there something about finishing school and a giggle-laden walk of shame before the term was out? Mussed-up white gloves or something?"

"We snuck away one day." Beatrice feigned a gasp of horror. "Away from the 'good' set."

"You mean the 'crowned cotillion crowd'?" he asked without thinking twice.

Beatrice had been so contemptuous of them then. The group of titled friends and extended family who seemed to drift across Europe together in packs. Hunting down the next in place, the next big thing so they could put their mark on it, suck it dry, then leave. The exact type of person she'd left him for. *Oh, the irony.*

When he looked across to see if his comment had

rankled he was surprised to see another small cynical smile in Beatrice's dark eyes.

Huh. Maybe she'd softened. Saw things now she hadn't before. Not that he and Beatrice had ever "hung with the crowd." Nor any crowd, for that matter. They had been a self-contained unit.

It had never once occurred to him that she was keeping him at arm's length from the affluent, titled set she'd grown up with. He'd never considered himself hung up on his low-income upbringing. The opposite, if anything. Proud. He was from a typical Northern family. Typical of his part of the North anyway. Father down the mines. Mother working as a dinner lady at the local primary school. Brother and sister had followed suit, but he'd been the so-called golden boy. Scholarships to private schools. Oxford University. An internship at London's most prestigious pediatric hospital before he'd returned to the part of the country he'd always called home.

Meeting and falling in love with Beatrice had just been part of the trajectory. *Local boy falls in love with princess.* Only that hadn't been the way it had played out at all. He hadn't known about Beatrice's past for—had it been a year? Maybe longer. Those two years at Northern General had been like living in a cocoon. Nestled up there in the part of the country he knew and loved best, hoping he'd spend each and every day of the rest of his life with Beatrice by his side.

He cleared his throat. "Sorry—you were saying about your friend?"

"*Si*—yes." Bea gave her head a shake, as if clearing away her own memories. "She's staying in Italy. Fallen in love with an Italian."

"Happens to the best of us."

Beatrice looked away.

He hadn't meant to say that. Not in that way. Not with anger lacing the words.

"It's a magical place up here. I'm glad I came," she said at last.

He nodded, turning to face the view. Despite the summer, snow still capped the high Alpine ridges soaring above the broad expanse of blue that was one of Europe's most beautiful high-altitude lakes.

"You know there's a little island out there?"

"Really? Uninhabited?"

"Quite the opposite. There's a group of monks. A small group living there… It's quite a beautiful retreat. Stone and wood. Simple rooms. Cells, they call them."

"Sounds more like a prison than a place of worship." Beatrice's eyebrows tugged together, but her expression was more curious than judgmental.

"No. The simplicity is its beauty. Gives you plenty of time to think."

He should know. He'd spent long enough in one of those cells, just staring at the stone walls until he could find a way to make sense of the world again. The friary was the reason he'd chosen to come here in the first place. He'd needed to hide away from the world for a while and atone for—he still didn't know what.

Failing himself?

Not fighting hard enough for Elisa's life?

Not fighting hard enough for Beatrice?

Those two years they'd spent together in England felt like a lifetime ago. He'd felt…*vital*—full of the joys of life. In his prime. When she'd told him she didn't want him anymore he'd just shut down. "Fine," he had said, and pointed toward the door. *What are you waiting for?*

He sure as hell hadn't found any answers when she'd taken him up on his offer.

And he was certain there hadn't been any when Elisa had died.

He'd found a modicum of peace when he'd gone out to that tiny island friary.

When one of the monks had fallen ill he'd brought him to the clinic here on the lakeside, had accepted the odd shift and found himself, bit by bit, coming back to life. Part of him wondered if the monk had been faking it. And when the clinic "just happened" to mention they needed full-time staff he'd thrown his hat into the ring. He'd been there almost a year now and—as strange as it sounded for a village several hundreds of years old—he felt a part of the place.

"They make some sort of famous Christmas cake— a special sort of panettone. I'm surprised you haven't heard of it."

"The Friars of Torpisi!" Beatrice clapped her hands together, her eyes lighting up as the dots connected. "Of *course*. I had some last *Natale*."

Again that faraway look stole across her face.

What happened to you, my love?

Jamie scrubbed a hand through his hair before stuffing both hands into his pockets again.

Perhaps some questions were best left unanswered.

CHAPTER THREE

"How can you do that?" Bea asked, finally pressing herself into the entire point of the walk. Laying her cards on the table.

"Do what?"

Jamie glanced over at her, his green eyes actively searching her face while the rest of his body remained turned toward the lake.

"Be so forgiving."

"I hardly think I'm being *forgiving*. We've got to work together. It'd be a shame to lose a good doctor because of water under the bridge."

Jamie's hands disappeared behind his back. Whether he was crossing his fingers to cover the lie or polishing a fist to take it out on a wall later, she didn't know. Either way it was a hard hit to take.

Water under the bridge.

No chance of reconciliation. Not that she had done a single solitary thing to earn his love, much less earn it a second time.

Even so…would it be crazy to take it as an olive branch?

"So you're not going to fire me?"

He looked at her as if she'd gone mad. "Is that what

you think this is about? I may be a lot of things, but I'm hardly a sadist, my love."

A surprised laugh escaped her throat. "I can think of a thousand other things you could call me besides—" She stopped, finding herself completely unable to repeat the words.

My love.

A thousand times she'd said them once. More. An infinity of moments she'd closed down all in the name of tradition.

"Why aren't you married?"

Shocked at the bluntness of his question, Bea froze as her mind raced for the right answer. The truth might push him away even further. Yank back his olive branch.

Just tell him. You owe him that much.

"The most immediate answer is that he was cheating on me."

Color flooded Jamie's face. The show of emotion meant more to her than she could say.

She continued before she could think better of it. "So I gave him back his ring and told him the wedding was off."

Jamie's shoulders broadened as he pressed himself to his full height. "He'd better have left the country if he knows what's good for him."

"He has." She had to laugh. "He's taken his new lover on *our* honeymoon."

"The tabloids must be loving that."

Jamie laughed, too, but she could see he was far from amused.

"I've been doing my best to avoid the tabloids."

"Probably just as well."

"Why? Have you heard something?"

"No, no." He held up his hands. "I hate those things as much as you do. They're...*toxic*."

"You've got that right."

He leant against the railing, his back to the view, and folded his arms across his chest. "You don't seem that upset for someone whose fiancé has ripped her future into tatters."

It's so much more complicated than I ever imagined it would be.

"I think you and I both know I never loved him."

There it was. The real truth. Whether or not it would make Jamie hate her more, or ultimately find a way to forgive her, only time would tell.

Jamie's jaw set hard. Long enough for her to wish she'd never said anything. Maybe it would have been better to pretend her ex had broken her heart. That there had been more of a reason than family obligation to her agreeing to the ridiculous marriage.

"Well, that's something anyway," Jamie said, holding his stance. Body taut, shoulders held back. He'd never hunched. Never shied away from anything.

Bea ran a finger along the railing, buying herself a bit of time before being truly honest. "For as long as I can remember my family and his were...were sort of *promised* to one another."

"The families, or you and their son?"

"Me and their son," she confirmed.

It sounded so clinical. Patriarchal. Hierarchal. Archaic. You name it. But that was what it had been. An arranged marriage cloaked in a foolish whirlwind of cocktail parties, whispered promises she'd hardly let herself believe—thank heavens—and her mother's long-sought joy. Her satisfaction that, finally, her daughter was behaving like a proper princess.

In other words, she'd taken one for the team.

"Your mother never really liked it that you came to England, did she? Worked in the A&E."

"Have you added mind reading to your skills list since I saw you last?"

Without even thinking about it she reached across and gave his forearm a squeeze. They'd always been like that. Touching one another. Confirming each cue— verbal or social—with a little hug, a little stroke on the cheek, a light brush of the fingers as they passed in a corridor too populated for them to get away with a proper kiss.

Jamie looked down, considered her hand for a minute, then looked back up into her eyes. "I always used to think I could read your mind, but after you left… Not so much."

She dropped her hand back to her side. "I could've handled that better."

"You could have stayed."

Tears leapt to her eyes, and for the first time since she'd laid eyes on him, Jamie didn't do a thing. No pad of his thumb wiping them away. No digging into one of his pockets for a fresh linen handkerchief. Just the set of his jaw growing tighter.

She *should* have stayed. Been true to her heart *and* his. Then she wouldn't be in this ludicrous position. Unmarried. Pregnant. Facing the future alone.

She nodded, letting the tears fall fat and unceremoniously down her cheeks, along and off her chin, darkening the light blue of her linen blouse. They were coming so thick and fast she didn't bother wiping them away.

"I thought I was doing the right thing. If I'd stayed with you—"

"If you'd stayed with me, *what*?" Jamie challenged.

"What would have happened if you'd stayed with me? We would've got married? Perhaps had a child by now? Not be here in this—" He swept an arm out along the vista when his anger collapsed. "Well…this is pretty beautiful. I don't regret *this*."

Beatrice spread her hands across her face and wiped at the tears, laughing despite herself. "You always could see the best in everything."

"You brought that out in me."

"No." She shook his words away. "I don't deserve that. You were good at that before I met you. It's one of the things that made me fall in love with you."

Jamie gave her a sidelong glance. "And what was it exactly that changed how you felt? Did you see something you didn't like? Or something you liked more in *him*? Even though you weren't 'in love' with him."

He hadn't needed to put up air quotes as he spoke. His voice had said it all. The glint of opportunities lost sparked in his green eyes, which flared to show her time *hadn't* healed the wounds she knew she'd inflicted in the way she'd hoped it might.

"Oh, Jamie." Her voice was barely a whisper, and her heart was doing its very best to leap out of her throat.

He could have said a lot of things. Accused her of leaving for the money. For the opulent palazzos she would have lived in. The parties, the traveling, the haute couture she would have been pictured wearing in all the glossy magazines, at all the parties where people cared about those sorts of things. Palaces and pistes. Beaches and ballrooms. The list went on and on, but none of those would have been the answer.

"Why did you do it?" he asked again, his voice hoarse with emotion.

"A little girl trying to please her mother, I suppose," Bea whispered, her voice breaking as she spoke.

She didn't suppose. She knew it. She'd hashed and rehashed it on an endless loop these past few weeks. And the answers she had come up with were sobering. It wasn't entirely her mother's fault. Her family's fault. Even tradition wasn't to blame.

At the end of the day, all the blame lay solidly at her own feet. *She* was the one who had left the man she loved. Put on that white dress. All that ridiculous lace!

The waste.

The heartache.

Heartache she couldn't admit to because, as Jamie had so bluntly put it, their relationship was "water under the bridge." Even if all she wanted to do right now was drop to her knees and beg his forgiveness. Plead with him to believe that she'd never stopped loving him. That she would do anything to make things right again. But it was impossible.

When her ex-fiancé had made it more than clear that she'd be raising her child on her own she had vowed never to enter into a relationship again. Too painful. Too many pitfalls.

And now that the one man she would have made an exception for was in front of her it was like stabbing a dagger into her own heart. But her choice was made. She had to continue alone. Live with the pain. With what she'd done.

There was no way in the world she could ask Jamie to love her child. Raise it. Love it as his own. Not after what she'd done.

She cleared her throat and forced herself to look him straight in the eye. "I guess you could say I fell in line. Our families—the di Jesolos and the Rodolfos—have known each other forever. Generations. It's what our people *do*."

She sought Jamie's eyes for some sort of understanding. Anything to make her feel the tiniest bit better... Nothing. Just a blank expression as if she'd been listing cement prices. His lack of response was chilling.

When he finally spoke his voice bore the toneless disappointment of a judge on the brink of laying down a guilty verdict.

"Do you *really* believe this was entirely your family's doing? That you didn't play *any* role in it?"

Bea's hands flew to cover her chest, as if protecting her heart from his words.

"Well, not entirely, no—but surely you can understand how—"

"No. I can't." He held up his hand, putting an end to her appeal. "Maybe it's culture. Maybe it's class. But *my* family has done nothing but make sacrifices to ensure my life was better."

"And is that your guilt for their sacrifices talking? Or righteous indignation because I made my own sacrifice at the di Jesolo altar? A sacrifice for the greater good of *my* family!"

Bea hated herself for the cruel words. Jamie was the last person she should be lashing out at. The last person whose forgiveness she should expect.

She'd been a fool to think he might be the one to go to for compassion. For one of those unchecked, bear hugs he used to give. The hugs that had assured her everything would be all right.

She steeled herself and looked him in the eye again. Nothing. The shutters had dropped.

This summer was going to be a test.

Penance for the mistakes she'd made along the way.

And, in the end, perhaps proof that she'd be able to put up with anything once her baby was born.

If she could survive the arctic gaze shredding her nerves right now she could survive anything. Raise a baby on her own. Teach him or her right from wrong... ensure they lived the life they wanted to live.

Steeling herself against that remote gaze of his, she turned to Jamie, matching his tone with a level of cool that took her by surprise. "Like you said, Jamie. People change."

Beatrice might as well have reached in and ripped his heart straight out of his chest.

Of *course* he'd bloody well changed!

Jamie set off with determined, long-legged strides after Beatrice, who had marched away, with quick, tight steps to start and then, when she hit the end of the promenade, stretched her legs into a run.

What did she expect? She'd *left* him. Yanked the world out from under his feet. Smashed his heart into bits. He'd been utterly dumbfounded when she'd left, had made it through each and every day since then through sheer force of will.

Eyes glued on that platinum blond head of hers, he pushed himself harder, even though he didn't have a clue what he was going to say when he reached her.

Tell her to leave.

Beg her to stay.

Either way, this *wasn't* how they were going to leave things. With her storming off in a huff because he wasn't rolling over and placating her ego. She'd left him once and he'd be damned if he was going to see the back of her again unless it was by mutual agreement.

Furious that he'd let things degenerate between them

so quickly, Jamie reached out and grabbed Beatrice's elbow. The move threw her off balance, so he quickly stabilized her with both hands, holding her square in his arms. The two of them were breathing heavily, eyeing each other in anticipation of who would make the first move.

Before he could think better of it he cupped her chin in his hand, tipped her lips toward his and kissed her as if his life depended upon it. At this very moment, tasting her, feeling her respond to him as passionately as she was, sure as hell felt as if it did.

As suddenly as the moment began it was over. He wasn't sure who had pulled back first or if they'd simply needed to come up for air. Either way, he was sure of one thing. Beatrice was right. She hadn't left him because she didn't love him. It was still there. The spark. The fire.

Knowing that made the whole scenario worse.

If he couldn't count on her to stick with him through thick and thin there was little point in asking her to try again. No way would he be able to pick up the pieces a second time.

He stepped back and away from her, his hands scrubbing at the back of his head as if his fingers could reach in and reestablish the order he'd only just put into place.

"I shouldn't have done that."

Beatrice didn't say anything, pressing her fingers into her kiss-stung lips. Her eyes were wide, red rimmed with the tears she'd already shed.

"Let me walk you home." He stuffed his hands into his pockets to stop himself from pulling her into a hug, stroking her hair, whispering to her all those things a man told a woman when he knew she was hurting and wanted it to stop.

"Don't worry." She shook her head, took a quick scan of the piazza as if to regain her bearings. "It's been a long day. I'd like to walk home alone, if you don't mind."

It came out as almost a question. Just the merest hint of her genuinely caring if he *did*, in fact, mind.

"Do you want to make this work?" he asked instead. "The working-together thing?" he continued when she looked up at him, eyes as wide as saucers.

"I do." She nodded, her voice more solid than he'd heard it all day.

"Well, then… Looks like we'd both better get some rest. Tomorrow's going to be a long day."

And without a second glance he turned and walked away.

CHAPTER FOUR

"AM I ALLOWED to take showers with this on?"

Bea smiled. Since when were thirteen-year-old boys worried about *showers*?

"He means *go swimming*," his mother interjected, rubbing a hand through her son's sandy blond hair. "*Il est mon fils*. He's my son and he's like me," she translated, though they had been speaking French for most of the time Bea had been circling the colored fiberglass wrap onto the boy's arm. "He's addicted to the lake. My little minnow."

Guillaume squirmed and muttered something about not being so little anymore. Probably a teenage growth spurt and a lack of awareness of his new gangly limbs were the reason behind his fall. It also explained why rock climbing might not have been the best choice of activity.

Bea finished off the task with a smile, smoothing the last bit of blue wrap onto his arm. "Good thing you were wearing a helmet."

They all turned to look at the multicolored helmet, which had received an almighty dent in the boy's fall.

"You know, your cast is made out of the same thing as your helmet. It should keep your arm safe until you heal, but unfortunately it's not one hundred percent waterproof. I've put a waterproof liner in there, and I can get you a waterproof sheath—but it's not a perfect guarantee it will stay dry."

"I can pretty much guarantee, now that you've said that, Guillaume is going to be in that lake straightaway."

Bea laughed. "If you can bear it, hold off until tomorrow. You want it to dry properly and make sure everything's set. After that—" she looked at the mother "—the main goal is to make sure his skin stays clear of rashes or any other irritation. If you have a hair dryer, use the cool setting to dry inside the cast if it does get wet."

The mother and son looked at each other and laughed. "Marie is *never* going to let me borrow her hair dryer!"

"Perhaps if you asked nicely, instead of teasing her all the time." His mother gave him an elbow in the ribs.

"Older sister?"

Mother and son nodded as one.

Bea busied herself with tidying away the packaging from the wrap, wondering if she and *her* child would share moments like that. The relaxed camaraderie. So different from what she'd grown up with.

Clearing her throat, she banished the thought. She had to get through the pregnancy first.

"A vacuum cleaner works just as well."

"Ah!" Guillaume's mother laughed again. "If only my son weren't allergic to cleaning! I doubt he even knows there's a vacuum cleaner in our cottage."

Guillaume pretended not to hear, tapping away at his cast, examining the multiple colors his fingers were already turning in the wake of the break.

"I can't wait to show Marie my X-rays. She'll have to take back everything she said about me crying for nothing."

Bea pushed back on her wheeled stool as the boy's

mother put her arm around her son's shoulder and pulled him in for a gentle hug. "It's all right to cry, *mon amour*. Strong men *should* show their feelings."

He wriggled in embarrassment, but didn't pull away.

Bea looked away again, fastidiously training her eyes on the paperwork.

It seemed every single thing in the universe was a little lesson, guiding her toward impending motherhood.

Moments like these would soon be in the pipeline for her. Trips to A&E. The frantic worry that her son or daughter would be all right. The relief, flooding through her when she was assured her child would be just fine. The love shining through it all.

"Let's get back to your *papa*, shall we, Guillaume? Show him your latest achievement."

The smile stayed on Bea's lips as she handed over the release papers, but inside, her heart had cinched tight.

That was the missing ingredient in her life. A father for her tiny little child.

Her fingers instinctively moved up to her lips, reliving that kiss. Even though it was a week ago now, in those few precious moments she'd thought maybe... just *maybe*...

"Is there anything else, Dr. Jesolo?"

Bea shook her head, unwilling to allow the wobble she knew she'd hear in her voice if she spoke.

Pointing the pair in the right direction, she curled her fingers around the cubicle curtain and tugged it shut, needing just a few seconds to compose herself. Another rush of tears. Another case of embedding the emotions of each of her patients straight into the fabric of her soul, of not being entirely able to retain her professional distance.

Hormones, no doubt.

All of a sudden Beatrice's eyes snapped wide-open. Was that really what she'd thought it was? Just the tiniest of flutters and yet...

Her hands slid instinctively across her belly... *Oh! Yes.* There it was again. Like having a butterfly inside her, but so much better.

Years of medical training told her it *couldn't* be what she thought it was. That precious little life letting her know that he or she was in there. It was far too soon to feel anything. There were all sorts of other possibilities. Medical explanations.

A need to pee. *Again.* An increase of blood flow to her womb, drawing her attention to the area. The fact that the low waistline of her skirt was becoming the tiniest bit more snug, despite weeks of morning sickness.

Either way, she believed the sensation *was* her tiny, precious baby letting her know he or she was alive in there.

"Can I get a hand here?"

Bea pulled her stethoscope around her neck and ran, not even bothering to take a swipe at the tears she didn't seem to be able to control. Happy or sad, they appeared on tap these days. Allergies, she told everyone.

Jamie.

Her focus was so complete as she ran to the triage area she hardly noticed that he had moved in alongside her as two gurneys were wheeled in by paramedics.

"Here." He handed her a disposable surgical gown. "Better put this on. Things might get messy."

"What's happened?" She saw Jamie's double take as she swept away the remnants of emotion before turning her full attention to the patients and the paramedic rattling off their status.

"Two women presenting with second- and third-degree burns."

"Where's my wife?" A man pushed through the swing doors, his eyes frantic with worry.

"She's here with us. Exactly where she needs to be." Jamie's solid voice assured the man.

"I *told* her not to use that kerosene stove. It didn't look safe. I *told* her it didn't look safe!"

Bea threw her attention to the woman on the gurney closest to her as she heard Jamie continuing to placate the man, convincing him to go back to the waiting room to be with his other children.

"Why are her clothes all wet?" she asked.

"When the stove exploded she jumped into the lake!" the woman's husband shouted over Jamie's shoulder.

"Second- and third-degree burns." Dr. Brandisi appeared on the other side of the gurney, his gloved hands at the back of his neck as he tied on his disposable gown. It was critical the wounds were kept as hygienic as possible. Infection was a burn victim's worst enemy. "We need to start cutting these clothes off."

Bea did her best to soothe the woman, although she was unable to run a hand across her brow as the flames had hit her forehead.

"What's your name, *amore*?"

"My sister!" The woman struggled to push herself up. "Is my sister here?"

"She's blistering. Only remove what isn't anywhere near the burns." Jamie's voice came through loud and clear as he took control of the team. "We need Brandisi and Bates with the sister. Her name's Jessica. Dr. Jesolo?" Jamie's eyes hit Bea's as she tied on a face mask. "This is Monica Tibbs. You're with me."

Bea nodded, not questioning his assignment for an

instant. To do so would waste precious time. Just a rough glance told her that somewhere around thirty percent of Monica's body had taken a hit from the explosion. The damage was significant.

The calm with which Jamie approached the chaotic situation infused everyone with much needed focus. Collectively, they went to work. Instructions, low and urgent, flew from doctor to doctor, nurse to nurse.

Bea didn't have time or any need to worry about the fact that Jamie was now by her side, carefully cutting along the length of the woman's trouser leg. Pieces of cloth stuck to her skin. It was hard to look at. Essential to treat.

"Jessica's lost consciousness." Dr. Brandisi's voice rose above the rest. "Can we get a check on her stats, please?"

"Where's the oxygen? We need to get some oxygen."

"It's impossible to attach the monitor tabs."

"Use your fingers. The woman's still got pulse points."

The tension in the room ratcheted up another notch. After a moment of taut silence and furious concentration a nurse rattled off some numbers. The voices rose around Jessica's bed, then dropped just as suddenly.

"What's going on?" Monica whispered.

"Can we get an intubation kit?" Dr. Brandisi asked.

"Anyone clear on the ambient temperature? We don't want to add hypo to the symptoms." Jamie threw the question over his shoulder to the stand-by staff awaiting orders.

"They're doing everything they can for your sister," Beatrice told Monica, taking as much of the her top off as she was able to, steering clear of the burns. Thank goodness it was cotton. A synthetic top would have melted instantly. "Hypothermia can be a problem if the room's too cool and there's a large burn surface."

"I never should've suggested making pancakes! It was ridiculous!"

"There's soot in Jessica's airway."

"Better that than losing oxygen."

"She's not breathing?" Monica rasped, lifting the oxygen mask from her mouth, her throat losing its battle for moisture.

Bea looked across to Jamie. He nodded. She knew that nod. *Go ahead and be honest*, it said. *But do it with care.*

Bea ran her fingers as gently as she could against the unburnt skin of the woman's cheek. "This team of doctors are exactly who she needs to be with right now. Let us focus on you."

"Give me a moment." Dr. Brandisi silenced his team as they prepared to intubate Jessica. "All right—we're in. Let's get her into surgery, people."

As one, the team flicked switches, unlocked wheels, tugged rolling IV stands close and moved toward the swinging doors that led to the small surgical ward.

"Is my sister going to be all right?" Monica tried to sit up again, screaming when her exposed arm brushed against the side of the gurney. "Cut it off!" she pleaded, her one good hand clutching at Bea's surgical gown. "Please—cut it off if you have to, but make the pain stop!"

"We're doing everything we can. As soon as your IV is in, the pain will begin to ease." Bea turned to the nurse hanging up the bag of electrolyte fluid. "How much lidocaine do you have in there?"

The nurse told her she'd used the standard calculation.

"Ten milliliters to a five hundred milligram bag?"

The nurse nodded.

"There isn't any potassium in the bag, right?"

"No. We've heard about the risks. Even up here in the hinterlands."

Bea's eyes flicked to Jamie's at the comment. She hadn't been questioning the nurse—just making sure all the bases were covered.

She returned her attention to Monica. This wasn't the time to bicker about whose pool of knowledge was bigger, even if her specialty *had* been trauma. Malnutrition and respiratory infections had been her bread and butter at the charity clinic in Venice, but today she was going to have to draw on every ounce of experience she'd had at Northern General. And rely on Jamie. This was *his* turf. His call to make.

"I know it's difficult, Monica, but if you could lie back it will help with the pain." Her eyes flicked to Jamie. Which way would he want to go with this?

"Have you done the fluids calculation for the first twenty-four?" Jamie asked. He had removed all the clothing he could from Monica's side and begun checking her circumferential burns.

"Four mils multiplied by the patient's body weight by TBSA?" She winced. She hadn't meant it to sound like a question.

"You've got it." He didn't sound surprised. "Make sure fifty percent of that is fed through in the first eight hours, the rest infused over the last sixteen. Are you all right to oversee this?"

"Sure." Bea turned to the nurse and asked for extra bags of the electrolyte solutions essential for rehydrating the patient, along with giving her a request to monitor the urine output.

"I'm swabbing for microbiological contamination."

Jamie looked to Bea. Again, as if reading his mind, she knew what he was saying. *Brace your patient.* It would hurt, but Monica had been in a lake. They had to know what germs they'd be fighting.

After talking Monica through the pain of the swabs, Bea returned her attention to Jamie. If he was needed for other cases she should show she was on top of this. Or was he babysitting her? Making sure nothing else had changed about the woman he'd thought he'd known inside and out?

Either way, it just showed he was a good doctor. It wasn't anything to get bristly about.

"Warm water wash before dressing, and then what would you like?"

"We'll need a CBC and ABG, a check on urea and electrolytes." Jamie turned to the nurse. "Would you please get Monica's blood glucose levels, B-HCG and an albumin test?"

"What *is* all that? Am I going to live?" Monica's hoarse voice croaked up through the list of instructions.

"We're doing our best to get you through this," Bea replied.

She would have loved to say yes. Make assurances. But burns this big opened a patient up to multiple complications. The tests Jamie had ordered were only the beginning of weeks, if not months of treatment. The poor woman would no doubt need extensive time with multiple therapists as her body was healed from its devastating injuries. Luckily, it seemed most of hers were second-degree burns—unlike her sister, who seemed to have taken the bulk of the fireball's heat.

"We need to get some saline into her. And some blood. Her heart's going to need all the help it can get." Jamie nodded at Beatrice to get the IV. "Anyone ascertained a blood type?"

"O positive," answered a dark-haired nurse, Giulietta. "And her husband said she doesn't have any allergies. Do you want me to organize a transfusion?"

"Not just yet. Let's see how she goes with the re-hydration solutions and lidocaine first. Dr. Jesolo, have you established the TBSA yet?"

Beatrice pulled a sterile needle from its packaging and prepared to inject antibiotics into the fresh IV bag. "To me it looks like thirty percent. Maybe a little bit more."

He nodded. "Good." His eyes flicked to Giulietta. "Can we get a call in to the burns unit in Pisa? These two are going to need to be transferred as soon as they're stabilized."

"They're from the UK. Is it worth putting a call into a hospital there? A medevac?"

He shook his head. The hospitals in the UK were terrific, but time was a factor. "Let's get her stabilized and en route to Pisa for the time being. We'll call in a translator if necessary."

"Yes, Dr. Coutts."

Another nurse filled her spot as quickly as Giulietta left.

"I'm just going to check on Jessica—are you all right on your own?" He knew what the answer would be, but wanted to triple-check with Beatrice. There was something a bit fragile about her today. Something in direct contrast to the slight bloom he'd thought he could see in her cheeks when she'd come in this morning. He'd been a fool to cross the line as he had with that blasted kiss, but it was too late to wish it back now.

"We're going to be just fine here. Aren't we, Monica?"

Jamie watched as Beatrice bent close to her patient's lips, listening intently as a message was relayed.

When she looked up at him, there were tears in her eyes. "Could you let Jessica know that her sister loves her?"

"Of course." Jamie nodded somberly as he met Beatrice's gaze.

They both knew how severe these two cases were. How, even if their patients survived the blast, their lives would be changed forever.

"Straightaway."

From the moment he entered the operating theater he sensed something was wrong.

The instant he heard the words *hypovolemic shock*, his mind went into overdrive.

Jessica's extensive burns meant her body couldn't retain fluids—crucially, blood.

Dr. Brandisi gave Jamie a curt nod when he joined the table, tying on a fresh gown as he did so. "We can't get enough blood into her. Or saline fluids. Her heart's beginning to fail."

"Raise the feet, please." It was a last-ditch attempt to try to increase her circulation, but a quick glimpse at her heart rate and pulse were sure signs that there was little hope. The atmosphere in the room intensified.

"I don't suppose there are any peristaltic pumps hidden in a cupboard somewhere," he said to no one in particular. He knew as well as everyone else that there weren't, and rehydrating the patient was critical. Despite the fact they were a midsize clinic, they simply weren't equipped to deal with an injury of this nature.

"Negative," Teo replied needlessly, his expression grim. "The chopper is on its way. Potassium levels are too high. Can we try to get more fluids in her?"

"She's going into cardiac arrest."

"Kidneys are failing."

"Temperature's falling. Let's not add hypothermia to the list, people!"

Jamie scanned the woman's chest. The burns were too deep to consider using the standard defibrillation equipment. They could try for open-heart surgery, but they simply didn't have the means of getting enough blood into her body to warrant any success.

As the team worked with a feverish intensity, Jamie did what he had promised. Jessica's chances were fading with each passing moment, and he sure as hell wasn't going to let her die without hearing her sister's words. He knelt low beside her, gently holding each side of her head as he did so, and passed on the message of love.

All too quickly the team had exhausted every means of keeping Jessica alive.

"Do you want to call it?" Teo stood back from the operating table, angrily pulling his gloves off and throwing them in the bin. No one liked to lose a patient. No one liked to make the call.

Jamie glanced up at the digital clock as he pulled off his own gloves. "Time of death—"

"The helicopter's here. Are you ready?"

Beatrice burst through the doors of the operating theater holding a mask in front of her face, her eyes darting around the room until they landed on Jamie.

"Time of death," he repeated, with more feeling than he'd anticipated, "nine-oh-seven."

Beatrice dropped the mask, a flash of dismay darkening her features before she quickly composed herself. She gave Jamie a quick nod. "I'll let the staff know. I might hold off on telling the sister until her transfer is complete."

"As you see fit," Jamie agreed.

It was always a delicate balance. Family desperate for information. Taking it hard. Losing the will to survive. Monica's burns were severe, and she would need every ounce of fight she had left in her.

He nodded his thanks to the support team and went out through the back of the clinic for just a moment to recover. Regroup.

Behind the clinic was a small courtyard, paved with big slabs of mountain granite. One of the nurses kept the flower boxes bright with fresh blooms. They were a cheery, lively contrast to the hollow sensation that never failed to hit him whenever their efforts failed.

He heard the helicopter rotors begin their slow *phwamp, phwamp*, building up speed and ultimately taking off, banking to the south to head for the burns unit in Pisa.

His thoughts were with Monica's husband, still in Casualty with his children, where the nurses and doctors were tending to their minor injuries. His holiday up in the mountains turned into a living nightmare.

Jamie wouldn't have wished what they were going through on anyone.

It was a vivid reminder that no matter how difficult he'd found it to see Beatrice these past few days, she was *alive*. While they were obviously still stinging from their breakup, neither of them was going to have to deal with the physical traumas Monica would for the rest of her life.

The poor woman would have to focus with all the power of her being on the silver linings. Her children had escaped injury for the most part. Her husband was fine, dedicated to his family and their welfare. Monica would bear the scars of this day forever, but in her heart she would be eternally grateful for pulling through.

He looked up into the bright blue sky, dappled with a smattering of big cotton-ball clouds. He picked one and stared, squinting against the brightness of the morning sun as it rose at the far end of the lake.

So Beatrice had left him to do right by her family. She had never been a woman to take a decision lightly, so there must have been something deep within her, compelling her to choose to fall in and play the good daughter. *His* family had made sacrifices for him. Life-changing sacrifices so that he wouldn't have to. What if he had been put in a similar situation?

He closed his eyes and let the sun beat down on his face.

His family wouldn't have *had* a similar situation, but he knew that if push had come to shove he'd have laid his life on the line for any single member. It would be two-faced of him not to expect Beatrice to do the same.

At the time her decision had hurt as badly as if she'd stabbed him and left him for dead. But she'd never said she didn't love him. Never said she didn't care. And when he'd kissed her… The sensation had kept him up near enough half the night. He knew what he had felt—and it was about as close to love as he dared let himself believe.

He opened his eyes, surprised to feel a soft smile playing on his lips. Tough start to the day. But it had given him some much needed perspective. A way to get through the summer with his heart intact.

It was at moments like these that Bea felt overwhelmed by the beauty of the human spirit.

The day had been a long one and having heard at long

last that Monica had arrived at the specialist burns unit and was receiving the best treatment she could get, Bea had felt the tightness in her chest loosen a bit. When the doctor changing shifts with her had mentioned the community's response to the accident she'd taken a walk down to the lake, and the sight that greeted her now set her heart aglow.

The lake was sparkling so brightly it looked as if it were inhabited by thousands of tiny stars, and out of respect for the family who had suffered such a heavy loss today holidaymakers and locals had joined forces, piling huge bouquets of flowers on the boat launch where the accident had taken place. As the sun set one by one people were releasing floating candles onto the lake. Hundreds of people had turned up. The overall effect—shimmery, magical, otherworldly—was healing.

"Quite a turnout."

A spray of goose bumps rippled up her arms. No need to turn around to guess the man behind the voice. But before she could think better of it Bea did turn, her body registering Jamie's presence and her brain still spinning to catch up, as if her skin remembered what it was like to be touched by him without a prompt.

Little wonder. When she'd agreed to the arranged marriage she had forced herself to preserve her time in England in a little memory bubble and hide it as far away as she could. How else would she have survived?

And now that she was pregnant... *Oh, Dio!* It was as if the bubble had been sliced open and her dream man had been put in front of her just in case she hadn't already known what she'd given up.

She was going to have to find a way to be stronger than this, better than this, when her child was born. There was no way her baby was going to suffer for her own madness-fueled mistake. Because it did boil down to just one. Leaving Jamie.

"Really good work today." Jamie tucked his chin down so that his eyes were on a level with hers. A move he'd once used to great effect to tug a smile out of her after a rough shift.

She swallowed before she answered, knowing those ever-ready tears would come if she spoke straightaway. "You, too." She went for a casual, buddy tone. "I'd almost forgotten how well we work together."

"I hadn't." He pushed up to his full height, eyes looking out upon the lake. "Look, do you see there, where the moonlight meets up with the candles? It's as if they're drawn to one another."

Unable to respond, she murmured an acknowledgment and looked back out at the lake.

Drawn to each other...

Just like the pair of them. She'd used to think their combined energies made them a force to be reckoned with. Now, with the situation she'd found herself in—correction, *put* herself in—she was a moth drawn to the flame. Falling in love with Jamie again would be all consuming. Something she wouldn't be able to come back from.

In a few months' time she would need to give all her energy to her child. Figure out how to pay the bills. Work. Breastfeed. Love. Laugh. Cry. All of it with one sole focus. Her newborn child.

So right here and now, opening up the heart she knew was near to bursting with love for the man she'd left behind wasn't an option.

They stood for a few moments in silence, gazing out at the lake. The area was crowded, and there wasn't much room. Someone trying to get a lakeside view caught Bea off balance, and despite her best attempts not to reach out to regain her balance her hands widened and found purchase on Jamie's chest. His arms automatically cinched around her back, creating a protective barrier by pulling her in close to his chest.

Bea was hit by a raft of sensations.

The scents she would have been unable to describe a fortnight earlier came to her now as clear as day. Cotton. Cedar. Spice and citrus.

The feel of the firm wall of chest her fingers hadn't been able to resist pressing into.

The memory of being able to tuck her head in that secure nook between his shoulder and chin, her forehead once getting a tickle when he'd experimented with growing a beard.

Despite herself, she laughed.

"What's so funny?" Jamie asked, pulling back to examine her.

"Do you remember when you wanted to grow a beard? It was wintertime, wasn't it?"

"Winter into spring," he answered, the memory lighting up his own eyes as he spoke. "That's why I ended up shaving it off." He scrubbed a hand along his bare chin. "That thing itched something crazy once the weather started warming up. What made you remember that?"

"Just popped into my head." A white lie. What else was she going to say? *Being this close to you made me want to nestle into your chest and relive some of the most perfect moments of my life?* Hardly.

"Memories are funny things." Jamie loosened his hold on her and then dropped his hands to his sides. "I've been having quite a few myself today."

Bea's forehead lifted, though it wasn't in surprise. How *could* he be immune to the fevered trips down memory lane she'd been tearing along from the moment she'd seen him again?

"Shall we?" Jamie tipped his head toward the square, where the crowd was less thick.

She shook her head. "I should probably be getting back to my apartment. I'm an early-to-bed sort of woman these days."

"No more double alarms?"

They both laughed at the memory and she shook her head. No. That had all changed.

"I'm up with the lark these days," she said, grateful for the reprieve from looking into Jamie's beautiful green eyes when he turned to forge a path through the crowd for the pair of them.

When they'd been together she'd slept like a log. So deeply she would turn off her alarm without even remembering having batted around in the dark to stop its beeping.

That had all changed when she'd returned to Italy. She'd blamed it on the one-hour time difference knowing full well it was nerves. A permanent feeling of foreboding, as if she *knew* marrying Marco would never bring her the joy loving Jamie had.

She stared at his back as he worked his way steadily, gently through the crowd. If she'd been with him she would never have…

Ugh. Sigh.

She would never have done a lot of things.

Like agreeing to have an IVF "honeymoon baby." Marco had pushed her into it so that no one would know he was infertile. Completely incapable of providing the Rodolfos with the heir they craved.

Not that she'd ever jumped into bed with him to see if the doctors had been wrong.

And not that he'd protested.

Having this mystery baby had never been a question for her. It was hardly the child's fault she'd agreed to marry someone whose pedigree rendered him more playboy than prince.

The only relief she felt now was that the baby wasn't his. The way things stood, the child growing inside her belly was one hundred percent hers and hers alone.

"Time for a drink?" Jamie asked over his shoulder, as if sensing the discord furrowing her brow.

She shook her head. "I shouldn't really."

"I won't bite. Scout's honor." He turned, crossed his heart, then held up his fingers looking every bit the Boy Scout she knew he'd once been.

"Are you still in touch with your old den leader?"

"Dr. Finbar?" He shook his head. "Not for a while." His gaze shifted up and to the right as he made a calculation. "Must be a year or so before I left since I saw him. I should've gone to see him before I up and went, but—" his gaze returned solidly to hers "—I wasn't at my best."

"I'm so sorry, Jamie. If I could have done anything—"

"No." He cut her off. "It wasn't you—it was a patient. Why I left."

Something in his tone told her that wasn't entirely true, but Jamie was allowed his privacy. His pride. He'd been the one left behind to pick up the pieces. To explain to everyone why she'd left after they'd seemed so perfectly happy with each other.

Being humiliated in front of the enormous crowd at her wedding had served her right. She wouldn't have been the slightest bit surprised to have learned Jamie had raised a glass at the news. A bit of schadenfreude for the embittered suitor.

"How is it you can even face me?" she asked, surprising herself as much as Jamie by the forthright question. "After what I did, I'm surprised you can even speak to me—let alone not hate me."

"Oh, my beauty. *Ma bella Beatrice...*" He pronounced it the Italian way, hitting each vowel and consonant as if he were drinking a fine wine. He stroked the backs of his fingers along the downy soft hairs of her cheek. "I could never hate you. I think I hated myself more than anyone."

A sad smile teased at the corners of his mouth. His lips were fuller than most men's. Sensual. She could have drowned in his kisses, and just the thought of never experiencing one again drew shadows across her heart.

"I can't imagine why you would feel that way. What would make you think so poorly of yourself?"

"Oh..." He clapped his hands together. "About a million reasons. Not putting up a better fight. Not—I don't know—challenging him to a duel? Confronting your parents? Showing them I was every bit as worthy as..."

He paused and swallowed down the name neither of them seemed able to say.

"Water under the bridge." The words rolled off his tongue as if he'd said them a thousand times before in a vain effort to convince himself it was true. "We're both grown-ups. We've moved on. Whatever happened, it happened for a reason, right?"

She shrugged and tried her best to smile, not really coming good on either gesture. The last thing Jamie was to her was water under the bridge. A moment of perfection embedded in her heart was more like it. "Sometimes I'm not so sure."

Jamie shook his head. A clear sign he didn't want her to plead with him. Beg him to try again as she so longed to do.

"We're on different paths now, Beatrice. But it doesn't mean we can't be on friendly terms for the length of your contract. So, what do you say?" He put out his hand in the space between them. "Truce? At the end of the summer you go your way, I go mine?"

A voice inside her head began screaming again and again. *No*, it cried. *No!* But a softer, more insistent voice told her that to do anything other than agree would be unfair. Cruel, even. He'd endured enough. And she didn't deserve him.

She and her baby would find another place, another way to be whole again.

She put her hand out and met his for a solid shake. "Truce."

CHAPTER FIVE

"It DEFINITELY LOOKS worse than it is, Hamish." Bea took a step back from her patient and gave him an appraising look. "The stitches should cover the worst of it, but opting out of wearing a helmet while kayaking...? Not a good move."

"But no one else was!" Hamish gave his chest a thump with his fist. "Scotsmen are *hard*!"

"Doesn't make them smart. You could've been a trendsetter. Using what's *inside* your head instead of bashing the outside of it on a boulder!"

She tried to keep the admonishment gentle, but threw him a stern look as she tugged off her gloves and popped them in the bin. He had a pretty deep gash in his forehead, and if it hadn't been for one of his friends pulling him back up into the kayak and keeping a compress on it until they arrived at the clinic he might easily have died.

"You're going to have to keep the dressing dry *and*—" she wagged an admonishing finger at him "—you need to let your friends know one of them is going to have to stay with you at all times for the next two days. Concussion watch."

"*Ach, no!* I've still got another few days here!" The young man protested. "I've been saving for *months*!"

"You could very well have a concussion." Bea pressed down on his shoulders when he tried to get up from the exam table and wobbled. "Any dizziness, nausea, headaches...all signs of a concussion."

"It's all right, Doc!" Her patient waved off her concerns and launched himself toward the curtains around the exam room.

"Hold on!" Bea ran the few steps toward him and tried to get under his arm to support him, but he pulled away and brought them both crashing to the ground.

Her instinct was to pull away. Protect her stomach. She knew the baby was still only teensy—tiny—but she'd already messed up her own life. She wasn't prepared to mess up the little innocent soul inside her.

Seconds later she felt a pair of hands pulling her up.

"Are you all right?"

Jamie's rich voice swept along her spine as she lurched into an upright position, far too aware of how close they were to one another. One arm was grazing against his chest. And her breasts. Ooh...that was a sensual trip down memory lane she didn't need to take. Especially with everything in her body on high alert.

Touch.

Sensation.

The pair of lips just millimeters away from her own. The bottom lip fuller than the top. Just perfect for nibbling. A bit of blond stubble around them, highlighting just how soft those lips were to touch in contrast to the tickle of his five-o'clock shadow...

"Beatrice?" She felt Jamie's grip tighten on her forearms. "Your patient is waiting."

Pregnancy brain be damned!

As quickly as she could, Bea wriggled out of Jamie's

arms, unsure just how many precious moments she'd lost to daydreaming about his mouth. And kissing it.

Another shot of heat swirled around her belly. *Santo cielo!*

"*Si, Dottore.* I'm fine. *Grazie.*" He could play the white knight all he wanted, but she needed to prove to herself she could stand on her own two feet.

"Are you sure you're okay to treat this patient?"

He rocked back on his heels, his eyelids dropping to half-mast as if he were suddenly in doubt as to her skills as a physician. Desired effect or not, it slammed her back into the moment. She might be a lot of things, but she was no slouch as a doctor.

"*Si, Dottore.* If you'll excuse me? Hamish and I have to finish our discussion about concussions."

"I think I'll join you."

Her eyes flicked to his, searching them for more meaning than she could glean from his neutral tone.

"In case Mr.—" He leaned over her shoulder to glance at the patient assignment board, giving her another waft of undiluted alpha Jamie. "In case Mr. McGregor, here, decides to take matters into his own hands again."

Beatrice didn't know whether to be relieved or furious. Her lips were dangerously close to tipping into a scowl, but ever the professional, she put on a smile, reminding herself she probably would need an extra hand in case Hamish decided to flee the scene again. Concussions were no laughing matter.

"Now, Mr. McGregor—" Jamie gestured toward the exam table "—what do you say we take another look at you?"

He knew he sounded like an uptight by-the-letter diagnostician, but it had thrown him off his axis when he'd seen Beatrice hurtling through the curtains as if in a full-on rugby tackle.

His every instinct had been to protect her. When he'd lifted her up and she'd pulled away from him as if he were made of kryptonite it had more than stung. It had riled him. Which meant he still cared—and that made the silent war he was waging with himself to treat Beatrice as he would treat anyone else even harder.

He had loved her with every pore in his body. And had spent every waking hour since she'd left trying to forget her.

Unsuccessfully, as was beginning to become wildly apparent.

Moving to Italy hadn't helped. The language, the food, the blasted snowcapped mountains were all reminders of her. He should have accepted the job in the Andes. He still could have had his snowcapped mountains, but also extra servings of beef charred on an enormous open fire and about twelve thousand miles between himself and his memories.

As if you could outrun something branded onto your soul...

"Just hold still for a moment," he heard himself saying, going through the examination by rote even as his mind played catch-up with life's strange twist of events. "I want to take a look at your eyes."

"I've already examined the cranial nerves," Beatrice said.

The exam area was small and she was close. Close enough for him to smell the sweet honey-and-flower scent that seemed to travel in her wake.

"Given that Mr. McGregor has had a *second* fall, I thought I'd just check again."

He felt a huff of air hit his neck. One that said, *Why*

are you treating me like a plebeian? You helped train me. You, of all the people in the world, should know I'm the best.

Who knew a little puff of air could contain so much sentiment?

"I'm not going to have to pay for this twice, am I?" Hamish asked, leaning around Jamie as if the only real answer could come from Beatrice. He pulled out the pockets of his shorts to show they were empty.

"No. All part of the service." Jamie leaned in closer to the young man with his medical torch, taking note of Hamish's various pupil responses and all the while pretending not to hear Beatrice's sotto voce grumblings behind him.

Caveman this...

Entitled Englishman that...

To her credit, she was saying it all in Italian, so the Scotsman appeared none the wiser.

Despite the fact that her venom was directed straight at him—like verbal darts in his back—Jamie smiled.

If someone had treated *him* like this, he probably would have responded in the same way. Boorishly barging in and repeating what was a standard exam was straight out of the Cro-Magnon handbook. But he hadn't liked seeing the look of terror on her face as she hit the floor, curling in on herself as if protecting a small child in her arms. It had frightened him. And though he might have closed his heart to the idea of loving her again, he damn well wasn't going to see her hurt. Not on *his* watch.

"Right, Mr. McGregor! It looks as though Dr. Jesolo has done her best by you. What did you recommend in regard to follow-up?"

He turned to Beatrice, only to receive a full hit of

Glaring Doctor. Arms crossed tightly over her chest. Foot tapping impatiently. One eyebrow imperiously arched as if in anticipation of another admonishment. Something told him not to laugh if he didn't want to turn that heated gaze to ice.

Through gritted teeth she began detailing what she'd presumably already run through with her patient. Rest. No kayaking or other contact sports—with or without a helmet—for at least forty-eight hours. A close watch by others on whether he was feeling nauseous, dizzy, light-headed, and some paracetamol—

"But no aspirin," Jamie interjected, suddenly feeling playful. They'd used to do this when they went on rounds together. See who could come up with the most obscure information on a case. Out-fact each other.

"I also made it clear to Mr. McGregor that if he loses consciousness, has any clear fluid leaking from his ears or nose, or feels unusually drowsy while awake, he should return immediately."

"Or has a seizure," Jamie couldn't help adding, knowing it would send that eyebrow of hers arcing just a little bit higher on her forehead.

"Or loses power in any part of his body. An arm or a leg, for example."

"And if he has a headache that worsens, that's a definite cause for concern."

"As is consuming any alcohol, engaging in stressful situations or losing eyesight."

This time he couldn't stop himself from smiling. She'd seen through him now. And was meeting him medical beat for beat.

"Perhaps he should also consider returning if he has problems speaking. Or understanding other people."

"You two are really freaking me out!" Hamish broke

into this verbal one-upmanship. "Am I going to totally *die* or something?"

They turned to him as one and began apologizing. Jamie took the moment to recuse himself from any further involvement in the case, faking a pained look at the same time. "I've got to dash. Lovely to see Dr. Jesolo has given such thorough treatment. All the best for the rest of your holiday. Toodle-pip for now!"

He took two long-legged strides, yanked the curtain open and closed it behind him and then looked up to the invisible heavens.

Toodle-pip?

His family would have had a right old laugh at the antiquated expression. One usually used by Britain's upper crust—not a working-class family like his.

He gave his head a shake.

Beatrice.

She was the only one who could put him in a tailspin like this. Truce or no—he was going to have to continue to watch his back if he wanted to be in one piece by the end of the summer.

He shook his head again and headed toward the assignment board to find himself a patient.

Toodle-pip...

Teo looked at Beatrice and Jamie as if they'd both morphed into mountain goats.

"What do you mean, you're not coming? *Everyone* on the last shift is heading out to the piazza for the Midsummer Festa. I think the crew inside are even taking it in turns to run out and get a bite to eat before drinks this evening."

He flicked a thumb toward the main square, where it seemed the town's entire population was headed.

"Gotta meet my missus. She's eating for two and I want to make sure I get a look-in."

Jamie didn't miss the sideways glance Bea shot him from the other side of the doorway they were inhabiting.

Was it hearing about "the missus"? Or the news that she was pregnant that had caught Bea out?

"C'mon, guys!" Teo persisted. "What are you waiting for? Grub's up!"

"Would you like to go, Beatrice? Get a taste of mountain living?"

"I've been to quite a few *festas*," she answered noncommittally, giving an indecipherable shake of the head. Then added, "When I was younger."

It wasn't a yes. But it wasn't a no. From the impatience building on Teo's face it was obvious he was taking it personally.

Okay. Bull. Horns. Time to seize them and make a decision.

"All right, I'll go."

Jamie and Beatrice spoke simultaneously, turning to one another in wide-eyed horror, then just as quickly recovering with an about-face to Teo and swiftly pasted on smiles.

Teo shot wary looks from one to the other. "I'm going to head off, but I guess I'll see you both in the square?"

"The piazza—yes." Beatrice nodded, as if she'd been the one to suggest going to the Midsummer Festa in the first place. "I haven't had cherry *crostata* in years. Just the time of year for it."

Her voice might have sounded enthusiastic, but she didn't make even a hint of a move.

Nor did Jamie.

Again Teo's eyes flicked from one to the other. "So..." he drawled in his lazy Australian accent. "Are either of you planning on going to this brilliant festival anytime in the near future? Or are you going to wait until you can sneak in under the cover of darkness?"

Jamie laughed. Too heartily.

His guffaw sounded about as genuine as Beatrice's giggle.

Not one bit.

Trills of genuine laughter sounded on the streets beyond them. Then came the sound of an orchestra tuning up for the musical entertainment. An opera diva giving an initial run at her higher range.

Strangely, the collection of sounds and the general buzz of excitement reminded him of a night when the two of them had scraped together their small incomes and plumped for a getaway in Blackpool.

The classic seaside resort in Britain might not have been to everyone's taste—particularly a princess raised with all the finer things in life within hand's reach—but Beatrice had loved it. The over-the-top light displays. The dance halls. The bright pink candy floss.

The memory hit a spot he had once thought he would never be able to return to without a wave of acrimony following in its wake.

They might never be lovers again, but he had really meant it when he'd called a truce. Tonight he would simply be putting his theory to the test: bygones should be bygones.

"Right, Dr. Jesolo. Let's not keep poor Dr. Brandisi waiting any longer. He's obviously desperate to join his wife."

"Girlfriend," Teo corrected. "She's not made an honest man of me yet. Although—" he glanced at his watch "—the wedding's got to be by the end of the summer.

The baby's due in October, and I want my child to have happily married parents when he's born."

Beside him, Jamie felt Bea stiffen. No great surprise when the words *happily* and *married* were bandied about, he supposed. Proof that money couldn't buy you happiness. Teo obviously had bundles of the latter, but not much money.

An idea popped into his head.

"How about at *Ferragosto*?"

"Aw, *mate!*" Teo feigned a few boxing jabs at Jamie. "That's *brilliant*. Alessandra will go nuts for that idea. A wedding *and* a festival for the price of one! What's not to love?"

Beatrice abruptly turned away. Wedding talk was probably not high on her agenda. A protective urge to steer the conversation in another direction took hold of him.

"Right!" Jamie clapped his hands, then rubbed them together. "Everyone's at their stations and ready for the next shift. I'm with Teo. Let's get a move on."

Jamie turned to Beatrice, his arm crooked, and a genuine smile began to form on his lips as she tentatively tucked her fingers around his elbow. He gave the tips of her fingers a pat. More akin to one a grandfather might give a granddaughter than a slighted ex-lover to a woman, but they were meant to be friends. And friends didn't caress, stroke or give one another unexpected passionate kisses that reawakened every part of the masculinity he hadn't tapped into in heaven knew how long...

"To the square?"

Beatrice nodded, her cheeks streaked with just a hint of a blush.

A hint of pride took hold in his chest. Though he knew it was best to keep things neutral, he couldn't help but enjoy having made an impact. Knowing he could still bring a touch of pink to those high, aristocratic cheekbones of hers.

"You're looking pretty as a picture tonight, Beatrice."

He meant it, too. Her short-cut hair accentuated the clean line of her jaw, and her dark brown eyes, always inquisitive, absorbed the flower displays already on show at the periphery of the square they were fast approaching. Her tongue darted out to lick her lips when they passed a *pasticceria*, its windows bursting with delectable pastries.

He didn't realize he was humming until Beatrice pulled back a little, her fingers still linked into the crook of his arm, and gave him a sidelong look.

He hadn't hummed since...

He knew exactly how long it had been.

"I'm still the same old me," Jamie said, when her expression remained bemused.

"Hmm..." Her lips tightened, then pushed into a moue before doing the little wiggly thing he'd used to be so familiar with. The telltale sign that she wasn't entirely sure of something.

"C'mon, Beatrice." He lowered his voice so Teo, who was talking away on his phone, wouldn't hear them. "Let's make the best of a—" He stopped, trying to find the best words.

"A bad situation?" Beatrice filled in the words he'd been about to say.

"An awkward one," Jamie parried.

She wasn't going to get away with making this harder than it already was. He'd endured more than enough angst on his own. Reliving those dark, lonely hours he'd fought and survived in front of her...? Not a chance in hell.

"Well—" she gave a quick laugh "—that's probably more accurate. But I have to confess I'm still reeling a bit." She changed the tone of her voice to mimic a film star of yesteryear. "Of all the clinics in all of Italy…" She trailed off, her dark eyes darting anywhere but up at his face.

A hit of defensiveness welled up within him. *He* had arrived here first. Well, not in Italy, but at the clinic.

"A clinic geared toward tourists was a good fit for me." *All things considered.*

"But an *Italian* clinic? I still haven't quite managed to figure out why they hired you."

"Thanks very much!" He feigned being affronted, knowing it wasn't what she meant. Even so, it felt a bit like she was drawing a line in the sand.

England—his turf. Italy—hers.

Well, too bad. It didn't work that way.

She laughed again, this time pulling her hand out of his arm to hold her hands up in protest. Though her hand hadn't been there long, his arm felt instantly cool at its absence.

"I didn't mean it that way. You know I think you're an amazing doctor."

Their gazes connected and he saw that she meant it. It would have been so easy to attach more meaning to the compliment. More sentiment. But that time had passed.

"I just meant I thought they would hire a fluent Italian speaker for the post."

"They did. Or near enough."

She turned to him, eyes wide with astonishment. "I didn't know that."

"There are a lot of things you don't know about me."

He swallowed the bitter words that might have followed. Some men might have done their very best to close off every last detail of a lover who'd chosen another path, but he had found it impossible. Their lives had been too interwoven. Beatrice's love of her home country had become as much a part of him as his Northern English heritage.

What was spring without stuffed zucchini flowers? Or winter without chestnuts? Scents, sights, smells—they had all vividly shifted when Beatrice had swept into his life like a refreshing spring breeze. Turning dull, dark England into a brighter landscape, only to plunge into darkness again when she left.

After a year of trying to block everything out but work, and then losing the young patient he'd grown far too close to, he'd needed that light again. And the closest he'd been able to get to rekindling that light had been to go to Italy.

"For starters," he began, by way of a gentler explanation, "you left your copy of *The Silver Spoon* behind."

"I thought you *hated* cooking!"

"Not anymore."

"But when we were together—" She stopped.

He wondered if she'd actually go there. Try to take him on a trip down memory lane neither of them seemed well equipped for. They'd effectively lived together during the second year they'd been together. Not officially—she'd still had her own apartment—but he doubted her roommate had ever seen her there. He couldn't remember a night when they hadn't fallen asleep, woven into each other's arms.

"I guess a lot of things have changed," Beatrice said finally. "Ah, *va bene*! Look at all the people!"

And just as quickly as they'd been held together by the invisible strands of the past, the strings had snapped with a hit of reality.

CHAPTER SIX

BEATRICE KNEW IT was feeble to duck out of the important conversation they should be having, but guiltily welcomed the approaching *festa*.

Exploring the past was too close to asking for a different future. One with Jamie in it. And she knew she couldn't go there. No matter how much it hurt, she'd have to pretend she was happy as could be with their collegial truce. There couldn't be anything more. She would never be able to forgive herself for what she'd done to him. The lies. The betrayal. If even the tiniest part of her thought Jamie could love her again...

She scrunched her eyes tight until she saw stars.

When she opened them again she saw an entirely different world from the quiet cobbled lanes they'd been walking through. Before them swirled a riot of color, music, laughter and scents that all but exploded in front of them when they rounded the corner into the teeming piazza.

"Looks like we've lost Teo to the crowds."

"Hunting down his fiancée, no doubt," Jamie said, scanning the sea of heads.

At six feet two inches, he was able to see across the top of most of the crowd. She'd always loved his height. Taken comfort in the fact that when she'd needed a hug he'd been able to rest his chin on top of her head, holding her close enough for her to hear the beat of his heart.

A shiver went through her—as if she'd just been in his embrace and then stepped away.

"Are you all right?" Jamie was already taking off his light linen jacket. "Here—put this on."

Without waiting for an answer he draped the coat over her shoulders.

How can you be so chivalrous?

The gesture was both cruel and kind. Kind because that was Jamie, through and through. Cruel in its vivid reminder of what she wouldn't have when her baby was born. Someone to look out for her. To care if she was hot or cold. Frightened or tired.

Another tremble juddered through her, despite the relative warmth of the night, though experience told her the high altitude would set a chill into the air soon enough. She tugged the lapels of his jacket over her shoulders and dipped her head to receive a deep hit of the scents she knew she'd never forget. Ink. Pine. Cotton.

Her shoulders shook against the fabric. The sorrow she'd carried with her all these years was being released in unforgiving waves, and icy tremors reminded her of the day she'd let such a good man go.

"Do you mind if we head over to the fire pits for a minute?"

"Not at all."

Jamie raised his arm as if he was about to drape it over her shoulders, as he would have when they'd been together. Then, his arm half-aloft, eyes blinking himself back to the present, he remembered otherwise and let it drop to his side.

Beatrice was half-tempted to slip her arms into the

sleeves of Jamie's jacket and grab hold of his hand. It was how they'd first realized they'd felt the same way for each other. A surreptitious moment of holding hands in a crowd.

It had been a busy night in Jamie's village. It was actually more of a town, but it had a warm, strong sense of community. Unlike tonight, it had been properly cold—wintry, even. She'd been all zipped up in a thick parka, with a wooly hat on her head designed in some silly holiday theme. A Christmas pudding? She couldn't remember, but she knew it had made Jamie's green eyes light up every time he had turned to her.

"What was that thing we went to?" She didn't look up at him, but could tell he'd turned to look at her. "The one where I wore the funny hat?"

He laughed before he answered. A soft faraway laugh, hinting at the genuine warmth they'd shared.

"Bonfire Night. *Remember, remember...*"

"The fifth of November," she finished for him when he left off with a slight lift to his voice.

It came back to her now, in a wash of distinct memories. Much like this evening, people had filled the historic English town—all thick slabs of stone and austere houses lit up by an enormous pyre in the very center of the square. Music had echoed off the walls and the scents of mulled wine and frying doughnuts had permeated the air. Fairy lights had twinkled from just about anything that was stationary—even some members of the brass band.

But more than any of those things Beatrice remembered Jamie insisting she leave the hospital after a forty-eight-hour shift to come out and enjoy the spectacle. They hadn't kissed. They might not even have hugged. She knew her cheeks had flushed regularly when he'd looked at her, and on the rare occasions when their hands had brushed against each other's…it had been heavenly. Like fairy dust sparkles lighting her up from the inside.

"Do you remember when you were almost speared by those two lads wrestling in Viking helmets?"

"How could I forget?" Bea smiled at the memory for, as frightening as it had been, Jamie had scooped her out of the way, lifting her up and swinging her out of reach of the one-pint-too-many brawlers as if she'd been made of air. Heaven knew she'd felt as if she were walking on air for the rest of the night.

Against her better judgment she let her fingers drop from their too-tight hold on the lapels of Jamie's jacket and let her hands swing alongside her as they strolled past the detailed flower displays. Thousands of buds and petals were arranged in intricate designs. Some religious, others nods to the Midsummer Festa's pagan origins. Either way, they were beautiful.

"It was the first time I ever had a sparkler."

Jamie stopped and stared at her, mouth agape in disbelief. "What? At the ripe old age of—what were you then—twenty-five?"

"Twenty-six," she corrected.

"You always did look young for your age." He winked in an obvious bid to let her know he was teasing.

Trust Jamie to retain his sense of humor in the situation. If she'd been in his shoes? *Ugh.* She didn't know if she could have done it. Swiped the slate clean and tried to work together. She could see he really *was* trying, and knowing that made her feel even worse.

There has to be a day when the guilt ends. When I can make my peace with him.

Her eyes shot up to the sky, barely visible for all the

light in the piazza, and she swallowed down the prayer, trying to make it a living, breathing part of her.

If she were going to raise her child she would have to find an inner peace.

"First time with a sparkler..." He shook his head again in wonder. "And there was me thinking you couldn't do *anything* new for a princess."

Bea's hopeful mood evaporated in an instant. She shot quick panicked looks around, fearful in case anyone had overheard, forgetting for a moment that nearly everyone within earshot wouldn't have the slightest clue who she was. The world's gossip magazine readers were looking for a brunette long-haired woman, grief stricken after those sensational altar revelations. Not a short-haired platinum blonde snuggling into her boyfriend's linen jacket.

Well, not *boyfriend...* But to an outsider up until about three seconds ago it might have looked that way.

"Too close to the bone with the princess comment?" Jamie asked, his expression unreadable.

No doubt it was a means of protecting his own feelings. Proof she couldn't help but hurt him when all he'd done was make a lighthearted comment.

Get over yourself! Prove to him you're the woman he once thought you were. Not the princess.

She held up two fingers and pinched them together to signify that, yes, unwittingly or not, his comment *had* stung a little bit.

"You know I never thought of myself that way."

She tried to shrug the moment away, but only ended up fighting the sharp sting of tears gathering high in her throat. She quickly turned away, feigning interest in a small stall selling exquisite posies of wildflowers.

"Signor!" She could hear the vendor appealing to

Jamie. "Buy your beautiful woman a small bouquet. *Va bene*. It is midsummer. Without flowers in her hand, she is naked!"

Bea chanced a glance at Jamie, relieved to see he that was laughing. Trust an Italian to insist a woman was naked without flowers. Especially when he was walking with his ex-girlfriend and didn't know she was pregnant from an anonymous donor.

He didn't owe her anything. Least of all…

Wait… Was he…?

"*Per favore, solo uno mazzetto*. To bring a smile to her face again."

There he was again. Indefatigable. The sympathetic, generous man she'd fallen in love with.

Just the sound of Jamie's warm caramel voice—the rich, deep-chested tone he'd used to use when he was trying to coax a smile to her face when she'd had a rough day at the hospital—told her he was doing his best to mend fences.

How could she let him know he didn't owe her a thing?

Bea silently smiled her appreciation, watching as he dug a hand into his pocket, rattling around for some change only to come up empty-handed.

He turned to her, and just as she realized *she* must be the one in possession of his loose change he tugged her around via the lapels of his jacket so that she was square onto him. Achingly slowly, he purposefully slid his hands down the lapels, just skidding along the tops of her hypersensitive breasts, pausing when her breath caught, then continuing until each of his hands found purchase on the edge of a pocket. His fingers dipped into the squares of linen, moving assuredly inside them, grazing her hips as he felt for coins.

Everything inside her was alight with anticipation.

When their eyes met, she knew he had felt it, too. The same thing *she* had felt when their hands had shifted and glanced across each other's time and again on that long-ago Bonfire Night. The tension between them had built until it had been virtually unbearable, until at long last Jamie had finally taken charge of the situation and grasped her hand firmly in his.

And from the moment they had touched...

Fireworks.

"I've got a better idea about where to find supper."

Jamie could hardly believe what he was saying. It was the smooth line of an assured lover. A man confident that if he made a move, he'd win the girl.

Was that why he was doing this? Trying to win back his girl?

A harebrained idea, given how it had ended last time. With him throwing himself into work as if it were the only thing keeping him alive. Neglecting his family. His home. Not that he'd ever been one to be house-proud. But what Beatrice didn't know was that the house of their dreams was sitting as empty as the day he'd bought it. If she'd waited just one more day to tell him her news...

There were so many ifs.

Beatrice was looking up at him, thick lashes framing those perfect chocolate-pot-colored eyes of hers, posy held up to her nose, cheeks still flushed with the remains of a blush. Her lips were nestled among the flower petals and every bit as soft. *Perfection.*

A shot of heat seized his chest as the memory of that stolen kiss worked its way back into his blood flow. Beatrice had made him feel more alive than anyone else in the world and when she'd gone—

Was it foolish or wise to hold on to his pride? Resist what came so naturally?

"What's this idea, then?" she asked, twisting back and forth like a schoolgirl behind her fistful of flowers. "Or are you going to keep it a secret?"

Excitement—or maybe it was just the fairy lights—twinkled in her eyes. She'd always loved an adventure. He had no idea what she got up to in her spare time here. Just went home, he imagined. He'd definitely not seen her in the square since the night he'd pulled her into his arms and reminded himself of everything he should have long forgotten.

She'd played with his heart.

And he'd lived to see another day.

What was that saying he'd learnt from one of the friars on the island?

He heard the monk's voice as clearly as he could now hear the diva launching into a beautiful aria by Puccini.

Che per vendetta mai non sanò piaga.

Revenge never healed a wound.

A renewed sense of purpose gripped his heart, then released it, repurposing the sensation into the first shot of pure happiness he'd felt in years. He would have to say goodbye to Beatrice at the end of the summer. That much was sure. But this time he would do it with his pride intact. His heart at rest.

"As we've lost Teo for the evening, we're going to be heading up on the chairlifts." Jamie gave her an appraising look as she gamely weighed up his proposal. "But first I think we'd better stop at one of these stalls. Get you a shawl. It might be a bit chillier where we're headed."

Beatrice's eyebrows rose. "Should I be worried? You're not going to lock me up in a cave or anything, are you?"

"That all depends," he countered, channeling the man he knew was buried somewhere deep in her heart.

"On..." Beatrice's smile was growing bigger. They'd done this dozens, if not scores of times before. Explored. Found new places to show each other. Watched the delight unfold.

"On how much you like cheese!"

Something flickered in her eyes. Indecision? A hint of reserve? That wasn't like her. To hold back.

Just as quickly it was gone.

"As long as there's plenty of hard cheese. It's my favorite these days."

"Not 'the gooier the better'?"

She shook her head and ran a fingertip along one of the flower buds in her posy before dropping it to her side. "No. I'm all about good old hard Italian cheeses these days. I'll leave the gooey ones to the French."

"All right, then." He offered her his arm again. "I see slivers of pecorino and shavings of parmigiana in your future."

He pressed his hand on top of Beatrice's when she tucked it back into the inner crook of his elbow—with greater comfort than earlier in the evening, he noticed.

A shard of warning sounded in his mind.

This is only temporary. This is putting the past to rest. If you can do this without kissing her, you can do anything.

By the time they got to the stall selling locally woven cashmere scarves, Bea was beginning to feel as if she'd stepped back in time.

Jamie was the very embodiment of… Well…*himself*. She knew it seemed ridiculous, but the man she'd fallen in love with was right here beside her, as if nothing had happened, no hearts had been broken… As if their lives had carried on as one.

And it felt so right. *Real*, even.

Would it be tempting fate if she just allowed herself one night of pure happiness?

"Here—what do you think of this one?" Jamie tugged a beautiful evergreen wrap from the midst of one of the piles. In one fluid move he unfurled the downy, soft cashmere and swirled it around her shoulders.

She brushed her cheek against the fabric, reveling in how silky it felt against her skin. There were fine threads of cream and mixed pastel colors woven throughout the scarf, giving it a greater depth…almost as if it were a wildflower meadow in the midst of an evergreen glade, seen from afar.

Jamie lifted a corner of the scarf and tested it along his own cheek. "Does it do the trick?"

A whirl of heat swirled around her as a vivid memory of Jamie lifting her fingers first to his cheek and then to his lips for a light kiss. Something he'd be doing right now if she hadn't bowed to her mother's wishes…

The tiny slice of space between them filled with warmth—the exchange of body heat melding them from two bodies into one—But there was another body. A tiny little baby she would love with all her heart.

A wash of longing poured through her so powerfully she almost lost her balance. If that baby was Jamie's…

She began to dig inanely through her handbag for her wallet. "It's perfect."

"Trade you for my coat?" Jamie was already handing a couple of notes to the vendor.

"You don't have to do that."

Why *was* he doing this? Each act of selflessness on his part only served to compound the ache of longing she felt for him. How was she ever going to channel the willpower to leave?

"Of course I do," he countered taking his change and helping Bea slip his jacket from her shoulders and rearrange the wrap.

The wrap was beautiful but, ridiculous as it seemed, just those handful of minutes wearing his jacket had felt heaven-sent.

"Jamie, honestly. You don't owe me a thing."

If anything, she owed him… Well, she owed him the truth for one thing, but since his knowing she still loved him would probably only make things worse, keeping her lips sealed was her self-assigned atonement.

"A beautiful woman deserves beautiful things. I never bought you beautiful things before."

"I never wanted *things*," she chided softly. "You know that."

He nodded. "Even so…"

His eyes flicked away, as if something else had caught his attention, but it was more likely for the same reason she found herself unable to hold eye contact with him for more than a few seconds at a time.

Too painful. Too perfect.

Two years ago the most natural thing for her to do would have been to go up on tiptoe. Give him a kiss. Swipe at his nose with her finger and tip his forehead to hers. The time they'd spent just breathing each other in…*otherworldly*.

She tugged at the edges of her sundress, fighting the instinctive urge to give her belly one of the protective strokes she so often found herself doing these days. A harsh reminder that she was still keeping secrets from Jamie.

Holding back this precious information was almost physically painful. Because Jamie had once been her port of call for all her thoughts. No editing. No filter. The only person in the world she'd been able to be herself with. None of the frippery and trappings that went with being a princess.

Her brother had cornered the royal market for their family. Why hadn't her mother been content just to let her go?

"Look at these tomatoes!"

She smiled, grateful for the change of tack as Jamie steered her toward a table groaning under a mountain of tomatoes bigger than both her fists joined together.

Beautiful deep reds, oranges and yellows. There were even some green tiger-striped fruits, all piled up in a magnificent display of the summer's early harvest.

"The North of Italy is far more generous than the North of England. My mother wouldn't believe her eyes!"

"My mother wouldn't know what a whole tomato looked like!" Bea shot back.

Both of them laughed, then said as one, *"La donna è mobile!"*

Woman—in this case her mother—was a fickle thing to be sure.

Jamie had heard more than enough stories of Beatrice's mother only deigning to recognize food if it was on a plate at a Michelin-starred restaurant. Deconstructed this... Reimagined that... If it wasn't à la mode, it wasn't in her mother's sphere of what existed in the world.

But she'd never been fickle about her choice for Bea's

intended. Her daughter would marry a prince. Such lofty heights for her white-coated daughter, more content in one-use-only surgical scrubs than a ball gown.

"And those peaches. They're the size of a house! They'd fill up the fruit bowl nicely."

Jamie pointed toward another vendor handing out slices of golden fruit dripping with summer sweetness. In true Italian style he was peeling them, then giving slice after juicy slice to wide-eyed passers-by.

Though she was tempted, the Italian in her had to insist upon being a purist.

"As you may recall, any *true* Italian would know these are from the South. Sicilian peaches are... Mmm..." A soft breeze carried a waft of perfumed air her way and suddenly she was ravenous. A pregnancy craving? Or just good old-fashioned hunger? She forced herself to regroup. "Their presence here is near enough sacrilege!"

"Like mayonnaise on chips?" Jamie parried, happily accepting a slice of freshly peeled peach from the farmer and making a big show of enjoying the sweet fruit, rubbing his belly to great effect as he swallowed it down.

"*Che schifo!*" Bea shuddered away the thought of gooey mayonnaise. "*Anyone* who knows how to eat a chip properly knows it's salt and vinegar if eaten with fish—but only by the seaside—or tomato ketchup if eaten with a hamburger."

Jamie smiled as she recited by rote the "training session" he'd given her. Bea had never eaten a chip in her life. She'd been astonished to hear they'd been a menu staple in his house when he was growing up.

"*A man needs to keep up his strength when he goes down the mines...*"

Jamie's father had been deadly serious when he'd told

her that. Right before sending his wife a saucy wink as he picked up a jug and near enough drowned his potatoes in the thick pool of shiny gravy Jamie's mother had magicked up from the small joint of beef she'd prepared.

That had been a heavenly afternoon.

One of only two times she'd met his parents.

Once it had been just in passing...it might have been that Bonfire Night. Near enough every house had emptied into the town square that night. And, of course, when they'd gone over for traditional Sunday lunch.

Not one ounce of shame had crossed Jamie's features when he brought her to the humble two-up two-down brick house in the middle of a seemingly endless swathe of similar homes. Ironic, considering she'd been too mortified even to consider taking him to her parents' palazzo.

One of the most lavish in the whole of Venice, It was her mother's work, of course. Her father would have been content with simpler furnishings. Less gilding. More wood. Less ostentation. More comfort. He often said a happy wife meant a happy life. It had been the spirit with which she thought she'd approach her arranged marriage. A happy husband meant...

Hmm... Maybe that was the problem.

Nothing really rhymed with husband.

James, on the other hand...

Blame. Shame. Tame. Flame.

She bit down on the inside of her cheek. Maybe that wasn't such a good comparison.

"C'mon—over here, you. No wandering off just yet. You're not getting away that easily." Jamie turned to her, a broad smile on his lips, a second slice of peach pinched gently between his thumb and index finger. "Why not try living dangerously?"

When their gazes connected it was as if he'd flicked a switch, blurring everything around them. All Bea was aware of was the light shining in Jamie's forest green eyes. The tempting slice of peach he was holding between them. His lips just beyond. Lips she knew would taste of peach juice and pure male strength...

He was a rock. He'd been *her* rock. And from the moment she'd left him she had felt more adrift in the world than at any other time in her life.

He slipped the slice of fruit between her parted lips, and for just one incredibly sensual moment her tongue and lips connected with his fingertip. The old Bea would have drawn it into her mouth, given it a swirl with her tongue, grasped the rest of his hand in hers so that she could taste the drops of peach juice on each of his fingertips. She would have met his gaze without a blink of shame, her body growing warm with desire as each second passed.

But she had no claim on him now. No right even to think the decadently sexual thoughts, let alone act on them.

As if reading her mind—or perhaps reminding her of where she stood—Jamie turned away, accepted an antiseptic wipe from the peach vendor, swiped his hands clean of the moment and threw it in the bin.

He turned back to her and smiled, as if they'd just been discussing the weather. "And how did little Beatrice become so au fait with the fruits and vegetables of the world?"

"My...my father, of course." She stumbled awkwardly over the words, and most likely failed miserably to cover the ache of longing she felt for him by adding a jaunty elbow in the ribs. "You know that."

"Yes, I do." Jamie nodded, his lower lip jutting out

for a moment, her comment having clearly hit an invisible target. "And there are a lot of things I don't know."

In equal parts Bea felt consumed by a wash of guilt and the powerful urge to tell him everything.

About the pregnancy.

About the separate bedrooms she'd insisted upon prior to agreeing to move into her ex-fiancé's palazzo because something in her just hadn't been ready to give herself to him physically.

The relief when her best friend had blown the whistle at the wedding.

The first full breath of air she had drawn after the wedding dress had dropped from her shoulders, then her hips, and plummeted to the floor in a huge flounce of silk and tulle. Part of her had wanted to shred it to pieces. The other half had just wanted to leave. Which was precisely what she'd done.

Only that time it hadn't hurt at all. Not even close to the searing pain she'd felt when she'd left Jamie.

With Marco, she had felt backed into a corner. Trapped by ancestral duty. Or perhaps, more accurately, by the little girl hoping, for once, to win her mother's approval. The more she thought about it, the more astonishing it was that Jamie had been able to rise above it now. Not just treating her civilly, but pretty much acting as if nothing had happened.

No. She gave her head a shake, knowing she hadn't pinned it down right. Jamie was better than ordinary old "civil." He was treating her with respect. Grace. Chivalry.

"All right, there?" Jamie bent down as he spoke.

Another reminder of his thoughtfulness. Her ex-fiancé wouldn't have noticed if she'd fallen silent, talked too much or even started dancing like a chimpanzee.

She nodded, doing her best to focus on Jamie's hand as he pointed out the small passageway across the square. If she turned to him now he'd see tears in her eyes.

"You feeling up to plunging through the crowds?"

"*Si.* Absolutely." Her voice sounded bright. Too bright. But it would have to do.

Being with Jamie… It was like being whole again.

But he was the one thing she would have to learn to live without.

A few minutes of weaving through the crowd later, they turned onto a small road with lighter foot traffic than the square.

"You sure you're still up for this? It may take an hour or two." Jamie turned and gave Beatrice a smile.

Her reaction was a bit delayed. As if her thoughts had been somewhere else entirely.

"Oh…" She tugged her new wrap around her shoulders a bit more snugly. Protectively. "An hour or two of cheese? Hmm… Let me think…"

Her hips swiveled back and forth beneath the light cotton of her dress. It was too easy to picture her long, slender legs beneath the fabric. The gentle curve and jut of her hip bones. His hands swooping along the smooth expanse of her belly before he slid them along the length of her thighs…

A tug of desire eclipsed his pragmatism. The number of times he'd pulled her to him, snuggled her slender hips between his own, fitted her to him as if they'd been made for each other…and then teased her away, holding her at arm's length, reminding her of the long shifts at the hospital they each had in store.

"We have all the time in the world to make love," he'd murmured into her ear, again and again.

Now he knew it hadn't been enough. A lifetime of Beatrice wouldn't have sated his desire for her. And he'd only had those two precious years.

"You know…you're right." He did a quick about-face, no longer able to go through with the charade of being "just friends."

She looked up at him, startled.

"About what?"

"It'll take too long. The chairlift and all. I'm not even certain they'll be open with the Midsummer Festa."

"What?"

"The *enoteca*. I've been up there a few times when I've needed a break from the clinic. A glass of wine… A bit of cheese and bread… It's lovely."

And it was. But going up there with Beatrice the way he was feeling… Chances were he'd tell her how he really felt. And he couldn't let her have access to that part of his heart. Not anymore.

"It was a silly idea in the first place. There's plenty to eat here. And you said yourself you weren't in the mood for gooey cheese. Um…what if we…" He looked past her to the square—busier now than when they'd left it, if such a thing was possible.

"Actually, Jamie…"

He knew that tone. The polite one. The well-mannered Principessa backing out of an awkward situation.

"I'm feeling a bit tired. Perhaps I'll just head off. We can go to the *enoteca* another time. Rain check?"

When he looked back at Beatrice she appeared to him as if through an entirely new prism…fragile. Delicate. Two things he'd never imagined her to be.

Feminine, yes. But for every ounce of grace and beauty she possessed he'd always thought of her as having a solid core of fierce intellect and passion. More than enough to stand on her own two feet.

"I'm happy to walk you back to your apartment. You're not too far from the clinic?"

"*Si*, an apartment in one of the *baita*." She held up her hand in the stop position and took a step away from him. "Don't worry about walking me. There's a little café downstairs. I'll grab something there. I could do with a quiet stroll."

Guilt swept through him. He wanted to pull her to him, wanted to push her away. "I don't mind, honestly."

From the look she shot him it was pretty easy to tell *she* did.

Hell. There wasn't exactly a guidebook on how to deal with the love of your life reappearing just when you thought you'd pulled yourself together.

"Thanks for the wrap." She threw the words over her shoulder, smoothing her hand along the fine cashmere, her feet already picking up speed. "It's really beautiful. *Buonanotte.*"

He said the same words as he spun in the opposite direction, felt the hard lines of a man trying to keep his head above water returning to his face.

It wouldn't be a *good* night. He felt it in his bones. It would be restless. His pillow would bear the brunt of his frustration.

He shifted course, taking a sharp turn into a *calle* that would deposit him at the only place he could burn off this excess energy for the greater good. *Work.*

Sure, it hadn't worked out well at Northern General, but one of the reasons he'd chosen a clinic for tourists was the limited chance of getting attached. People were in, out, referred, transferred, never to be seen again. Only rarely did they see a patient twice. Enough times to start caring? Just about never.

He gave his hands a quick rub, forcing the doctor back into this man he'd not seen for a while. Peach slices? Cashmere wraps? Those were things lovers shared. Not platonic colleagues.

He steered his thoughts away from the glow he'd seen in Beatrice's eyes when he'd slipped the peach between her gently parted lips. There were bound to be people who enjoyed a bit too much high-altitude revelry on a night like tonight. Sprains, dehydration, the occasional fallout from a silly brawl over the last piece of prosciutto... They would keep him busy. The staff at the clinic wouldn't think anything of him showing up to relieve them for an hour or so.

A huge boom sounded not too far-off. He looked up to the sky, his eyes adjusting to the darkness and then the explosion of colored lights.

Instantly he dropped his gaze and sought out Beatrice's pixie cut. She should be seeing this. They should be watching it together. Hands brushing. Shots of heat igniting his every nerve ending as if he was discovering what it meant to be a man for the very first time.

He looked up into the sky one last time then turned back toward the clinic with a shrug.

Fireworks.

They weren't all they were cracked up to be.

CHAPTER SEVEN

BEA KNEW SHE should be at home, but restless sleep was worse than a bit of focused work, right? Just the idea of going back to her lonely apartment, with its plain single bed, and no green-eyed pediatricians lying in wait to pull up the covers and have a good snuggle...

"Are you sure you're happy to cover for me?" Rhianna handed over a stethoscope, not even waiting for an answer.

"You said a couple of hours, right?"

She smiled as Rhianna turned her Irish brogue up another notch and launched into an assurance that, with heaven as her witness, she'd be back before Cinderella had a blessed thing to be worried about.

Bea pursed her lips and gave them a little wriggle. The fairy-tale princess reference wasn't lost on her, but a quick glance to Rhianna, who was busy slicking on a fresh layer of lip gloss and lavishing her lashes with a thick coat of mascara showed she was being silly.

Stop being so sensitive!

Bea sat down on the long wooden bench and undid the straps of her sandals to change them for her sneakers, surprised to see her feet were a tiny bit swollen. Pregnancy symptom? Her mind raced through all the worst-case scenarios swollen feet at this point in a pregnancy might mean, then gave her head a sharp shake.

Probably just too much walking in flat sandals and having all her hopes and dreams plummet to the soles of her feet. Or something like that anyway.

"Ooh!" She put on a cockney accent and repeated something she'd heard a teenager say the other day as she gave her feet a rub. "My dogs are *barking*!"

"Hold on, there." Rhianna ducked her head down so she was level with Beatrice's eyes. Quite the feat now she'd popped on impossibly high cork-heeled sandals. "Is that you backing out already?" She swiftly pulled out her mobile phone and held it at arm's length. "Am I going to have to send a text to the lads and tell them no?"

"The lads?" Beatrice raised her eyebrows. She'd heard of a few summer romances beginning to blossom among the collection of seasonal staff, but...*lads*?

"Sure!" A blush appeared on Rhianna's cream and freckled complexion. "There's a whole squad of 'em over here—from Denmark, I think. They're all blond and rugged, and I'm sure half of 'em are called Thor."

"Thor?" Beatrice intoned drily.

"Or Erik." Rhianna struck what she guessed was meant to be a Viking pose, waved away Bea's disbelief, then adroitly twisted one of the male doctors' shaving mirrors to her advantage, lowering her eyelids to half-mast to receive a whoosh of eyeshadow as she continued her story. "They're up here on some sort of epic paragliding trip, or some such. One of them was in earlier today. He had a right old bash on his thigh from where he'd landed on some gravel instead of the meadow he'd been aiming for."

She gave a swift eye roll. Clearly the injury hadn't stood in the way of a bit of flirtation.

"Either way, they're all down at the piazza and looking mad keen for some company, if you get my drift. A couple of the chalet girls and I are going to play Eeny-Meeny-Miny-Mo!" Her eyebrows did a swift little jig as a naughty grin appeared on her lips. "I'll tell you what, Dr. Jesolo. They're a right handsome bunch of lads. If there's any left over, I'll be sure to keep one for you when I come back in."

Despite herself, Bea laughed. She'd never really been that boy crazy, but she certainly remembered the giddy feeling of looking forward to a night out…the swirls of frisson…the nineteen trips to her wardrobe to make sure she'd put on just the right skirt or blouse or dress, only to turn away from the mirror and start all over again.

With Jamie it had never really been like that, it had just been…*easy.* Sure, she'd wanted to look her best, her sexiest, her most desirable, but he'd always had a remarkable way of making her feel beautiful. Even at the end of a day's long shift, when her hair had been all topsy-turvy, her makeup long gone and the shadows under her eyes had predicted a need for lots of sleep.

Quickly she finished tying her shoe and pressed herself up from the bench.

A bit too quickly as a hit of dizziness swamped her.

"Whoa! You all right there, girl?" Rhianna swooped in and steadied her. "You've not been out on the lash, have you?"

"No." Bea shrugged herself away from her colleague, trying her best not to look ungrateful. "Just got up a bit too quickly, that's all."

"Would you like me to get you some water or anything? A wee lie-down before I head off?"

"No." Bea shook her head firmly. "Absolutely not. Off you go. Have a good night, all right?"

Rhianna tipped her head to the side, her multicolored eye shadow on full display as she gave Bea a sidelong glance. "You're absolutely sure?"

"Absolutely sure about what?"

Both women turned sharply as the door to the locker room swung open.

Bea's heart swooped, then cinched tight.

One glimpse into those familiar green eyes told her she might be better off saying no.

"Dr. Jesolo here's a lifesaver!" Rhianna jumped in.

"Oh?"

If she'd thought Jamie had flinched at the sight of her he was showing no signs of any discomfort now. Just the cool reserve of a man who...

Wait a minute.

"Aren't you meant to be off tonight?" Rhianna veered off topic. "*And* you?" She wheeled around, her index finger wiggling away as if she were divining water instead of looking for answers. "What are the two of you doing here when the whole of Torpisi is out celebrating the longest day of the year?"

Collectively they reacted as a huge boom of fireworks sounded in the distance. Well, not Jamie. He was still frozen in the doorway, as if someone had sucked every last inch of joy out of him. *Terrific.* No guessing that her turning up for a few hours of burying her head in the sand had ruined his own plan to do the exact same thing.

Great minds...*per carita*!

Rhianna was the first to recover, pulling a sky blue pashmina out of her locker and swirling it around her shoulders. "Dr. Jesolo—this is your last chance. I'm telling you it's good *craic* out there."

"*Craic?*" Nice to have a reason to look away from

Jamie. She hadn't known how powerful his not-happy glare was before.

A shard of guilt pierced through his skull. *Because you didn't bother to stick around.*

"Sure, you know good *craic* when you see it, Bea. A party. A good time—fun."

She took a quick glance between the two of them, clearly immune to the thick band of what-the-heck-are-you-doing-here? thrumming between them.

"What with Dr. Coutts being here when I guess he doesn't have to be they can spare you, sure? This is grand. You don't have to cover me at all—right, Dr. Coutts? You're all right here, aren't you? Happy to let the lovely ladies go out for a wee bit of gallivanting?"

Rhianna looked up to Jamie, seemingly undaunted by his unchanged expression. And then, just like that, it brightened.

"What a delightful idea." He unleashed a warm smile on Rhianna. One of those smiles Bea had used to get when she'd suggested they either stay on at the hospital for a couple of extra hours, just to talk through some cases, or go to bed early.

Ouch.

"Don't let me stand in the way of some gallivanting. Just the thing for a pair of young maidens on Midsummer Day."

"That's exactly what I was saying." Rhianna turned to Bea, arms crossed over her generous bosom with an I-told-you-so expression on her face. "C'mon, girl. What's the point of being up here in this rural idyll if you don't run into the arms of a Viking?"

"Oh, it's Vikings tonight, is it, Rhianna?" Jamie dropped her a playful wink, clearly no stranger to the young doctor's quest for a summer romance. Or seven.

"Please. Feel free to go, Dr. Jesolo. We've got more than enough staff. Unless you were hoping for an early night?"

Bea opened her mouth to protest, then clamped it tight shut again. Where she should have felt a sting of hurt that Jamie was trying to get rid of her, she decided to take up the gauntlet from another direction. She wasn't the only one who'd told a fib in order to burn off some energy at the clinic.

"Actually, I was really looking forward to a few hours here. Special research on a—" she quickly sought a reason from the ether "—on a dissertation I'm writing."

"A dissertation?" Disbelief oozed from Rhianna's response. "What are you wasting time writing a dissertation on when you could be having fun? Isn't that the point of working up here?"

Bea's gaze flicked from Rhianna to Jamie. No way was she getting cornered into going out for a bit of *fun*!

Um...wait a minute.

"Dr. Coutts?" A nurse stuck her head in the doorway. "We've got someone I think you should see right away."

"I'll go." Bea pulled on her white coat, ignoring Rhianna's plaintive sigh and mumblings about leading horses to water—or something like that anyway—and swept past Jamie.

But not before getting a full lungful of Northern-British sexpot disguised as a surly doctor. *Humph!* She'd have to start holding her breath when she passed him from now on.

"I'm pretty certain *I* was the doctor requested."

Jamie was matching Beatrice step for step as she hotfooted it toward the waiting room.

"It doesn't matter, really," the nurse said, jogging a

bit to keep up with the pair of them. "It's a lady. Mid-thirties, I'm guessing. She's presenting with severe gastrointestinal pain. I just thought—"

"I'll get it."

Jamie and Beatrice spoke in tandem, each with a hand on the swinging doors leading to the waiting room, their eyes blazing with undisguised sparks of frustration.

"What shall I tell the patient?" asked the befuddled nurse.

"Tell her I'll see her."

Again they spoke as one.

And then, as quickly as the fire had flared between them it shape-shifted into laughter at the ridiculousness of it all.

"You go ahead." Jamie swept a hand in the direction of the waiting room.

"No, really, I'm fine—"

A scream of pain roared past the double doors, jarring them out of their increasingly ridiculous standoff.

"Two heads are better than one?"

Jamie enjoyed the spark of recognition in Beatrice's eyes at his roundabout invitation to join him. It had been his oft-used excuse for pulling her into a consultation back at Northern General.

The adage still held true, and immediately dissolved any tension between them.

When they pushed into the room a flame-haired woman was staggering from a chair, one hand clamped to her back, one clutching her stomach. "Please help me! I can't stand it any longer!"

"Right you are, madam—oops!" Jamie swept under one of her arms, only just stopping her from falling to the ground.

"I want to lie down!" the woman howled. "Or crawl. Or *something*. Just make it stop!"

From her accent he could tell she was North American. There was a wedding ring on her finger. The flesh was puffed up around it. It looked like swelling. Water retention?

A quick glimpse down and he saw shiny white tennis shoes on her feet. The American tourist telltale. Not Canadian, then. He'd keep his maple syrup and moose jokes to himself.

"She had some of those cheese-stuffed flowers." A rusty-haired man with the most remarkable sky blue eyes rushed over from the desk, where he had been filling out some paperwork. "Marilee, honey, I *told* you not to try the flowers. They're probably hallucinogenic."

"Do you mean the pumpkin flowers?" Beatrice asked gently.

"Jesse, I'm going to *kill* you for making me try those things—ooh! Make. It. *Stop!*" She doubled over again and her husband tucked himself under her other arm.

"Those are the ones," Jesse said, sending quick looks to Jamie and Beatrice, his gaze taking on a dreamy aspect as he continued to speak. "They were deep-fried. Filled with some sort of soft cheese and a truffled honey. We were at the *enoteca*. The one up at the top of the chairlift. Have you been there?"

He looked at Beatrice, who shook her head and gave him a rueful smile before looking behind her—presumably for a wheelchair.

"I'll tell you… I thought they were delicious. I'm Joseph, by the way, though Marilee here calls me Jesse. Her very own Jesse James," he continued with a laugh, giving a quick squeeze to Beatrice's arm, seemingly oblivious to his wife's pain. He let go to shoot a pair of invisible revolvers, only just catching his wife as she stumbled and unleashed another despairing howl.

"I'll get a wheelchair," Beatrice said in a low voice to Jamie.

Jamie nodded, then stopped her with a hand on her elbow as she turned to go. "Make it a gurney." He glanced around until he found the nurse who'd signed the woman in. "Name?"

"Marilee James."

"All right, Marilee. We're just going to get you—oops! Easy, there, I've got you. Over this way, love."

Beatrice had magicked a gurney out of the ether and was already pushing it through the waiting room door.

"Now, if I can just get my colleague to…" He flicked his eyes from Bea to Marilee, which, true to form, Beatrice understood as "Come over here and help me get her up on the gurney because the husband's not much use."

After a handful of awkward maneuvers, the sturdy but fit-looking woman was up and on the gurney.

"Mrs. James—"

"Call me Marilee. I can't stand the formal stuff… *Ooo-eee*… It hurts. Do you think it was the clams, Jesse?" She reached back and grabbed her husband's hand as he tried to keep up with the moving gurney, squeezing it until it was white. "We should never have had seafood up here in the mountains. This is *not* the vacation of my dreams you promised!"

"I know, my little cherry pie. But we'll get it right. I'm sure they have loads of medication they can give you here for the pain." He shot anxious looks in Jamie's direction as he pulled the gurney.

They did. But only if they knew what was going on.

"Have you been sick at all? Vomiting, diarrhea?" Jamie tipped his head toward an open exam area. "Let's get her in there for an abdominal exam. Can you call up to X-ray? We might need a—"

Marilee's scream drowned out his instructions to Beatrice, who stood, calm as she always was in a crisis. He could almost see the medical terminology whizzing past her eyes as her mind did its usual high-speed race through possible prognoses.

"She hasn't been sick," said Jessie. "Not at all. And we only had the clams about half an hour ago. Lovely, they were. All sorts of garlic and some kinda green thingy. A little chopped-up herb."

"Appendicitis?"

Jamie threw the word softly to Beatrice, who nodded one of those could-be nods and then parried with a whispered "Spleen?"

"No, it wasn't that. Something more like parsley, but Italian-style. Mountain grass?" Jesse looked to his wife, who answered him with an I-don't-know glare.

"Are you having any trouble passing wind, Mrs.— Marilee?"

As if to prove she wasn't, the woman rolled to the side and rather dramatically passed a healthy gust of wind.

Beatrice turned to Jamie and rather spectacularly managed a straight face as she said, "Perhaps passing wind isn't the trouble after all. Can you tell us where the feeling is most acute, Marilee?"

She put a hand on the woman's belly, doing her best to work around the fact Marilee seemed unable to remain stationary for more than a few seconds.

"My back!" Marilee plunged a hand behind her and then quickly grabbed one of Jamie's hands and one of Beatrice's and dragged them to the center of her belly, pulling her knees up to her stomach as she did so. "Oh, my sweet blazes. It's wet. I feel *wet*! Am I bleeding?"

Jamie shot Beatrice a worried look. This was more than a case of gastroenteritis.

"Pseudocyesis?" Beatrice whispered, tucking her shoulders down and dropping a quick shrug.

False pregnancy was a far reach, but...

"Psuedo *what*? Don't bother whispering. Little Bat Ears, my Jesse calls me." Marilee tightened her grip on Jamie's hand.

"That's right, my little sugar pie." Jesse beamed from the far end of the gurney, his eyes suddenly widening. "Oh, my blue-blooded ancestors! Marilee, your dress is all wet."

"Marilee?" Jamie quickly untucked his hand from hers, seeing the situation for what it was in an instant. "Why didn't you tell us you were pregnant?"

"Uh..." Jesse held up his hands—minus the invisible pistols this time—and started backing up. "Hang on there a minute, Doc. My Marilee may be a lot of things. But pregnant is most certainly *not* one of them."

Marilee pushed herself up on her elbows and shot wild-eyed looks between each doctor, her cheeks pinkening as the rest of her face paled.

"Let's get you lying back down here—all right, Marilee." Jamie moved to the side of the gurney, gently pressing on the woman's shoulders and only losing eye contact to indicate to Beatrice that she should do a vaginal exam.

Beatrice quickly shifted down to the foot of the gurney, snapping on a pair of gloves as she went, and deftly blocked Jesse's view.

After a surreptitious glimpse, and the most infinitesimal of nods to Jamie to tell him that he'd made the right call, she turned to Mr. Jesse James and began to guide him to a chair adjacent to his wife's gurney.

Jamie replaced Beatrice, barely containing his astonishment at what he saw. Thank goodness Beatrice had stayed behind. He'd need someone who could keep their head on their shoulders for this one.

"How're your midwifery skills, Dr. Jesolo?"

"All right." Beatrice threw a look over her shoulder as she gowned up.

Jamie grinned. "That's good. Because Mrs. James is crowning."

"What the heck are you people on about?" Marilee cut in. "I just ate some funny cheesy flowers, is all!"

"Marilee, I think you'd better lie back and ask your husband if you can hold his hand." Jamie kept his voice as calm as possible. "It looks like the pair of you are about to become parents."

He shot a look over to Beatrice, who was popping on a fresh pair of gloves and unfurling a disposable surgical gown.

"Doctor?" Bea held out the gown for him.

He swiftly stepped into the gown and for one brief moment their gazes caught and meshed as if they were back at Northern General. Madly in love. Meeting challenge after challenge with dexterity and skill.

And that was when she knew she had never—not for one second—stopped loving him.

"There is no chance at all there is a baby inside me," Marilee was busy explaining. "We've been married over eighteen years. Exchanged rings the first day we were legal, then spent the next seventeen trying to have a baby. Isn't that right, Jesse? Then last year we decided to give up. It was just going to be you and me. Why, I think the last time we—"

She stopped midsentence and reached out for her husband's hand.

"Do you remember the last time *before* the last time? Not last night's last time, but the *other* last time?"

"Sugar bean, I don't know what you're talking about—unless you mean the last time we—oh... Do you mean...the whipped cream night?"

"Mmm-hmm... Thanksgiving?" She teased the memory up a bit more, her voice dipping an octave, to a lower, more sultry tone, saying something about pumpkin pie and cinnamon-hot spices before lurching back up with a sharply pitched gasp.

As hard as she tried, Bea couldn't contain the crazy feeling of sisterhood she felt with Marilee. Against all the odds, the American woman was going to have a child!

She'd be doing the same in a few months' time. Granted, she'd be on her own—Jamie wouldn't be there, asking if she'd eaten bad clams, and there would be the press to contend with eventually because she wouldn't be able to hide away forever—but...a *baby*! The explosive joy of it warmed her chest and recharged her, as if she'd just woken up from a perfect night's sleep.

"You're going to be all right, Marilee. If you thought about this for seventeen years, you'll have read a fair few books on what to expect."

Wide-eyed, Marilee looked up, panting through a hit of pain and doing her best to nod.

"I've read 'em all. And nearly each one of them mentioned getting painkillers. That's all I was hoping for when we came stumbling in here. Just a couple of pills to take the edge off and then we were going to get back for the rest of the fireworks—weren't we, honey bun?"

"Sure were, sugar bee. Now, look what you've done! Thrown everything all off-kilter. We're going to miss the grand finale."

"I think you two are going to have one exciting grand finale of your own to the evening," Jamie said. "You're fully dilated, Marilee. This baby's going to be here in the next few minutes."

Bea glanced across at him, enjoying the warmth of his smile. She knew he loved babies every bit as much as she did. He hadn't been the least bit shy about telling her he hoped to be a father to a fleet of little ones.

It wouldn't be fair to ask...

"Dr. Coutts, are you sure you're seeing everything straight? Are you *positive* it's a baby?"

Bea had to stem a rush of emotion as Marilee's voice caught and grew jagged as she well and truly began to take on board how enormous a turn her life was about to take.

"How could you not have known?" Jesse threw up his hands. "I thought you were meant to throw up or go off your favorite foods or something?"

"I most certainly did no such thing," Marilee shot back indignantly, then went quiet. "Or did I...? I can't remember. Maybe after those oysters on Valentine's Day, but... Jesse James!" She threw the argument back at her husband. "How could *you* not have noticed? Aren't men supposed to be fine-tuned to a woman's breasts getting bigger or something?"

She shot Bea a glance to garner some support for her argument. The best Bea could come up with was a who-knows? face. This was her first surprise pregnancy. She'd certainly heard about them, but... Well, everything about her own pregnancy had been planned down to the microsecond.

Not so much a surprise as a secret... Even if her ex-fiancé had held out until the wedding, he probably would have run for the hills once the baby was born. Perhaps his infertility was nature's way of stating the obvious. The man wasn't meant to be a father. Just as well, he'd hit the road before they'd had to worry about divorce proceedings.

Bea smiled as Marilee grabbed her, then tightened her grip on her hand, pulling her in for a stage-whispered "At least he knows it's his."

"How could I not, my little sugar plum pie? That Thanksgiving dinner was the best..." He looked up to the sky, swiped at the beads of sweat accruing on his forehead. "That was a real doozy."

"I sure do love you, Jesse." Marilee's eyes filled with tears.

"I love you, too, Marilee. There isn't a single other woman on the planet I would have a child with just when I thought we'd have the whole rest of our lives to play."

"You mean—" Marilee's eyes widened. "I guess this *does* take the cliff-jumping trip to Mexico off the agenda for a while."

"We'll get through it, Marilee." Jesse tipped his head down and dropped a kiss on his wife's forehead. "We always do."

As the scene unfolded Bea was finding it harder to keep a check on her emotions. Her family wasn't one of those so-called traditional European families—lavishing each other with kisses and bear hugs and the smother-love Italian mothers in particular were renowned for. Jamie's was. Open arms. Broad, unaffected smiles. Unfettered affection...

All the light she'd felt about her own pregnancy abruptly disappeared into a deep pool of fears.

She'd be a single mother.

Alone.

Her mother was the last person on earth she'd go to for advice. Her nanny would be a better source of wisdom than—

No!

She was going to do this.

But it's scary.

She had to do this.

All on your own.

Bea took a surreptitious glance at the couple, now reaching for each other's hands, trying to grasp the magnitude of what was happening to them, and felt a pure bolt of envy rocket through her.

She could have had this. Maybe not the surprise labor part—but she could have had this with Jamie. She hadn't been sure, but something had told her Jamie had wanted to ask her to marry him. They'd walked past that beautiful old stone house, paused and daydreamed enough times. It would have needed so much work…

"Here you are, Jesse. Why don't you keep your wife's forehead cool with this cloth? And, Marilee? Perhaps we should get a pillow under your head, there."

Bea huffed out a sigh, trying her best to disguise it as a reaction to the misstep she took as she turned away, no longer able to remain neutral as the couple began to shed tears of joy as the news sank in.

She'd misstepped, all right.

In so many ways.

She was—what was it now?—ten weeks along and not one person had noticed a single change in her. Not that there was anything dramatic this early on, but even so… Her breasts were a bit bigger than when she'd first found out. And though she hated to admit it, she was going to have to do some internet-shopping pretty quickly to get some bigger pants.

Bea glanced at Jamie, quietly, deftly at work, sliding a pair of stirrups down from the end of the multi-purpose gurney. She knew it was crazy to look to him for reactions to this pregnancy that had clearly taken this pair by surprise, but she couldn't help wondering what Jamie would think if he found out *she* was pregnant. Keeping it secret had seemed the best thing at the time. The wisest thing. If he were to know, would he—

No. No, he wouldn't. And, no, you shouldn't, Bea silently chastised herself, before realigning her focus to Marilee.

"How about slipping your feet in these, love?" Jamie eased her tennis shoes off, then carefully slipped each foot into a stirrup.

Marilee grinned and giggled at the instruction, and then quickly her features crumpled in agony as another contraction hit. It was a sign for Bea not to get hopeful. She wasn't pregnant with Jamie's baby. And that simple fact made a world of difference.

"You've got a lot to answer for, Jesse James," Marilee hollered, in between biting down on her lip and doing her best to mimic Bea as she started to show her how to control her breath.

"Nice and steady, there, Marilee." She glanced across at Jamie, who gave her a nod. "You ready to start pushing?"

Sweat was trickling from the poor woman's brow. This was a lot of information to take in at once. A dream vacation turning into a—a dream baby? It was definitely the last souvenir the couple had anticipated bringing home from their European journey.

"Shall I get that cloth back in the cool water for you, Jesse?"

"You can get my wife some drugs, is what you can do," Jesse asserted, as if he'd been recalling a TV medical drama and remembering it was *his* turn to demand an epidural.

Jamie, having spread a paper cloth over Marilee's knees, was taking another look. "I'm afraid we're a bit too far along for any painkillers."

"We?" Marilee barked, trying once again to elbow herself up to a seated position. "We are talking about *me*, and *I* think it is high time you gave me some!"

"Breathe. Remember to breathe, Marilee. Just a couple more pushes and we're there."

Jamie ducked behind the blue paper towel, his hand already on the crowning head of the little one. Beatrice had wrapped her hands around Marilee's and was breathing along with her, murmuring words of encouragement.

Every bit of him longed to look across at those dark brown eyes of hers. Share a complicit smile. Revel in all that was yet to come for these soon-to-be-parents. But today was yet another vivid reminder that none of that would be coming for *him*. Falling in love again would be a big enough miracle, let alone having a family with someone who wasn't Beatrice.

"It stings! Really, *really* stings!" Marilee managed through her deep breaths.

"That's a normal sensation to feel. Especially without any painkillers." Jamie put up a hand to stop Marilee's knees from catching his head in a clamp. Given the madness of the situation, it probably would be fitting.

"Can't you give her *anything*?" Jesse was throwing panicked looks between him and his wife, whose face was scrunching up as she bore down for another push. "Gas? Ether? Knock her out with something? I can't stand to see my little sweet honey bear in so much pain!"

"Oh, no—we wouldn't want her to go to sleep now..." Jamie's jaw tensed as he cupped one hand beneath the baby's emerging head.

"Why the hell not? She's in *agony*!"

Jamie's own features tightened as Marilee's scream of primal pain reached epic proportions. Within seconds he was helping the rest of the little form wriggle free, uncoiling the tiniest bit of umbilical cord from its foot, tipping it back to prevent any blood or amniotic fluid from going into his lungs.

And, yes, Beatrice was there, as if he'd summoned her out loud. The same rhythm. The same ability to read his mind. No matter what chaos reigned between the pair of them on a personal level, he knew he could rely on her to be one hundred percent professional.

She gave the baby's mouth and nose a quick suction with a bulb syringe, and then, with the umbilical cord still attached, he reached across and laid the now-crying child on his mother's stomach.

"And miss the birth of your son..."

The Jameses gasped in disbelief, their eyes clouding with tears as they took in the sight of their red-haired son.

"Jesse Junior," Jesse whispered, tickling the tip of his son's teensy nose with his index finger.

"Jesse Walton Junior," Marilee added with an equally

starry-eyed expression, her finger teasing at the clutch of fingers making up her son's miniature fist.

"J. W. Junior. My little boy."

As the couple carried on with their cooing, Jamie quickly clamped the umbilical cord, while Beatrice gave the baby a bit of a wipe to clear some of the vernix from his skin. Jamie could hear her agreeing, that, yes, he was the cutest baby she'd ever seen and, no, she'd never been through anything like this before. Yes, she *did* think he weighed enough, and he *was* long enough. She answered all the questions as calmly as if she'd done this a thousand times before, and as joyfully as if she'd never before experienced the magic of seeing a newborn.

He delivered the placenta and made sure his patient was clear of any cuts or tears.

"Not a one?" Jesse exclaimed, all the while giving his wife the thumbs-up. "That's my girl!"

Bea magicked the baby away to weigh and measure him, and put a little tag on his wrist—even though they had no obstetrics ward in the small clinic, so he would most likely be their only newborn tonight and there was no one to mix him up with.

A hit of longing struck him so suddenly when Beatrice reentered the exam area, holding the swaddled baby in her arms, that he had to turn away. She would see right through him.

Pulling in a draught of air, he swallowed back the sharp sting of emotion. That micromoment couldn't have been more pronounced. He could have sliced each second into a hundred frames. A glimpse into what fatherhood would feel like. Pride. Unchecked love. A bit of fear as to whether he would be able to do the best by his child—and its mother...

He forced himself to turn around again, only to clash

and connect again with Beatrice's dark-eyed gaze. She hadn't moved. Had frozen on the spot as if the moment had been as laden with emotion for her as it had for him.

He felt as if his chest was being crushed, and his heart was barely able to provide the simple pumping action required to keep him alive... Because without Beatrice in his life...

Jesse was walking across the room to retrieve his son. Jamie barely noticed when he elbowed him out of the way.

"Now, you just hand that little whippersnapper over here, Dr. Jesolo. Daddy and Mommy are going to take care of him now."

Bea looked up, her dark lashes beaded with tears, her sole focus on Jamie.

"So..." Jesse looked between the pair of them, "What about the two of you, huh?"

Jamie cleared his throat, tore his gaze away from Beatrice, forcing himself to face reality. "What *about* us?"

"When are you two going to have a child?" Marilee joined in, arms extended toward her husband to regain possession of her newborn.

Jamie hadn't meant to laugh. The idea had been far from ridiculous at one point in their lives. But now? *No*. Children weren't on the menu.

He glanced across at Beatrice, who had backed up against the curtain, her expression stricken as if the question had caught her completely off guard.

Marilee's brow crinkled. "You're obviously together, or you wouldn't have been shooting all those doe-eyed looks at one another when the baby came out, wouldja?"

"Oh, no." Beatrice pulled the curtain back and took another step away from Jamie. "We're not... We're not a couple."

"No!" Jamie shook his head and popped on a smile, as if people were always honing in on the fact that he was just pals with the woman who had smashed his heart into smithereens.

I messed that up a long time ago.

"If you'll excuse me? I'm just going to get a vitamin-K jab for your little one."

When the Jameses raised their eyebrows in alarm he assured them it was standard practice. Nothing to worry about.

When he headed out into the corridor there was no sign of Beatrice.

Being with her, watching her hold that tiny child in her arms was as close a glimpse as he'd get to believing he and Beatrice could start again.

Yes, they had history. And there was a part of him that wasn't sure he'd entirely forgiven her for leaving. Or forgiven himself for breaking his Hippocratic oath by getting too close to his patients. Too emotionally involved.

Which was exactly what he was doing right now. Superimposing someone else's emotions onto his own hollowed-out heart.

He might be able to forgive Beatrice for leaving, but how would he ever be able to trust that she wouldn't do it again? Pick up and leave when her mother unearthed another prince or far-off royal for her to wed in order to uphold the di Jesolo name?

More important… He needed to stop pointing the finger of blame.

He'd had a chance to fight for his true love and he hadn't done it. Had just stood back and watched it happen.

He *deserved* this. Deserved the searing heartache.

The bleak, unfulfilling future as a bachelor... The single bed. The sleepless nights. All in a vainglorious attempt to escape the wretched truth.

He had let her go.

Let her walk out of his life as if she hadn't meant a thing.

It wasn't his place to forgive. He saw that now. It was hers.

CHAPTER EIGHT

"At last!" Teo pulled his head in from the window. "This must be the first day without rain in—what?—a fortnight?"

"Something like that. It's not been the best of summers, has it?"

Jamie gave Teo a clap on the shoulder, before turning around and nearly careening into Beatrice as she went out to the waiting room to fetch a patient.

"Apologies!" He raised his hands and backed off, trying his best to ignore her sidelong look as she slipped through the swinging doors, leaving a trail of fresh linen and honey in her wake.

They might have called a truce, but polite chitchat wasn't making working with Beatrice any easier. If anything, the surprise-baby night had only made him more aware of just how singular a woman she was. An amazing doctor. Kind and generous. Calm in a crisis. Quieter than he remembered her being back in England, when her laughter had been able to bring a room to life. Still every bit as beautiful.

It didn't help that she had taken to life in the village as naturally as dewdrops to a flower petal. She had well and truly blossomed in the past few weeks. There was a lovely pink bloom to her cheeks, and a…a softness about her that complemented her slender figure.

He scribbled out a prescription for a patient he'd just seen—a regular at the clinic owing to his severe asthma, who'd had the temerity to scrunch his face up when he saw Jamie was going to be the doctor and asked for Beatrice instead.

"Such a lovely young woman. Don't you think so, Dr. Coutts?"

The cheek! He'd been there for a year and had yet to have *anyone* request him. Then again…he hadn't exactly been himself. Before or after she'd arrived. And no doubt he'd be a right old curmudgeon when she left. There was no winning at this game.

"Dr. Coutts?" Rhianna held out a tablet to him so he could check another patient's stats.

Jamie started. He'd been staring at Beatrice. *Again.*

"Yes…good." He scanned the stats. "I think she's good to go. Can you give her a couple of extra ice packs for the journey back to the campsite?"

"Will do." Rhianna nodded with a smile. "And Dr. Coutts…?"

Jamie turned away from staring at the platinum blond pixie cut, astonished at how short his attention span was. "Yes—sorry?"

"It's good to see you in—" her eyes traveled over toward Bea "—in such good spirits."

She gave her eyebrows a little happy jig and tossed him a knowing wink as she rejoined the mother and teenage daughter trying out new crutches in the wake of a freshly sprained ankle.

Jamie gave his face a scrub. Was he that transparent? He knew he hadn't been able to hide it at Northern General. Hadn't felt any need. He'd been in love.

He tried shrugging it off. Just because Rhianna was having a torrid summer romance with one of the adventure-tour-group guides it didn't mean every single person in the clinic needed to be floating on air. Someone had to keep his feet firmly grounded. He was *British*! Made of stern stuff. He could make it through the summer without falling in love again. As sure as the sun would hit the horizon every day of the week, he could keep himself emotionally off-limits.

He forced himself to focus on the patients board until, a few minutes later, he found himself unable to drown out the sound of a crying baby.

He turned and saw a mother handing her infant over to Beatrice, who expertly tucked the baby into her hands using *his* "magic trick." The special hold he'd been taught by his mentor that never failed to stop a baby from crying.

Fold the right and then left arm across the child's chest, use an index finger to prop up the little chin and tip the child to a forty-five-degree angle. Place your other hand along its nappy and rock it. A bit like a baby jig, but gently. Slowly. And in... That's right... In just a few seconds a smiley, relaxed baby.

He vividly remembered teaching Beatrice the technique. The light in her eyes when she'd had a success on her first try.

Beatrice looked up, perhaps feeling the weight of his gaze upon her?

And when their eyes met...

Lightning strike.

It never failed to amaze him.

Bea's gaze dropped to the child for just a moment before she returned it to meet his eyes, and in that instant of reconnection he saw something in her he hadn't seen before. Was it—longing for a *child*?

As quickly as their gazes had clicked and meshed, Beatrice's attention was straight back on the mother, discussing the reason for their visit. A rash on the infant's leg, from the looks of things.

"Dr. Coutts?" A nurse was holding out a phone for him as Beatrice disappeared behind the curtain of her cubicle. "You've got a call from 118."

His pulse quickened. The Italian mountain-rescue team.

"This is Dr. Coutts. What's the situation?"

He listened silently as the caller detailed an accident. An accident involving a school group on holiday from England. A massive landslide. A bus. Crushed roof.

Regular medics were en route in the helicopter, but they needed ground crews because of the number of children involved. The fire department was on their way, too, but they needed more medical personnel. Did they have anyone free?

He glanced up at the clock. It was late afternoon. They'd have a few hours of daylight left, and they were precious.

"We've got another shift coming in a couple of hours. For now I can get together a team of three or four. More to follow."

It would have to do.

He quickly called one of the ambulance drivers on the radio to come and meet them at the clinic entrance.

When he turned around Beatrice was waving off her patients—a happy mother and a giggling baby.

"Dr. Jesolo, can you suit up for an emergency rescue?"

If she wasn't keen to participate, she didn't let it

show. Just nodded and headed off to the supplies area. A true professional.

"Dr. Brandisi?" He flicked his thumb in the direction Beatrice was heading. "Suit up. We've got a long night ahead."

Teo gave him a quick, grim nod, finished up with his patient and the pair of them headed off to change.

"Steel yourself," Jamie warned Teo—the most anxious and excited father-to-be he had ever encountered. "This one's full of children."

"Children?" Bea had caught the end of Jamie's warning as she tugged on a red jumpsuit. "What age?"

"A group of eight-year-olds, I think. Hiking holiday. Wilderness skills or something. About twenty-plus counsellors and a few parents."

Jamie's expression was flinty. A sure sign that he was steeling himself from the inside out for the worst-case scenario.

If there was any time she needed to keep her emotions at bay, it was now. Carrying a precious life inside her had not only ramped up her hormones, it had opened up her heart in a way she hadn't imagined possible. As if carrying a child herself had made her a proxy mother to every other child she encountered until she could hold her own beautiful baby in her arms.

"Fatalities?"

Jamie gave a sharp nod. "Definitely the driver. Thrown through the front window on impact. Lacerate carotid." He huffed out a tight breath. "We should get an update on our way up there. Have you all got your run bags?"

Teo shouldered his large emergency travel bag and picked up Bea's bag with his free hand.

"Don't worry—I can get that." She didn't want special treatment. Not yet anyway.

Teo gave her a look. One that said she hadn't been hiding her pregnancy symptoms as well as she thought she had. "I'll carry it to the ambo. When we get there you're on your own. But call me if you need anything. No heavy lifting, all right?"

She glanced across at Jamie, relieved to see he was busy rattling through a list of medications they'd require in addition to what was already on the emergency vehicle.

"Is he..." Teo began, eyes gone double wide with disbelief.

"No!" Bea shushed him as quickly as she could. "Just—I need this job, all right?"

She pulled her fingers across her lips in a zip-it-up-pal move, but not in time to stop Jamie catching the end of it.

The vertical furrows between his eyes deepened. "Everything all right with you two? This is going to be intense. We don't have time for any disputes between colleagues."

"No, mate." Teo stepped forward, all business. "We're all good here. Just trying to be chivalrous and it got Dr. Jesolo's dander up a bit—didn't it, Bea?"

He turned and gave her a complicit wink. He'd be quiet. *For now.*

Which was just as well because she knew the coming hours were going to be tough.

The minutes of their ride to the accident ticked past in a merciless silence. Each doctor was shoring up their emotional and mental reserves as information began trickling in on the ambulance driver's radio.

Bea felt as though mere seconds had passed when the ambulance lurched to a stop and they opened up the back.

Cars were already backed up along the narrow mountain route—the only way to the summer resort at the foot of the Alpine glacier. And up beyond there was some hastily put-up emergency tape.

Bea could see the fire crew already on-site, and heard the loud, shrill screech of metal on metal reverberating against the exposed chunk of the mountainside laid bare by the devastating landslide.

Each shouldering their emergency packs, the three doctors took off at a steady jog to reach the overturned bus, precariously hanging to the cliffside. When they arrived, Jamie led them to the head of the 118 team.

"Dr. Coutts, good to have you on-site." The man stepped forward and gave him a quick handshake. "We've got to shoot off with two of the most critically injured patients. Will you be all right taking charge?"

Jamie nodded. "Anything in place yet?"

"Only the triage sites. I'll leave assignments up to you. We've kicked off with START." He glanced over at the helicopter, its rotors already beginning to whirr into action.

"START?" Bea looked to Jamie. She wasn't familiar with the acronym.

"Simple triage and rapid treatment." He nodded across to a lay-by near the bus, where large plastic ground cloths in bright colors had been laid out. "Red, yellow, green and black. Critical, observation, minor or walking wounded, and expectant."

"Expectant?" Bea gave a little stomp of frustration. What a time for her English to be failing her.

"Deceased or expected to die," Jamie said, his green

eyes following a pair of fire crew members carrying an adult-sized body bag over to the black tarp. He looked back to Bea, concern tightening his features. "It's harsh, but essential if we're going to get to those who require critical care."

"I'll help with the crew tagging up at the bus—all right, Doc?" Teo took off at a run when he received Jamie's okay.

"Let us know if you need a hand," he called after him, and then placed a solid hand on Bea's shoulder. "Are you up to this? Do you want me to get someone else on board?"

"No. Absolutely not."

She shook her head clear of the fog of information overload. No matter how distant he'd been over the past few weeks, she took strength from his touch now. From knowing he was there. If she ever wanted anyone at an emergency situation it would be Jamie. The calm at the eye of any storm.

"Where would you like me?"

"Are you up for the critically wounded? I'll be there. Working between you and Teo."

She nodded. Despite everything, she knew she flourished at work with Jamie by her side.

"Let's get to it."

"I need an extra pair of hands over here!"

Jamie called across to Beatrice, who was downgrading a child she had resuscitated to the yellow crew. Another life saved.

"What have you got?" She was there in an instant.

He glanced across at her as she knelt on the other side of the young boy he was tending to, relieved to see the hesitation he'd noticed in her when they'd arrived had completely vanished. She was one hundred percent focused now. Exactly what the situation warranted.

And then she saw it. The long shaft of thin metal impaling the boy in the lower part of his chest. She glanced up at the boy's face, her eyes widening, then quickly regrouped into a smile as she felt the boy's gaze on her.

"Well, look at what you've gone and done!" Beatrice chided the boy teasingly, her eyes not leaving his for an instant.

"It's pretty cool, isn't it?" the boy answered.

"This is Ryan." Jamie pulled a hard plastic brace out of his case. "He's got quite a few ideas about his own treatment, but first I think we need to slip a neck brace on him. What do you say, Ryan?"

The boy began to nod in agreement, then winced.

"Easy, *amore*," Beatrice cautioned. "I love your enthusiasm, but how about we keep all responses verbal rather than physical?" She held eye contact with the boy until she'd received an okay and a smile. "And is this little bit of extra equipment coming or going?" Her eyes shot to the small blood stain slowly spreading out from the wound on the front of his T-shirt. Ryan had yet to spot it.

"It's one of the tent poles," Ryan volunteered shakily. "I was holding the tent kit in my seat so I could be ready to set up camp."

"You sound like me when I was in the Scouts." Jamie smiled at the memory of his escapades in the woods. When being a child was all that he'd had to worry about.

"I'm not a Scout," Ryan corrected. "I'm a wilderness expert! If my leg's broken, we can pull out this tent pole and break it in two and then use it as a splint. And if it grows too dark, I can start a fire with my flint stone. It's here in my pocket."

He began moving his hand toward his jeans pocket.

"Hold on there, pal. No need for fires just yet. Your leg's looking all right. Let's just try to stay as still as possible, okay, Ryan?" Jamie laughed at the boy. "As much as I'd like to take it out, I think Dr. Jesolo will agree with me that the tent pole is probably holding more together than ripping it apart."

Beatrice gave an affirmative nod. A surge of energy heated his chest. This was what it had been like in "the good old days." A real team. Better than that. A dynamic duo.

"What would happen if you took it out?" Ryan asked after giving a disappointed sigh.

"Well…" Jamie rocked his weight back on his heels. He always had to play things carefully with his pediatric patients. Kids were smart. They liked information and they could tell when he was holding back. Then again, they were *kids* and as enthused as Ryan was, terrifying him with details about bleeding out wasn't the object of the game.

"What do you say we leave it in place until we get you to a proper OR? That way if there's any blood loss they'll be able to sort you out straightaway. In the meantime we're going to hook you up to an IV to get some fluids and a bit of pain relief running around your system. How does that sound?"

"Cool! I've always wanted to see what it was like in an operating theater. Especially if I'm arriving in a helicopter!"

"Are you planning to be a doctor?" Beatrice asked, while Jamie began cutting away the youngster's shirt so he could get a better look.

He laughed along with her when Ryan announced

that he planned to set up his own clinic in the woods to treat both humans *and* bears.

"Oops! Try your best not to move, *amore*."

Ryan's breathing shifted as they laughed, quickly becoming labored, indicating that the pole might have nicked one of his lungs. Pneumothoraxes could be fatal. But they didn't have to be.

Jamie did a quick run of stats. "Blood pressure is stable. Pulse is high."

"Not surprising, given then circumstances. When is the next helicopter due?" Beatrice asked, giving him a quick glance before they both turned to look up at the darkening sky. Dusk was just beginning to set in, and getting as many of the children out of the bus before the sun set was crucial.

"When do I get to ride in a helicopt—ow! It hurts."

"I know, mate. We're going to get you something for the pain." He looked across at Beatrice. "We can't use topical numbing agents. Can you hold on to the pole while I check if it's a through and through?"

"Me?" Ryan asked in disbelief.

"No, *amore*. I'll do that," said Beatrice. "You just concentrate on staying still. I know it's tough, but you're doing so well."

Beatrice gave Jamie a nod, indicating that she was ready, quickly folding the trauma pads he handed her in half and then placing them on either side of the metal rod.

"How many more pads do you need?"

"Are you pulling it out?" Ryan's voice was straining against the pain now.

"Not yet, Ryan." Jamie ran a hand along the boy's creased brow. "We're just seeing how far this bad boy has penetrated."

"A couple more pads, please." Beatrice held out a hand. "That should be enough to stabilize the rod up to the halfway point. Enough to turn him over and check for the through and through."

Jamie quickly handed her the extra folded dressing pads, which she laid crossways to the layer below, gently pressing on them as Jamie slipped both his hands under the boy's side and ducked to take a quick look.

"No." He shook his head, lowering the boy as carefully as he could back to the ground. "It didn't come through."

"Aw…" Ryan lifted his hand to the tent pole but Jamie quickly trapped the small fingers in his own, pressing them firmly to the ground. He couldn't help but laugh. "Were you hoping for a through and through, pal?"

"A little…" Ryan tried lifting himself up again, and instantly started gasping for air.

"I'm just going to put this oxygen mask on you, Ryan. It should help your breathing." Beatrice lowered her voice and continued to speak, ducking her head away from Ryan's eye line to Jamie's as she did so. "Do you think the pole could've cracked any ribs on entry?"

"Tough to tell at this point. Best thing we can do is stabilize him as much as possible and get him to a hospital."

Jamie tugged his medical kit closer. He'd need to pull out the works on this one.

"Ryan?" A mother's frantic tones broke through the hum of voices. With so many children injured and receiving treatment, only a mother would be calling for one boy in particular. *"Ryan!"*

The calls began to fade as quickly as they'd risen. From the sounds of it she'd made a quick scan of the medical triage site and, having missed her son, was now working her way back toward the crash site.

Jamie pressed down on the boy's shoulders, knowing he would want to respond if it *was* his parent.

"Mum?" Ryan fought for breath to say it again—scream it—but found himself fighting for breath. Tears sprang to his eyes as he whispered, "I want my mum!"

"I know you do, mate. We'll get her, but you've got to stay put—all right?" He looked up to Beatrice. "Can you find her? Ryan? C'mon. Stay with us, mate. Can you tell me what your surname is?"

"Cooper…" Ryan's voice was barely audible as the blood began to drain from his face.

"There's swelling of the subcutaneous tissues," Beatrice said quietly.

"I'm going to have to put in a chest tube."

"Thoracotomy?" she asked.

"Needle decompression. Are you all right to find the mother?"

If he acted fast, he could get it done and restore the boy's oxygen flow. It would be less frightening for the mother to see her son with a needle and a valve in his chest than gasping for breath.

"Absolutely. I'll check on the helicopter, as well."

The low-altitude trip to the hospital might necessitate a chest drain, as well. He'd wait for Beatrice to return to put that in.

Jamie nodded his thanks, noticing as she rose, how her hands slid protectively to her stomach. It was the second or third time that day he'd seen her repeat the gesture. He wondered if she'd hurt herself—got a cut or scrape in all the frantic lifting and carrying of children from the bus to the triage tarps. Adrenaline ran so high during incidents like these it was easy enough to get injured while trying to help those in need.

She was gone before he could ask. Jamie shook his head, turning to his medical kit to rake through his supplies. It was hardly the time to speculate on things that weren't critical medical issues. Then again, maybe his not paying attention was what had lost him Beatrice's affections in the first place.

But his not paying attention now could cost this child his life.

Jamie blinkered his vision so it was on Ryan, forcing himself to drown out all of the other stimuli whirling around them. The sirens, the crying children, the screech and scream of the fire department's Jaws of Life still extracting children from the seats that had virtually fallen like dominoes in on each other.

The fact they'd only lost the driver so far was little short of divine intervention. Three children had already been flown out to a large hospital near Milan. Ryan was the last critical case they had here. The yellow team were busy with a lot of cuts, sprains and a few broken bones. The compound fractures had already been sent off by ambulance. So it was just him and Ryan right now on helicopter watch.

He pulled on a fresh pair of gloves, and by touch located the second intercostal space on Ryan's chest. Using his other hand, he swiped at the area with an iodine-based swab, then deftly inserted a large-bore needle just above the boy's third rib. Holding the needle perpendicular to Ryan's chest, he leaned in, listening for the telltale hissing sound of air escaping.

A sigh of relief huffed out of his own chest at the noise, and he quickly set to removing the needle, leaving the catheter in place while opening the cannula to air.

"Ryan? *Ryan!*"

Jamie looked up from securing the final piece of tape to see a woman running at full speed toward him, calling out her son's name.

Beatrice was just behind her, one hand on her belly as it had been before and the other on her back. When her eyes met Jamie's she stopped cold, her hands dropping to her sides, her expression completely horrified.

As quickly as he'd registered her dismay, it disappeared, and Beatrice joined the woman who had dropped to her knees beside her son and began answering the inevitable flood of queries, her hand slowly, but somehow inevitably, creeping to the small of her back.

A thousand questions were running through Jamie's mind and they should have all be about his patient. But every single thought in his head was building up to one shocking realization.

Beatrice was pregnant.

"The helicopter is on its way back." Bea braved looking into Jamie's eyes. "They think it'll be here in ten, maybe fifteen, minutes." Flinching at the wobble in her voice, she just prayed no one else noticed it.

"Right."

The monosyllabic answer was all the proof Bea needed.

Jamie knew. She'd seen it in his eyes. He knew she was carrying a child.

She'd been doing her best to hide the intense cramping that had hit her throughout the afternoon, but this latest bout of running must have exacerbated things. Fear suddenly gripped her. Her concentration on the injured children had been so intense she hadn't bothered connecting the dots.

She was twelve weeks pregnant now. Still within that window where miscarriage was, for many women, a constant worry. She'd never been pregnant before, so had no idea how her body would respond to pregnancy. So far it had been the typical symptoms: tender breasts, nausea and sharp hits of fatigue. She'd been careful. Or so she'd thought. Keeping her shifts at the clinic to a minimum, but regular enough so as not to raise any alarms.

"I think you will need to go with Ryan."

She only just heard Jamie through the roar of her thoughts.

"No." She shook her head solidly. "Absolutely not. His mother should go with him. There's not much room on the chopper."

"Which is why *you* should go. Mrs. Cooper..."

Bea watched as Jamie did what he did best. Calmed. Soothed.

"We can get you transported down to the hospital so that you'll be there in good time to meet him coming out of surgery."

"Oh, no..." Mrs. Cooper began shaking her head, too worried to take on the looks shooting between Jamie and Bea.

Why couldn't he just stay out of this?

"I absolutely *insist* that Mrs. Cooper flies with her son to the hospital," Bea finally interjected as she and Jamie tossed the subject back and forth over Ryan's supine form. No need for the eight-year-old to have a battle over his transport reach epic proportions when all he needed was to hear his mum's voice and the uplifting whir of a helicopter on approach.

"Excuse us for a moment," Jamie said, giving Mrs. Cooper's arm a quick squeeze before rising and tipping his head toward a clearing a few meters away from the triage site. He stopped there and turned to face Bea, his expression deadly serious. "You need to go to the hospital."

"What makes you think that?" She knew she was buying time, but telling Jamie she was pregnant because of a ridiculous cover-up of her ex-fiancé's infertility now...? It would be madness.

Suddenly the shame of it all—the full impact of just how far she had gone to keep the family name golden—hit her like a ton of bricks. Had she really thought she could keep her pregnancy secret? And why should she?

Having this baby was the one good thing that had come out of that mess and yet here she was again—hiding the truth despite her vow to do otherwise.

Bea blinked, certain she could hear Jamie replying to her question, but all his words were beginning to blur. A swell of nausea began to swirl and rise from her belly as a sharp pain gripped and seized her. She reached out. Her thoughts were muddled. No matter how many times she blinked, her vision was blurring. And as the swell of sensations reached critical mass, darkness fell.

CHAPTER NINE

Bᴇᴀ ʜᴇᴀʀᴅ ᴛʜᴇ beeping first.

A heart-rate monitor. She shifted. The sensation of wires sliding along her bare skin brought her to a higher level of alertness. They were taped on. She could feel it now. High up on the exposed skin near her clavicle. On her belly… She wiggled her left hand. There was a clip on her finger.

The heart rate was her own.

Panic seized her and she squeezed her eyes tight shut against the dark thoughts.

Please let my baby be alive!

Not yet ready to open her eyes and face what might be a dark reality, she listened acutely, forcing herself to mark the cadence of the small pips indicating her heart rate.

After a swift rush of high beeps the sounds leveled to a steady rhythm. Faster than normal, but not surprising under the circumstances. She was pregnant. Her heart rate was *meant* to be elevated. Her heart was pumping more blood—an ever-increasing amount as the baby grew—through her womb, her body, her heart.

Beep. Beep. Beep.

Like the beats of a metronome, the heart monitor

was telling her she was stable. But all her thoughts were for her child.

Another layer of awareness prickled to attention when she heard light footsteps and the sound of a door opening. Then the sound of Jamie's voice. His wonderful, caramel-rich voice. Assuring a nurse in English that Beatrice must have just had low blood sugar or not enough sleep. He was sure that there wasn't anything to be worried about. Not yet anyway. Best to leave her to rest for a while. In private.

She heard the nurse leave but not Jamie.

For a few blissful moments her thoughts took on a dreamlike quality. She was together with him. They were going to have a child together. Be a family.

Everything in her relaxed, then just as quickly tensed as the click of the door reminded her that they were in the Torpisi Clinic. She was pregnant by a stranger. Her secret was now public.

She swallowed. This was the moment she'd been dreading most. The judgment, the disappointment and ultimately the indifference she was sure she would see in Jamie's eyes.

Her pulse quickened as she heard him approach, tug a wheeled stool across to her bedside. She felt his touch before her eyes fluttered open to see his handsome face.

His hand was lifting to tease away the tendrils of hair no doubt gone completely haywire over her forehead when he noticed she was awake. He pulled his hand away and pushed back from the side of the bed—as if he'd been caught trying to steal a kiss and she were Sleeping Beauty.

If only things were so simple.

Her fingers twitched. Aching to reach out to him. To hold his hand. Feel the warmth of his touch. The desire was urgent. Insatiable. Her hands began to move toward her stomach when fear gripped her. She wasn't ready to go there yet.

"How are you feeling?" Jamie asked from the other side of the room, where he was briskly washing his hands as if scrubbing them with antiseptic would erase everything he'd been thinking or feeling.

She'd heard that tone so many times before. The caring doctor. The doctor who was there to help, but was keeping his emotions in check because he had to.

He shook the water off his hands and turned to her as he toweled them dry.

She parted her lips to speak, surprised at how dry they were. "Thirsty..." she managed, before closing her lids against the deep green of Jamie's eyes.

"Here." He elevated her bed with the electronic toggle. "I've got some water for you."

He handed her the glass, holding the base of it as she took a sip and then braved a glance at him.

Jamie knew. He knew she was pregnant. Why else would he have had her put in a private room? Hooked up monitors to her belly? And yet he still had room in his heart to be kind. Gentle. Caring for her in a moment that was making it more than clear that she'd chosen another over him.

She ached to blurt out the real story. Tell him it wasn't what he thought. Tell him she'd loved him all along. But to explain the whole ill-conceived story would only diminish what he must already be thinking of her. *Very little*.

She'd seen it in his eyes as the weeks had passed. That famed cool British reserve coming to his rescue time and time again. Just when she'd thought they'd be able to try out a fledgling friendship... *Slam!* Down had gone the shutters, crushing her hope that...that what? She could turn back time and have him back again?

Even the tiny part of her that was still a dreamer didn't stretch *that* far.

"Does your...?" Jamie stopped, swallowed, then began again. "Does he know?"

Bea nodded her head—yes. It was the single blessing she had in this scenario. That man would never be able to lay claim to her child.

But would any other man?

Would Jamie?

"How long have you known?"

She sucked in a deep breath. That was a much harder question to answer. Obviously the treatment had given her more than a ballpark date, but something in her had lit up within days—too early for a test but she had just *known*.

"A couple of months. More..." She was past telling white lies now. All she wanted to know was that her baby was going to be all right.

Just tell him.

Tell him everything.

"I'm guessing you fainted because of lack of food. A bit of dehydration. Sometimes a low iron count can contribute. Have you been taking supplements?"

She nodded. She had. Of course she had. Everything had been done by the book except reducing stress and making sure she always had a snack in hand. But it wasn't as if anyone had anticipated the bus crash. She'd just have to be more careful in the future.

Jamie crossed the room again and tugged open a drawer. He pulled out a little bag of almonds and held them up. "You should keep some snacks on you. At all times. Nuts, cheese, apples... There are all sorts of healthy tidbits you can keep without much bother. It's a bit early, but have you been tested for gestational diabetes?"

Shamefully, she hadn't. Whenever she thought about the baby she thought about the absurd mess she was in, and went right back to not thinking about it.

"I must've been out a long time," she said finally. "To get back here and not even notice."

"You were." Jamie nodded, his brows cinching together as if he were trying to piece together the bits of puzzle he'd only just been handed. "We got you into an ambulance straightaway. Sometimes when low blood pressure and a handful of other factors collide, fainting is the body's way of rebooting itself. Though it's not like *you* need explanations about what's happening..."

"I'm human as well as a doctor," she said softly. "It's always good to have reminders. An outside eye."

To have you.

Jamie let the words hang there between them without responding.

Bea pressed her back teeth together. It was time to face facts. She was still wearing the khaki pedal pushers she'd had on earlier. There was no telltale wetness between her legs that might indicate that things had gone horribly wrong.

"I didn't take the place of any of the children?"

"No." Jamie sat down on the stool he'd pulled up to Bea's bedside, his eyes on the monitors as he answered. "Most of the children were treated on-site. Those who needed extra care, like Ryan, were flown to Milan. It's easier to get blood supplies there, specialized surgeons, that sort of thing..."

Beatrice couldn't help it. Now that she knew she hadn't elbowed some poor child out of critical transport to a hospital, she blurted out the question she hadn't yet dared to ask. "Is the baby all right?"

"A full exam hasn't been done yet, but if it's miscarriage you're worried about, you can rest easy. I've listened for a heartbeat. Your baby is alive and well."

He sat down on the stool he'd pulled up to her bedside so that they were at eye level. He ran his finger along the rim of her water glass.

Beatrice watched as that finger, long and assured, wound its way along the glass's edge, skidding up and over the area where her lips had touched it. Whether it was a conscious act or not, it stung.

And yet…he had kissed her. Although it was so long ago now it almost felt like a dream.

"Right!" He clapped his hands together. A bit loudly for the small exam room, but it wasn't as if they were having the most casual of exchanges. "How about we take a look together, then?"

Of all the moments Jamie had imagined having with Beatrice, it had never been this.

Giving her an ultrasound scan for a baby that wasn't his.

"Let's get some more water in you. If you can get this whole glass down, we'll be able to see it—your baby—better."

She nodded and started drinking.

He turned to get the screen in place, gather the equipment, willing the years of medical training he'd gone through to kick into action. Enable him to take an emotional step back as he once again turned toward the woman he'd thought he would one day call his wife and apply gel to her belly.

Now that she had unbuttoned her top and shifted her trousers down below her womb, he could see the gentle bump beginning to form. Fighting the urge to reach out and touch it, to lay his fingers wide along the expanse of the soft bulge, Jamie forced himself to rerun the past few weeks like a film on fast-forward.

All the bits of discordant information were coming together now.

Beatrice looking beautifully aglow one moment... gray or near green the next.

The light shadows below her eyes he knew he'd seen more than once... He'd written them off as postwedding stress, but now that he knew she was pregnant...

Everything was out of whack.

"I'm just going to put some gel on."

"It's going to feel cold."

They spoke simultaneously, then laughed. One of those awkward laughs when the jolt of connection reminded a soul just how distanced they'd become from the person they loved. Jamie looked away before he could double-check, but he was fairly certain Beatrice was fighting back tears.

Everything in him longed to pull her into his arms. Comfort her. Hold her. Touch her. Kiss her as he had on that very first day. But how could he now that she was pregnant with *that man's* baby?

Ba-bum. Ba-bum. Ba-bum.

"You hear that?" He kept his eyes solidly on the screen, but despite the strongest will in the universe he felt emotion well up inside him. Beatrice was going to have a child. A beautiful...

"I'm just taking some measurements, here."

"Twelve weeks," she volunteered through the fingers she was pressing to her lips. "It's been about twelve weeks."

The date put the baby's conception date somewhere

right around the wedding date. Too close for it to have been a shotgun wedding.

He swallowed away the grim thought. Beatrice might have left him for another man, but he knew in his heart that she never would have cheated on him. On anyone. This child would be Marco's.

"The measurements look good. The baby's about seventy millimeters. A good length."

"Tall?"

"Not overly—but you're tall. The baby's bound to inherit some of your traits."

Her ex-fiancé was tall, as well. Not that he'd spent any time reading the tabloids. Not much anyway.

"Oh, Jamie. Look!" Beatrice's gaze was all unicorns and rainbows as she gazed upon the screen. "She's perfect."

"Or he," Jamie added. It was still a bit early to tell. Maybe two more months. The tail end of Beatrice's contract.

Beatrice was taking no notice of him, waving to the baby. "Hi, there, little girl," she kept repeating. Then to Jamie, more solidly, "She's a little girl. I can tell."

She lifted her hands and moved to caress her belly, only to remember the gel. She pulled them back, accidentally knocking Jamie's arm away from her stomach, and the image dropped from the screen.

"Oh, no! Bring it back! Sorry—please. *Per favore*. Just one more look."

When he turned to look at Beatrice both her hands were covering her mouth, and the tears were trickling freely down and along her cheeks as she took in the fully formed image of her child. All the tiny infant's organs were up and running at this point. Muscles, limbs and bones were in place. Beatrice was showing all the telltale signs of a parent who didn't care one way or the other if a child was a boy or a girl. She was just a mother, thrilled to discover her baby was healthy.

"Do you have plans to tell the father how the baby is doing?"

He didn't know who was more shocked by the question. Himself or Beatrice.

"I—" Bea looked to the black-and-white image on the screen again, then back to Jamie. "He doesn't want anything to do with the child."

"He—he *what*?"

"He didn't—*ugh*!" She scrubbed her hands through her hair. "When I called off the wedding he told me I could do what I liked with the baby."

Saying it out loud made her shiver at the coldness of his words. It was a *life*!

"But—" Jamie shook his head, visibly trying to put the facts in order. "What a coward." Disdain took over where disbelief had creased his features.

"We did it so it would appear to be a honeymoon baby."

The look of pure disbelief was back. Jamie shot it at her and it made her raise her hands to protest, then drop them as if anvils had suddenly fallen into them. "Calling the wedding off wasn't a scenario I had envisioned having to prepare for."

Jamie shook his head, obviously at a total loss for words. She didn't blame him. If she was hearing the same thing from a friend... Well, if it was a friend in similar shoes, from a similar background... She'd heard worse. *Much* worse.

"I know this isn't how things are normally done—"

"Certainly not where *I'm* from," Jamie intoned.

A surge of indignation shot through her. "That's not fair. I've never judged where you've come from. Not in that way."

"You must've judged it to an extent. Decided it—decided *I*—wasn't good enough for you."

All the words drained from Bea's arsenal. "Is that what you think?"

"I think a lot of things, Beatrice, and not one of them involves you getting yourself knocked up by someone who doesn't have the backbone to step up and give a name to his child."

Bea was still reeling from his turn of phrase. "Knocked up?"

It sounded so coarse. Crude, even, the way he'd put it. She might have stooped low to a lot of things, but she had done everything for a reason.

"How dare you? I did this—all of this—for my *family*. Obligation. Duty..." One of her hands pounded into her open one as she continued. "That's how one 'steps up' in a family like *mine*."

For a mother like hers, you upheld tradition. Even when it came at a price.

Jamie took a final glimpse at the image on the screen, then turned to her, his expression an active tempest. The calm of his voice was so still and steady it almost frightened her.

"Beatrice, I don't think I should be involved in this any longer. Perhaps you can find a local obstetrician...?"

"No." She reached out to Jamie as he dropped the scanning wand on the tray next to the monitor and turned away from her. "If the press find out about this they'll have a field day."

"I'm afraid that's really not my concern."

The words landed in her chest like daggers.

"But you—" She stopped herself when she saw his shoulders stiffen and he took another step away from her.

She had no right to ask him for his help.

"This isn't my battle to fight," he said finally, after he'd cleaned his hands and thrown away the paper towels.

He was right. Of course he was right. But something deep inside her wanted to fight this out until there wasn't the tiniest shred of possibility.

Now that he knew everything…

But he didn't know everything. That was the point.

And wasn't his strong reaction because he was feeling the same things she was? Being together. Working together. Having a scan of her baby—

Screech!

Okay. Deep breath. She knew she must be coming across as an absolute screwball now, but the Jamie she knew and loved—

She still loved him. And when you loved someone… did you let them go free or fight?

You fought until there was no choice but to let him go.

"Why did you kiss me?" Bea pushed herself up and looked him straight in the eye. She had to know. Had he felt anything close to the full-on fireworks display she had when their lips had touched for the first time in two years…? Had he felt the magic when physical sensation had melded with powerful emotions and those two forces had joined together?

It had been pure seraphic bliss.

Jamie didn't seem to be taking the same rose-tinted journey down memory lane that she was. Thunder and lightning crashed across his features, rendering his face implacable.

"Everything was different then! I wouldn't have kissed you if I'd known."

"What? So it was all right to kiss me when you thought I was just a runaway bride?"

"You're going to be a *mother*." He turned away to yank some more paper towels from the dispenser.

"It's not what you think."

"Really?" Jamie wheeled on her, eyes flaring with indignation. "Because I don't believe you have the remotest idea what I'm thinking."

"I have a rough idea," she whispered, no longer able to hold his gaze.

Everything in her longed to run away from this moment. Find another village, another country, another continent to hide away in. But hiding could only last so long. She had a truth to face up to, and until she did she didn't deserve to be a mother, let alone have an ounce of Jamie's respect.

If the last few weeks had taught her anything, it was that hiding the truth from Jamie—no matter how hard she tried—was an impossibility. He was the beacon that drew it from her. Demanded it of her. He was her true north and she owed him an honest answer.

She stretched her arms out toward him, knowing he wouldn't fall into them as she ached for him to do, but at least the gesture would speak a thousand words she couldn't voice.

Jamie shook his head, refusing to move any closer.

"How can you have even the slightest idea of what I am thinking, Beatrice? Your life... You've made decisions that took away any right to know what I'm thinking."

"Those decisions had nothing to do with how I felt about you, though."

"How could they not?" He spread his arms out wide and looked around the room, as if there were a crowd assembled in a courtroom. A jury keen to pass judgment one way or the other. "You *left* me, Beatrice. Left me to marry another man. Now, I'm sorry it didn't pan out the way you envisioned it, but you're pregnant by another man and, like it or not, he's going to be part of your future."

"But I'm *not*."

Jamie gave his head a sharp shake, his hands latching onto his hips. "What do you mean you're not? We saw the baby. Alive and kicking." He pointed to the scan where the black-and-white image remained. "Whose is it if not his?"

"I don't know."

Bea's chest nearly exploded with relief. She'd said it. Said it and it nothing had happened. Well, nothing yet anyway, because Jamie's jaw was twitching and she knew what *that* meant. He had something to say, but he was going to wait until he was ready so that whatever it was would come out with surgical precision.

Before he leapt to any other conclusions she began explaining. She told him everything. About her ex-fiancé's infertility. The high expectations for a honeymoon baby. The demand for a male heir to the Rodolfo name. Their agreement for her to have the IVF treatment. The moment she'd walked away after discovering his infidelity.

Despite the gravity of the situation, she burst out laughing. "Isn't it hilarious that she's going to be a girl?"

"We're not going to know that for another eight weeks."

* * *

"We?"

The word hung between them like an offer of something more.

Everything in him fought to return Beatrice's smile. *We.*

Two little letters.

Far too much history.

Though she didn't move, he heard the word again.

It ran over and over in his mind, as if he was trying to extract every ounce of meaning he could from the moment.

Her voice was full of hope. *Hell!* He could see it in her beautiful brown eyes. Trace it through the flush pinking up her cheeks, its heat adding even more red to her full lips.

But what was she asking of him? To forget the past? Forget that she had chosen her family and another man over him? The thought riled him.

Family, eh?

That wasn't how family worked where *he* came from.

After all his family had done for him—the sacrifices they had made—he would have a hard time telling them where to go if they didn't approve of the woman he loved. Maybe…

No. This was an entirely different scenario now. Perhaps Beatrice was good old-fashioned scared. He was a familiar entity, and she didn't want to go through this alone. But another man's child? A stranger's?

The way this whole crazy story was unfurling, Jamie couldn't help but think Beatrice was a stranger to him now. The woman he'd known wouldn't have done any of those things. It was time she owned up to her behavior. Accepted some responsibility.

"I think you should try to find the father," he said finally, after the silence became unbearable.

Beatrice threw him an odd look. "He's anonymous."

"What?" Confusion rained through him like nails. "Did aliens come down to earth, abduct the Beatrice I knew and once truly loved and replace her with *you*?"

She stared at him for a moment. As if processing the accusations. The facts. But he knew it wasn't as if any of this rang true with the woman he'd once known. The time he'd spent with Beatrice had definitely been a fairy tale compared to this nightmare.

Beatrice sat up in the bed, pulling her shirt closer around herself even though the monitors were all still attached. She reached unsuccessfully for a blanket at the foot of the bed, and for one not very nice second Jamie felt like picking it up and throwing it over her. Just hiding her away from sight.

"The treatment was anonymous."

He blinked and forced himself to pull her back into focus. Her eyebrows tugged together, then lifted, her expression changing into something a bit brighter. "I did stipulate that, whoever he was, he must have at least a drop of English heritage."

The words slammed him in the chest and sucked out the oxygen when he heard himself echoing Beatrice. "English?"

"English," Bea repeated, her eyes solidly on his as she gave a wicked little laugh. "That was my little secret at the clinic. No one knows—well, now you know...but no one else knows." She gave her stomach a reassuring pat and pulled her top down close, as if to warm it.

If possible, the atmosphere in the small exam room flexed and then strained against the swirl of information Jamie was trying to make sense of.

A flash of a future that might have been his slammed into his solar plexus. *He* should be the one fathering that little boy or girl growing in Beatrice's womb. *He* should be the one to soothe it, rock it to sleep while his wife caught up on her sleep. He should be the one to tickle its nose, read stories in the middle of the night even though he or she wouldn't be ready yet to hear about Treasure Island or Cinderella. Holding the tiny infant in his arms.

The tug of longing he felt in his chest near enough suffocated him. The harsh reality was that it *wasn't* his child. And it wasn't his future to dream about.

"Your fi—how did he become infertile?"

Bea's shoulders lifted and collapsed in a deep sigh. "I'd love to make a joke about Italian men and tight underwear, but it's a bit more complicated than that."

"He didn't—he wasn't unsafe with you, was he? Did he hurt you at all?"

Jamie fought the urge to go to her, pull her into his arms, instead channeling all his energy into tightening his fingers along the counter's edge—as if pressing the blood out of himself would make her revelations hurt less.

Why hadn't he done more to keep her by his side?

You just let her go.

"No." Beatrice shook her head, her upper lip curling a bit, as if she were reliving an unpleasant memory. "We never consummated our relationship. For a number of reasons."

Her features changed, as if even saying the words was akin to tasting the most sour of fruits.

As quickly as she'd sunk into a sigh she sat up tall, charged with an invisible shot of energy. "I need to get out of here."

She tugged off the monitor tabs and turned her back

to Jamie. Shirt buttoned and tucked into her trousers, after a quick swipe and clean of the gel that had so recently helped give them access to that little baby inside her, she turned to him with a renewed sense of purpose flaring in her dark eyes.

"Jamie, listen. My cousin has offered me the use of his chalet in the next valley over. It's blissful. I went there once in the winter season. I have a couple of days scheduled off. Is there any chance I could convince you to come with me? Let me explain everything. Give you a chance to ask all the questions you must have."

A knock sounded on the door. The nurse called in and said that she had an update about a couple of the children who had been flown to Milan and one who was here at the clinic.

Jamie wanted more than anything to ignore it. To go to this "blissful" chalet and start asking the pileup of questions jamming in his throat. See if there was even the tiniest sliver of hope that they could start something new.

But he wasn't there yet. Couldn't pair the woman he'd loved with the one in front of him—drowning him in a flood of off-key information.

"Sorry." He pulled a fresh white coat off of the back of the door. "Duty calls."

An hour, later Bea felt ready. Refreshed after a restorative walk along the lakeshore and a power nap that seemed to have supercharged her.

She was ready to fight for her baby. *And* for her man.

When Jamie stepped out of the back door of the clinic he looked exhausted. More tired than she'd ever seen him. And she knew it had nothing to do with work. The second their gazes connected, she knew her battle to win him over was already lost.

"Shouldn't you be at home? Resting?"

The words in another context, another tone would have been soothing. Caring even. But at the sound of the brittle tone they'd been delivered in all the impassioned reasons to try again Bea had planned to stack at his feet like Christmas presents were swept away.

"I thought I'd come in and do a couple of hours. Relieve anyone who was at the crash site."

"I think it's best if you don't." Jamie squared his stance to hers. "I know your contract runs until the end of the summer—early September, wasn't it?"

She nodded, her tongue weighted to the bottom of her mouth with disbelief. *He was going to fire her.*

Not wanting to hear what was coming next, she shook her fingers in a wide just-stop gesture that anyone with half a brain could have read.

And yet he continued, as if purging a poison from his own body.

"I think it's best if you don't come in anymore. I'm sure we'll be able to get through the next few days with relief staff. Until we can get someone permanent in."

He spoke as if in a trance. The words coming out in the dull, staccato tones of an automaton. As if his hollowed-out heart would never know the joy of love again.

Part of her wanted to rush to him. Take her hand and press it to his chest, feel for the beat of his heart. She knew it was there. Knew blood pumped through his veins the same as hers. And yet...

This Jamie frightened her.

This Jamie was saying goodbye.

"If you've left anything, I'll get someone to bring it by. I presume you'll stay in town overnight?"

Her shoulders slumped with defeat as she watched his cool gaze drop to her lips, then to the dip of her clavicle. The swoop of bone and flesh he'd used to trace with the pad of his thumb before dipping his head to press hot kisses into the hollow at the base of her throat.

Heat clashed with icy cold as the sensation of his gaze and the memory of his touch collided.

She shut her eyes against the memory, willing herself to focus on the child she was carrying. The love she and Jamie had once shared. And when she opened her eyes again...willing to bare her soul to him for one last shot at being together...he was gone.

CHAPTER TEN

BEA PULLED THE covers around her shoulders, not quite ready to admit that it was morning even though the sun was already peeking through the shutters she could never bring herself to close.

Bah! Who needed another sunny day when it was raining inside her head?

Pragmatism told her that her behavior was bordering on depression.

Her heart said otherwise.

She'd laid it on the line. As good as reached into her own chest and handed Jamie her heart with a ribbon and bow on it and a little tag attached. *Take me.*

She pulled the sheet up and over her head and gave a small groan. She'd already cried as many tears as her body would allow. Cried until she'd fallen asleep. And even then it had been restless, fraught with terrifying dreams. Darkness. Unseen dangers. Cliff edges. Racing vehicles. Natural disasters. Anything and everything she'd ever been frightened of gathered together in a dream to lure her into the most harrowing of chases for survival.

Well…

She cracked an eye open and let the morning sounds of the town register.

She'd survived.

Just.

There was a part of her that still wanted to curse Jamie. Scream at him for not standing by her at this time of crazy, urgent need. The other half of her knew she had no right. All of this was a nightmare of her own making.

All of it save her inability to stop loving him.

It was time to let go. She knew it now.

No matter how cruel his looks, how callous his words, she knew she would love Jamie until the end of time. It was as if the first time she'd met him, he'd lit a single candle in the center of her heart. A pure flame that had refused—no matter what she had thrown at it—to be extinguished.

True love could never die.

But perhaps it could change form.

The harsh, unforgiving speeches she would normally be giving herself were impossible to drum up.

Had she…? Was this her first step in forgiving herself?

Her hands slipped to her belly. The only way she could go on was to forgive herself for all she had done. Everything—no matter how insane it had seemed—had been done with love in her heart.

Had it landed her in the deep end?

Most definitely.

Would she make it to the other side?

A smile tweaked at the edges of her lips.

Of course she would.

No matter how down she felt, it was time to find the reserves of strength lying somewhere deep within her and protect and care for the baby she was carrying on her own.

The phone rang and she let out a groan. Anyone who knew her would hear that her throat had been rasped raw with sobbing the night away. Maybe she should call in sick.

A fresh bloom of tears clouded her eyes.

There was no work.

She'd been unceremoniously fired.

Sighing, she batted her hand about on the bedside table until she hit the phone and pulled it under the covers.

"Pronto?"

"Don't go out this morning."

Bea sat straight up in bed, pulling the covers around her as if they would shield her from whatever news he was about to spill.

"Jamie?" She knew it was him, but the message he was conveying wasn't computing at all.

"The press. They're all around your *baita*. The clinic, too. They got a photo."

"Photo?" She shook her head, the information still not entirely registering.

"Of you... Me. Your hand on your belly."

She shook her head again, willing her brain to play along. Sort everything into the right place.

"When?"

One-word responses seemed to be all she was capable of this morning.

"Yesterday at the accident scene. There was press everywhere."

Her fingers flew to her mouth. Of *course* there had been. She'd been so engrossed in work she hadn't even thought to consider...

The accident scene came back to her in vivid snapshots.

Emergency tape cordoning off the onlookers... Had

there been photographers among the crowd? Mobile phones?

Definitely.

The flash of cameras as they lost the light?

Paparazzi at a crash site?

Or a keen-eyed tourist trying to make some extra money.

Had anyone called out her name?

She shook her head again. It was so hard to remember.

Helicopters flying in and out.

One helicopter hovering… Something a medical chopper would never do… *Press.*

A man on a motorcycle, trying to talk his way past the *polizia di stato* overseeing the slow flow of traffic trickling down the mountainside past the crash site. He'd had a camera, long lensed, resting on his thigh… and then she'd stumbled.

She squeezed her eyes tight against the memory.

"Beatrice?" Jamie's caramel-rich voice was edged with worry. "Are you still there?"

"*Si*—yes." A logjam of words caught in her throat, and in the end all she achieved was a cry for help. "I— I'm not sure what to do."

"I know what you're *not* going to do…" And in a steady, assured voice, Jamie began detailing how to get out of this outrageous predicament.

She let his voice do what it always did. Pour down her insides like warm caramel, pooling at the base of her spine where it turned molten. Fiery. A lava-hot core of resolve.

Bea swung her legs out of bed, pressing her toes against the cool wooden planks of her apartment, taking strength from his assured tone that she would be fine.

"Close your shutters. Take a nice shower. Put on a loose-fitting dress. Find a hat. If you don't have one, I'll bring one."

"You'll bring one? What are you talking about?"

"I'm coming over. Don't open your door to anyone but me."

"Jamie, what are you talking about? I thought—"

I thought you wanted me out of your life.

"Never mind what I thought. I can't have my patients' welfares compromised because of the press outside."

Ah.

The patients. Of course.

"I'm going to drive up to the back door. Your landlord will let me in. Don't even be tempted to leave your apartment until you're certain it's me."

"It's really not your concern."

"It is now," he bit back, his voice as grim as she'd ever heard it. "You made it my concern the second you stepped into my clinic."

He was lashing out. She knew that. He'd never asked for everything she'd brought in her wake.

Her eyes worked their way over to the suitcases she'd already packed, the clothes she'd set out to make an early departure, before the full impact of Jamie's demand that she leave had kept her cemented to her bed.

She would leave on her own. No matter how hard it would be not to fight for the man she loved with all her heart, the life she'd thought they could share together, she would leave so *he* could survive.

"I'll get a taxi." She flicked an app open on her *telefono*. "There's a train leaving in a half an hour. I'll be on it. Just—" She swallowed back the tears stinging her raw throat. "It's really okay."

"It really *isn't*, Beatrice."

Why was he making this more difficult than he had to? For both of them?

"I've already spoken to the local police about an escort. Do you know the fastest way to your cousin's chalet? The one you mentioned yesterday? I can get some security in place before we arrive if you let me know what the address is."

"Wait! *We?*"

Leaving on her own was going to be harrowing enough. She'd just made the tiniest of baby steps toward making peace with herself and already it was torn to shreds. *Deep breath in...*

"Jamie. Surely I can get past a couple of paparazzi on my own? I know I'm no pro, but I have managed a few in my time."

"Beatrice, there are *dozens* of them."

Jamie's words crystalized in her brain as he spoke... then froze icy cold as he continued.

"Even more here at the clinic. You're trapped."

The phone clattered to the floor as her hands instinctively wove around her belly, protecting the tiny life inside. The fist-sized baby she'd vowed to take care of no matter what.

Something fierce and powerful rose within her. A mother's elemental chemistry at work, protecting what she and she alone could give life to. This was *her* battle. And hers alone.

She scooped the phone from the floor, took swift strides to the windows and pulled the shutters closed against the invasive glare of the tabloid press. There was an underground garage she could leave through. Calls she could make.

Part of her felt like striding out in front of them all, holding a press conference, pouring her heart out so the world would know once and for all that being a princess was far from living "less than a whisper away from heaven," as one of the tabloids had put it right before her disastrous wedding.

"I got myself into this mess. Thank you for your help."

She parted her lips again to wish him well in life, but stopped herself because the only words she knew would come tumbling out if she continued would be the three most beautiful and yet cuttingly painful words of all...

I love you.

She held the phone away from her ear and with great remorse pressed the little red symbol that would end the call. Then swiftly, through the blur of tears now flowing freely down her cheeks, she deleted the number.

It felt like cutting off a limb. But at long last she felt pride at her decision. A long-awaited fragment of self-respect that she knew would only continue to grow.

Jamie stared at the phone with an equal mix of terror and fury churning through his veins.

She'd hung up on him.

He was trying to *help*!

Surely she could see he was trying to help.

He stuffed the phone into his pocket, his gaze snagging on the tabloid newspaper in front of him. The picture took up nearly three quarters of the page. Beatrice was front and center. She was wearing the regulation emergency-care jumpsuit, so it wasn't obvious she was pregnant. Even now he knew it was still difficult to tell. There was a soft arc where he'd scanned her belly yesterday, but nothing so pronounced it was obvious. And yet...

He shook his head, willing himself not to relive the

moment where he'd first laid eyes on the child grow-ing inside Beatrice's womb. *Useless.* No matter what he did—eyes open, closed, half-mast—none of it worked. He could still see that baby—still feel the thread of empathy... *No.* It wasn't empathy. He'd seen hundreds of babies inside hundreds of wombs in the course of his medical career, and held even more in his arms as a pediatrician.

But he'd never felt for any of them what he'd felt for this one.

Love.

Electricity crackled through him as the thought took shape and grew.

Of *course* he loved the child.

Because he loved Beatrice.

It was why he hadn't been able to sleep. Why every-thing, despite being in the full bloom of summer, had seemed gray, dull and lifeless since he'd all but kicked her out of the clinic. Of his life.

It explained his ridiculous knight in shining armor attempt. By telephone.

The memory curdled when he tried to give it a softer edge.

It had been little less than cowardly.

He had given himself a way out by ringing Beatrice from the safety of his office, instead of elbowing his way past all those ridiculous camera-wielding journal-ists. Beatrice was right to have hung up on him. They were photographers—not armed snipers lying in wait to kill anyone.

Though they *were* stealing her right to live her life the way she chose. Just as he'd done by rejecting the baby she was going to bring into the world.

She wasn't mad. Or foolish. She was brave. Loving.

Selfless, even, to bring a child created in such calculated circumstances into the world and love it as if she *hadn't* lost everything in the process.

A fire started in his gut. Beatrice shouldn't have to do this. Hide away from the press. Sneak out of her shuttered apartment under the cover of darkness or hidden behind another disguise. Be fired for being— what?—the love of his life?

So she was pregnant because of an attempt to do the right thing by a family so interwoven in the traditions of the past that she'd agreed out of loyalty?

He knew loyalty.

He showed it to his patients. He gave it willingly to his own family. Would lay down his life for them.

He glanced at the newspaper again.

Mystery Knight in Shining Armor for Venice's Runaway Principessa!

Hardly pithy, but no one needed to read the wordy headline to understand the one thing that photo showed.

He was in love with Beatrice.

It was there for all the world to see.

She was reaching out as the darkness of her faint began to consume her, and the expression on Jamie's face as he stretched out his arms to catch her was one of the harrowing anxiety of a man who would lose a part of himself if he lost her.

There was no chance Bea was going to risk another set of heartbroken-princess headlines.

Jilted Again!

Always the Fiancée...Never the Bride!

Destined to be Alone...Forever.

Well, screw that!

If she was going to leave, she was going to leave with her head held high.

One long shower, a session in front of the mirror and a bit of prevarication over the blue dress that flattered her olive skin or the green that definitely showed her small baby bump later...and she was ready to go.

Her heart rate accelerated as the elevator doors opened to the wide foyer on the ground floor of her apartment block...the last open space before she opened the doors to the world...

"Jamie?"

She looked over her shoulder, as if half expecting the press to jump out of some invisible closet and scream "Surprise!" All the while snapping away, taking photos of her looking shocked. But there was no one. No one except for Jamie, standing there as handsome as ever, blond hair curling over the edges of his shirt collar, green eyes holding her in their steady gaze.

Her gut instinct was to run to him, throw herself into his arms and weep with relief that she wouldn't have to go through any sort of charade with the press. The other instinct? The other instinct was hopping mad that he was there at all.

Wasn't *he* the one who had pointed the way to the exit yesterday?

Wasn't *he* the one who had refused to consider trying again?

Wasn't *he* the one to whom she had lost her heart all

those years ago and against whom no one else would compare? *Ever*.

She put one foot in front of the other and made her way across the foyer, through the doors and out onto the street, Jamie keeping pace with her the entire time. He swept out in front of her, down the steps and toward his car.

"Madame..." He opened the passenger door of his dark blue 4x4—a typical rugged Alpine doc vehicle. "Your carriage awaits."

Bea stayed rooted to the spot. *No way.* She wasn't going to let her heart go on this crazy merry-go-round ride again. She'd been through enough emotional joyrides and not a single one of them had been fun.

"What did you do?" she heard herself ask in a voice that didn't sound natural.

Jamie had the grace to look the tiniest bit bashful before he admitted, "I told them you'd left the clinic and were headed to Milan. Something about going to a hospital ward..."

The edges of her lips twitched. But he didn't deserve to win her smile. Not yet anyway.

"What type of ward?" she asked, her fingers still retaining their firm grip on the handles of her wheeled luggage.

"A maternity ward," he answered, the twinkle in his green eyes flashing bright.

The tiniest glimmer of hope formed in her chest.

"Oh, really? And what is it exactly I'm meant to be doing there?"

"I don't think you'll be doing *anything* there," he answered, his voice growing thick with emotion. He tipped his head toward the car. "What do you say we get you out of here? Before they figure out someone might've given them duff information."

Her hand swept to her belly. She couldn't do this again. Not if he was just offering her a ride to so-called freedom. It would just be a few days in a holding pattern until she came up with a new plan. A new place to hide away.

That wasn't how she was going to face life anymore. She was a handful of months away from being a single mother. It was time to stand on her own two feet. Even so...he *was* looking terribly earnest. It would be rude not to ask what his plan was.

Wouldn't it?

She gave her hair an unnecessary shake and showed him her haughtiest look.

"What exactly are you proposing, Jamie?"

"I'm proposing we get out of here," he said, taking a determined step toward her. "I'm proposing you consider forgiving me for acting like a boor."

Bea shivered despite the warm summer breeze as he took yet another step. Only a handful of stairs stood between them. She had a chance. A chance to turn around...flee. Escape with a bit of her heart intact.

Her fingers pressed against the warm curve of her belly.

"I'm also proposing," he continued, taking the steps in a few swift, long-legged strides and pulling her hands into his, "that we get out of here before any straggling paparazzi come by. C'mon!"

He tipped his head toward the car and reached either side of her to pick up her bags. She caught a warm hit of evergreen and...honey? Candle wax? She'd never been able to put a finger on it, but the scent had always been Jamie.

She would accept the ride and then she would say goodbye.

Loving a stranger's baby was a big ask. Just knowing he'd forgiven her, knowing she could leave with true peace between them, stilled her restless heart.

He dropped her a wink. "C'mon. I know a girl who has a cousin who has a chalet somewhere out there in the wilderness. Let's get out of here."

Jamie knew the only way to stop himself from popping the question on the torturously long thirty-minute car ride was to fill the car with opera. Beatrice loved listening to the beautiful arias of Puccini, so he scanned his phone's music library until he found the file he'd been unable to delete when she'd left.

Even catching a glimpse of it had been like swallowing bile up until today. But today? Seeing it there on his phone was like receiving a hit of much-needed sunshine on a rainy day.

As if he'd called up to the heavens and ordered it the clouds shifted away one by one until, when at long last they reached the hidden-away chalet, the sky was a beautiful clear blue and the sun shone brightly down on the broad spread of mountain meadows surrounding the estate.

Beatrice gave him the code for the gate, and when they drew up to the house she turned to him, her face taut with nerves. "You'd probably be best just leaving me here. I'll be all right."

"I am not doing any such thing, Beatrice di Jesolo." He was out of the car before she could stop him and around at her side, opening the door and pulling her hands into his as he dropped to one knee.

"I was hoping not to do this next to the footwell of a beat-up 4x4, but if there's one thing I've learned this summer it's that waiting is a bad idea when it comes to you."

Beatrice's brow crinkled. "What do you mean?"

"I was a first-class idiot, Beatrice. Two years ago when you left I should've put up a fight. Proved I was the man for you. Maybe I wasn't. But I've grown a lot since then."

A dark sigh left his chest, leaving the bright hope of possibility in its wake.

"And I hope you will believe me when I say I've grown the most since you've come back into my life."

"What is it you're saying, Jamie?"

"I'm saying I love you. I'm saying I want to marry you. I've *always* wanted to marry you. I'm saying I want to be a father to the child you're carrying and any other babies you and I might create as we live out our lives of wedded bliss."

He pulled her hands into his and dropped kisses on each of them.

"We've missed too much time together, Beatrice. Time I don't want to risk losing again. Please say you'll marry me?"

He looked straight into her eyes, praying that what was beating in her heart was the same fiery, undying passion beating in his own.

"Beatrice di Jesolo, will you do me the honor of becoming my wife?"

For one heart-stopping moment a crease of distress

flashed across her features, before dissolving into the most beautiful smile he'd ever seen.

"You're absolutely sure?"

"Positively."

"My family is insane."

"Mine is *too* sane," he countered. "It'll make a nice balance."

"Your mother-in-law will be a very…uniquely challenging woman," she said warningly.

"I've been told I have a way with the ladies." He dropped a wink and rose to his feet so he could look her square in the face. "I'll win her over."

Beatrice's eyebrows lifted. "You have to win the bride over first."

"So it's a yes?"

"This *is* what you want?" she asked. "Mystery baby and all?"

She gently pulled her hands from his and swept them along the small swell beneath her cotton dress.

"Mystery baby and all," he replied, more solidly than he could even have imagined. He meant it. He wanted this baby. To love it. To raise it. To read stories to it while it was still in the womb and for every day after. "You are the love of my life, Beatrice. I can't let you get away again."

Tears popped inito her eyes as she nodded her understanding. "*Si, amore.* It's a yes."

He didn't need to hear another word. Whooping with joy, he swung her around before pulling her into his arms for a kiss that was long overdue.

Sweet, sensual, loving, impassioned… The kiss embodied it all.

When at long last they broke apart, heads tipped together as if any more space between them was an impossibility, he whispered to her again, "I love you, Beatrice."

"I love you, too, Jamie. Forever and a day."

EPILOGUE

BEA PUSHED THE shutters back so that the morning sun could flood into the bedroom, barely able to contain her fizz of expectation. January in Britain had never seemed so beautiful. Frost still covered the fields beyond the house—just as Jamie had described when he'd told her about the single winter he'd spent here on his own, with only the wood burner for company.

Well, a lot had changed since then.

A knock sounded at her bedroom door, and before she could cross to answer it Fran's face appeared in the door frame, wreathed in smiles.

"And how is the happy bride-to-be?"

"Happy!" Bea said, laughing as she spoke, feeling another jolt of enthusiasm crackling through her veins. She beckoned Francesca in and twirled around. "What do you think?"

"Beautiful!" Fran's fingers flew to her lips as emotion stemmed anything else she'd planned to say. "Jamie's going to go wild with desire when he sees you!"

"Hardly!" Bea swatted at the air between them, allowing herself a little twist and twirl to show off the A-line cap-sleeved dress she still couldn't believe she fitted into. "Eight and a half months pregnant, swollen feet and chubby cheeked is *not* how I was expecting to walk down the aisle."

"Oh, don't be silly," Francesca parried, flopping onto the old-fashioned bed with an added bounce or two. "You tried it the other way and that was clearly not singular enough for you. Surely your mother—"

"Uh-uh! No, you don't!" Bea feigned horror as she turned to her hodgepodge of a dressing table, pulled together from a packing box and a precariously balanced mirror she'd found in the attic a couple of hours earlier.

She lowered herself onto the packing crate in front of it, ensuring she swept the short train of champagne-colored fabric to the side as she found purchase on the slats. Her mother would be having an absolute hissy fit if she could see her right now.

"We already tried it her way, and the reason you're here and not her is because I thought I could rely on you not to go all Principessa royal this, royal that on me. We both know that is *not* a recipe for success."

"I don't know..." Fran pushed herself up from the bed and wandered over to stand behind her friend, their gazes connecting in the mirror. "It worked out pretty well for Luca and me."

"You and Luca have an entire village at your disposal!"

Fran's musical laugh filled the room. "It was a great day, wasn't it?"

"Amazing. Enough glamor to tide my mother over until my brother decides to get married."

"*Pfft!* Hardly!" Fran rolled her eyes. "I suppose Dad *did* go a bit over-the-top with the catering, didn't he?"

"You should see what *my* father brought over. His suitcase was full of food and nothing else!" Bea's hand swept across the arc of her swollen tummy. "*Oof!* I think this baby girl is going to be part focaccia and part wedding cake if the past few weeks are anything to go by! Italian made, that's for sure!"

Fran took up a lock of Bea's hair and started weaving it into an intricate plait along her hairline. "You're still convinced it's going to be a girl?"

"She," Bea answered solidly. "I'm sure of it."

"I thought you weren't going to find out?"

"We haven't, but... You should know by now—a mother can sense things."

Fran stepped to Bea's side and put her hands on her own growing belly. "It's madness, isn't it? The two of us pregnant at the same time?"

"Jamie would say it's the world proving to us that we can show our mothers how it's *really* done."

"Jamie would say anything to make sure you're here with him in this beautiful home, about to embark on a beautiful life together." Fran grinned, returning to her role as wedding hairdresser. "It's so great the hospital is only a fifteen-minute drive away."

"Mmm..." Bea nodded. "Great for work and great for when my water breaks!"

"I can't believe how much your hair has grown. It's *so* beautiful now." Fran pulled an apologetic face in the mirror and rapidly covered. "I mean the platinum thing was good for a while, but—"

"Well, you're not supposed to dye it when you're pregnant, are you? And it wasn't really *me*," Bea said, pulling a face in the mirror. "A lot of things weren't me over the past couple of years, but now...?"

She looked around the huge old high-ceilinged room, its corners stacked with boxes yet to be unpacked. Only the antique bed and the cradle beside it—lying in wait for its little occupant to make an entrance—were already made up and ready for use.

"Now I'm finally at home."

Jamie glanced at his watch again, his brow crinkling further when Luca gave a rich, throaty laugh.

"Relax!" He clapped an arm around the nervous groom. "I thought the whole point of having your wedding at your house was so you could enjoy yourself!"

"It would be *completely* enjoyable if my bride would ever—" Whatever else he'd been going to say vanished. There, at the doorway to their centuries-old sitting room, was an angel.

Beatrice had never looked so beautiful. Her dark hair had been magicked into an intricate updo. Miniscule little plaits and curls of mahogany hair outlined her perfect face. Lips full and pinkened with emotion rather than lipstick. He knew she hadn't put on a lick of makeup since she and her mother had agreed to disagree on "the true aesthetic of a princess." The swoop and swell of her stomach made his heart skip a beat.

A husband and a father all in the space of a month.

The celebrant they had chosen for their simple ceremony cleared his throat, and Beatrice's father jumped up from the armchair where he'd been making friends with Francesca and Luca's latest canine companion.

"Beatrice! *Amore*..." He raised a fist to his mouth to stem a sob. "You look beautiful," he added in English as he reached out his arm for her to take.

There was only a handful of steps to take from the doorway to just in front of the French windows, looking out onto the sprawling back garden and the farmers' fields beyond, but with each step Beatrice took Jamie felt his heart pound with greater conviction and pride than he thought he had ever felt before.

When Beatrice's father dropped a kiss onto his daughter's cheek and passed her hand over to Jamie's he whispered something in Italian—clearly meant for his future son-in-law's hearing. Jamie's mind was too scrambled to translate it perfectly, but he got the gist. *Take care of my little girl.*

He gave him a nod. There was nothing that would stop him from loving and protecting the woman by his side ever again.

Time took on an otherworldly quality, and it seemed that just a few moments later Jamie was pulling his beautiful wife in to him with one hand, while the other tipped her chin up so he could seal their wedding vows with a kiss.

When at last they broke apart he swept the tears of joy from her cheeks as the tiniest wedding party in history applauded their brand-new union.

"Are you ready to start your life as Mrs. Coutts?" he asked before they stepped away from the "altar."

"Only if you're ready to go and get the car keys," she replied, both her hands swooping over the rich arc of champagne fabric swaddling her belly as she sucked in a sharp intake of breath.

"Are you…?" Jamie looked at the other faces in the room, each as wide-eyed as he was. "Do you mean we…?"

Beatrice nodded, the smile on her face near enough reaching from ear to ear. "A husband *and* a father. All on the same day!"

Jamie ran a few steps toward the Victorian-tiled foyer for the keys, then doubled back to his brand-new wife and took her hand in his, forcing himself to take a steadier pace as they walked to the door.

He barked out orders to Fran to get Beatrice's shawl, to Beatrice's bemused father to find the prepacked suitcase and to Luca to grab the wedding cake.

"You planned this, didn't you?" he whispered into his wife's ear. "The best wedding present of all."

She answered with a kiss, and by the time they had broken apart everyone had whirled into action and it were in place to head off to the hospital for an entirely new escapade as husband and wife.

"Mrs. Coutts?" Jamie swept open the door and scooped up his wife. "I know this isn't the doorway you were expecting to go through after we were married, but are you ready for the next stage of our adventure?"

"With you by my side?" she asked, nestling into the crook between his chin and shoulder. "Every day for the rest of my life."

* * * * *

If you enjoyed this story, check out these other great reads from Annie O'Neil

HEALING THE SHEIKH'S HEART
HER HOT HIGHLAND DOC
SANTIAGO'S CONVENIENT FIANCÉE
THE NIGHTSHIFT BEFORE CHRISTMAS

All available now!

MILLS & BOON®

EXCLUSIVE EXTRACT

What happens when the forbidden passion between
Dr. Adam Cordeiro and his best friend's sister,
Natália Texeira, becomes irresistible?

Read on for a sneak preview of
THE DOCTOR'S FORBIDDEN TEMPTATION
part of Tina Beckett's sizzling **HOT BRAZILIAN DOCS!**
miniseries

Adam leaned sideways and kissed her cheek. "See?
Painless. That wasn't embarrassing, was it?"

"No, I guess not." She smiled.

"Your turn, since the fortune was for both of us." He
presented his cheek to her.

The second she touched her lips to his skin, though, he
knew he'd made a huge mistake in asking her to reciprocate.
The kiss hit him just beside his mouth, the pressure warm,
soft and lingering just a touch too long. Long enough for
his hand to slide to the back of her head, his fingers tunneling
into her hair. Then before he could stop himself, his head
slowly turned toward the source of that sweet heat until he
found it. Leaned in tight.

Instead of her pulling away, he could have sworn the
lightest sigh breathed against his mouth. And that was when
he kissed her back. Face to face. Mouth to mouth.

It was good. Too good. He tilted his head to the side,
the need to fit against her singing through his veins. He
captured a hint of the coffee she'd drunk, and the wine, his
tongue reaching for more of the same.

He forgot about the meal, the fortune cookie...everything,
as the kiss went on far beyond the realm of the words platonic
and friend and into the hazy kingdom where lovers dwelt.

Every moment from this morning until now seemed to be spiraling toward this event.

A soft sound came from her throat and the fingers in her hair tightened into a fist, whether to tug free or pull her closer, he had no idea. Then her mouth separated from his and she bit the tip of his chin, the sharp sting jerking at regions below his belt, a familiar pulsing beginning to take over his thoughts. If he didn't bring this to a halt now...

Somehow he managed to let go of her hair and place both of his palms on her shoulders, using the momentum to edge her back a few inches. Then a few more.

"Nata...we can't do this." The words didn't seem all that convincing. "Sebastian would kill us."

Don't miss
HOT BRAZILIAN DOCS!:
THE DOCTOR'S FORBIDDEN TEMPTATION
FROM PASSION TO PREGNANCY
by Tina Beckett

Available September 2017

And if you missed them earlier:
TO PLAY WITH FIRE
THE DANGERS OF DATING DR CARVALHO

www.millsandboon.co.uk